PEN

A VILLA

Guy Bellamy was born in Bristol but has lived mostly in Surrey. After National Service in Germany with the RAF, he went into journalism and has worked on newspapers in Cornwall, Bournemouth, Brighton and Fleet Street. He has written several short stories for *Punch*, and his previous novels include *The Nudists* (Penguin 1987), *The Secret Lemonade Drinker* (Penguin 1988), *In the Midday Sun* (Penguin 1989), *The Tax Exile* (Penguin 1990) and *The Sinner's Congregation* (Penguin 1991). He is married and has a young daughter.

Rave reviews for *The Nudists*:
'Whip-crack wit and street-smart prose ... funny, caustic and gloriously readable' – *Evening Standard*

and *The Secret Lemonade Drinker*:
'One of the wittiest books I've read in years'
– Erica Jong

'The nearest we novel reviewers come to an understanding of heavenly bliss' – Auberon Waugh

and *In the Midday Sun*:
'The blue skies blacken very funnily indeed'
– *Mail on Sunday*

and *The Tax Exile*:
'A very funny book' – *Sunday Times*

and *The Sinner's Congregation*:
'High comedy ... high entertainment' – *New Yorker*

'Crackles with aphorisms ... a powerful novel'
– *Daily Express*

GUY BELLAMY

A VILLAGE CALLED SIN

PENGUIN BOOKS

PENGUIN BOOKS

Published by the Penguin Group
Penguin Books Ltd, 27 Wrights Lane, London W8 5TZ, England
Penguin Books USA Inc., 375 Hudson Street, New York, New York 10014, USA
Penguin Books Australia Ltd, Ringwood, Victoria, Australia
Penguin Books Canada Ltd, 10 Alcorn Avenue, Toronto, Ontario, Canada M4V 3B2
Penguin Books (NZ) Ltd, 182–190 Wairau Road, Auckland 10, New Zealand

Penguin Books Ltd, Registered Offices: Harmondsworth, Middlesex, England

First published by Viking 1991
Published in Penguin Books 1992
1 3 5 7 9 10 8 6 4 2

Grateful acknowledgement is made to Jonathan Cape, Charles Scribner's Sons (an imprint of Macmillan Publishing Company) and the estate of Ernest Hemingway for kind permission to reproduce the extract from Ernest Hemingway's *A Farewell to Arms*, copyright 1929 by Charles Scribner's Sons, renewal copyright 1957 by Ernest Hemingway.

Printed in England by Clays Ltd, St Ives plc

For Carole and Kate

PART ONE

• Cold Front •

My neighbours are not merely patient
and loftily resigned to distress; they
are still groping, dimly, for an enjoyment
of life which they have not yet realized
to be unattainable.

George Bourne
Change In The Village

[illegible]

[illegible] back journey [illegible]

[illegible]

[illegible] was [illegible] of his [illegible]

[illegible] the [illegible]

always imagined that if [illegible] could only [illegible]

[illegible]

1

VANNER WAS STAYING OUT LATE to avoid the sexual demands of his wife. His appetites in that direction had been quashed by the tension-filled twelve-hour day, the 100-mile there-and-back journey, the lack of sleep and the skimped meals. Feeling drained as usual, he looked at the pint of lager in front of him that promised a rare moment of peace in a day that had frazzled his nerves.

Toby Beauchamp was staying out late because he always did. He had only been to bed completely sober once in ten years, and what a long night that had been. He hated going home early. It shut down the day and seemed such a waste. How many evenings did he have left?

Toby was fifty-five but seemed younger. With his good looks, his silver hair and white moustache he looked like a man you vaguely remembered from an early British film comedy. In the bar of the Fox he was a regular fixture because he lived alone, worked for himself and did as he pleased.

'How did you escape?' he asked.

'I abseiled out of the bathroom window,' Vanner told him. Vanner was thirty but his plump figure and tired face made him look older than his years. For most of the time he operated on the edge of exhaustion and his face was haggard. Toby always imagined that if Vanner could only arrange enough sleep for one month his face would probably look quite different.

'She's probably put an electronic tagging device on your ankle. Tell her that a man with a half-million-pound mortgage deserves a drink in the pub,' he said.

'I was joking, pal,' said Vanner. 'I'm still on my way home from work.' He picked up his drink and wondered if Suzanne would be asleep. It would depend on how much wine she had managed to consume during the day. One night, after a frenetic day in the money market, he had been to see some pornographic films in the hope that their explicit sexuality would kick-start his crumbling libido, but they were so lurid that he'd felt queasy and it was several days before he could think about women's bodies again.

The pub in which the two men sat had oak beams and brass horseshoes and, tonight, a roaring log fire that created the cosy atmosphere that pubs were supposed to have; it was hardly surprising that almost everybody in the village was to be discovered in here at one time or another.

The landlord, a plump and harassed man named Barry, looked as if he had spent too much time enjoying his own product, but he had managed to fit other pleasures into his life too. His fourth wife, Sylvia, even plumper but less harassed, was herself on her third surname. From her previous marriage she had brought her two children to add to Barry's four and now they had more of their own. This protracted ordeal in motherhood could not entirely eradicate a flirtatious streak in her nature which was revealed indiscriminately to any male customer who loitered in her company.

It was directed now at a new arrival in the bar, a heavily built, somewhat untidy man with a boyish face which suggested that his forty years had been lived at a much slower pace than Paul Vanner's thirty.

'Hallo, Harry,' she said. Her upper lip twitched in what she imagined was a sensuous manner, but to Harry Grant it looked as if she was hyping herself up before disembowelling a live snake.

'I'll have a bitter,' he said. Harry Grant seldom flirted himself these days, having painfully gathered the impression over the years that behind every voluptuous woman was a homicidal maniac claiming to be her husband. 'Toby? Paul? Drink?'

The two other men at the bar produced empty glasses in a matter of seconds.

'What's the news, Harry?' asked Toby Beauchamp. 'Are they going to build a nuclear-waste reprocessing plant on the green?'

'Nothing so exciting, I'm afraid.' As he was the district reporter for the county newspaper people expected Harry Grant to come into the pub to tell them what was going on, when he had actually come in to find out. 'The bus service is going to be cut is the only news I have, but it won't affect you rich men in your big cars.'

Harry Grant was always conscious of the wealth that surrounded him in this village. In the last decade of the twentieth century, making money had become the most popular activity even among those people who had no trace of materialism in their characters. Ten years of Thatcherism, it seemed to him, had killed the public's interest in leisure and pleasure and focused its attention on the accumulation of wealth to such an extent that merely to have made money sent people to bed happy, even after a day in which they hadn't actually enjoyed themselves. And the most remarkable thing about this obsession with wealth was that it didn't seem to make any difference to anyone's life. Harry couldn't tell in the pub which man earned £40,000 a year and which earned £140,000: both had comfortable homes, smart cars, foreign holidays; both seemed to spend most of their waking hours at work. Once you made more money than you spent it didn't seem to Harry Grant to matter what you earned.

'Money is no consolation,' said Paul Vanner, 'if you've got the sex drive of a wether.'

'You've bought the Manor House and you've got a Ferrari. You can't have everything,' said Toby Beauchamp.

'If you city slickers had a sex life as well it wouldn't be fair on the rest of us,' said Harry Grant holding up his beer. 'I don't think this has matured in oak vats under the sage eye of the cellar-master.'

'I should hope not,' Sylvia told him. 'It's best bitter.'

'Well, pour it back in the horse and give me a lager. At one time the ale was safer to drink round here than the water.'

'It still is,' said Toby. 'Have you seen what comes out of your tap these days?'

Harry Grant took his new pint of lager and gave Sylvia a nervous smile. Like many overweight women she dressed in black which he felt gave her a menacing air.

He was relieved to hear that it wasn't all gasps of success in Vanners' bedroom. The wheels seemed to have come off his sex life, too, and he was sustained by a series of carnal fantasies, the latest of which had him addressing a roomful of grateful nuns while standing naked before them on a chair.

He said: 'Being a reporter round here is a bit like being a swimming instructor in the Negev Desert. Why don't any of you ever do anything newsworthy? Where are the antique auction rings and the witches' covens? Where's the arson and the rape?'

'We're deficient in the pillage department too,' said Toby Beauchamp. 'And quite right. Peace and quiet is what we want. It's part of the pleasure of living in Sin.'

Compton Sinbury – its name abbreviated to Sin by many of the residents who derived a childish pleasure from telling others where they lived – lay at the foot of sloping fields where chalk met sandstone, and was built round an oblong village green. At the top of the green was the church and at the bottom, facing it across the grass, was the public house, the Fox. That had been renamed too. A poor painting of the eponymous beast on a new inn sign had prompted the customers to refer to it as the Flatulent Ferret. Behind the public house was a river which meandered across north Hampshire and, at the corner of the green, passed beneath a medieval five-arch bridge which carried the people of Compton Sinbury to both the railway station and a new motorway.

The green itself with the bridge in the background was a much-photographed scene of English country life and had adorned many a magazine cover. The pictures were usually taken when the cricket team were entertaining visitors on the green; many of the photographers who arrived to capture this portrait of rural calm stood far enough back to get the duck pond covered with water lilies, at the top of the green, into the foreground of their picture. The ducks had their own tiny house with a roof that somebody in the distant past had thatched, and the photographers liked to include that too.

Compton Sinbury was so old that Iron-Age farmers had built their huts here centuries before the birth of Christ. In medieval times they had made glass in the village, using local sand and wood. Even within living memory the people who didn't work on the farms were likely to be farriers, wheelwrights, cobblers, saddlers or thatchers. But the last thirty years had seen more change than the previous three hundred. The thud of the hammer in the smithy had been silenced. The village forge had been replaced by a garage and petrol station. The muddy rutted streets were now immaculate Tarmac, and there were Mercedes in double garages where once there were broughams in barns. The Meadow Estate, an upmarket quadrangle of modern detached houses, had replaced one of the farms, but another, Mr Garrity's, still survived on the edge of the village with a mixture of grazing, cereal and potatoes – the proportions endlessly juggled to cope with changes in the quotas for milk and cereals.

As fewer people could earn a living from the land, the village, which had once been the home of pioneer peasant farmers, milkmaids and yokels, was now merely a pleasant place to live and its popularity affected its prices. The businessmen, lawyers, money brokers and estate agents had moved in, attracted by the peace and quiet as much as by whitewashed, timber-framed walls and thatched roofs. They disappeared in their large cars in the morning and returned, mysteriously enriched, in the evening to drink gins in the Flatulent Ferret. Their presence, or the presence of their wives, enlivened the village. The list of activities which appeared from time to time on the notice-board outside the village hall which stood next to the church at the top of the green would have kept a much larger community busy: amateur dramatic society, flower-arranging circle, women's institute, judo classes, ladies' tap class, rambling club, art society, writers' circle, chess club, handbell ringers, young wives group – all these and more helped to keep boredom at bay.

In some ways it was a maverick community. When other

villages in this peaceful part of the world had risen to fight the plans for a motorway that would cut across southern England missing Compton Sinbury by no more than a mile, the residents, mostly attuned to mobility, kept a judicious silence, realizing that London would soon be less than an hour away in the Porsche. When a small airfield was mooted for the fields beyond Garrity's farm the expected outrage never occurred. It was seen not as a noisy intrusion on the peace of the countryside but as a useful and easily affordable amenity that might benefit any one of them.

It was through accepting, even welcoming, change that the village had survived and prospered. Strangers still arrived with the hope of separating the residents from some of their money, but they were no longer itinerant tinkers, knife-grinders and hurdle-makers; today they were charity collectors or representatives of firms who built swimming pools. Nobody sat down to an evening meal of horsebeans and turnips, and no family now had a pig in the back garden. The original occupants would be amazed to see what had happened to their dowdy, oil-lit homes. Tastefully converted, whitewashed and freshly thatched, the cottages, with roses round the door and luxury bathrooms, now cost exactly a hundred times more than their first owners had earned in a lifetime of exploitation.

Compton Sinbury prospered today because the residents prospered. With very few exceptions they found no difficulty in guiding more than their fair share of the country's money supply into their bank accounts, an enviable accomplishment that left no residue of guilt. In each case success was attributed not to luck or even a capriciously bestowed talent, but to hard work.

To earn his £200,000 a year (£100,000 salary, £60,000 commission, £40,000 bonus) Paul Vanner got up at five o'clock every morning to catch a train that would get him to his bank in London by seven-fifteen. It was then afternoon in Tokyo and the yen was still in business. He was never home before eight.

Harry Grant worked seven days a week to augment his

newspaper salary with articles and stories for whoever would pay for them. Toby Beauchamp presided over a thriving development company by packing six days a week with car journeys to possible sites and telephone calls to possible builders, often simultaneously.

Among the few exceptions in this oasis of affluence was Terry Wallace, a young man of twenty-five who, handicapped by both a speech impediment and a sleepy brain, was called, even to his face, One-cell Tel. He eked out a meagre existence by being apparently everybody's odd job man, prowling the village in a battered yellow van in search of work.

He was accompanied occasionally by an old man named Barnaby who had spent his earlier years restoring furniture, a talent that today he found difficult to sell. Barnaby was sixty-six and lived alone in a bungalow left to him by his parents, where he spent much of his time tending a potato patch.

What Compton Sinbury lacked was a celebrity, living or dead. Other villages were sustained by their historical associations or by the eminence of a long-dead resident. In Chawton the shops flourished because Jane Austen had lived there and written three novels in a large house that was now a museum. Only a few miles away, visitors flocked to Selborne because Gilbert White had studied the habits of the fauna and the cycles of the flora to such effect that his volume on the subject had run through more editions than any other book in English apart from the Bible.

Compton Sinbury's most famous inhabitant had been a nineteenth-century multiple rapist on whom not even the most esurient local businessman could construct a tourist industry.

2

NEIL KENNEDY and his family arrived in Compton Sinbury with the snow. His heavily laden, red Ford Escort crept over the five-arch bridge and was confronted with a village green that was now white. Beside him was his attractive blonde wife, Gwenda. Behind them, strapped into her baby seat, was their noisy three-year-old daughter, Lindy. Further behind them was a furniture lorry.

'It's pretty,' said Gwenda Kennedy as they drove up beside the green. 'What does it mean – Compton Sinbury?'

'Compton means valley of the fields,' said her husband. 'But you don't have to know that. The locals call the place Sin.'

The Kennedys had told their friends that they were leaving London because it was no place to bring up a child. They said they wanted to see her play on grass and not cement, to breathe fresh air, pick fruit and learn the names of birds. But the truth was less hopeful.

Neil Kennedy was an actor who had been hailed as a future heartthrob in his teens with his bright eyes, his black curls and his deep voice. But he was now a slightly jaded thirty-year-old and too many late nights and too many drinks had made him look older. The big parts on the big screen which had once seemed to be a certain part of his future had never quite materialized, and he was surviving now on brief appearances in domestic soap operas and voice-overs for television commercials.

Moving west was an economy that had been forced on the Kennedy family. The house that he had bought in Islington when he was a rising star and earning good money had gone up in value to such an extent that he was able to put a nought on the end when he sold it. You could always sell in London and buy cheaper in a village and now he had a big detached four-bedroom house for £150,000 and £20,000 in the bank. If things didn't improve he could always move west again – the way things were going he could end up cleaning a multi-storey car park in Penzance.

The damage to his fragile ego was the opposite of what a man needed in his egotistical profession, but these days you had to adapt to survive. South Africa had belatedly discovered that apartheid didn't work and Russia had belatedly discovered that communism didn't work. Neil Kennedy was discovering that Neil Kennedy didn't work.

At the top of the green they passed a parade of shops and turned right, then right again into the Meadow Estate. Neil Kennedy was relieved to see that he wouldn't have to get the car out to go to the pub.

He pulled into the drive of Number Thirteen, his tyres making fresh tracks in the snow.

'Is this our house, daddy?' Lindy had already unstrapped herself from her baby seat and was climbing into the front of the car to get out. She had blonde hair like her mother but with her father's curls.

'This is it, kid.' He went round to the back of the car to get some cases. He was a stocky man, not much taller than his wife. He had once won the part of a boxer in a TV film because no other available actor had the same credible physique.

Gwenda Kennedy, a slim figure in jeans and a sweater, made impatiently for the front door which she unlocked and pushed open. There was an air of efficiency about the way she moved as if she still had her high-powered job in London and every minute must be thoroughly used.

Their wedding pictures, taken on the pavement outside a London register office, caught them both looking as if they were about to dash off to get on with something more important.

Some people found empty houses depressing but Gwenda Kennedy, gazing down at a vast expanse of herring-bone parquet, saw this as a challenge. It was much bigger than their home in London.

'It's a big garden,' Lindy said, having rushed past her to the French windows.

'That will keep your father busy.'

Neil Kennedy came in, loaded with suitcases.

'What will?' he asked.

'The garden. It's big.'

'Gardening is a hobby for people who don't have anything better to do with their time,' he said. He had not come to this rural refuge to spend his Sundays prowling round the proliferating garden centres, examining secateurs and shears, pots and plants, barbecues and bird tables – it could give him the feeling that he had been edged into premature retirement. He joined his daughter at the window.

'Daddy,' she said, 'shall we make a snowman?'

'I was just going to,' he told her. 'Do you want to help?'

Neil Kennedy never forgot that his daughter had not asked to be born. He opened the French windows, stepped out on to the patio and began to gather snow with his bare hands. Disillusioned with his career, he was beginning to feel that the more he saw of children the less he liked adults. He had discovered to his surprise that the conversations with Lindy were more interesting than the conversations with his friends. He also had a feeling that a sharper intelligence was involved in their chats in the toy room. Assumptions were challenged, fresh light thrown on old problems, a clear eye picked out something that had been overlooked for years. Like a neophyte journalist she kept asking: where? when? why? how? The ultimate revelation was that sometimes he didn't know the answer.

'What does the snowman have for a nose?' he asked her.

'An orange.' She had a favourite video called *The Snowman.*

'Well, until we do some shopping we haven't got any.'

'Let's use a stone,' she suggested.

Gwenda came out to look at their handiwork.

'Where's the furniture?' she asked.

'It probably missed the turn-off and is on the way to south Wales.'

'Well, I'm going to look at the shops,' she said. 'We need food.'

Neil Kennedy always felt uneasy when his wife went shopping. Keeping this family in funds was like trying to fill the bath with water when she had hidden the plug. Gwenda was the sort of woman who went into Marks and Spencer to buy a sandwich and came out with three dresses. She seemed to forget that she was no longer earning a big salary in an advertising agency which was where they had met when he was making a television commercial.

'I gave up a top management job to sing "I'm a little teapot" at a mother and toddler group,' she complained to him once, and he knew the frustration that she was enduring. The frustration was more than just professional. Nobody had warned them how demanding a child could be. Lindy never slept during the day and hardly slept at night when she would climb into their bed and disrupt their own sleep. It was an exhausted family that sat down to breakfast every morning.

When he took Lindy back into the empty house to warm their hands he began to wonder who he was going to meet among the local country bumpkins and how long he would last here. Would he be spending his leisure hours in the company of slow-talking yokels for whom a journey to London was a once-in-a-lifetime experience, shifty folk with straw in their hair and a physical strength that was balanced by their mental weakness? How long he would stay here was a financial question to which he did not have the answer. It lay partly with his agent in London who seemed to experience huge difficulties these days in finding him work.

The £20,000 he would be left with after this little move gave him a false sense of well-being, even though he knew that it wasn't only the removal expenses that would eat into it. There were new carpets and curtains to buy, a larger dining room table that wouldn't cost much less than a thousand pounds, a proper bed for Lindy and, according to his wife, a portable television for the kitchen. He could well imagine that there would be many other things which would be necessary before this empty house could be converted into a home.

The bills he had paid last month without moving had come to nearly £1,500 (car insurance £236, rates £582, gas £182, electricity £149, sundry credit cards £300). The figures were scarred, if only temporarily, on his brain and didn't even include the normal everyday expenditure on food and drink.

He heard the sound of a pantechnicon arriving in the drive and went out to open the door.

The first thing he would do in the morning was go round to establish a good relationship with Mr Kirby who, his bank had told him, was the manager of the local branch.

Felix Kirby was in the bathroom snipping hairs in his nose with a pair of nail scissors. He hated Monday mornings and the thought of another long week. For most of the time he hated his life. When he had gone into the bank in his teens his ambition had been to work in the Bank of England or, at the very least, to have held the managership of a big branch in the city where he would have been at the throbbing centre of the country's finances. But now, at fifty-two, he had been consigned to the bucolic stupor of Compton Sinbury for more than twenty years. He had a lovely house on the green and the bank was only next door – but the bank owned the house and when they retired him he was going to have to find a home. He had no choice now but to press on, to endure, to survive. The worst part of the marathon, he told himself, was the last twenty-six miles.

He looked in the mirror and ran a comb through his sandy hair. He wore a permanently serious expression, having once been told that when he smiled he looked like a gibbering idiot. He would gladly have missed the next bit of the day, breakfast in the kitchen, with its demands for early morning conversation. What my life needs, he thought, is a fast-forward button.

Breakfast television was blaring as usual in the kitchen, introducing a half-awake nation to the newest star in the pop world who seemed to have even less talent than most of his predecessors. Felix Kirby's idea of a pop song was Guy Mitchell singing 'Sparrow In The Treetops', but this acne-ridden idol seemed to have won the approval of his ten-year-old daughter,

Rachel, who was ignoring her muesli to absorb his bellowed message.

He looked at Rachel, with her straight back and bright, alert face and could hardly believe that his sporadic sex life had produced such a pearl. She cruised through her lessons, drew like a born artist and read books so quickly that she had already finished the entire works of Charles Dickens. She behaved so well in the company of adults that Felix Kirby was slightly perplexed to discover that he was already treating her like an equal.

He walked over to the window to see what the January weather had to offer and noticed that the grilles outside the window needed painting. His conception of himself as a prisoner was heightened by these grilles which were intended to discourage thieves. He had an idea: he would rename this house Wormwood Scrubs.

His wife Nadine put a plate of scrambled eggs and bacon on the table and poured him a cup of tea.

'Sit down, Felix,' she said. 'You'll be late for work.'

Nadine was fifteen years younger than he, but whatever prettiness she had had when he married her sixteen years ago had been replaced by a certain bland plumpness in her thirties; her conversation was of last night's television, supermarket prices and royal brides of whom he had never heard. Felix Kirby, his head full of other things, bounced between boredom, anger and depression.

Her grandmother, he had once been told, had lived in a shed at the top of the garden because her grandfather wouldn't allow her in the house. This piece of domestic history appealed to Felix Kirby: family tradition, custom and practice. Could he install his wife in a shed?

He looked across at her but she had settled down with a cup of tea and the morning newspaper. His assistant at the bank made love to his wife three times a week even when they weren't talking, or so he said. It wasn't a bit like that in this house.

She looked up from her paper. 'What is overweight, undersexed, lazy, not very bright and can be horribly bad-tempered?' she asked.

He paused with his scrambled egg halfway to his mouth. How was he to deflect this little taunt?

'The giant panda,' she told him and returned to her paper. She thought that what he actually reminded her of was a koala, snoozing in the fork of a eucalyptus tree. It was an animal with no personality because it was given everything it needed without having to make an effort.

She did everything for her husband and he ignored her. Suzanne Vanner hardly cooked her husband a meal and spent all her time and money in clothes shops, hairdressers and beauty salons, and her husband adored her.

It was only her permanent feeling of guilt that made Nadine Kirby accept the injustice of her situation. She turned to the holiday pages and wondered whether they would get abroad this summer. The writer was enthusing about the Italian Adriatic. Holidays provided hope.

'How many times would I have to cycle round the green to cover a mile?' her daughter asked, released now from the pop star's thrall.

Her father stood up and looked at his watch. 'Four, I should think,' he said. 'When do you go back to school, anyway? The Christmas holidays seem to last until Easter.'

'Thursday,' she said, smiling at him. 'I'm going to measure it.'

Why am I such a miserable bastard? he thought as they went out of the front door together. Look at that girl, riding into the future full of hope and excitement. When you stopped looking forward to the future you started to die.

Across the green Harry Grant was watching Rachel from the front window of his 300-year-old cottage. He wondered how long it would be before somebody noticed her resemblance to him – not just the black hair and the broad nose but the piercing eyes that looked as if they missed nothing. Felix Kirby, with his sandy hair and long face, was nothing like her.

Harry Grant was sitting at his typewriter trying to earn some money. It was positioned so that he could look out of his front window not because this was the corner of the world whose news he was supposed to report for the *County Gazette*, but because the pauses between his sentences were so long these days that he liked to have something to look at while he was thinking.

The turmoil of Fleet Street, or wherever the national newspapers resided these days, held no attraction to Harry. The noise, the bustle, the malevolent hysteria which animated the offices of the daily press did not suit his placid nature. He was a country person.

Of course the news that emerged from a village like Compton Sinbury was not important enough to justify his full-time presence in the village. (The last big story had been in 1929 when the village policeman had been thrown in the pond for interfering with the annual bonfire night.) So Harry was dispatched two or three days a week in his Ford Mustang to newsier venues like the crown court or the county council where the important stories happened.

But his heart was in Sin, his rustic dormitory, where the screech of a magpie was the most potent assault his ears had to endure. Covering flower shows, antique fairs, bring-and-buy sales and charity coffee-mornings among people whom he knew seemed an almost perfect existence. He knew that some men would sneer at the modesty of his aspirations, but they were the same folk who secretly envied his idyllic life.

The telephone rang. It was Dakers, his news editor at the *Gazette*.

'What's the big news in your locale this week, Harry?' he asked. 'Any dogs run over?'

'I believe the vicar belched last week,' Harry told him. 'I'm trying to get an interview.'

He consulted his diary. There was a recital of secular music from the sixteenth to the twentieth century tomorrow night. The day after he was himself giving a talk to the women's institute on 'media influences'.

'Sounds quiet,' said Dakers. 'Can you do court tomorrow?'

'Love to,' said Harry, and replaced the phone.

He returned to his old typewriter. He had stuck a satirical

quotation from C. P. Scott to its top: 'Truth is a very rare and precious commodity. We must be sparing in its use.'

The sheet of paper that he had rolled into the machine bore only a single sentence: 'Have you ever noticed how ill people look who work in health food shops?'

It was the start of a whimsical article that he was writing for a magazine, urging readers to ignore all experts, but the second sentence was proving elusive. The tripewriter is being difficult today, he thought. Perhaps a visit to the potting shed would help.

He stood up for a while and watched Rachel Kirby cycling carefully round the green and then went out to his back garden and to the potting shed. He had turned the potting shed into a bar with a brick-built counter and four stools, glasses and bottles on the shelf behind and posters and souvenirs hanging from the walls. There was even an old sixpenny fruit machine. He poured himself a gin and sat down.

The hours that he kept were not those of other people. Sometimes he dropped in to the potting shed in the early morning. Sometimes he went to bed in the afternoon. But he always started the day early, waking at dawn and listening to his transistor radio. He had become interested in fatstock prices and worried about the Far East long bond.

It's a funny life that I lead, he thought. By most commonly accepted standards I would be regarded as a failure. The formula for success was not what they had told him at school. He knew men with tremendous talent but no drive who were broke; and others with no talent but great energy who were rich. It was effort that counted and it was effort that he had always refused to make. He promised himself that it wasn't laziness but a clear-headed recognition of the real pleasures that his life had to offer: peace and enjoyment of the countryside, the company of friends, a beautiful seventeenth-century cottage and – the vital ingredient – time to appreciate all these things.

There were gaps, of course, but there were gaps in everyone's life. He did not know his own daughter. And that summer of passion with Nadine Kirby had never been equalled in the ten years since it had ended with Rachel's birth. It hadn't been so easy for Nadine to skip knickerless across the green for their dangerous assignations once there was a baby to look after, and by the time she had grown a little her mother had acquired caution. Now she greeted Harry like an amiable neighbour.

He poured himself another gin and remembered the horror of his cleaning lady when Nadine had first dropped in to see him. Alarmed by the prospect of illicit sex she had stayed on in an attempt to forestall it, busily cleaning the carpet around their feet. 'Nature abhors a vacuum cleaner, Mrs Sainsbury,' he told her.

He was proud of his little jokes and had once hoped that some of them would reach a bigger audience but they never got beyond the crepuscular sub-editors at the *Gazette* office.

They had blocked his 'fête worse than death' joke every summer for fifteen years.

Barnaby Barton sat in the rocking chair that he had lovingly restored many years earlier, reading a book and waiting for the postman. The squalor of his surroundings came as a shock to his remarkably few visitors, the more fastidious of whom took a bath on reaching home. The carpet in his living room had three holes in it, the rest of it being protected by dust, fluff, old shoes, unwashed clothes, screwed-up newspapers and various evil-smelling piles of something that might have been discarded food or, more likely, the noisome evidence of a recent visit by one of the village's dogs who, in the absence of human company, were encouraged to drop in.

The reason why Barnaby was waiting for the post was that on every Monday morning for more than a year the postman had brought him an envelope containing a £10 note. He had long since ceased to wonder where this money came from; the neatly typed envelope with a late-Friday postmark was now a part of his life and he didn't know how he would get through the week without it. His old-age pension and the odd jobs that were provided by One-cell Tel kept him alive in the bungalow that his parents had owned, but the cost of many pints of

Guinness in the Flatulent Ferret required extra resources and Barnaby could remember when every advertising hoarding assured him that Guinness was good for him.

He turned the pages of his book and yearned for the spring when he could get out to his potato patch. In a few weeks he would get potato tubers and sprout them in the shed. His garden was over an acre and the potatoes were a wonderful source of income in the summer, usually providing him with a couple of days in Brighton. In March he would plant some early ones and then spend April watching for frost. He looked out of his window at a grey sky that threatened more snow but there was no sign of the postman.

The book that he was reading was a novel he had collected from the mobile library that came to the village every Thursday. It was a fat novel by a British actress who now lived in America and there was sex on every page. There were words and phrases that Barnaby didn't understand and sometimes he didn't understand the sex. There were things that men and women did to each other that nobody had ever told him about and it was hard occasionally to work out exactly what was happening.

He had never had enough sex and he now knew that he would never make up for what he had missed. Even among today's liberated women there wasn't much call for short, bald 66-year-old men with red noses.

Of course he had looked quite different in 1942 when as a healthy eighteen-year-old he had chased Lydia Baxter. That had been sex all right in the shadow of one of old Mr Garrity's haystacks. It had been what came afterwards that poisoned his life.

Lydia Baxter hardly had time to tell him that she was pregnant. She lived in the next village where her father was the solicitor, the chairman of the parish council, the treasurer of the church and the pillar of moral rectitude that set an example to the others. His errant daughter was not going to be allowed to marry somebody like Barnaby Barton, nor would she be permitted, in the moral climate of 1942, to stay at home and allow her bastard to bring disgrace on the family.

The last that Barnaby knew was that her father had paid for her to catch a boat to Halifax, Nova Scotia, where he had a sister, and she had never been heard of again.

Blighted in his hopes of marriage, thwarted in his professional ambitions as a furniture restorer, and frustrated in his sexual desires, he was a lonely and bitter man with many strange ideas spinning round in his head.

The whiff of baronial feudalism that permeated the air of Compton Sinbury kept him in place. Many of the people he had grown up with were already dead but only he appeared to miss them. Life was like a party where nobody notices or cares who has already left. He had always expected to be dead by sixty himself and was quietly embarrassed still to be here.

He saw the postman leaning his bike against the shaky gatepost and come up his path clutching a solitary letter. Barnaby put down his book and went out to collect it from the mat.

Inside, as usual, was a £10 note and nothing else. He pulled it out and studied it gratefully. The picture of Florence Nightingale on the back, with her intelligent face and central parting, reminded him of Lydia Baxter whose picture he still kept on the mantelpiece.

Many times over the forty-eight years he had hoped that any letter the postman dropped through his door would be a message from her. Sometimes over a few pints of Guinness he could imagine her arriving at his door with their child, seeking a home.

He knew that it was stupid and only a dream. But the dream would not go away.

3

Nobody could remember why the first hour of the week in the Flatulent Ferret had been designated Men's Hour but at noon on Sunday the men appeared in the bar with a punctuality that never faltered and it was one o'clock before their wives joined them.

They saw Toby Beauchamp as the incubus behind this male club, a lonely misogynist whose interests did not coincide with theirs. The idea of Men's Hour was an irritant to some of them although preparing Sunday lunch kept them at home anyway.

The conversations that they missed would have been of little interest to them, passing from the incompetence of Britain's sportsmen to the weakness of her politicians and thence to the all-absorbing subject of money and how to get it. But occasionally they couldn't pass up the opportunity to discuss the absent sex.

'The real trouble with women is that they don't take men seriously,' said Paul Vanner, clutching a pint of lager. This was the only day of the week that he allowed himself to unwind, and his old jeans and yellow sweater were an official declaration that this was playtime. Saturday had once been for relaxation as well but lately Suzanne had a list of domestic chores ready for him, having seen little of him for five days of the week. It was the additional price you paid for buying a huge house: there was always something that needed to be done.

'I think that's because a lot of women become convinced quite soon after their wedding that they've married an idiot,' said Harry Grant. 'Of course, quite a few of them have.'

Harry did not regard any day as a holiday; he was always on duty with an ear cocked for the news. But while he waited for a jumbo jet to crash in flames on the green, or some simple-minded local like One-cell Tel to go berserk with a 12 bore and slaughter a dozen villagers, the Flatulent Ferret was as pleasant a place as anywhere to cradle his Bell's whisky.

'Thank you for that *aperçu*,' said Toby Beauchamp. He sat at the counter in the corner of the room and the other two men sat beside him. He was wearing a light-brown suede jacket over a pink shirt; he never wore a tie. His shoes were suede too, which seemed unwise with the snow still lying in patches outside, but he had driven the hundred yards or so to the pub in his Porsche. The corner seat in the pub seemed to belong to him and only a stranger would take it when he was in the room.

The three of them faced Barry, the landlord, who today had several children hindering his progress on the business side of the counter. He was one of those many men who seemed surprised to find that noisy and demanding children were the natural consequences of their disordered sex lives, and he moved among them looking confused as if he wondered who they all were. The latest additions the previous year had been twins. 'Two for the price of three,' he called them.

Toby told him: 'The connection between sexual pleasure and the birth of babies is a mistake. It produces unwanted children and reluctant parents. Sex should be a chore.'

'What makes you think it isn't?' Paul Vanner asked. He loved the friendly cosiness of the Flatulent Ferret, its boisterous conversations and, not least, the feeling of hope that only alcohol could produce in him. At the other – the top – end of the green people were coming out of church and perhaps they had emerged with feelings of hope, too, but they never seemed to Vanner to smile as much.

Felix Kirby came in looking as glum as usual. With him was a younger man nobody knew, in jeans and an old denim shirt.

'I'm in the chair,' said Toby. 'Pint of bitter, Felix?'

Felix was wearing a dark blue blazer and grey trousers,

believing that a bank manager should never look too casual when customers could see him.

'Thanks,' he said. 'Can I introduce you all to Neil Kennedy? He has just moved to the Meadow Estate.'

'What will you drink, Neil?' Toby asked, looking at the curly-headed newcomer. 'Don't I know you?'

Kennedy shook his head, depressed that this was what people always said to him.

'The glowing rectangle!' said Toby. 'I've seen you on television.'

'Neil's an actor,' Felix announced. 'He was in one of those soap operas recently.'

'And have you settled down?' Toby asked.

'I've got to settle up first,' Kennedy told him. 'What's it like round here? Beautiful countryside? Lovely walks? Hills to climb?'

'I'm a toper, not a topographer, old son. Why? Are you a family man?' He made 'family man' sound like a tethered goat.

'Don't tell him,' said Vanner. 'Toby is the village gossip.'

'And when gossip is scarce he invents a story and lures the truth towards it,' said Harry Grant. 'I work on the *County Gazette* and I'd like to do a piece about you.'

'You must be hard up for news,' said Neil Kennedy, taking a gin that had finally appeared. 'It's a quiet village, is it?'

'Things have changed,' said Harry Grant. 'The market for handmade boots and gaiters isn't what it was. Some interesting people live here though.'

'Like who?' Felix asked.

Harry Grant looked round the bar but could only see Barnaby Barton and One-cell Tel ensconced in a corner after a Sunday morning money earner cleaning windows.

'Barnaby and One-cell Tel are rather amusing,' he said.

'Amusing?' said Toby. 'Two half wits don't make a wit. Nothing happens here, Mr Kennedy. They don't even play cribbage in the pub any more. People like us are killing the place, do you see? Paying fancy prices for houses that were unfit for human habitation a few years ago. Your genuine sprout picker can't afford to live here. Farmer Garrity has to bus workers in, the local school is in danger of having to close because all the wealthy new arrivals send their kids to private schools elsewhere, and the social life of the place is reduced to exclusive dinner parties.'

'It's called progress,' said Felix Kirby. 'You didn't need a bank here in the old days. If anybody saved anything they stuffed it in their mattress. Now we've got young men like Paul with half-million-pound mortgages.'

Paul Vanner nodded at what he took to be the bank manager's approval.

'Never let it be said that nothing ever happens here because of the newcomers. Why don't you all come round to my place on Friday for a few hands of poker?'

'His place is a gigantic manor house in four acres with tennis court and swimming pool,' Harry Grant told Kennedy. 'You can't miss it.'

'Poker would be fun,' said Toby Beauchamp. 'I'll keep Friday evening clear.'

At one o'clock other customers began to arrive in the bar, and not long afterwards it was crowded with people who were never seen on licensed premises at any other time of the week but who regarded Sunday lunchtime drinking as an event that it would be a social blunder to miss. The good attendance was bolstered by a widespread and somewhat optimistic conviction that people couldn't discuss you behind your back if you were quite visibly present.

To some people these once-a-week tipplers were intruders at a private club, but to Harry Grant, whose business it was to know all he could about the people who lived in Sin, almost everybody was interesting. He looked round the crowded bar at all the couples who enjoyed this civilized Sunday ritual of a leisurely drink before the roast beef.

The Granthams were interesting because their son, now fifteen, had not eaten anything except mashed potatoes and beans since the age of three. Doctors, psychiatrists and hypnotists had all failed to wean him from his austere diet. His father, Harry knew, secretly attributed it to a six-month row he had had with his wife over one of his affairs when the boy was three. Now there was still no sign that the boy would ever eat anything else.

The Porters were interesting because of their unusual sex problem. He had spent his teenage years making love to girls in cars and had subsequently discovered, to his horror, that he couldn't get sufficiently aroused for sex unless he was in one. He had to get out of bed and go down to the garage where he would sit fantasizing in his old Cortina before haring upstairs with an erection. 'It can't be true,' Harry Grant had said when he was told about it. 'That's how it is at *chez* Porter,' he was assured.

Listening to them talking in the bar, Harry concluded that they still had problems.

'Darling, I know we started to make love last night,' said Mrs Porter, a trim brunette with sleepy eyes, 'but did we finish?'

The Wyatts were interesting because he had admitted after several years that he had once been a homosexual teenager in the Merchant Navy before straightening himself out and getting married when he was twenty-three. They now had two rather colourless children, but the big event in their life together was Mrs Wyatt's decision, after a decade of pandering to the requirements of her husband, to embark on a lesbian relationship with a social worker in Bournemouth. For one family to have so thoroughly traversed the sexual spectrum was, to Harry, a source of endless conjecture and fascination.

Eddie, the man in the blue anorak, was interesting because of the curious way in which he had lost his job. For twenty years he had been a train driver, hauling commuters from the green fields to the grey streets of the city, but there was something about Eddie's trains which made them irresistible to those people who were tired of this world and curious about the next. Six suicides had selected his trains to hurl themselves in front of – his window on the world seemed to be full of flailing limbs. Eventually he was incapable of taking a train into a station if there was a passenger standing on the edge of the platform in the rain without an umbrella. Eddie's trains hovered teasingly short of the station and passengers could get neither in nor out. Delays disrupted the schedules, and commuters harangued the railway staff who had to persuade everybody to stand back before Eddie would agree to move. British Rail were sympathetic. Every driver expected one or maybe two suicides in a long career, but six in twenty years was too much for one man to take. They moved him to the ticket office from where he peered nervously at the queues as if somewhere among their number was a man who was planning to garrotte himself in the booking hall.

Gwenda Kennedy, who had not heard of Men's Hour, arrived soon after one quite accidentally, and cast a shrewd eye round the room at her new neighbours. She had brought her daughter with her and was quite prepared to do battle with the landlord but saw immediately that in a welcome breach of the law the room was full of children.

'Bring her in,' said the landlord, who seemed to be knee-deep in children himself. 'It's bloody cold out there.'

'Isn't there a law?' she asked.

'Not in Compton Sinbury,' Barry told her. 'I get fed up myself with all those "no dogs or children" lines in hotel adverts. No wonder this country is raising a generation of thugs. You never get a chance to civilize the kids when they're young.'

'I'll have a dry white wine,' Lindy said.

'You'll have lemonade,' her mother told her.

Intercepting a glance between this new arrival and Neil Kennedy who was discussing poker with Paul Vanner, Harry Grant decided that this must be Mrs Kennedy and offered to pay for the drinks.

'She's a bright child,' he said.

'Too bright,' said Gwenda Kennedy. 'Her parents are exhausted, but that's the way we decided to bring her up. I think that the characteristics that a young adult needs – confidence, forcefulness, initiative – are precisely those which the typical English parent has knocked out of the child before it is ten. We're going to let Lindy run.'

Harry Grant was about to introduce himself but Neil Kennedy came over.

'This is Harry Grant. He's a reporter who wants to write about me,' he told his wife.

'Don't do that, Mr Grant. He's conceited enough.' She turned to her husband. 'We had a visitor. I didn't catch her name but she was a neighbour who obviously wanted to be friends. Dear God, I haven't got time for the friends I've got already.'

'What did you say?'

'I told her that I'd put her name on the waiting list and if a friend died she could become one.'

Neil Kennedy winked at Harry Grant. 'I can see we're going to be popular here,' and strolled back to Paul.

'The trouble with neighbours is that they live next door,' Harry remarked.

Gwenda Kennedy twirled her wine glass and looked at the people who clustered round the L-shaped counter in this bar. The bar itself, with its oak beams, brass horseshoes and open log fire was just what she had expected, but the people were not. An unmistakable aura of money hung over most of them – their clothes, their accents, their cool assurance suggested to her somehow that if life had ever been a struggle it was a struggle that had been resoundingly won. In the wine bars of Islington, which she had recently deserted, the pale faces of the preoccupied regulars betrayed a tension that was missing from the relaxed, weather-beaten features in here. What they sought so desperately in Islington had been annexed long ago in Compton Sinbury and stashed in the discreet ledgers of a bank.

A woman came in wearing a fur coat. She removed it immediately to reveal a bright flowery dress. She went up to the overweight chap who was talking to her husband and gave him a peck which seemed to Gwenda Kennedy to owe more to past services than future expectations. She was a startling woman with bright eyes, long black hair and the sort of figure that newspaper editors liked to feature on their pages. Gwenda Kennedy began to feel a surge of envy at this glittering creature but was distracted by a tug on her sleeve.

'Are we here much longer?' Lindy asked. 'If so I'd like champagne.'

Champagne was her favourite drink and smoked salmon her favourite food. Sometimes Gwenda Kennedy wondered what she was going to make of school meals.

'Lead is very dangerous and we get it in food, water and air,' said a woman alongside her.

'If we give up food, water and air we'll be okay?' a man asked.

The woman in the flowery dress came over and introduced herself. 'Suzanne Vanner,' she said. 'Such a sweet little girl you have.'

'Gwenda Kennedy. I'm afraid she's a handful.'

'We've been trying to have a family for years but can't seem to click.' She gazed over her shoulder towards her tired husband. 'Haven't I seen that man on television?'

'Probably,' said Gwenda Kennedy. 'He's an actor. Also my husband.'

'Neil Kennedy.'

'Very good. Not many people remember his name.'

'How marvellous. We're absolutely starved of celebrities down here.'

'I'd hardly call him a celebrity.'

'Oh, I would. I remember him in that naval film. Trapped in a submarine.'

'That was before I married him. Is that your husband he's talking to?'

'Yes. The one with no children. He's so busy earning £200,000 a year he hasn't the energy for anything else.'

Gwenda Kennedy looked at Suzanne Vanner then and decided that she had been drinking before she ever reached this bar. To mention your husband's salary just like that was not normal behaviour. Nevertheless, now that the subject had been brought up it seemed legitimate to pursue it.

'How on earth does he earn that much?' she asked. 'He looks too young.'

'The city. The money market. Chief spot dealer, whatever that means. I hardly know what he does. Money isn't real up there.'

Neil Kennedy came over to fill his wife's empty glass.

'This is Suzanne Vanner,' she told him. 'She remembers you in a submarine.'

He looked at her and wondered how somebody so stunning could be attached to the tired, overweight man he had just been discussing poker with. 'Luckily it was a film set,' he said. 'I get claustrophobia in a telephone kiosk.'

'You looked bloody sexy in that uniform,' said Suzanne Vanner. 'What are you doing now?'

'I'm the man holding the biscuit that the dog jumps up for in the advert.'

'So you are!'

'It took three years at drama school to learn how to hold that biscuit. What are you drinking, dear?'

'Wine.'

'A drink, Mrs Vanner?'

'Suzanne. Let me introduce you to some of these people.'

'I've met Mr Kirby, the bank manager, and the reporter chap.'

'Harry Grant. Well, come and meet some of the others.'

An uneasy quarter of an hour followed for the Kennedys as a sea of faces and quickly forgotten names were paraded before them. Muttered welcomes in a range of accents reaching from Buckingham Palace to the cowshed floated their way, and they were only saved from further embarrassment by the vocal protests of their daughter.

'We must get her out of here,' Gwenda Kennedy said. 'She's beginning to annoy people.'

'Well,' said her husband when the three of them were walking home, 'what did you think?'

'About what?'

'Your fellow villagers. Your new neighbours. What did you think?'

'I thought what a sleazy, money-grabbing, self-opinionated bunch of shits.'

Though Toby Beauchamp's comfortable existence was regarded with envy by many of the residents of Compton Sinbury, whose lives had rather more stress without the regular consolation of huge cheques from various estate agents, the object of this envy occasionally saw his life quite differently. His large Georgian house stood in splendid isolation, with its own riverside garden, on the other side of the five-arch bridge, just a stone's throw from the green and, more importantly, the Flatulent Ferret. It was beautifully furnished and meticulously cleaned two mornings a week by old Mrs Hockley who carried out her duties in a silence that was not the least of her assets.

And yet his life seemed sometimes to be as empty as his big empty house. The solitude that he had once valued seemed now at fifty-five to be indistinguishable from loneliness. The money that might have financed a family life quietly multiplied in several bank accounts, many of them offshore, with no obvious purpose in view. And unaccustomed to giving or receiving love, he was conscious of the underuse of certain faculties he had been given.

Studying himself in the bathroom mirror on this Monday morning he noticed that a white hair had now appeared in his eyebrow, a further sign that life from here was a downward journey. Soon the ailments that arrived with age would join him on that journey. In bed at night he contemplated the horrors in store with an imagination that was made vivid by his loneliness. Last night he had imagined himself ending up like one of those unfortunate men in some benighted corner of the globe who carried their balls around in a wheelbarrow.

It was his misfortune to have been irresistible to some very unalluring women. He had been told once that attractive women steered away from him because they thought his good looks would make him vain. And so their plainer sisters, finding him ignored by their rivals, threw themselves at him with a wanton longing that had practically driven him to vows of celibacy.

Only once had he allowed himself to become enmeshed in an affair of passion and the experience had cooled his ardour for ever. Miranda was a rich man's wife and one of the luxuries she had awarded herself was a proficient but discreet lover. Toby came to the role like a man born for stardom.

Their two-year affair took him from murky hotels in Bognor to passionate weekends beneath the pink dome of the Negresco in Nice. While the rich man pursued lucrative deals in Singapore and Hong Kong, Toby pursued the rich man's wife.

He wasn't a self-employed property developer then, but the paid slave of a development company whose astonishing profits first gave him the idea of going out in business on his own. It was a decision that was hastened by the taste of the high life that Miranda's money provided: lobster and champagne, caviare blinis and vodka chasers. These had not previously featured in his diet.

It was his experience at the hands of Miranda that gave Toby Beauchamp the somewhat jaundiced opinion of the opposite sex that he was prone to express in the Flatulent Ferret. Miranda conducted their affair in the confident belief that it was her money that bound him to her; when she discovered that what Toby actually wanted was her she was deeply hurt. She seemed to believe that he had strayed beyond the bounds of their agreement and made assumptions that he wasn't free to make. She also found the idea that she should ditch one of the 500 richest men in England for a clerk in a building firm profoundly offensive.

Toby was given his dismissal in a brief phone call that he never forgot. He felt like a pair of shoes that were being cast aside because they didn't match the new outfit. But the bruise that survived was to his heart and not his pride.

He yearned for Miranda, whether it was in Bognor or Nice. His dreams were filled by her and his wallet carried her picture. It was a year before he felt completely operational and had regained sufficient confidence to start his own business. But he resolved never again to expose himself to the risk of so much pain.

He borrowed money at terrible interest rates, bought land and built. The profits were so huge that the interest rates became an irrelevance.

Once, at a charity dinner at the Dorchester, he had seen Miranda a dozen tables away with her portly husband. He waved a friendly greeting but got no response. Perhaps she hadn't wanted to explain who he was. More likely, Toby thought, she needed the glasses that she was too vain to wear.

The song on the radio in his bathroom said that it was easy to remember, so hard to forget. He could have written the words himself.

Downstairs he went into the small room which might in other circumstances have been a toy room for the children and which was actually his office. Almost from habit he punched up the debits and credits on his home computer and then consulted his diary. He had evidently decided some time in the past that he should visit the flats' site this morning to check on the builders' progress. There seemed to be a direct correlation between the speed of the work and the frequency of his appearances on site.

Toby Beauchamp had several works in progress at the moment, all of them calculated to deliver him a sizeable profit and none of them requiring very much effort on his part. This morning's little venture had begun when he had noticed two almost derelict cottages for sale on the edge of the village. 'Ideal for do-it-yourself expert' was the estate agent's coded language.

The cottages were of no interest to Toby but there was a third one next to them in much better order with a beautiful flower-filled garden at the front. If he could buy all three he would have a piece of land he could do something with.

The young couple who had just bought the cottage for £120,000 were not pleased to see him.

'We wouldn't dream of selling it,' said the wife. 'It is exactly what we always wanted.'

The husband seemed less certain. 'What sort of price were you thinking of?' he asked.

'Whatever you like,' said Toby smiling. 'You'll be able to afford a much bigger house and it would be a good time to buy. Interest rates have forced the prices down.'

'Name a price,' the man repeated.

'I'll pay you £1,000 a month now for the next six months for an option to buy it while I try to get planning permission.

If I get it I'll give you – you paid £120,000 and it's probably gone down to a hundred by now. I'll pay you a quarter of a million.' Toby knew that a quarter of a million sounded much more than £250,000. The wife gaped.

'Well,' she said, 'we ought to think about it, darling.'

'No need to think,' said the man.

There was never much doubt that Toby would get planning permission: his secret cheques to the planning officer were sent to the Isle of Man. Driving to the site this morning, he wondered what the profit was going to be on this little enterprise in the present economic climate. He had bought the other two cottages for £50,000 each, and the whole site had cost him £356,000. The ten flats that he was now building there would surely sell for at least £80,000 each. It was such an easy way of making money that he often wondered why more people didn't do it.

He was keeping busy now because he didn't know how long it could last. The way the opinion polls were leaning, Labour's tax-and-spend welfare state would soon be back, curbing enterprise and penalizing success.

He parked his blue Porsche behind the builder's Sierra. A sticker in the Ford's back window said HONK IF YOU BONK. Toby Beauchamp wondered what it meant.

Where three cottages had stood for almost a hundred years there was now a sea of mud. The builder and his three workmen were putting in the footings and it made a depressing picture. Toby was never happy until something that bore a passing resemblance to the architect's drawings began to rise above ground level.

'Listen,' he said. He always began with 'listen' when he couldn't remember the name of the person he was talking to. 'How's it going?'

The builder sucked on a cigarette that he had clearly rolled himself. 'Concrete goes in tomorrow,' he said. 'We had the building inspector round and he thought we should go a bit deeper, so we went down a spit or two which held us up. We'll be up and away soon.'

'How long will it take?'

He received the reply that builders always gave him. 'It'll be done when it's done, Mr Beauchamp.'

Toby smiled and nodded. It seemed to be the rule of today that nobody had enough time to do anything properly, but builders were one breed who would not be hurried.

'Do a proper job,' he said. 'I've got to find buyers for these flats.'

Back in his Porsche a little later, he gazed at the depressing scene that he had created. There was nothing quite so muddled and chaotic as a building site in its early days; it was always difficult to imagine that anything good was going to emerge from the shambles, but Toby had seen the miracle often enough now to feel a sense of pride at what he was achieving. With a little more money he could do for Sin what Washington Irving did for the Alhambra!

He drove down country lanes. The crows strung out on the telephone wires looked, he thought, like a piece of sheet music. He remembered then that he had a lunch date with Felix Kirby. The bank manager, grateful for such a large account in a tiny branch, took Toby every month or so to La Palme d'Or, a restaurant in a converted farmhouse in the country that was the only eating establishment within ten miles to have found its way into one of the good food guides.

He was sitting at his usual table in the corner, sipping a Pernod. His long face and sandy hair somehow made him look older than Toby although he was three years younger. He had a thing about keeping fit and had recently been seen jogging, but to Toby it seemed that the more activities he engaged in to fend off old age, the older he looked.

'You want to get rid of that Porsche and get yourself a car with a bit of style, Toby,' was his opening remark. 'What about a Bentley?'

Toby sat opposite him and smiled. 'I couldn't justify that,' he said.

'That's the new language for can't afford it, isn't it? I think you can afford it. I'm your bank manager.'

A waiter appeared promptly and Toby ordered a gin. To

Felix he said: 'We don't want to make anybody envious, do we?'

Felix Kirby laughed. 'Round here? You'd have to go some to do that. This must be one of the richest villages in England and you don't have to work in a bank to know it. A bloke came to my front door the other day and asked if I wanted to buy an aerial picture of the village. Once I'd got it I discovered that nearly everybody has got a swimming pool in their back garden. You don't find out things like that till somebody sells you an aerial picture.'

Toby wondered what it must be like studying the swollen bank accounts of your neighbours while pinned to the miserable salary of a bank employee. Felix was such a grave companion that these lunch dates were sometimes hard work. If a person's success was to be judged by either their wealth or their happiness he was, on both counts, a failure.

'I haven't got a swimming pool, Felix,' he said.

'No, you've got your own stretch of the river.'

They both ate steaks and afterwards dabbled with a little cheese. It was over the port that Felix Kirby tossed a question across the table that ruined Toby's lunch. Exploring his mouth with a toothpick, he paused to ask: 'Who's Brynwyn Rolfe?'

That is what is called 'a curving ball question', Toby thought. Brynwyn Rolfe was the chief planning officer of the local council, the man whose recommendation in nine cases out of ten, meant that planning permission was granted for a new building.

'Who *is* he?' Toby stalled.

'You keep paying him cheques to the Isle of Man. He's on your payroll, is he?'

Toby could hardly imagine that Felix did not know who Brynwyn Rolfe was. His name was seldom out of the local paper. How many people were there with a name like that?

'He's a man I keep losing bets to,' he said uneasily.

4

PAUL VANNER got up at five o'clock that morning as usual. He found it easy now. Other people screwed up their faces in horror at the hours that he kept but they didn't earn £200,000 a year. They talked disparagingly of 'telephone-number salaries' and then waited for him to pay for the drinks.

He poached an egg and made himself a cup of tea and then headed for the bedlam of the office. Suzanne had another three hours of sleep to enjoy as he drove to the station in his Ferrari, past the Flatulent Ferret, over the bridge and half a mile down the country lanes to the station. The station, serving such a tiny village, would have been axed years ago had it not been on a main line to London from resorts in the south-west.

Other cars turned into the station yard as he arrived, all of them driven by women. The wives disgorged their husbands and then drove off with the car. At one time Suzanne Vanner had done this until it dawned on her that, if her husband bought her a white drop-head Mercedes, the Ferrari could stay at the station all day and she wouldn't have to get up at five o'clock in the morning.

As Vanner stepped on to the platform the 5.55 to Waterloo pulled in. He had got the timing of this journey down to split-second perfection and only the bloody-mindedness of the railway's staff could disrupt it. He read a financial magazine that he had bought the previous evening – the newspapers were not on sale at the station when he left – and one quick hour later he was at Waterloo. From there he got 'The Drain', the Tube from Waterloo to Bank, on which nearly all the passengers were reading the *Financial Times*. He emerged among glassy skyscrapers and walked briskly to his office. It was already seven-fifteen.

There were about 450 different banks in London and Vanner was the chief foreign-exchange dealer for one of them, an international bank near Moorgate. There was nothing surprising about his colossal salary. On a good day he could make his employers 250,000 dollars.

It was the best job in the world when things were going well, but easily the worst when things were going badly. When he reached the fourth floor twenty dealers in shirt sleeves were already at work. Some were in the spot market – the instant deals where settlement was made in two days – others in the cash market, looking at interest rates, and a third group were trying to guess the future in the forward foreign exchange.

Vanner took off his jacket and sat down in front of three green screens, two telephones and a battery of speakers. Two of the screens were news-information services and the middle one was a Reuters dealing machine on which he could communicate with the world. Keeping up with the information was important. He remembered the day when the dollar dropped two cents because of a rumour emanating from Tokyo that Ronnie had suffered a heart attack. The victim had actually been a show-business personality called Lonnie.

Looking at the screen now, Vanner decided that it was going to be a quiet morning. The market was confused because the dollar had gone up despite some bad trade figures yesterday.

Some people described economics as common sense made difficult but Vanner thought that foreign exchange dealing was an example of perfect competition. There were lots of buyers, lots of sellers, lots of *players*, all with equal information. The fastest won and he was very fast. He was absorbing information now through both eyes and his ears.

From one of the speakers that competed with others for his attention he could hear Schupke, down among his number crunchers on the Swiss desk at the money brokers half a mile away, shouting '45–50 in small', and remembered that he was going to meet Schupke to discuss an investment idea over a drink in the City Circle at lunchtime.

He put the thought from his mind and went for a stroll round the office to get a feeling about the market. Men stared at screens, talked into phones, listened intently to the crackling speakers. In one corner Pritchett was trying to identify the trend in dollar–yen dealing with a four-hourly price range chart on his screen.

London was amongst the world's biggest markets in foreign exchange dealing, partly because it covered all the time zones. Clocks along one wall told him that it was 7.30 in London, 8.30 in Zurich, 14.30 in Singapore and 15.30 in Tokyo. It was 2.30 in the morning in New York but they would be in their offices before it was lunchtime in London.

It was a game that everyone was joining which was good news to Vanner. The more *players* the better. Even the corporates – sick of exchange fluctuations hitting their prices – now had foreign-exchange departments that struggled to ensure that the 12 million dollars they would be paid for their product next November would be worth the number of pounds sterling that they would receive if the dollars were paid to them today. The rates had never moved in the past as they moved now. It was a volatile market and the men in this room could not afford to lose their concentration. In a quiet market one commercial order could move everything.

'What's cable in 5?' somebody shouted. He wanted to know what sterling was against the dollar in the amount of £5 million. Nobody could remember why the sterling–dollar exchange was called 'cable'. It probably referred to the good old days when the means of communication between London and New York was a cable under the ocean.

In the good old days this had been a gentlemanly business, with telephones and telexes and trust and tranquillity. But hyped-up Yuppies baying for lucre and desperate to justify their inflated post-Big Bang salaries had changed all that, along with the new technology. Vanner could sell 10 million dollars to Tokyo in a matter of seconds without talking to anyone. It was all done with words on his little green screen in an atmosphere only slightly less frenetic than a football riot.

But Vanner didn't resent the other Yuppies. In fact he had recruited several from the most unlikely sources. One had previously operated in the thoroughly vilified world of house sales; another had actually been a barrow boy. Education could be a hindrance in this business. Young men had wandered in with their degrees in economics and not known the time of day. If you asked them to turn off the light they had forgotten what the job was by the time they reached the switch. You couldn't teach anyone how to do a deal, how to make a price.

It was a quiet morning but by lunchtime, when he left the office to meet Schupke, he was 50,000 dollars in front.

The money brokers occupied several floors of a large building in the city and on every floor people were shouting. In each room about a dozen men sat round a large table with a microphone at their mouth and a battery of communication technology in front of them. Hanging from the ceiling four screens told them all about the world spot currency market, with the last five updates against the dollar in all the major currencies.

Each room dealt with a different currency. In the Swiss-franc room, a grey room with grey carpets and a grey ceiling, Schupke sat with a faraway look in his eye and a telephone to each ear. In one ear, all linked up on one line, he was listening to Tokyo, Hong Kong and Singapore; in the other he was getting news from Zurich. At the same time, like the others, he was shouting into his microphone which went to the eight clients that he handled, including Vanner's bank.

When one of the dealers received a price the others took up his shout to relay it to their own customers. Soon everybody was shouting the same thing.

'Forty-five bid not large!'

'Forty-five bid not large!'

'Off it.'

'Forty to forty-five small top!'

When there were no prices to quote there were other things to shout.

'Swiss I need.'

'Anyone quote, please?'

'Price anyone?'

The prices they were shouting were the last two digits after the decimal point which would have been of no interest to the general public but meant a lot if you were Paul Vanner. When they shouted '56–61!' they were selling Swiss francs at between 1.6556 and 1.6561. To Vanner, buying 10 million dollars' worth, the difference was 5,000 Swiss francs.

Schupke was only twenty-five but looked about forty. He had already had one nervous breakdown and was seeing a hypnotist about his drinking. His eyes now had the same distant look when he wasn't listening to four simultaneous telephone messages as when he was, and his face was white. His fair blond hair was almost white as well. To Vanner he looked like an albino.

In the City Circle he drank two glasses of red wine, while Vanner sipped champagne and listened to the latest developments in Schupke's frenzied life. The highlight of the last six months, apparently, had been when he caught gonorrhoea in an apple orchard in Dublin, but Vanner was in no mood to listen to the sexual triumphs of others.

'You had an investment idea you wanted to discuss,' he said.

Schupke changed the subject abruptly, like a television presenter who had just received new instructions from his producer through an invisible device in his ear – or, perhaps, a money broker who had just heard bad news from Hong Kong.

'Cars,' he said.

'Cars as an investment?' Vanner asked. 'They're the things that drop in value the second you buy them.' He knew that Schupke was obsessed with motor-racing, which he described as 'the epitome of brinkmanship', but Vanner's interest didn't extend much beyond owning a smart one. Recently he had been wondering whether to sell his Ferrari and buy an Aston Martin Volante.

'You have to buy the right one,' Schupke said, ordering more wine. 'It used to be houses as an investment. Now it's cars which is much better because there's no capital gains tax. The car I have in mind for you is called a Ferrari Daytona. The last one was built in 1973 and they only built 1,300 between '68 and '73. I know where you can buy one.'

'How much?'

'It's £300,000. I'd buy it myself if I could afford it. It'll be worth a million in three years.'

'Are you sure?'

'I'm not going to give one of my most important clients a bum steer, am I?'

Vanner looked at his albinotic friend. 'No,' he said. 'You're not.'

He found the idea irresistible but wondered whether he could afford it.

'It's a lot of dosh,' he said.

'What the hell,' said Schupke. 'America has spent more than she's earned for twenty years. Skip the Hellenic cruise this year!'

On Vanner's income of £200,000 a year he paid £76,000 in tax and another £60,000 in mortgage repayments on the half million he had borrowed to buy the Manor House. That still left £64,000 for the baubles which his wife seemed to find indispensable, most recently a drop-head Mercedes and a conservatory.

Schupke was saying: 'According to a survey by Debrett, 84 per cent of the nation's wealth is owned by 43,000 people. That leaves 16 per cent for the other 60 million.'

Vanner thought that he could borrow £200,000 from the bank where he worked and pay it off at £20,000 a year. If Schupke was right it would only be for three years anyway. The money that he had been dumping regularly in a building society would make up the rest.

'I'll buy it,' he said. 'Can I use it?'

'I think you're supposed to do a couple of thousand miles a year to keep it turning over, but what you really want is a safe place. A garage showroom is quite a good idea. They've got all the security and insurance, and they can always put a P.O.A. notice on the windscreen.'

'What's one of those?'

'Price on application.'

'I hoped it stood for preposterous offers accepted.'

Vanner ordered another glass of champagne. The bar-room conversation in here was unlike the chat that he enjoyed in the Flatulent Ferret: at his elbow a bright young couple in smart suits were betting £1,000 on the number of atoms in an ozone molecule.

He patted Schupke on the shoulder. 'You're going to make me enough money to pay off my mortgage, pal,' he said. 'Have a drink.'

Suzanne Vanner was having a drink in the conservatory at the Manor House. The house was much too big for her and sometimes when she was alone in it she found it hard to relax; she was haunted by the feeling that there was somebody else here somewhere. But Paul had wanted a home on which he could one day reap a large profit. 'Over a certain period of time houses double in value,' he had said. 'When that happens it's better if it cost half a million in the first place.'

It stood on four acres with its own paddock, swimming pool and tennis court. The house itself was more than two hundred years old but it had been tampered with so much it looked almost Regency. All five bedrooms had *en suite* bathrooms, and downstairs a warren of small rooms included a butler's pantry, a boot room and a scullery. A library that had been built on the back by the previous owner now housed a snooker table, a recent enthusiasm of her husband.

The conservatory was the newest part and had been ordered by Suzanne to replace the 1940s' loggia. Its centre-piece was an outsize ottoman, covered in cushions, on which she now sat with a very large gin.

If I don't have a man soon, she thought, the top of my head is going to come off. She put down her drink and lay back, remembering with a smile the afternoon she had done something rather unusual with a garlic baguette.

But there wouldn't be any need for that today, she told herself. She picked up her drink and walked restlessly back into the house. The *hausfrau* role wasn't to her taste. If there were not going to be any children she would ask Paul for the money to open a small shop.

Through the front window she could see Terry Wallace a hundred yards away opening the gate at the end of their long drive. Soon his battered yellow van was trundling towards the house. He climbed out of it in his usual yellow T-shirt and jeans and rang the front doorbell.

'You wanted some logs chopped, Mrs Vanner?' he asked. His speech impediment meant that she had to concentrate when he spoke.

'Indeed I do, Terry,' she said. 'Come in.'

He stopped behind her in the hall and looked about him.

'Nice house,' he said. 'Your husband paint it?'

Suzanne Vanner laughed at the suggestion. 'My husband is more autistic than artistic, Terry. Would you like a drink?'

One-cell Tel was not accustomed to being offered drinks when he called at the big houses to do their dirty jobs and he followed her gladly into the conservatory. She was wearing some sort of housecoat which stopped just above the knees to reveal shapely naked legs. The conservatory contained a variety of plants, some of them six feet high, pine-wood chairs and what looked like a double bed covered in richly patterned cushions.

'Would you like gin, Terry? Or are you a vodka man?'

There was a fridge, he now saw, in a corner. It was full of bottles.

'Vodka,' he said, watching her.

She poured him a large one and brought it over. His face was very manly and rather handsome, she thought. People called him One-cell Tel and said that he was a brick short of a load, but he didn't seem to her to be very different from most other men who were startlingly childish once they had been lured away from their own special subject. The only difference between men and boys was that men's toys cost more.

'Sit down, Terry,' she said. 'The logs can wait.'

He sat on the edge of the ottoman and wondered what this was about. You had to behave carefully in other people's houses or you didn't get any work. He stared at her bare l which had suddenly become closer.

Suzanne Vanner, with a newly-filled glass of gin in he hand, looked down at him.

Across the back of his right hand was tattooed the word, TSAR. The inch-high message was in red, shaded with blue. People were vaguely intimidated by these four letters which carried a hint of power, a suggestion of tyranny. Some were impressed that One-cell Tel had even the slightest knowledge of Russia's turbulent history. They could not know that, always unlucky, he had been cruelly unfortunate to have discovered in a travelling fairground one of the country's few dyslectic tattoo artists on the night that he had decided to have STAR engraved on his fist.

'Have you much work on today?' she asked. She wasn't quite sure how to handle this now. A brighter man would already have got the message and slipped a friendly hand on her breast. Perhaps she should fling herself open to him with a lover's shamelessness and watch his face brim with desire.

'It's quiet in January,' said One-cell Tel.

She could not imagine what sort of life he led with humble jobs that were far from regular, and payments that were far from generous. But she could imagine Paul now, frantically busy in his office, juggling huge quantities of money and talking into two phones at once. What was the point of having a husband who made four thousand pounds a week if he was too tired to make love to her?

She took another swig of gin and then put her glass on the floor and knelt down beside it. Leaning forward, she undid the belt in his jeans and unzipped his fly. Then she stood up and let her housecoat fall to the floor.

He looked up at her nude figure.

'That's nice,' he said.

'You're an odd job man,' she told him. 'I've got an odd job for you.'

5

THE CALLERS AT HER FRONT DOOR four days later had a different game in mind.

Toby Beauchamp, Harry Grant and the new arrival Neil Kennedy stood on the step in the cold, their hands deep in their pockets and their breath coming out in white clouds as if they were all smoking.

'There's a game of poker here tonight,' said Harry Grant, 'according to your husband.'

Suzanne Vanner looked at them as if five hundred years had slipped away and three serfs had arrived at the Manor House to pay the thegn their rent.

'And when did old two-pumps-and-a-squirt vouchsafe this gem?' she inquired balefully.

The three men looked at each other, uncertain whether this was a question that required a precise answer. They had all arrived, carless, at the Flatulent Ferret and walked the two hundred yards or so to the Vanners' baronial home, wrestling with a five-bar timber gate with oak posts at either end and then braving a bitterly cold night in the long trek up the Manor House's drive. The least they wanted now was an invitation into the warmth which presumably existed on the other side of this big front door.

'What is it?' asked Suzanne Vanner, receiving no answer to her first question. 'The Men's Hour annual outing?'

'Suzanne,' said Toby Beauchamp, 'are we to infer that you are opposed to gambling in your house?'

'I'm opposed to gambling anywhere, Toby, particularly with my money.'

'Is Paul in?' Harry asked, irritated by this obstruction to the evening's fun. He toyed with the idea of demanding the organ grinder and not the monkey but he didn't like the look in Suzanne Vanner's eye. She had obviously been drinking.

'No, he's not,' she replied promptly. 'He's gone to look at another Ferrari.'

This seemed to wrap the subject up and soon afterwards the three men found themselves taking the long walk back down the Vanners' drive.

Neil Kennedy felt cheated by the débâcle on the doorstep. He had taken the trouble to withdraw £1,000 from the bank that morning and had looked forward to skinning these three simple country folk. In his younger, carefree days when stardom loomed and money never seemed to be a problem, he had frequently sat down at poker tables in London's fashionable casinos and stared down hard-faced Arabs and hostile East Enders before emerging with a full wallet.

'She runs him, does she?' he asked.

'It seems that way,' said Toby Beauchamp. 'I was looking forward to a game of cards.'

'Get your Porsche out,' said Harry Grant. 'I know a little club in town near the office.'

'Are you a member?' Neil Kennedy asked, cheering up.

'All the *Gazette* staff are sort of honorary members. They've got poker, blackjack and roulette.'

'Roulette?' said Toby Beauchamp disdainfully. 'Bingo in a dinner jacket. I like to feel playing cards in my hand and think I'm in control of my fate.'

As his Porsche cruised along country roads that had been intended for slower and smaller forms of transport, he wondered how much money the others were prepared to lose. He had brought a couple of thousand himself, convinced that in poker, as in life, he who had it won; nobody was going to bully him with a hefty bet that left him unable to prove his private conviction that he had the better cards.

Harry Grant had brought £500 which was what he could afford to lose without lying awake in bed afterwards, cursing his folly. If the worst happened he could write an amusing article on the agonies of poker and recoup the money in a long hard day.

The Wali of Swat – a name that nobody could explain – stood beside a car park on the edge of the town. A solitary playing card adorning its fascia was the only clue about what went on behind its darkened windows. Climbing out of the back of the Porsche, Neil Kennedy could only smile at the comparison with lavish casinos he had patronized in London.

They were greeted by the owner, a short, cheerful Italian with greying hair called Gino who welcomed Harry Grant as if he were important.

'The power of the press,' said Toby Beauchamp as they were ushered down a corridor and into a small bar. 'What will you drink?'

Neil Kennedy patted the pocket that held his stake to make sure that it was still there and said that he would have a gin. They had lost Harry Grant during their journey to the drinks: he was signing them in and arranging their admission to the poker school.

Ten minutes later he returned and Gino escorted the three of them into a room at the back where six men sat round a big green baize table playing cards. A seventh, in black suit and bow tie, was dealing.

The cashless society did not extend to casinos where credit cards were not wanted and only currency notes were greeted with enthusiasm. They laid their money out on the table and were given chips. The lowest was £5, the highest £1,000.

Neil Kennedy began to feel unlucky directly he received his first cards. They were playing five-card stud and he was given a king and an eight. He risked £5 to see a dud third card and folded his hand.

It was worse when his first cards were good, encouraging him at some cost to stay in. Once, convinced that he was on his way to a straight, he spent £300 only to receive the wrong card at the end.

'What a poxy hand,' he said.

'It cost you enough,' said Toby Beauchamp.

Toby was winning. The right cards were coming his way

and when one of the resident gamblers raised the stakes to frighten him off he stayed with them, gazing expressionlessly at the dealer. On one hand, when he began with aces back to back, his third card was an ace as well and he went on to win £800 with a full house.

Harry Grant was playing carefully and going up and down. His cautious approach avoided big losses but it prevented big wins as well.

Somewhere they could hear an ivory ball hurtling round a roulette wheel but none of them was concerned with mindless ventures like that. Here you might suddenly have to pay £500 to stay in the hand and it was necessary to concentrate, to remember what cards had already gone. This was real gambling.

Occasionally Gino would appear to ask who would like a drink. It was an indication of the seriousness at the table that, although drinks were free, the only requests were for coffee.

As Neil Kennedy's money began to disappear his mood turned sour. He began to suspect that the dealer was feeding certain cards to the regular punters, and took a dislike to his neighbour, a blond, middle-aged man who, Kennedy decided, had the short haircut and ridiculous moustache of a predatory poof.

The chips seemed to be stacking up in front of Toby Beauchamp. Even sitting at the bar in the Flatulent Ferret he had looked like a man who acquired money effortlessly.

Neil Kennedy counted his own chips. He had £300 left.

The dealer, a young Italian with fierce good looks, shuffled the pack adroitly and slipped them each two cards, one down. He had given Kennedy two kings, back to back. Staying in he collected a queen and another king and waited tensely for his fifth card.

The blond man seemed to have nothing: an ace, a jack, a nine. His fifth card was an ace. Kennedy's was a jack.

He looked round the table and bet all his money on his three kings. It was a hand that would have won many of the pots tonight. But when he revealed his hidden third king, the blond man revealed a hidden third ace.

'You look a trifle lachrymose, old son,' said Toby Beauchamp.

'I'm well gutted,' Kennedy told him.

'Life's a bitch, isn't it? Do you want to borrow a grand? I can't stop winning.'

He pushed chips to the value of £1,000 towards Kennedy who cheered up temporarily. But the trend had been established and would not change. The full houses were never quite complete, the straights would never quite fill out. Money trickled away when even the good hands were not quite as good as someone else's.

Harry Grant was one of the beneficiaries of this run of ill luck. Without possessing any of the acknowledged requirements for success at poker – a steel nerve, a rat-trap memory, an iron mask and a cool contempt for the money itself – he had quite simply received better cards. Once he realized that he was £500 in front he began to enjoy himself. In this smoky den, where all conversation had died, hundreds of pounds went backwards and forwards across the worn green table. From each pot the house deducted 10 per cent and Harry Grant imagined that if they sat here long enough all the money that had been at risk would eventually end up in the hands of the Wali of Swat.

He smiled across at Neil Kennedy who looked tense. The five cards in front of him would be a straight if the hidden card was a queen. He seemed to be considering the size of his bet. Finally, with a great display of reluctance, he pushed the £600 in front of him to the centre of the table. Either he had the straight or he wanted the others to believe that he had.

Harry Grant had three jacks and folded his hand. He wasn't going to risk his winnings now. The blond man showed two kings and two tens. Toby Beauchamp didn't seem to have anything very much and the others had abandoned this hand after three cards.

Like a man making a supreme sacrifice, the blond gambler eased £600 towards the dealer. Neil Kennedy turned his card over to reveal that he indeed did have the queen, but immediately the blond man flipped his to show a ten. A full house beat a straight.

'Scumbag,' said Neil Kennedy.

He stood up and left the table in search of the loo. He walked down a poorly lit corridor, following the signs, and found himself in one of those lavatories where you have to hold the seat up with your knee while you pee over your shoe.

On a Monday morning in February when the sky was beginning to hint that better weather was in store, Barnaby Barton waited by his front door for the arrival of his weekly £10 note. He could see Mrs Mortimer next door brushing her step and looking round for somebody to talk to, but her idea of a conversation was her talking for half an hour and everybody else listening, and Barnaby stood well back from her field of vision.

Instead of the postman with his anonymous gift there appeared a man in a grey trilby and dark overcoat, carrying a black briefcase. Barnaby, alarmed, withdrew into the malodorous seclusion of his bungalow, fearful of an invasion by officialdom and an influx of questions and forms. His dread of officials from whatever desk-filled office was unthinking and deep-seated, and owed nothing to reality at all.

The man was knocking on his door now, an importunate rap that demanded an immediate response. Barnaby steeled himself and opened the door by no more than a few inches.

'Mr Barton?' the man said briskly.

Barnaby nodded as if he was reluctant to commit himself, a cautious admission that provoked a torrent of words.

The man was from an Anglo-American oil company that had been conducting geological surveys across a swathe of southern England. Their researches had suggested the presence of oil beneath a tract that cut through Compton Sinbury and they wanted to install a few drills to test their findings. Barnaby Barton's acre was right in the middle of the most promising stretch of land and what the oil company wanted was 'permission to look'.

Barnaby said: 'What about my potatoes?'

The man in the trilby looked at him and almost visibly

modified his judgement about 'the bungalow man' as he was called back in the office.

'There is a fee,' he said.

Barnaby smiled a crooked smile. He had met people like this before.

'How much do I have to pay?'

The man, his impression confirmed, gave up hope of being invited in and opened his briefcase on the step. 'No, we pay you, Mr Barton. Compensation for disruption. It would be several hundred pounds. It depends how long we take. All you have to do is sign this form.'

Barnaby looked at the form suspiciously, but there was no misunderstanding what the man had said. Several hundred pounds. We pay you. Oil wells in the garden. He took the Sheaffer pen that was being offered to him.

An hour later, his new £10 note in his pocket, he walked into the village to meet One-cell Tel who wanted him to help remove some tiles from a roof. The familiar yellow van was already parked outside the Arts and Craft shop at the top of the green where this work was due to take place, but it wasn't work that Barnaby Barton was interested in any more.

'I'm not working today, Tel,' he told Terry Wallace.

The younger man, who was already unstrapping a ladder from the roof of his van, asked: 'Why's that, Barney? Are you ill?'

'I've got oil in my back garden. They're going to drill for it.'

One-cell Tel smiled at him. 'Give over, you daft bugger,' he said.

'It's true. I've had a man come to see me.'

'You let me down today, Barney, and there'll be no more work.'

'I don't need to work, Tel. I've got oil.'

'You've got oil on the brain, Barney. Out of my way. I've got to strip this roof.'

Left on his own on the pavement, Barney found himself looking into the window of the Arts and Craft shop. It was a shop that was finding that arts and crafts were not quite sufficient to sustain it in so small a village, and prominent among the items displayed temptingly in the window was a stetson hat.

Barnaby went in. It was a perfect fit even if it did make a dent in his Guinness money. But that didn't matter. There was compensation for disruption.

He arrived a few minutes later in the Flatulent Ferret where his stetson was greeted with quiet guffaws. He took off his raincoat but couldn't bring himself to remove the hat.

'I've got oil,' he told Barry. 'In my back garden.'

'Good for you,' said Barry, pulling a pint of Guinness.

Barnaby took the drink to a corner of the bar and sat down. Most people ignored him and as usual he felt excluded in here. Life was a bit like watching television: he was never in the scene himself. But he would be. He imagined sudden wealth and the touching arrival of Lydia Baxter, begging forgiveness. The thought raised sweat on the back of his neck.

When he went up for his second pint Harry Grant came in.

'I drank too much in here last night,' he said. 'I walked home with quite a stammer.'

'Barney's got a story for you,' said Barry. 'He's got an oil well in his back garden. I think he's come unglued.'

'I have though,' said Barney, and immediately embarked on a long and rambling account of the visit he had received that morning.

Harry Grant listened, confused. 'If this was a video I'd press re-wind,' he said.

'I'd press fast forward,' said Barry. 'He doesn't seem able to get out of this sentence.'

'It's a life sentence,' said Harry. 'Barney, slow down and give us the facts in sentences that have full stops at the end.'

'There's a fee for disruption,' said Barney. 'My potatoes are going to be late.'

Harry Grant could see that there was a story here somewhere but finding it in this conversational fog was more than his hangover would permit.

'Let me buy you another Guinness, Barney,' he said. 'It looks as if you've blown your beer money on a hat.'

Barnaby retreated to the corner again. These people would

soon have to stop treating him as a joke figure and take him seriously. It was only money that earned respect in Sin. He stumbled out to the toilet in the corner of the bar. The graffito on the wall said 'The penis mightier than the sword'. He stared at it uncomprehendingly.

'It wouldn't belong to him anyway,' said Harry Grant. 'Mineral rights belong to the Crown.'

'Don't tell him that – he's having his moment.'

'And who gets rich? Not us. Do you remember when North Sea oil was going to change the economy of this country? And what happened? We've got worse balance-of-payment figures now than before they found it, and our petrol costs more!'

Barnaby emerged from the toilet with an idea that would make people give him the respect that he was going to deserve. He finished his drink, put on his coat, and wandered back down the road to his bungalow. The sign on the gate said THE BUNGALOW. He went into his shed at the back and found some paint.

In a couple of minutes white paint had obliterated this name which had been his boring address since he was a boy. He went back into the shed and found some blue paint and then sat and waited for the white paint to dry.

An hour later he had painted his home's new name on the sign. It was difficult after the Guinness but it was readable. It said SOUTHFORK.

When the bright red Ferrari Daytona arrived on a transporter, Paul Vanner stood in the drive taking photographs of his spectacular acquisition. He had wanted to drive it from the garage in Leicester where it had been cosseted by its previous owner, but the risks of bumps and dents on Britain's crowded motorways had persuaded him to forgo this pleasure. He watched the men push it into the corner of his huge garage and felt a tremor of concern that his conspicuous prosperity depended on debts whose size would unhinge the average citizen. He now had to add £20,000 a year in repayments to his bank for the car loan to his £60,000 a year mortgage. If borrowing money was truly the first step to great wealth, he must be halfway there.

'It's a good-looking car,' said Suzanne, patting the prancing black horse on the front of the bonnet.

'Enzo's masterpiece,' said her husband. 'A motoring legend.'

Suzanne Vanner was uncertain what attitude to take towards this gaudy new arrival. On the one hand it looked like extravagant self-indulgence of the worst male-chauvinist sort; on the other, Paul was adamant that it would be worth £1 million in three years, and, whatever his failings, his talent for making money could not be questioned.

'I now have a classic car in my portfolio,' he said when the transporter had gone. 'Do you realize that in 1970 these cars cost less than £7,000?'

There was little he didn't know about the Daytona now, about its sturdy square-tube chassis and its wishbone suspension. They had taken it from stop to 150 miles an hour and back to stop within a mile. It was the ultimate in *gran turismo* cars and there would never be any more of them.

'A pity you didn't buy one in 1970,' said his wife opening a door to look at the two hammock-like seats.

'I was ten and my pocket money didn't run to it. Anyway, this one wasn't built until 1973. You will notice the M registration number-plates.'

'It's only done 32,000 miles in seventeen years.'

'I told you. It's an investment. You're not supposed to drive the thing.'

But he was itching to take it out, to cruise past the Flatulent Ferret, over the five-arch bridge and up to the motorway where there were always plenty of boy racers who thought they were Ayrton Senna or Alain Prost. When this elegant monster roared past them at 160 miles an hour they would be returned to humbling reality.

The problem was insurance. Once he had decided not to fetch the car from Leicester he hadn't pursued the question of insurance except for fire or theft. Schupke, the man who had urged him to buy this Italian miracle, had warned him that insurance to drive it, even with the promise of limited mileage, could be as much as £7,000 a year. It was going to take an effort of will to spend £7,000 on a few joy rides and after the money he had spent on buying this car today it might be some time before he could gear himself up for that effort.

And there were to be other demands on whatever money he had left, as he learned when he managed to drag himself away from his new toy and carefully lock the garage door.

'You can spend some money on me now,' Suzanne told him when they had gone indoors.

'And what do you want, Mrs Vanner?' he asked nervously.

'A little shop. I want to open a boutique.'

Neil Kennedy was erecting a swing in the garden for Lindy. Winter was getting warmer and he liked to see her out of doors. He had succumbed to this piece of expenditure during a shopping expedition with his wife who felt that she was keeping in touch with the world if she could escape from the endless domestic demands of her daughter and wander through a department store from time to time. Now he was wrestling with blue tubular steel and yellow polypropylene ropes, trying to create from the tangle a swing that looked like the illustration in the instructions.

His efforts to embed the four legs securely in the lawn brought solemn applause from his daughter who seemed to be getting more pleasure from his attempts at construction than she ever would from the finished article. When it was completed she applauded him again and he gave her a theatrical bow. He was determined to enjoy her now, having a dark suspicion that the euphoria which greets babies has turned to something else less ecstatic a few years later when it can be seen what the baby has become. A rebel with green hair? An addict of white powder? An empty chair at the dinner table? The joys of parenthood could be short-lived.

She climbed on the swing and he gave her a push. Thirty pounds, he thought. What am I doing spending £30 on a swing? There had been few more depressing moments in his life than when he handed Toby Beauchamp a cheque for the

£1,000 that he had borrowed and then lost in the casino. Money spent was frightening enough in his present situation; money lost induced feelings of panic.

Gwenda was talking about getting a gardener in time for spring, and hinting that her restricted life would be more tolerable if they had a cleaning lady. Both ideas struck him as wasteful and unnecessary. He seemed to have the time to do some gardening, and Gwenda was the sort of woman who would clean the house before the cleaning lady arrived so that she wouldn't think them grubby.

The £20,000 that he had acquired as a result of the move to Compton Sinbury was having chunks knocked off it, and there were no monthly replenishments as with the bank accounts of other men. He guessed that a quarter of it had gone already – on the move, on new furniture and on the disastrous visit to the Wali of Swat.

And yet . . . he could not rid himself of the idea that a second visit to the casino would repair the damage created by the first, and that the last result had been a freak. After all, he had won many times at casinos in London. His mistake had been that his stake was too small to endure the inevitable reverses. Anybody who had won £10,000 during a night's gambling had probably been three or four thousand down at some stage: it was only those with plenty of money who could survive the troughs and reach the peaks.

A few days later in the Flatulent Ferret when Toby Beauchamp revealed that he had won more than £3,000 at the poker table and would be very glad to visit the club again, Neil Kennedy was the first to agree. Harry Grant, a victim of that dangerous feeling of invincibility that a single casino win can engender, said that he would like to be included in the party. Only Paul Vanner, his gambling aspirations quashed by the frisky chatelaine of the Manor House, cried off.

Neil Kennedy withdrew £5,000 from Mr Kirby's bank and arrived at the Wali of Swat with a glorious feeling of impregnability, but cushioned by his stake he was tempted to place lavish bets on mediocre cards that neither convinced nor deterred the resident experts. Soon he was losing quite heavily and when his luck briefly changed he did not have the money to capitalize on his good fortune.

At half past three, as Gino appeared with the fourth cup of coffee, Harry Grant had won £80, Toby Beauchamp had won £2,000 and Neil Kennedy was sitting white-faced and empty-handed.

6

IN THE FLATULENT FERRET Men's Hour had skipped lightly over the familiar territory of man's misfortunes and become marooned in a spelling contest in which diarrhoea and pterodactyl had eliminated most of the contestants.

Harry Grant, finding himself humiliatingly among the vanquished – humiliatingly, because he alone earned his living writing words on paper – gazed at flirty Sylvia behind the bar and wondered how she behaved in bed. In a room full of men almost any woman looked attractive. And spring was on the way. When the sun came to Compton Sinbury and bright summer dresses revealed smooth shoulders and shapely legs he had a powerful urge to saunter through the village in dark glasses and a hat, exposing himself to any woman who would be kind enough to notice.

'I need a woman with a fine pair of legs,' he announced, as if this would shortly be provided.

'The only legs I am interested in now are legs of lamb,' said Toby Beauchamp. 'English, not New Zealand. Well, go and find yourself a woman, Harry. Detection, affection, connection.'

'Rejection, dejection,' said Harry. 'This bleary-eyed old stud is on the skids.'

'You can always tell Harry's fans,' Paul Vanner said. 'They're the ones waving their pension books.'

'Talking about pensions,' said Harry, 'how is your big red investment?'

'Sitting in the garage growing more valuable by the minute.'

'If interest rates go up again I think your gearing could be a bit iffy, old son,' Toby told him.

'Don't mention it,' Paul Vanner said, shaking his head. 'Half a million for a house, three hundred grand for a car. And I'm only a simple boy with a way with figures.'

The enormity of his outlay merely for the house and the car which most people took for granted brought a thoughtful silence to the bar. The log fire crackled behind them and a child howled in one of the rooms inside. Suddenly Toby Beauchamp's face assumed the expression of a man who is aware of an earthquake that nobody else has noticed. He placed his vodka on the counter. 'It's a woman,' he said. 'Is this Men's Hour or what?'

'What is occurring?' Vanner asked.

Gwenda Kennedy, in a short red dress and brown suede jacket, had come into the bar on her own.

'Yes, it is a woman. I've seen them before,' said Harry Grant. 'I'd like to lie on top of her and go up and down. Look at those legs!'

'English or New Zealand?' Toby asked.

She came up to the bar and put a £20 note on the counter. 'A bottle of champagne,' she said to Barry, 'and an ice bucket.'

'Where's Neil?' he asked.

She ran her fingers through her blonde hair and shrugged. 'The last time I saw him he was standing on the lawn singing Happy Birthday to a fictitious guinea pig called Roger. He was being a father.'

'It's Men's Hour,' Paul Vanner told her. 'Did he forget?'

'Or has he sent you as an honorary man?' Toby asked. '*In absentia?*'

In her earlier incarnation as an account director with a leading advertising agency Gwenda Kennedy had been quite accustomed to cowing males, and in the self-confident world of advertising they were not easy to subdue. Bright, forceful, imaginative and, above all, ambitious young men had seemed to lose a little of their assurance when she was handling the campaign. Falling for the practised charms of a less than successful actor had caused her much heart searching, but she was trapped by a biological imperative. A successful career was no substitute for motherhood for a normal woman, and marriage and motherhood required quite different qualities from those she had deployed with such success in her job. She had quietened down and played her new role of housewife with a judicious restraint that had secretly surprised her. But, she told herself, she could still handle this bunch of half-baked schoolboys.

'Men's Hour, is it?' she said. 'Where's the train set?'

'Where's the what?' asked Paul Vanner.

'That one over there looks old enough to go with the girls,' said Gwenda, taking her bottle of champagne from an ice bucket that Barry had provided. 'You boys shouldn't be afraid of them. It's all part of growing up.'

'We're not afraid of them, we're escaping from them,' Toby told her. 'You're intruding on a haven of sanity here.'

'Three men and not a child between you,' said Gwenda Kennedy. 'I wonder what you get up to when you're on your own? And what do you all talk about in here? The football results? Your hangovers? Your martyrdom? How you have to stand here and drink while your women cook lunch, entertain the kids and answer the phone?'

'As you so rightly point out, we don't have any kids,' Toby told her. 'Having children is an expensive and exhausting experience that usually ends in disappointment.'

'A good job your mother didn't take such a cynical view,' said Gwenda Kennedy. 'Look what the world would have missed.'

'Why do people call you cynical these days when you tell the truth?' Toby asked, looking genuinely mystified.

'What we talk about in here is money and how to make it,' Paul Vanner said. 'So our wives can buy champagne.'

'I didn't know I could afford it until my husband was persuaded to lose money at poker,' said Gwenda Kennedy. 'It suddenly dawned on me that a few bottles of bubbly were well within the family budget. Would anybody like a glass?'

Normal drinks were pushed to one side as glasses of champagne appeared.

'Men's Hour seems to be better with women,' Harry said, 'Toby never buys us champagne.'

'You're learning, Harry,' said Gwenda Kennedy. 'There's a whole world out there beyond pints of lager and wet dreams. You should put some sweets in your satchel, get your tricycle out and explore.'

'There's a fallacy at the back of your implication, Mrs Kennedy,' Harry told her. 'If you care to drop round to my potting shed some time I would be glad to clear the matter up.'

'My implication is that you should get yourself a wife. I didn't mean somebody else's. You're supposed to find your own.'

At that moment Suzanne Vanner came in wearing a yellow track suit.

'You've missed the news again, Harry,' she said. 'The vicar had a stroke during his sermon. Of course it was some time before anybody noticed. They thought he was being his normal incoherent self.'

'What happened?' Grateful as he was for news and sorry though he felt for the vicar, he was not about to let his consumption of free champagne be interrupted by something that could be adequately dealt with later.

'Well, he keeled over apparently and was taken off in an ambulance. I wasn't there myself, I was playing squash. It does me more good quicker.'

'Did they have to scrap the service?'

'I believe they did. They don't have a substitutes' bench of vicars, do they? If one is carried off the game is abandoned.' She turned and saw Gwenda Kennedy pouring her a glass of champagne. 'What are you doing here already? Did you gatecrash Men's Hour?'

'Boys' Hour,' said Gwenda Kennedy.

'She's a revolutionary,' Toby Beauchamp said.

'They were very good boys once I had bought them some lemonade.'

Suzanne Vanner took the glass and smiled. 'Is Neil working?'

'In a manner of speaking. He's cooking the lunch.'

'Blimey, how did you manage that?'

'He's doing penance,' said Gwenda Kennedy.

Neil Kennedy was in his garden throwing a Frisbee at the squirrels. It was the nearest he would get to the blood sports that he imagined to be a staple of country life and the squirrels stood up on their hind legs and watched his erratic lobs with a nonchalance that was almost impertinent. This exercise was to amuse his daughter who seemed to require new experiences at half-hourly intervals. Last week it had been the dolphins at Windsor, yesterday the skyway safari at Chessington.

The joint was in the oven: he could remember when joints were what you smoked. The potatoes had joined it in the baking tray, the cabbage was cut up and the wine was in the fridge.

Neil Kennedy was, as his wife said, doing penance – and expiation for losing £7,000 of the family funds at poker involved rather more than buying a box of chocolates. Another man would have concealed the loss but, despite being an actor, he was such a bad liar that he had to spend his life telling the truth. He sometimes thought that Gwenda would prefer it otherwise.

'I want a Philip steak,' Lindy had told him as he pursued his womanly role in the kitchen.

'Fillet steak, Lindy,' he said. 'We're having beef.'

'I don't like beef.'

'The alternative is starvation.'

'Ice cream is best.'

When the Frisbee-throwing had lost its audience he took her indoors and persuaded her to play with her Talking Bus, from which a strange voice asked for letters of the alphabet which she had to place in cube-shaped spaces on the side of the vehicle. He was curious about whether the microchip which must be hidden at the heart of this modern toy was going to produce a more literate generation of toddlers than the world had ever seen.

He gathered together the newspapers and sat at the kitchen table. If the Sunday papers grew any bigger, Monday would have to become part of the weekend. He flipped through them restlessly. There was a major philosophical cleavage in the government and a siege at Strangeways prison. He had reached the television reviews when the phone rang. It was Howard, his agent.

'Sorry to call you on a Sunday, Neil. I kept ringing yesterday but there was no reply.'

'We were at Chessington, entertaining Lindy. Have you got me a job? We're dying of hunger down here.'

Howard laughed uneasily. There were more glamorous earners in his stable, self-adoring creatures with household names who could make more money opening a supermarket than Neil could earn in a fortnight's acting.

'I've got you a voice-over on a TV commercial for Tuesday. That's why I'm ringing you today. Ten o'clock at Willy's studio in Soho. Okay?'

'*Give me an A*,' said the Talking Bus.

'Sorry?' said Howard. 'Have you got somebody with you, Neil?'

'It's Lindy's Talking Bus.'

'It sounds pissed. What about the commercial?'

'I'll do it. God knows, I need the money. Have you got anything else lined up? I could use the work, Howard.'

'There's a new serial planned by the BBC called *Hot Air Rises*. I've put you up for the role of a middle-aged husband.'

'Couldn't you get me a speaking part?'

Howard's cackle reverberated down the line. 'How is married life, by the way?'

'Fine. My wife's in the pub and I'm peeling the potatoes.'

'You're ahead of your time, Neil. Me, I still use whores.'

'Aren't you worried about diseases?'

'I don't think I give them any.'

Howard's abrasive chuckle returned to punctuate the conversation. It worried Neil Kennedy who felt, with some reason, that his agent no longer took him seriously. The actor had not fulfilled the promise he was showing when Howard took him on his books, but they had enjoyed many a fine evening together, and Howard kept him on now more out of loyalty to an old drinking partner than with any hope of a huge return.

'There's a new panel game in the pipeline,' he said. 'They're going to do a pilot show and see how it looks. It's called *Be Rude* and I might be able to get you a chance on it. The idea is that participants are invited to be as rude as possible to each other in sixty seconds. It's not your style, I know.'

'Too true, Howard. But if they put me up against Cliff Richard I'd have a go.'

'In the meantime I'll put the script of *Hot Air Rises* in the post and you can have a look at it.'

'Do that.'

'How's the wife-swapping going?' Howard had a lurid picture of life in the country which nothing Kennedy told him could dispel.

'Fast and furious,' he said obediently.

He hung up and went over to put the cabbage on. The Talking Bus was still addressing his daughter. '*No. You Are Wrong. That is an E!*' He went back to the newspapers in search of entertainment. For most people most days were what you got through in the hope of something better.

Gwenda returned looking flushed. She was carrying a half-empty bottle of champagne and it was quite clear that ninety minutes in the Flatulent Ferret had effectively removed the subject of poker losses from her mind.

'Hallo, house-husband,' she said. 'Is everything in order?'

'How was Men's Hour? Are they still a sleazy, money-grabbing bunch of shits or have they developed some endearing qualities?'

'They are lovely, charming, talented human beings,' she told him.

'Who says so?'

'The champagne.'

Two days later she drove him to the station after breakfast.

'It's just as if you were a normal husband,' she said as he climbed out of the Ford. 'Catching a train to town to earn the housekeeping.'

'I am a normal husband,' he said irritably. 'We don't all have to be pen-pushers.'

But as the train rattled its way towards London her remark

began to rankle. Everybody he knew these days seemed to be making much more money with far less work than he had to get through before he saw a cheque. His inability to earn at an adequate rate had now been compounded by his loss of much of the family's capital in a card game. He wanted to work – highly paid, richly rewarded work. But most of all he wanted his £7,000 back.

He opened the steel briefcase that he always carried to jobs like this to convince the neurotic executives in the advertising world that here at least was one businesslike actor. From it he pulled the script of the first episode of *Hot Air Rises* which had arrived from Howard in the post that morning.

The part of Julian had been ringed in the list of characters and he flipped through the pages to see what he had to say.

JULIAN: Clive was struggling. I knew that if he didn't get his figures up he'd be out the door. This job's all about territory management, running a patch.

WYN: Forget work, darling. It's so nice to see you home before midnight. Would you like something to eat?

JULIAN: Could do.

WYN: Would you like Monday's dinner or Tuesday's dinner?

JULIAN: Let's forget food and eat in bed.

WYN: Oral sex is out, I'm afraid. I've got a throat infection.

JULIAN: It's an ill Wyn that blows nobody.
(*Canned laughter.*)

Neil Kennedy read this with mounting horror. Who produced this junk food for the mind? Who were the triple-distilled cretins who bought such pap and foisted it on to a stupefied public? His disillusionment with the business didn't even stop short at his fellow actors who dutifully recited tenth-rate drivel so that they could drink gin with tonics. Why was it, for instance, that when you turned on television or radio you knew immediately whether it was an actor acting or a real person talking? Because actors didn't sound like real people which was precisely what their precious talent was supposed to be about. And he wasn't any happier these days when he got away from the twentieth century's magic and returned to the theatre's roots, a stage, a proscenium arch and, with any luck, some curtains. There he found himself haunted by a quotation from Updike: 'The unreality of painted people standing on a platform saying things they've said to each other for months is more than I can overlook.'

What I'd really like to be, he thought, is a pizza chef in Nice.

At Willy's studio in Soho a disparate group of people had gathered with the joint intention of promoting the fortunes of a furniture warehouse on the North Circular: representatives of the advertising agency, staff of the film company and the taciturn head of the furniture warehouse itself all stood around in a darkened room and an atmosphere of scarcely concealed nervousness. The film company was anxious to please the advertising agency and the advertising agency were desperate to satisfy the rigorous demands of the man from the furniture warehouse. Neil Kennedy arrived to discover the usual edgy mood of transparently bogus bonhomie.

'Here comes the voice,' said Willy, a bearded man in his thirties, whose ownership of this small, thriving film company had made him rich but haggard. 'How are you, Neil?'

'Fine.'

'Here's the script. Okay, let's see the film.'

The room was like a small cinema with a screen at one end, and they all sat in low seats and watched the 30-second film.

'They want a hard-sell voice, Neil,' Willy said. 'Do your usual. It shouldn't take ten minutes.'

Neil Kennedy had been hired for an hour for a fee of £250. If it only took him ten minutes he would regard it as a result, but these little jobs were seldom over that quickly. There were too many cooks tending this particular broth, too many different people to please.

When they had seen the film twice, the engineer got up from his console desk and showed him into a small cubicle where he donned headphones and looked out at Willy.

'We'll put the words on now,' came the message in his headphones.

Neil Kennedy looked at his script. He could hardly bring himself to utter the words, but he forced himself to look at the screen when the film started. Each time a black stripe had moved across the picture from right to left he had to speak.

'E.J.C.'s fantastic summer sale is now on!' he announced. The picture showed a warehouse that looked like a maximum-security prison. The stripe appeared. The picture changed.

'This chair for only £450!' Another picture. 'Three-piece suites from £990!'

'Put more variation in the inflexion,' Willy's voice said in his headphones.

'Dining-room tables to suit every room!' Neil Kennedy said, changing the modulation of his voice.

He looked at his script: there was only one more line. He waited for the stripe to appear and cross the screen.

'It's all in E.J.C.'s fantastic summer sale!'

The screen went blank and he got up and left the cubicle. They had to wait now while the engineer mixed words and music at the right level.

'That's going to be okay,' Willy said. 'Money for jam, isn't it, Neil?'

It didn't seem to be money worth talking about when the man who evidently owned all this furniture came across and introduced himself. He wore a very expensive blue suit and had a fleshy face with the hard, piercing eyes, Kennedy imagined, of a trainee rapist.

'Elvis Corrigan,' he said, offering a hand. 'I've seen you on television.' Presumably, thought Kennedy, his middle initial is J. 'Very good in that thing about motor bikes.'

Neil Kennedy tried to remember whether he had ever appeared in a television programme that featured motor bikes. It was always possible that Elvis J. Corrigan was thinking of somebody else.

'If I were an actor,' his admirer excitedly persisted, 'I would take great pleasure occasionally in pretending to be somebody else. You know – to see how people reacted to another person. I suppose we'd all like to be somebody else at one time or another.'

'I think I'd be quite happy to be somebody with your business empire,' Neil Kennedy told him.

Willy interrupted them to say that the film was now ready for final approval. As usual, Kennedy was surprised at his cheerful, forceful delivery. It did not reflect in any way what he had felt, sitting alone in the cubicle.

'Just fine,' said Elvis J. Corrigan. 'That'll bring in the punters.'

But Neil Kennedy was thinking about something else that the furniture tycoon had said, and suddenly he knew how he would get his £7,000 back – and a bit more besides.

7

THE UNDISTURBED SERENITY which was what attracted people to Compton Sinbury was a mild irritation to Harry Grant whose job it was to engross newspaper readers with exciting accounts of what was happening in the village. Creating drama from tranquillity was the impossible challenge that he faced every week.

A desperate quest for news took him one evening to the village hall, built at the top of the green in 1878 in memory of some local benefactor. The event was the quarterly meeting of Compton Sinbury Parish Council, a sober body of a dozen local worthies who were re-elected unopposed from time to time because there was nobody else available who could match their boredom threshold. They discussed car parks and street lighting and overgrown verges and, most regularly of all, dog mess on the village green.

But tonight there was a fresh item on the agenda, placed there by Miss Daisy Balcombe, a spinster of seventy whose tenuous grip on reality was the source of much ribald laughter and frequent embarrassment. Under 'any other business' she wanted to raise the subject of Anglo-French relations and, specifically, the possibility of Compton Sinbury being twinned with a suitable place in France.

'Most villages are twinned with somewhere on the continent,' she told the meeting in her terribly upper-class accent. 'It provides the possibility of reciprocal visits, educational trips by children and, with the freedom of movement following 1992, could be beneficial financially to Compton Sinbury.'

The chairman, Colonel Arbuthnott, thought that this was one of Miss Balcombe's more lucid contributions to meetings of the parish council, but his heart sank. Although four years younger than Miss Balcombe, he had not been abroad for forty-six years since he had arrived home on a stretcher after some unpleasantness in the Hürtgen Forest while attached to the 4th Infantry Division. If he thought of French villages today, he thought of 1415, St Crispin's Day and a village called Agincourt.

'You have recently been abroad, Miss Balcombe, I believe,' he said, as if he was inquiring about a recent arrest for soliciting. 'Is that what brought this on?'

'Indeed it is, Colonel,' said Miss Balcombe. Her nose curved like an eagle's beak. 'I have just been on holiday in Gascony and came across the ideal twinning partner, a little place in the department of Gers between Bordeaux and Toulouse. It's a little medieval town with a sixteenth-century cathedral and it's full of history. I ate in a wonderful restaurant called Table des Cordeliers that had Gothic vaults. It's on a tributary of the Garonne and the nearest airport, Bordeaux, is only an hour or so away.'

Harry Grant scribbled in his notebook. This was a story. It might even produce a free trip to France.

'It owes its prosperity today to the trade in Armagnac, and one of its most famous residents,' said Miss Balcombe, consulting some notes, 'was Montluc, the leader of the crusade against the Albigensians.'

But Colonel Arbuthnott, who had already heard far more than he wanted to know, was raising his hand. 'Miss Balcombe,' he said gently, 'what is the name of this favoured place?'

'Condom,' said Miss Balcombe.

'Condom?' said Colonel Arbuthnott.

'Yes,' said Miss Balcombe. Her accent made 'yes' sound like 'knee-yarse'.

Colonel Arbuthnott, a man of guile and irony, fixed the speaker with a basilisk gaze. 'Miss Balcombe, do you know what a condom is?'

'I've just told you, Colonel,' said Miss Balcombe briskly. 'It's a town between Bordeaux and Toulouse.'

Colonel Arbuthnott looked sick.
'Sin – twinned with Condom,' he said. 'Terrific.'

In the strained silence of the Wali of Swat, cards slid across the table and soon afterwards money slipped across the table too.
The visitors tonight had made a change in their team. Neil Kennedy, who had announced sadly that he could no longer sustain the losses, had been replaced by a man with more money than he could use. Paul Vanner's belated opportunity to visit the club had been created by his wife's departure to the Midlands to visit her ailing father. Counselled by Toby Beauchamp to make sure he had the resources 'to face the big guns' he had brought £10,000 in £50 notes and was sitting now trying to recall the subtleties of five-card stud poker which he hadn't played for years.
Harry Grant had arrived reluctantly, talked into making up the numbers despite a secret conviction that he had already used up what luck was coming his way in this somewhat dingy environment. Winning and then losing, he seemed to be taking two paces forward and then two paces backward in a financial dance that was leading him nowhere.
Gino, the owner, came in with coffee, and stood beaming while a hand was played to its conclusion.
'Gentlemen,' he said. 'If I may interrupt.' The lights above the table glinted on his greased hair. 'I have a request. There is a gentleman, a visitor to Britain, who wants to play tonight. He sent a friend to ask permission, and I am allowing him to play as he's a guest in this country.'
A heavily set man with a black moustache, who had sat silently through every game so far, asked: 'Who is he?'
'He's an Arab,' Gino told him. 'A sheikh. His younger sister is training at the nursing college and he has rented a house in the country to look after her moral welfare. It's the Moslem way. Apparently he gets bored sitting in this big house on his own all day and so he sent an English friend down to see me. You know, the Arabs love to gamble.'
'He should bring a few shekels into our little game,' said Toby Beauchamp.

'Shekels are Jewish,' Paul Vanner told him. 'You mean dinars.'

'Lucky you being in the currency market. I nearly made a mistake there.'

The air of expectancy which Gino's announcement had created had subsided half an hour later when no visitor had appeared. But just after midnight the door opened and Gino ushered in the Arab sheikh. He was a stocky figure with a big black beard, dark glasses and the Arab *ghutra* on his head, a square of white cloth, folded cornerwise and held in place by two circles of fine black wool rope. He was wearing a black *dish-dasha*, a long-sleeved woollen shirt that reached to the ground. He carried a large leather bag.

He raised a hand and said in a gravelly voice: 'Salaam-alaikoom.' The men round the table smiled and nodded at this apparent salutation.

When Gino had shown him to a chair at the table, the sheikh put the leather bag at his feet and placed both hands flat on the table. There were rings on most fingers.

'He speaks no English,' Gino said to the dealer. 'He'll tell you with his hands.'

The sheikh did not react to this message but sat, motionless and untouched, like a man in a time capsule. When the dealer shot them each two cards, the sheikh cupped his hands to examine the one that was face down and then pushed both cards away. It was a quarter of an hour before he received cards that persuaded him to stay in.

As the betting progressed the sheikh reached down into his leather bag and came up with a fistful of £50 notes which were immediately changed into chips for him. Whatever the bid he raised it, defying the others to stay with him. If his hidden card was a king he had a good hand and the eyes of the other players swept furtively round the table to see how many kings had been used.

When the players received their fourth card the sheikh produced another £5,000 from his bag and pushed the bundle towards the dealer to be turned into chips.

A mixture of doubt and panic began to pervade the table.

People who were quietly confident about the strength of their hand discovered that they were not *that* confident. Reasonable bets began to look like ludicrous gambles. An element of high risk began to enter their calculations.

Only the silent man with the black moustache refused to be intimidated by the contents of the leather bag. He slid £5,000 worth of chips towards the pot and waited for his last card. It did not appear to improve his hand and when the sheikh raised the bet to £10,000 he folded and swore quietly.

Watching his money disappear, Paul Vanner began to wonder what he was doing there. His huge salary arrived only with a prodigious effort. Did he need to fritter it away? His house was going up in value, the Ferrari Daytona was quietly appreciating in the garage. What more speculation did he need?

Toby Beauchamp was discovering what it was like to lose money in the Wali of Swat for the first time. He did not like it. Once he had a straight which ought to win a pot at this table but the sheikh had raised the ante so much as each card appeared that Toby was going to have to pay £6,000 to find out whether it was good enough this time. He discovered that he wasn't that curious.

Harry Grant had almost dropped out of the game. He had arrived with his usual £500 and now he had £400. He was not anxious to lose more and so was not exposing himself to the chance of winning. He still accepted the first two cards but then pushed them away without betting.

Nobody knew how much money there was in the leather bag, but after two hours the pile of chips in front of the sheikh was quite enough to dishearten the others. The chips were there to be won, stacked temptingly as a challenge, but you needed almost as many chips yourself to get in the ring with them unless you were prepared to risk serious financial injury.

A last desperate bid by the man with the moustache to get back into this game brought the session to a halt soon after three o'clock. He had three kings showing and every card he received had made him look stronger than the sheikh. He stayed in, matching the influx of Arab money, hoping for a full house or a fourth king. By the time his fifth card – a seven – arrived he had paid £8,000.

The sheikh indicated with one finger pointed at the pot that he would bet the maximum, and found it necessary once more to delve in his bag.

'Don't bother,' said the man with the moustache and stood up.

'I've finished too,' said Toby Beauchamp. 'For good, as it happens.'

Paul Vanner looked at the empty space where his chips should have been. 'I lost £10,000. Whose idea was it?'

'I lost seven,' said Toby. 'That's my last game of cards. How did you get on, Harry?'

'I seem to have lost a hundred. Couldn't we find a less expensive hobby?'

They walked out to the Porsche without talking again, feeling more stupid than angry.

When the sheikh's hoard of chips had been converted into bank notes by a respectful dealer, who had rarely seen such a masterful display of bluffing and bullying, he stuffed them into his leather bag and zipped it up. He walked from the club without speaking, up the corridor and out into the street where a black Mercedes was waiting with a driver in a peak cap. The sheikh climbed into the back seat.

'Drive me home, my good man,' he said.

Gwenda Kennedy was watching her husband kiss another woman whose bikini top became askew in the passion of the embrace. It was an old film in which Neil had played a small part eight or ten years ago, resurrected now to fill a gap on late-night television. It was depressing to see how he had aged, and eerie to think that if he died she would still be watching him and hearing him in one of those third-rate movies from the past.

She looked across to the sofa where Lindy had finally fallen asleep. Other people's three-year-old children were asleep by seven but this one was still disrupting the evening at ten o'clock, running, shouting, thinking of games and even attempting to dictate the channel that they would watch on the television.

When she first became pregnant Gwenda Kennedy had expected to be back at work within a year, her child looked after by some amenable nanny, but the child was so active that she couldn't bring herself to inflict her on anyone else. Her conversation was a continual surprise.

Tonight Gwenda had told her: 'Daddy was there when you were born.'

'Yes, I know,' said Lindy. 'I saw him.'

'You *saw* him? Did you see me?'

'Well, only your legs,' said Lindy, laughing.

Her mother was still pondering over this remark as she watched the film.

At eleven o'clock she switched it off and carried her daughter upstairs. Neil was obviously having a late drink in the Fox, or the Flatulent Ferret, as these country folk called it. Gwenda Kennedy had come to the country reluctantly, feeling herself shunted from the warm centre of the universe for humbling financial reasons. But now, as her eyes became accustomed to the green and her ears became used to the silence, she found a quality of life – peaceful and yet interesting, circumscribed and yet safe – that was beginning to suit her.

She climbed into bed after another exhausting day with Lindy and was asleep within minutes. When she was woken by the key in the front door she looked at her watch and was astonished to see that it was nearly four o'clock. She could not believe that her husband had either the stamina or the money to drink this far into the night and she sat upright in bed and put on the light.

She heard his footsteps on the stairs and prepared herself for a drunken entrance. But he came in quietly, grinning like a man in a toothpaste advertisement, and dumped a leather bag on the bed.

'Don't tell me,' she said. 'You've got a part-time job as a burglar.'

'Sort of,' he said, sitting down. 'Blimey, I'm knackered.'

'What have you got on your face?'

'Make-up. You remember. I'm an actor.'

'Not in the middle of the night, you're not. Neil, what have you been doing?'

'Gambling.'

He picked up the leather bag, unzipped it and held it upside down above her, shaking it endlessly as more and more banknotes floated down in front of her.

'Gambling?' she said. 'I thought you had given that up?'

'How much do you think is there?'

'I don't know, but I'm going to find out.'

He sat watching her as she counted the money, enjoying seeing her expression change. The count took a long time and in its early stages she seemed to be smiling. But the smile was replaced by amazement which was eventually succeeded by something that looked ominously like anger.

'Forty-nine thousand pounds,' she said, looking at him. 'You *won* £49,000?'

'Not that much,' he said laughing. 'Twenty thousand was my stake money, and I'd lost £7,000 on earlier visits. My overall profit is £22,000.'

Something in his wife's expression told Neil Kennedy that he had just made his first mistake of the evening. He had intended to keep this gambling expedition to himself but he was so exhilarated by his success that discretion had fled. His wife may have been half asleep, but she was alert enough now to spot the part of his story that he should never have mentioned.

'Your stake money was £20,000? Where in the hell did that come from?'

'The bank.'

'We don't have that much in the bank, Neil.'

He stood up, feeling slightly nervous. 'Banks lend money, dear. It's what they're for.'

'Against what? The house? We haven't got anything else.'

'We wouldn't have lost the house. We'd have had to take out a small mortgage to repay the bank.'

She lay back on her pillow and closed her eyes.

'I think I'm dreaming this. We're struggling to survive and you're out borrowing thousands of pounds to gamble with.'

He collected the money that was now strewn all over the bed and returned it to his leather bag. His nervousness had been replaced by frustration and resentment.

'We're £20,000 better off than we were this morning. I may be going mad, but I thought you'd be pleased.'

There was no reply from the pillow and he took the bag back downstairs and tried to sleep on the sofa. He had endured an equally difficult conversation about fourteen hours earlier with Felix Kirby at the bank and his nerves were frayed. He rolled off the sofa and poured himself a whisky.

Felix Kirby had been sitting idly in the bank when his assistant told him that Neil Kennedy would like to see him. He was day-dreaming about faraway places with sunshine and coconuts and wondering how, out of the whole enormous world with its pleasures and possibilities, he had managed to end up in this sterile cell.

Neil Kennedy came in wearing the sort of expression that Felix Kirby was deeply familiar with: it combined a formal respect with the nervous grin of an anxious supplicant.

'Hallo, Neil, sit down,' he said. 'What can I do for you?'

'I want to borrow some money,' he said.

'How much do you need?'

'Ten thousand pounds for twenty-four hours.'

'Twenty-four hours?' said Felix Kirby, alerted immediately to something odd. He was quite used to lending £10,000 to all sorts of people. They replaced their furniture or built a conservatory or bought a car and paid the money back with appropriate interest over three or five years. But lending that amount for a day not only suggested some sort of reckless investment, it also produced little for the bank in the way of interest.

'I have fifteen or sixteen in the bank,' Neil Kennedy said. 'I need twenty. I want to withdraw ten of my own and borrow ten.'

'Why don't you withdraw fifteen of your own and borrow five?'

'Well,' said Neil Kennedy, looking uncomfortable, 'I want something left in the bank if anything goes wrong.'

'Goes wrong?' said Felix Kirby. 'The more I hear the less I like it. What is the money for, Neil?'

'A speculative investment.'

'For twenty-four hours?'

Neil Kennedy nodded. 'For twenty-four hours.'

Felix Kirby leaned over his desk. 'I don't want to be difficult, Neil, but it sounds . . . unusual.'

Neil Kennedy felt that his grand plan was under attack before it was even assembled; he decided that this probing would have to be resisted.

'You hold the deeds of my house,' he said. 'I have no mortgage.'

'Oh, quite,' said Felix Kirby, retreating a little. 'But I'm here to offer advice as well as financial help and I thought you might care to discuss it.'

'I'd rather not if you don't mind.'

Mr Kirby pressed a buzzer which summoned a secretary from the next room. Soon pieces of paper were being laid out in front of Neil Kennedy, all of them requiring his signature. Half an hour later he left the bank with £20,000 in his leather bag.

When he returned a day later he didn't bother to ask whether he could see Felix Kirby. He walked straight into his office.

Felix Kirby was reading his post and looked surprised as a leather bag was opened in front of him. Bank notes poured on to his desk.

'Forty-nine thousand pounds,' Neil Kennedy told him. 'Could you credit it to my account and deduct your ten and the interest?'

'Thank God for that,' said Felix Kirby. 'I was frightened that you were going to do something silly.'

PART TWO

• Warm Feelings •

It is my belief, Watson, founded upon my experience, that the lowest and vilest alleys of London do not present a more dreadful record of sin than does the smiling and beautiful countryside.

Sir Arthur Conan Doyle
'Copper Beeches'

8

FROM THE CORNER OF THE BEDROOM WINDOW in his council house on the outskirts of the village, One-cell Tel was watching a topless girl mow the lawn next door. He had glanced out of the window to see what the chances were of rain and found himself looking at a bare-breasted beauty with long blonde hair mowing the grass in a pair of pink briefs. His heart pounded. His mouth went dry. On the Colemore Estate this was not how people tended their gardens.

He retreated into his room and stood on the bed so that he could see her but she could not see him. She was doing the job briskly and her breasts bounced as she glided over the grass. Either she thought she was not overlooked, or she didn't care. When she bent to empty the grass box her breasts swung like two rugby balls. One-cell Tel, scared to blink in case he missed something, felt his eyes beginning to burn.

He wanted to go downstairs to find out who this lovely creature was but he couldn't abandon his vantage point while she was mowing. He stood transfixed on his unmade bed watching the girl go up the lawn (back view) and then, as he caught his breath, turn and push the mower towards him. Not once did she look up to see whether anyone was watching.

When the grass was cut she pushed the mower towards the house and was lost to view. One-cell Tel got off the bed feeling giddy. His sex life wasn't such a triumphant affair that he could remain coldly impervious to the beautiful body on the lawn. In fact, since his unexpected seduction by Mrs Vanner in the conservatory, it had only involved himself in daily bouts of increasing frenzy.

The temptation to return to the conservatory had been almost overwhelming and his resistance to the idea had not been helped by an inviting phone call from Suzanne Vanner herself who had wanted a job done on the wire netting surrounding her tennis court. But One-cell Tel occasionally found himself drinking in the Flatulent Ferret at the same time as Paul Vanner and what had happened already frightened him more than enough.

He went downstairs to the kitchen where his mother was making some sort of pie. His father had died in a bar in Brighton many years ago while losing a bet that he could drink a pint of whisky.

'Somebody moved next door, mum?' he asked.

His mother, a little old lady with grey hair and a bun who never seemed to stop moving, nodded.

'Widow called Mrs Gray,' she said. 'Come up from Cornwall in a house exchange. She's got a daughter called Cathy but I haven't seen her yet.'

'I have,' said One-cell Tel. 'That's a nice name, isn't it? Cathy?'

'Yes, dear,' said Mrs Wallace.

Her son wandered out of the kitchen, trying to recall the picture of Cathy's breasts. He decided that he would send her a nice present. Actions spoke louder than words, particularly words that came from somebody with his speech problems.

Suzanne Vanner sat in her Victorian button-back chair in the Manor House and wondered if she might be pregnant. It would be a cruel irony if a baby were to appear after the sexless months she had endured with her tired husband, and an impossible development to explain to him.

She was sitting in the drawing room which was also the dining room. The view from the windows was of an archway of laburnum that led to the tennis court. The contents of the room itself had been bought separately and bore no relationship to anything else. The parquet floor was covered with a big Persian rug. A large, round rosewood table stood in the middle of the room and was used if there were guests for dinner. A huge sofa, upholstered in tweed, stood against one wall quite near a mahogany sideboard. Flowers, plants, magazines, bronze candlesticks and pieces of china were strewn almost haphazardly round the room. Only the marble chimney-piece with club-fender had been there when they arrived and seemed, unarguably, to belong.

Suzanne Vanner had never had any money and neither had her husband. They had both been brought up in poor homes where bills piled up on the mantelpiece until one sacrifice or another enabled them to be paid. Her father had spent his life earning little money as a clerk in a factory where punctuality was valued higher than talent, and she had spent her childhood learning not to spend. 'The best way to teach young people about money is not to give them any,' he said. 'Then when they get some they'll realize its value.' There was something in this because even in her teens, when she was earning money herself, she thought two or three times before buying anything while her friends squandered their weekly wages in a matter of hours.

These days her father's meanness had developed into an obsession that verged on illness, a condition vividly demonstrated during her recent visit by his removal of the second hand on his watch because he thought the battery would last longer.

Paul Vanner's family had, if anything, even less money. Home had been a council house in Stepney where his school reports had not suggested that he would ever be able to afford anything better. But a messenger's job in the City at the age of sixteen had opened the doors to an exciting world where education was irrelevant and the rewards were stupendous. Illiterate yuppies drove £50,000 cars and lived in penthouse flats. Paul Vanner discovered that he had a talent that was suddenly prized above all others: he could make a deal.

When they met in a wine bar he was already earning £40,000 a year and seemed to be spending at the same rate. After a life of financial caution, it was a characteristic that she found deeply attractive. He was drunk on lager and wearing a blue peak cap which had 24 HEURES DU MANS on the front. It emerged that he had just spent over £5,000 on a weekend in France watching a car race, a journey made in somebody's private jet.

Suzanne was working then in a ladies' dress shop, despite the urgings of her friends that with her startling looks and long hair she should become a model. But she had a dream that she would one day have her own shop and the career of a model was a short one.

Paul Vanner bought her a drink without even asking whether she wanted one. His verbal foreplay, too, seemed to cut several corners.

'Going to bed with me is a bit like cooking a meal for Egon Ronay,' he told her. This proved not to be the case, a discovery she made a couple of weeks later in the Royal Bath Hotel in Bournemouth. Their wedding in Hammersmith was a Bacchanalian orgy.

But when they had sobered up she found it easy to steer him towards her childhood ambition of a large house in a beautiful village in the country. Looking round the room now she wondered whether they deserved it – whether they were people who were equipped to handle money. Never having had the chance to develop the elusive attribute of taste, they had furnished the Manor House in an unforgivably random fashion that would have horrified the cultured and elegant magazines that she now studied so diligently.

On breakfast television a man was talking about 'the jorker of the tuf' and she turned, interested, to the screen before realizing that he was discussing a jockey who was the joker of the turf. She punched up the headlines on teletext and read the first two:

HUSBAND ACCUSED OVER BODY IN GARDEN
WANTED MAN IN COMA BY WOMAN'S BODY

It was always good to know, she thought, that other people's private lives were even worse than your own. She turned off the television and dreamed of a shopping spree in Geneva, of sunshine in a Tuscan orchard.

She had a glass of wine in her hand, she suddenly realized,

but could not remember how it had got there. Sipping it, she wondered whether her husband was punishing her for marrying him.

'Pretend he's not there,' Nadine Kirby had said to her once. 'That's the only way to share a house with a man.'

She put on a coat and went out. It was a pleasant March morning and she decided to walk to the shops.

She was heading for the little supermarket that was next to the post office at the top of the green but then she noticed a CLOSING DOWN notice in the window of the Arts and Craft shop that was two doors away. She went in.

The shop was run by a pale man called Davey who moved amongst his exotic goods with a distracted air as if he couldn't remember how they got there or what they cost. He was rumoured to be a painter with a hoard of unsold canvases.

'What's happening?' she asked him. 'Are you really closing down?'

'Afraid so,' said Davey, wandering slowly towards her. 'This is not a going concern.'

So you're going, she thought. He was one of those people who stood six inches closer to you than was really necessary and she was assailed by the rancid fumes of his cheap cologne.

'Who's taking the premises?' she asked. This was just the sort of shop that she had imagined opening.

'Nobody yet and it'll be a brave man. The people round here have got money all right, but they don't like spending it which is probably why they've got it in the first place.'

'Perhaps it will be a brave woman. Have you got the agent's name?'

She thought that Paul had almost been won round now to the idea of her opening a boutique. The big shift had come when she had hinted that if she had something to do she would drink less. But at first he had insisted that they couldn't afford it.

'I'm not rich like the rich are rich,' he told her. 'When I buy something big I've borrowed the money. When they buy something big they've sold a few shares.'

'But you're so good at borrowing money, darling,' she replied. 'Not everybody knows how to do it. And this isn't an extravagance, it's an investment. Like the Ferrari.'

An opportunity to improve the sepulchral atmosphere that had hung in the house like a fog since his win at the Wali of Swat came to Neil Kennedy with the arrival of his wife's birthday. He rang up Nadine Kirby and asked if Rachel could babysit, and booked a table at La Palme d'Or. Gwenda Kennedy was less enthusiastic about birthdays than some people because its appearance emphasized for a few months that she was older than her husband, but she had promised herself a dinner at La Palme d'Or ever since they moved to Compton Sinbury.

'I suppose we have to spend the money on something,' she said as they crept along country lanes in the Ford Escort. The countryside was losing its winter bareness and dressing for spring.

After dark La Palme d'Or carried on its farmhouse exterior strings of twinkling lights that gave it the appearance of a grotto. Inside it was warm and cosy. The Kennedys were shown to a corner table that he had specifically reserved, and from there they could observe the select collection of customers most of whom carried with them an air of disdain, as if they were wondering who had left a Ford Escort outside. Short of going to London, being seen in La Palme d'Or was the highest social peak available.

A captain of industry, whose £2 million mansion sat on top of a hill nearby, was dining with a large party in the middle of the room. At an adjacent table was the local MP, a former sailor, who had been delivering ignored speeches from the back benches for a quarter of a century. He was a man who, since 1945 at any rate, liked to keep out of trouble, and this was as close to his disputatious constituents as he cared to get. At another table was a dramatically made-up lady of about seventy whose high-kicking talents had enlivened many a West End musical even before the MP went to sea.

Neil Kennedy sought to disturb the tidy and complacent

behaviour that seemed to rule among the tuxedoed diners in these elegant surroundings by asking the waiter as he waved a large gold menu before him: 'Have you got any Australian wild pig?'

But the waiter had recognized him from some television appearance and was only too keen to enter into the spirit of things. 'I don't know, sir,' he said. 'I haven't met all the customers yet.'

When he had served them, first with melon and ham and then with leg of lamb, he returned to loiter at Gwenda's side as if her company was preferable to others on offer. 'Is everything all right, madam?'

'No,' she told him. 'I'd like some more butter and a new man. Mine's corked.'

For her birthday her husband had bought her a new dress in black and gold which she was wearing now. She was trying to balance her pleasure at the dress with her knowledge that it was gambling that had produced the money to pay for it. But the money was in the bank now and it seemed silly to let it lie there. Her husband was pouring her some Roederer Cristale champagne instead of her usual white wine.

'What else are you going to spend your ill-gotten gains on?' she asked.

'You know what I want,' he said. 'A holiday.'

Gwenda Kennedy could see why, after three years of being tied to the house by the demands of her daughter, of sleepless nights and nappy changes and odd meals and endless child's games, she needed a holiday; but her husband's need, after 'resting' periods between infrequent jobs which were invariably longer than the jobs themselves, did not seem so pressing.

'You can't lie on a sunny beach with a three-year-old, nor go on a safari in Kenya,' she said.

'Think of something else. Money is no problem.'

'America,' she said. 'I've got to get there one day.'

Neil Kennedy was delighted. One of the biggest bugbears of marriage had been that it always posed an obstacle to travel. The instant holiday had vanished from his life. Trying to get three people moving in the same direction at the same time had proved so impossibly difficult that there had been very little movement at all.

'Right,' he said, grabbing the chance. 'The sooner the better. I might be heavily involved with a dreary TV series in a minute and it could mean a lot of weeks with no time off.'

'That *will* be a shock to the system, dear,' said Gwenda Kennedy. 'What I'd really like to do is go over there and live like an American for a month. I wouldn't want to stay in an hotel. I saw an advertisement in a magazine last week. There's a firm in London who arrange house swaps. You go and live in somebody's house over there for a month while they come and live in yours.'

Neil Kennedy had always hoped that an acting role would get him to America but the years had produced nothing more exciting than ten days in Portugal.

'New York or the West Coast,' he said. 'That's what we want.'

'I imagine the choice is restricted by who you are swapping houses with. Can they find somebody who wants to stay in Compton Sinbury?'

'Just the sort of place Americans go for. A real English village.'

Gwenda Kennedy finished her lamb and looked across at the sweet trolley. 'Shall I write to this firm in London then?' she asked.

'Tomorrow morning,' said Neil Kennedy, momentarily distracted by a new arrival. 'Look, there's old Toby with a very sinister-looking gentleman.'

Toby Beauchamp's guest seemed to be ill at ease. He looked covertly round the room, noting each guest in turn as if somewhere among them was a man who had been hired to wipe him out. When he sat down he chose a seat that gave most of the diners the back of his head. Toby Beauchamp, in contrast, seemed wonderfully relaxed in a new light-brown check suit and, unusually for him, a pink silk tie. He greeted the waiter with a joke and plucked his serviette from the table with a boyish flourish.

'I'm not sure this is the best place for us to meet,' said his guest, Brynwyn Rolfe. 'Property developers and chief planning officers are best not seen together in public.'

You're paranoid, thought Toby. 'You're paranoid,' he said. 'I wanted to buy you dinner and this is the very best place to do it.'

Brynwyn Rolfe shook his head. 'It shouldn't have been on my patch. One councillor in here and I could face a lot of embarrassing questions.'

He was a small man with horn-rimmed glasses. He had spent his childhood on the Lleyn Peninsula and got out of Wales at the first opportunity in search of a standard of living that didn't seem to be available in Pwllheli. Today his greed always got the better of him.

It took the menu now to console him. His eye ran down the long list of free food and a more satisfied expression settled on his plump red face. He sniffed his Valpolicella and then drank from it.

'I'll have a T-bone steak,' he said. 'No starter.'

He hadn't eaten very much of it when Toby told him: 'Your paranoia isn't entirely misplaced. I had a little shock myself the other day.'

Brynwyn Rolfe stopped in mid-chew. 'A shock?'

'Yes, I had lunch with Kirby, my bank manager, and he had spotted your little cheques. He thinks you're on my pay roll.'

'Jesus, Toby, I *know* Felix Kirby.'

'He pretended he didn't know who you are. He pretended that he thought you were some bloke in the Isle of Man as that's where the cheques keep going to.'

'What are you telling me?'

'That's all. I think we can count on the discretion of bank managers, don't you?'

'I don't count on the discretion of anybody. Every bastard's out to get you is my philosophy, boyo.'

'Well, perhaps we ought to alter the arrangement. That was one of the things I wanted to discuss with you.'

'How do you mean – alter it?'

'I could pay cash.'

'And I have to keep flying to the Isle of Man with it? Forget it.'

'Why don't you form a company? Get your name off the cheque.'

'I looked into that once. Forming a company creates other problems on the tax front. Why don't you shift your account to somewhere where the manager hasn't got time to riffle through your old cheques?'

'I'm not going to do that. I want a bank manager who is a friend.'

'Well, let's hope he is one. You've worried the hell out of me.'

The steak seemed to have disappeared despite the worrying intrusion of Felix Kirby and now the wine was vanishing fast too.

'You know,' he said, dabbing his mouth with his serviette, 'that this is a prison job? For you as well as me.'

Toby smiled, more to reassure his guest than out of a conviction that what he was saying was untrue.

'I doubt it.'

'Well, don't doubt it. I know the form. It's all happened before, we're hardly in unknown territory. If Kirby's smelling something I'm not happy. We have to make a different arrangement or the deal's off.'

'Brynwyn, if it comes to it I will personally fly to the Isle of Man and deposit the money in your account in cash. Stop worrying.'

Brynwyn Rolfe nodded slowly. 'That might be the best idea.'

'Good. Now the other thing I wanted to discuss with you. You know that piece of land between the meadow and the garden centre on the road to the station?'

'I know it.'

'What do you think the chances of half a dozen homes there are? If they have to wait until I've got planning permission they'll put the price up. If I buy it without I can get it for a song.'

'Buy it,' said Brynwyn Rolfe.

One-cell Tel looked for Cathy for more than a month but he never saw her. He didn't see her in the village or even on the estate. Worst of all, he never saw her in the garden.

He peered often from his bedroom window and noticed with impatience the length of her growing grass; he waited in the front room after breakfast to see if she left for work; and he laboured unnecessarily on his van in the drive in the hope that she would emerge from the house next door. And all the time he wondered what to buy her. He wanted a present that would make her sit up, a gift that spoke to her sexual nature. Cathy Gray did not look like the sort of girl who would appreciate flowers, and her figure did not suggest that she would welcome chocolates. His mind returned to the subject again and again but it didn't reach the conclusion that he was groping towards.

And then, one hot day in April, he looked out of his window and nearly cried out. She was standing on the lawn in the nude. She was laying a rug on the lawn to lie on and her bottom was offered up to him. He climbed on the bed and gaped.

Suddenly she decided that the grass was too long to lay her rug on and she vanished briefly and returned with the mower. She was going to cut the grass in the nude! One-cell Tel swallowed hard and, feeling that this was more than he deserved, promised to be good for ever. He wished that he had a camera with one of those zoom lenses he had heard about. He could get some pictures here that would sustain him during the lonely evenings and provide him with the private entertainment that he needed.

Watching her stride naked up and down the lawn he felt excitement and then discomfort in his jeans which he hastily unzipped to liberate his growing organ.

She moved gracefully, her slender, sylphlike figure almost too light for the manly job of mowing grass. He liked it when she was coming towards him and he could see her big breasts and the blonde triangle of her pubic hair, and then he liked it when she turned and he could watch her trim bottom moving sexily up the lawn. He smiled to himself as he realized that he had not yet seen Cathy Gray with clothes on.

When the grass was cut she found the rug again and laid it on the lawn, and then she lay down on her back and closed her eyes. Her long hair, spread out around her head, made it look as if she was floating on her back in a pool.

One-cell Tel stared at her in his frustration, wondering what present he could possibly send her that would put her in his debt. And then to a mind deranged by lust, an idea came. He very rarely had an idea but his concupiscent vigil had produced one now. The answer was in his hand!

He would send Cathy Gray a gift that she would really appreciate and understand, a life-size replica of his erection, sprayed, perhaps, with gold paint.

He wasn't sure how such a model could be obtained without damage to his most delicate regions, but he was a handyman accustomed to finding solutions to life's smaller technical problems.

Driving down the M23 with a chattering child behind her and a comatose husband on the front seat at her side, Gwenda Kennedy wondered whether transporting her family across the globe would really achieve very much. She seemed to be taking her domestic problems with her – all the way to St Louis, Missouri, where they were to spend a month in what Americans called a condo. St Louis had not been their first choice but the house-swap firm in London had on their books, oddly enough, somebody in St Louis who wanted to stay in or near Compton Sinbury. She imagined that a pleasing picture of the village green had appeared in a magazine over there and captured an American heart. She had studied the map and decided that St Louis was as far south as Gibraltar and should therefore be a little warmer than Sin at this time of the year, but she was beginning to fear that life would be the same relentless chore – shopping, cooking, cleaning, washing, ironing and mending, while trying to cope with Lindy's never-ending demands.

Neil Kennedy was asleep beside her after a very late night in the Flatulent Ferret where his trip to America was unanimously regarded as ample justification for a few late drinks.

'Holiday ale,' Toby Beauchamp called it, ordering champagne by the bottle. 'Visit Kansas City for me. It doesn't look as if I am going to make it.'

'You won't want to come back,' said Paul Vanner. 'We'll never see you again.'

'I'll leave you my Ford Escort, seeing as you're fond of cars.'

'Good. I can give it to my milkman as a Christmas tip.'

When he woke up, in the long-term car park at Gatwick Airport, he felt a tremendous sense of exhilaration at the prospect before him. He had been owed a holiday for a long time, and a flight to America seemed a wonderfully exciting idea after a long period of self-denial that poverty and a baby had combined to impose. He jumped out of the car and began to lift their luggage from the boot.

'What airline is it?' Gwenda asked.

'Air Icarus,' he joked.

'How does the plane stay in the air?' Lindy asked.

'Magic,' he told her. 'Have we got enough trinkets to entertain this child on the flight?'

'A bagful. She's got terrible wind problems, I'm afraid. Do you think it's excitement?'

'My bottom's noisy today, isn't it?' Lindy confirmed.

When they reached the airport building on the car-park bus, he hurried to the check-in desk, still feeling the beneficial effects of last night's champagne.

'I want to fly to America,' he said. Getting no reply from the girl who was studying her terminal, he added helpfully: 'In a plane.'

'I think we can arrange that, sir. Is that all your luggage?'

When they had gone through passport control he looked at the departure board for his flight and was surprised to discover that people were flying to places that he had never heard of: Heraklion, Monastir, Alghero. Outside planes were climbing into the clouds with a frequency that he found reassuring.

'I want chocolate,' said Lindy. He bought her Maltesers. His wife accused him of 'sneaking the affection of the child through lazy bribery' but Neil Kennedy thought that keeping his daughter happy over the next twelve hours was his major objective.

They strolled round the duty-free shop, bought nothing and then found a seat and waited for their flight to be called.

'It's amazing,' he said. 'We've actually got ourselves organized enough to fly off on a holiday. I never thought we'd manage it.' He wanted to add that it was all due to poker, but he decided that he didn't want to spoil the holiday atmosphere.

Gwenda Kennedy, relaxed at last now that there was nothing she could do, shook her head.

'The most amazing thing to me is that we found an American who wanted to stay in Compton Sinbury.'

9

IN HIS THREE-STOREY CONDOMINIUM in St Louis, Missouri, Duncan Baxter was snapping instructions into a cordless phone. 'Forget the ads, Jack. I've taken care of them for the rest of the summer.' Never a man to do only one thing when there was the possibility of doing two or three, he wandered across the room and began tossing socks into a suitcase. 'You got it, Jack. Doctor Baxter has prescribed a little R. and R. No phone calls unless it's a goddamn emergency.' He found his three favourite polo shirts and dropped them on top of his khaki walking-shorts. 'A month, Jack,' he said. 'That's the plan.'

Some men would have worried about leaving Jack in charge of five tyre stores, but Duncan Baxter had assembled his best collection of managers so far. All Jack had to do was look after the city branch and liaise with the other stores. It had only taken thirteen years to reach this beautiful situation – thirteen years to get his name off the front of his overalls and up on the billboard on Highway 44: BAXTER'S TIRES: THE BEST FOR LESS. Thirteen years to reach a personal quarter of a million a year, including the pizza franchises.

Jack would do fine. They all needed a little soothing which was why they were managing Baxter's stores and not their own. At least he could count on Al to run the three pizza franchises in his absence. Investing in 'Chicago's Own' pizza was the smartest thing he had done in a long time. Baxter's business major had finally paid for itself. Despite pressure from friends, Baxter had stuck to his faith in a one-crust franchise. 'When you sell only the best, who needs variety?' He winced every time he saw that slogan, but it worked. Old Henry Ford was right.

He stared out at the woods while he stepped into his sweatpants. The back yard rolled down to a muddy swarf. Beyond it was the beginnings of Rockwood State Park, in which he had promised himself a daily jog. He had promised himself many things, and he'd delivered most of them. As far as exercising went, he probably got enough of a workout running up and down these damned stairs.

At forty-seven he was a tall, upright man with the strong muscular body of somebody younger, but the stresses of creating his own little business empire had already turned his hair silver. He pulled on his old Reeboks, made in Britain. Perhaps he would pick up a couple of pairs while he was over there.

He stuck his wallet into his hip pocket and went out into the sunshine. It was 92 °F. The air-conditioning in his new condo was so good that he was never quite ready for the weather outside. He got into his Mercedes and drove to Straubs in Webster Groves.

It was his maid, Sharon, who had told him that he should fill the freezer for the Kennedys; she had even given him a suggested list although why she should know anything about the preferred tastes of the English – a fussy and quirky race from what he'd been told about them – he couldn't imagine. He supposed that her knowledge, like most knowledge these days, came from a television.

He stocked up on staples: pitta, Brie, taco shells and salsa, currently his big indulgence. The English were supposed to love sweets, so he bought a half-gallon of Edie's Rocky Road (nuts and chunks of chocolate with miniature marshmallows), ice cream, a box of Dove bars (choc ices on a stick) and New York cheesecake – all things that Baxter would dearly love had he not heard the insistent rapping of middle age on his front door.

Sharon's list said Marmite and he had to go on to The Cheese Place to find it. 'What the hell is this stuff?' he asked. 'At seven bucks a crack it had better be good.' He unscrewed the lid off the little brown jar and sniffed. It was obviously an acquired taste. He let the girl sell him some water biscuits too.

If this is their idea of delicacy, he thought, perhaps he should take a couple of frozen pizzas to Britain with him.

When Sharon arrived to take him to the airport she'd had another idea. There should be flowers delivered to the Kennedys soon after they arrived.

'Only a woman would have thought of that,' he said grudgingly. He rang Rich Zengel, the florist. He stuck with Rich Zengel partly because his store was on Baxter Bend. It was good to have a sense of identity.

The journey to the airport was not something that he was looking forward to. He hated being a passenger more than he hated the prospect of the dumpy little redhead behind the wheel of his prized Mercedes. He wanted to drive to the airport himself but he needed to check that she could handle the car.

'Which way do you want to go?' she asked. She seemed pretty comfortable and he wondered whether she had borrowed the vehicle before without asking him.

'Stick to the straightforward route. Big Bend to 270, all the way up to 70 and Lambert Field.'

Slumped on a TWA jumbo two hours later, somewhere over Cleveland or Pittsburgh, he began to wonder about the wisdom of this strange mission and its likely outcome; but the curiosity had been gnawing at him for too many years and this was the only way that he was going to kill it.

It had taken all those years to get his mother to talk. The idea that there were some subjects that were not available for discussion had been instilled into him early on, and for a decade or two he had obediently refrained from raising the matter. But she was sixty-six now, living in a luxury that she had never known in Miami Beach, and he had begun to fear that she would take her secret to the grave. Slowly, over a long tea at the side of her apartment's pool, he had extracted the story.

As the jumbo embarked upon its long haul across the water, he tilted his seat back and tried to sleep. The *Post-Dispatch* lay unread on his lap as he pictured the country that he would soon be landing in. He had never been to England but these days television made you feel that you had spent weeks in a country you had never seen. And now he could see Big Ben, policemen in strange helmets, a murky river winding its way through a cloudy city, wild men in Union Jack shorts hitting complete strangers. Already he was glad that he didn't live there.

He landed in bright sunshine that didn't seem to have produced any heat. He waited in line with women with unshaven legs and louts in leather jackets. Did everyone in England smoke? Baxter had recently succeeded in forcing employees to restrict their smoking to an anteroom beyond the main garage. At the store in Clayton it was against the law.

As soon as he was through customs he bought himself a sweater. It cost 125 dollars and he could have bought the same sweater at Dillards for less. He pulled it on and looked at his change. These coins must wear holes in your pants pockets.

The next job was a hire car but before that he decided to try the beer. He had been warned but he was curious. It was warm and tasted dreadful. More than anything else, he was already thinking, I'm going to miss the condensation beading on a frosty glass.

The car-hire people were as offhand as he had expected. There was something about an island race that he had read somewhere: it wasn't so much a fear of foreigners as a lofty disinterest in them. But his American Express card seemed to smooth the way, and he was soon behind the wheel of a Ford Sierra on a small road with far too many vehicles around him. Once behind a wheel these guys were pushy bastards.

Driving on the left-hand side of the road was a novelty that he had been looking forward to; his map, on the front seat and to his left, seemed to be in the wrong place, but he soon became used to it even as he wondered why the English tried so strenuously to be different. He smiled as he remembered the snotty voice of the man in immigration.

'And what, Mr Baxter, is the purpose of your visit to Britain?'

The reply had shut him up for good: 'I've come to find my father.'

In the bedroom of his house on the Colemore Estate, One-cell Tel was experimenting with plasticine. The experiment was not a success. He sat on his bed with his trousers round his ankles, wrapping the plasticine gently round his erect penis, but after that things started to go wrong.

Getting the erection in the first place was not a problem. These days tumescence arrived with the sound of a lawn mower, regardless of who was pushing it, and there were plenty of people cutting their grass today. But the firmness was proving difficult to maintain. Under the clammy touch of the plasticine what was rigid became flexible, and when the prototype wilted the plasticine caved in too.

He looked at his distended organ covered with bits of plasticine and wondered whether he was going mad. What would the next step have been, anyway? If he had waited until he could extract himself from the plasticine, what would he have done then?

Plasticine, he saw now, was not the answer. He wasn't sure he knew what was.

He glanced at his watch because he had a little job waiting for him at the village hall. He saw that he was already late and pulled his jeans up in a hurry. He arrived at the hall, in the company of quite a lot of plasticine, ten minutes later.

The job was to pick up, fold and stack two hundred chairs that had been used at a meeting last night, and put out thirty trestle tables in three carefully designated rows for an exhibition in the hall tomorrow. It took him an hour and before he had finished a group of people had arrived, impatient to set out their exhibits for the morning.

They consisted of colourful little shiny models of animals and birds – ducks, horses, elephants – all of them in bright colours. In the same translucent material were a few domestic items: lamps, book-ends, pen-holders.

One-cell Tel, who wouldn't have noticed what the exhibition was if it had been the portrait busts of Jacob Epstein, was fascinated by these gleaming creatures.

'How do you do them, then?' he asked a lady who was arranging a menacing circle of yellow cats round a red bird.

She looked at him, not sure that she had understood.

'Polymerization,' she said and then noticed his vacant expression. 'You make a mould and pour in the resin and bingo! Pretty, aren't they?'

'Tell me again,' said One-cell Tel.

When Suzanne Vanner gave a dinner party she had people in to do the food. They were smuggled almost shamefully into the old tile-floored kitchen with their mysterious packages and baskets before the guests arrived, and their secret labours enabled Suzanne to emerge triumphantly at just the right moment bearing pheasant in rich red wine and Stilton cheese sauce, or duck, or venison. It was a little expenditure that her husband thoroughly approved of because he knew that if his wife cooked the meal he would be roped in for several tedious duties himself. She was never slow to accuse him of helping too little in the work of running a home; his usual reply, that he got up at five o'clock every morning and worked for twelve hours a day was never accepted as a sufficient excuse for his domestic inactivity.

Tonight he was lurking in the snooker room, practising long pots, while the married couple who ran the freelance-catering business prepared a banquet in the kitchen. He found snooker very relaxing, particularly if he was playing on his own and didn't have to cope with the unwelcome possibility of defeat. He sent the blue ball the length of the table. It rattled in the jaws of the pocket and came out again. He picked it up and dropped it in – it had nearly gone down, anyway.

Suzanne came in with a glass of champagne for him. She was friendlier when guests were coming; they had to be forged together, a couple.

'Get in the party mood,' she said. 'I hope you're going to wear a suit?'

'Of course, my love. How are Have-potato-peeler-will-travel getting on?'

'Everything's going fine. I'm about to lay the table.'

He took the champagne and drank a little. 'This is all to announce that you're opening a shop? Who's coming?'

'There'll be seven of us. Felix and Nadine, Toby and Harry. And the Kennedys were keen that I should invite the American chap who's taken their house for a month. I rang him up and he said he'd be delighted.'

'I haven't seen him yet.'

'Well, I expect he'll find the Flatulent Ferret eventually.'

An hour later, at the time he had been given on the phone, Duncan Baxter, in a white seersucker suit, found the Manor House. He had spent a day or two sleeping off his jet lag and trying to edge himself into the British time zone, and now felt ready to meet a few of the local inhabitants, to find out what the English were all about. It was a walk of no more than a few hundred yards, the lady had said on the phone, but after he had crossed the green and walked up the long drive to the Manor House he saw a blue Porsche, a red Ferrari and a white drop-head Mercedes, so not everybody in Compton Sinbury walked. He took a peek round the back before he rang, and saw a swimming pool, a tennis court and a paddock, but no sign of any horses. The grounds must have run to at least four acres. And he had always understood that the Brits were hard up! He had expected the owners of this spread to be getting on a bit, with the fruits of a lifetime's work laid out all round them, but the door was opened by an attractive woman in a red dress who was not a day over thirty.

'Are you Mr Baxter?' she said. 'I'm Suzanne Vanner. Do come in.'

'Duncan,' he said. 'Call me Duncan.'

Inside, half a dozen people were standing around in a conservatory drinking champagne. Only one of them was a woman, a small, slightly overweight blonde with a pleasant face. Suzanne Vanner introduced her as Nadine Kirby. Her husband was a tall, morose man with sandy hair who shook his hand as if uncertain that he would get his own back. Mr Vanner, who was called Paul, looked like a big, spoilt child with a chubby face and tired rings round his eyes that gave him a fishy look. The other two men, a plump bespectacled chap called Harry, and a very dignified older man named Toby, seemed to be drinkers.

'Mr Baxter – *Duncan* – has taken the Kennedys' house for a month,' Suzanne Vanner announced. 'And this is his first visit to England. He's from St Louis.'

'St Lewis, not St Loo-ey,' said Duncan Baxter. 'It's a British misconception.'

'We got it from a song,' said Harry Grant. 'What on earth made you choose Sin?'

'Sin?'

'It's how we pronounce Compton Sinbury.'

'Ah. I've come to look up a man.'

A bell rang somewhere and they were shown into an outsize room with panelled walls and a large round table laid out for dinner at its centre. Duncan Baxter looked at the chandelier over his head and the mahogany sideboard and the Persian rug and imagined that this was how every Englishman dined at night. The Vanners were acting as waiters, with the aid of a gold-wheeled trolley, but the food had evidently been prepared by servants in the deeper recesses of the house.

'What I want to tell you all is that I'm opening a shop,' said Suzanne Vanner when the wine had been poured and the pheasant distributed. 'Felix here is lending the money and you, Harry, are going to give me some publicity in your newspaper. Toby isn't going to be much help unless he's a transvestite in which case he can become a customer.'

'For you, anything,' said Toby Beauchamp. 'What are you going to call this shop?'

'Suzanne's,' said Paul Vanner. 'I suggested Paul's but it didn't sound right. It's going to replace the Arts and Craft shop at the side of the green. There are easier ways to make money, but my wife fancies a shop.'

'Tell us some easier ways,' said Duncan Baxter who was curious about how these people made such a comfortable living.

'You can make £7,000 over the weekend if you've got £7 million to put on the overnight money market. I do it every week.'

'For yourself?' asked Duncan Baxter, looking astonished.

'Only indirectly, unfortunately. I work in the money world. I find that the nearer you get to the stuff the more you are likely to earn. I mean, if you're a scientist or something money doesn't really get on to the scene, does it?'

'Well,' said Duncan Baxter, 'I guess scientists aren't interested in money.'

'They aren't even interested in people,' said Suzanne Vanner.

'Did you know,' said Nadine Kirby, remembering something, 'that scientists said that heavier-than-air machines would never fly just before the first flight?'

'How typical of men's rigid thinking,' said Suzanne Vanner. 'They had only to throw a stone to realize that they were talking balls.'

'Who said,' asked Toby Beauchamp, 'that the scientists were men?'

'Toby is our resident misogynist,' said Suzanne Vanner. 'Are you married, Duncan?'

'Not yet I'm not.'

'You should try it. A loving home. Adoring kids. A wife who always knows where you are.'

Listening to this summation, Paul Vanner wondered what his wife was describing. 'A woman who always knows where her husband is, is called a widow,' he said.

'You've got to watch the women over here, Duncan,' Toby said. 'They sandbag you round the back of the head and drag you up the aisle before you regain consciousness.'

Harry Grant, whose latest sexual fantasy was living naked on a desert island with Kylie Minogue, said: 'Some of us escape though. We've got far too much respect for our women to even contemplate giving them two hours of ecstasy.'

'Two hours?' said Nadine Kirby. 'Are you sure, Harry?'

Harry Grant stared back at her, surprised at the intervention. Was the champagne and wine affecting her? She wasn't normally so indiscreet, and now Felix Kirby was looking at him as if he had picked up a message in the air. Felix was not a great star of the dinner party circuit. Thirty years in an office had diminished his horizons and confined the possibilities of his conversation. But he had stirred now.

Harry Grant decided to move the conversation on quickly. 'How are you finding Britain, Duncan?' he asked. 'I suppose it's a bit quiet after St Louis? It's so quiet round here you can hear a mouse get a hard-on, as one of your compatriots once put it.'

Duncan Baxter, disconcerted by the prurient drift of the conversation, said that he found Compton Sinbury a delightful change from the lifestyle that he was used to. It wasn't, of course, a large enough stage for the entrepreneurial energy he deployed in Missouri but it had a peace and charm that, frankly, he had not expected to find.

Toby Beauchamp wondered why all Americans sounded as if they were president. They all seemed to have the same classless confidence. 'The only interesting thing that has happened around here lately is that the vicar had a stroke in the pulpit and died,' he said.

'I didn't know he died,' said Nadine Kirby.

'He definitely died,' said Harry. 'They buried him last week. Don't you read my newspaper?'

She gave him another long look. 'When I get time, Harry.'

When the pheasant had been replaced by raspberry pavlova, and the wine had induced a feeling amongst most of them that they had been sitting there for some years, Duncan Baxter turned to Harry Grant and asked: 'You a reporter?'

'Sort of,' said Harry, 'but not the frenetic type we see in the moving pictures that you are kind enough to send us. It's more whist-drive results than organized crime in Arizona. Golden weddings, amateur dramatics, sponsored walks, wine tasting, that sort of thing.'

'No crack? No dope? I thought you called this place Sin?'

'I'm sure there's plenty of dope but Scoop Grant hasn't found it yet,' said Nadine Kirby.

'You come across a guy called Barnaby Barton in your travels?' Duncan Baxter asked Harry.

'Barney?' said Harry. 'I know him well. We all know him. He's sort of the village character.'

Duncan Baxter looked at him in a way that revealed rather more interest than Harry had expected, so he went on. 'He's a kind of pathetic figure. No family, no money, no job most of the time.'

'What work does he do, when he is working?'

'Anything that's available. No task is too menial for Barney.'

'A funny thing happened the other day,' Toby told them. 'A man from a petrol company called on him and asked for permission to conduct tests in his back garden. They were looking for oil. By the time they came back to do them he'd changed the name of his bungalow to Southfork and bought a stetson.'

'What happened?'

'There was no oil.'

'I'm afraid Barney is a class-one simpleton,' said Suzanne Vanner. 'Why do you ask about him?'

'He's my father,' said Duncan Baxter, staring at his pudding.

'Oh, oops!' said Suzanne Vanner, putting her hand to her mouth. 'I'm terribly sorry. I didn't even know he'd had children.' She filled his wine glass as if to compensate for her gaffe.

'Are we to take it that you've never met?' Felix Kirby asked. At last there seemed to be a conversation that he could join.

'Never seen the man,' said Duncan Baxter, picking up his wine.

'Well, all I can tell you is that you're going to have great difficulty in accepting him as your father,' said Harry Grant. 'Resemblance there isn't.'

'How does he come to be your father, for Christ's sake?' asked Nadine Kirby.

'The same way your father came to be your father,' Duncan Baxter said, smiling for the first time. 'It all happened a long time ago. Jesus, I'm forty-eight this year.'

'And Barnaby went to America in 1942?' Harry Grant asked. 'What was he doing? Dodging the bombs? I thought his peregrinations never took him further than the pub.'

Duncan Baxter ran his fingers through his silver hair. 'I don't know whether Barnaby Barton has ever been to America or not. From what you say it sounds unlikely. What happened took place here. In 1942, when we were locked in deadly battle with Hitler, Mussolini and Hirohito, there was a girl who lived round here called Lydia Baxter. She and Barnaby Barton had some sort of affair. It may be hard for you to imagine, but they were both eighteen then. Lydia became pregnant and her father, who was a local solicitor and chairman of the council, was an old-fashioned country gentleman who was horrified at the disgrace. Nor, apparently, did he fancy Barnaby as a son-in-law. Lydia was sent to Canada where she gave birth to me and I was given her name. We moved to America when I was ten, and she's never returned here or had any contact with her family since.'

'And Barnaby doesn't know you're here?'

'He doesn't know I'm alive.'

'He doesn't know he's alive, half the time,' said Harry Grant.

'Did he ever marry? I used a detective agency in London to establish that he was still alive and living in Compton Sinbury, but they couldn't find out whether I had any half-brothers or half-sisters.'

'I think it's a miracle that he reproduced himself once,' said Toby, 'if you will forgive me for saying so. I think you can be quite confident that you're not going to bump into any relatives.'

'I think I'd better get the port,' said Paul Vanner. 'We don't normally get stories as good as this over the dinner table.'

In the Kirbys' pink bedroom Nadine was watching television from the comfort of her double bed. In the bathroom next door her husband was whistling Guy Mitchell's 'My Truly Truly Fair' through his teeth and trying to track the onset of baldness with two mirrors. He emerged in a pair of grey pyjamas, smelling of toothpaste.

'An interesting evening,' she said, without looking up at him.

He sat on the edge of the bed and took off his slippers, a

birthday present from Rachel. 'I never know what to make of the Vanners.'

'Oh, they're head over heels in love,' his wife told him, still watching the television that was perched like an intruder on a chest of drawers.

He didn't know what to make of that, either, and didn't answer. He had never understood the expression. Heads were *supposed* to be over heels, weren't they?

'I didn't know you were lending money to Suzanne to open a shop,' she said after a while.

'Do I ever discuss bank business with you?' he asked. He got into bed and lay on his back. On the television a man was talking to a man on a television: face-to-face communication had died there as well as here. He tried to remember a joke he had thought of in the bank the other day, and then it came to him: marriage is like money – not worth saving if the interest is too low. Then he remembered something else.

'You've had an affair with Harry Grant,' he said.

This unexpected assertion succeeded in capturing her attention, but she was so surprised that she could only repeat it.

'An affair with Harry Grant?'

He couldn't remember why he had said it now, but there had been something over dinner – a look, a remark, a reaction of some sort – that had convinced him that Harry Grant had been to bed with his wife.

'That's what I said.'

'You're not going loopy, are you?' she said. She found the remote control in the folds of the duvet and reduced the sound from the television. 'Whatever gave you the idea?'

'Something that happened tonight.' He remembered what it was. 'He was talking about making love for two hours and you gave him a look and said "Are you sure, Harry?"'

'Well, I would say that, wouldn't I?'

'It was the look. It wasn't what you said.'

'And what was this look exactly?'

'It was a woman looking at a man she'd been to bed with. You can't confuse it with any other look because there's no other look like it.'

'Yes, there is. A woman looking at a man she *wants* to go to bed with.'

'That's a different expression altogether.'

'How would you know?'

But his imagination had raced too far ahead now for him to even notice this barb. He could picture moonlit trysts with the reporter when Felix was working late as he did at the end of every month, secret drinks in Harry Grant's infamous potting shed. He said: 'I'm going to speak to him.'

She disguised a tremor of alarm. 'You're going to ask Harry? He'll put you right.'

'It won't be what he says. It'll be the look on his face when he says it.'

'Have you become an expert in physiognomy all of a sudden?'

'It's all part of a bank manager's armoury. Who's lying, who can be trusted. I never listen much to what they're saying. I just look into their eyes as they're saying it.'

'They must think they're visiting a cracked hypnotist.'

'Nevertheless, it seems to produce the right decisions on my part.'

Nadine increased the television's volume again to put an end to this. She imagined that Harry would be quite capable of dealing with Felix when he arrived, a decade late, with his questions and his suspicions and his new-found expertise in masks and veneers.

'Turn the television down if you must have it on,' he said. 'You'll wake Rachel.'

Duncan Baxter sat in the Kennedys' kitchen reading the Sunday newspapers. Having flown over three thousand miles to see his father he was finding some difficulty in completing the last eight hundred yards. Now he was here he had no idea what to say. His mother had warned him that the trip would be a disappointment and that there was no point in making it, but curiosity about the man who was his father had evolved over many years. 'He was nothing special,' she had told him. 'He's probably a clerk in a council office now.'

What he had heard over the Vanners' dinner table suggested that even this modest assignment had proved too onerous for Barnaby Barton, so that now the prospect of embarrassment loomed, of stilted conversations and awkward silences. Duncan Baxter told himself that there was no rush, he had a month. Ideally he would like to see his father first at a distance, perhaps walking in the village, so that he would know what it was that he was dealing with.

The English newspapers carried the same stories every day, just like the news broadcasts on television: a helpless obsession with inflation; a new food-poisoning scare; a young royal, waving fatly from the steps of a plane; the endless procession to the grave in Ulster.

He pushed the papers to one side and decided to go down to the public house at the foot of the green for a beer. Perhaps he would find some of the people he met last night. They had seemed nice enough in their strange English way. It wasn't always easy to tell when they were joking and sometimes when you knew that they were there was a brutal edge to the humour. It was hard to see, when you talked to them, how they had ever built an empire, won a war or got the Falklands back. There was obviously a murderous streak concealed beneath the Brits' well-known civilized façade.

In the Flatulent Ferret Toby Beauchamp was discussing cash flows with Paul Vanner. They both stopped talking to welcome him.

'You have stumbled across a little local institution called Men's Hour,' Toby Beauchamp told him. 'The women don't come in until one o'clock.'

'You ban the women? Back home the ladies'd have your scrotum in the ice box for that.'

Toby Beauchamp shivered slightly at the image. 'We don't ban them,' he said quickly. 'We sort of discourage them. We have to have an hour of pleasure a week.'

'Excuse me? You only enjoy an hour a week? This is a *strange* country. Can I buy you fellows a drink?'

'It's my round,' Paul Vanner said. 'What'll you have?'

'Didn't I drink enough of your hooch last night?'

'Today is another day. Try the bitter. Your turn to pay will come.'

Duncan Baxter tried the bitter and decided that it wasn't so bad after all.

'That was an extraordinary story you told us last night,' Toby said, lighting a small cigar. 'When are you going to see him?'

'I'll get round to it.'

'He could come in here this morning.'

'If he does don't tell him who I am.'

'Certainly not. I don't want to be the one to give him a heart attack. Don't Americans ask about your Christian name? I mean, Americans are all called Milt or Buck or Irv or Abe, aren't they?'

'Not all of them, but I must admit I've never met a Toby. What do you do, Toby? What paid for the blue Porsche?'

'He's a property developer,' Paul Vanner said. 'He buys land cheap and gets permission to build on it. The last of the old goldmines.'

'And you, Paul? A bank?'

'The currency market,' said Toby. 'The first of the new goldmines.'

'There's a lot of money swilling round here,' said Duncan Baxter thoughtfully. 'My old pa seems to have missed out on it.'

'Not everybody's loaded,' Toby assured him. 'Harry Grant isn't rich.'

'Where *is* Harry?' Vanner asked. 'Have we received a doctor's certificate?'

The door opened as he spoke but it wasn't Harry Grant who came in.

Duncan Baxter saw shuffle into the bar an old man with round shoulders, wearing the sort of raincoat that Columbo had, and an absurd stetson hat. He walked to the counter without giving or expecting greetings, and nodded to the big man who was already drawing him a pint of Guinness. Slowly he pulled some coins from his coat pocket and put them on the counter, counted them and then plunged his hand into his pocket in search of more. It wasn't clear at the end of all this whether there was enough, for the man behind the counter swept them up and said 'Okay, Barney' before dropping the cash in his till.

'The stetson keeping your head warm, Barney?' he asked.

'Heat escapes through your head,' was the reply in a surprisingly deep voice.

Duncan Baxter followed all this with growing dismay. He knew directly he saw the hat that this man must be his father, but he had managed to hope for a few moments that stetsons were suddenly the fashion in Compton Sinbury (if one had been bought round here recently, why not two?). And then the barman had called him Barney.

He watched the old man make his way to a table in the corner where he greedily drank an inch or two off his Guinness. And then, not bothering to look at anyone else, he pulled a tin from the pocket of his shabby raincoat, and began to make his own roll-up cigarette with his hat still firmly in place on his head.

'Jesus Christ,' said Duncan Baxter.

Harry Grant sat in his front room reading the Sunday newspapers. He bought several every week and they all seemed to be getting bigger, sprouting fresh sections devoted to arcane matters that barely concerned him. As a dutiful journalist he waded through the multiplying pages, absorbing miscellaneous information that he doubted he would ever need.

Frogs made love only once a year but when the big occasion arrived it lasted for twenty-four hours. Perhaps that was why their eyes bulged. He looked at his own eyes in the mirror. They seemed to bulge, too. He suspected that he should stroll up to the church to see who was deputizing for the late vicar, but the Vanners' port had quelled all desire to move.

Somebody was moving though: he could hear footsteps on his gravel path. The doorbell chimed and he went out to find Felix Kirby on his doorstep. He was wearing a blue blazer and white trousers that pronounced that this was Sunday, but his face was not that of a man who was enjoying his day off.

'Felix,' he said, 'come in. Is my overdraft so bad that the bank manager has got to visit me?'

'Nothing to do with the bank, Harry,' said Felix Kirby, following him into the cottage's small front room. 'It was something that happened last night.'

'What happened last night was that I drank too much port,' said Harry when his visitor had lowered himself into a very old armchair. 'It's going to take a supreme effort to get me to Men's Hour.'

He never knew quite how to take Felix Kirby. He was a very serious man who couldn't even take a holiday in Spain without first reading ten books about the country, and yet there didn't seem to be anything there beyond a gaunt, somewhat forbidding appearance. Perhaps he was a hologram.

'Something else happened last night,' he said now. 'In short, I got the distinct impression that you had been to bed with my wife.'

There had been a time when Harry had prepared himself for this: he had a speech prepared, an expression ready. But that was ten years ago and he had long since forgotten his lines.

'What *are* you talking about, Felix?' he said. 'Me? The celibate scribbler?'

'It was the way she reacted last night to your remark about two hours of ecstasy. A man knows his wife, Harry.'

'Perhaps you could remind me when this beautiful experience occurred? We bachelors live on our memories of such things.' He was vaguely disconcerted by the close look that Felix Kirby was giving him, as if he had a piece of dirt on his nose.

'I've no idea when it was. I was hoping that you would tell me.'

'I'd gladly tell you, Felix. Be proud to. Your wife is a lovely woman. Would it help if I made it up? After all, I am a journalist.'

Felix Kirby continued looking at him. 'I just want you to tell me the truth, Harry. I've got a position here. If my wife has been putting it about I'm entitled to know.'

Harry Grant stared back at him. For some reason Kirby reminded him of a story he had written once for the *Gazette* about a bored man whose hobby was attending funerals.

'I'll tell you the truth, Felix. Apart from social occasions in the Ferret, or evenings like last night at the Vanners', I doubt whether I've spoken to Nadine four times in ten years. It's strange, considering we live opposite each other but our paths never seem to cross. I regret it, but there it is.'

Watching the reporter's eyes, Felix Kirby saw that this was true. He couldn't understand how he had misread his wife's response last night. He felt as if he had made a bad decision in the bank.

'I may have made a fool of myself,' he said. 'I may owe you an apology.'

Relieved now, Harry was prepared to joke.

'Not at all. A night in bed with your wife would square the balance sheet, as you bankers put it. Now you've brought the subject up I'd love to sleep with Nadine.'

'Don't joke, Harry,' said Felix Kirby, standing up. 'It hasn't been a laughing matter for me. But I can see that I do owe you an apology. Will you come to the pub and let me buy you a drink?'

'That's something else I wouldn't say no to.'

The usual roast beef and Yorkshire pudding was waiting for Felix Kirby when he returned at two o'clock from the Flatulent Ferret. Nadine, familiar with his punctual ways, was already carving it.

'Where's Rachel?' he asked. The Sunday lunchtime drinks and Harry's convincing replies had put him into a rare good mood.

'She's writing an essay in her bedroom. She's entering a competition.'

'What a bright girl she is. I wonder where she gets her brains from?'

The question reminded her. 'I saw you going across the green to talk to Harry.'

'Yes, I dropped in.'

'Did you ask him whether he had been to bed with me?'

'I did.'

'What did he say?'

'He said he'd love to,' replied Felix Kirby cheerfully.

Nadine Kirby left the room to conceal her smile. 'Rachel darling!' she called gaily. 'Lunch is ready.'

10

ONE-CELL TEL was sprawled face down on the floor of his bedroom – supported by his elbows and his knees and, in the lower part of his body, by a bucket.

The bucket contained a silicone–rubber moulding-compound into which One-cell Tel had plunged an erection induced by a view of the lawn-mowing next door. He had added enough catalyst to the contents of the bucket to make it set quickly and had been told in the shop that it would cast at room temperature in two minutes. Helped by the high viscosity, the initial experience had been surprisingly sensual and he had no difficulty in keeping his erection for the required two minutes.

His problem, now that the mould had set, was in losing it so that he could extricate himself from his ridiculous situation. He was held firm, locked into a bucket by an erection that wouldn't subside.

He tried to counter his tumid condition by thinking about sexless things: semolina pudding, a bus queue in the rain, the House of Commons; but his panic-stricken quest for detumescence was thwarted by the whirring of the mower next door. She was naked again – that was what had delivered him in the right shape into this trap in the first place – and lying on the floor he could imagine too easily her lovely body, now turning brown as it floated over the grass, revealing everything. The thought of what he would see if only he could stand up made it impossible to bring the necessary degree of concentration to a semolina pudding which, in his current crack-brained circumstance, had, anyway, begun to acquire sexual attractions of its own.

The consolation that he had definitely created a mould was no consolation at all as long as he was attached so humiliatingly to this bucket. Bus queues in the rain, the House of Commons. But Cathy appeared naked in the rain with the water running down between her breasts, and the House of Commons was only a phrase he had heard and brought no picture to his mind.

The spell was broken by his mother's footsteps on the stairs. The prospect of her coming into the room and discovering her son spreadeagled over a bucket with his trousers round his ankles worked wonders on his anatomy and suddenly he was free. He stood up quickly and was relieved to hear that his mother had not come upstairs to visit him.

He pulled his trousers up and discovered that he felt too tender to risk looking out of the window. Instead, he went across to his wardrobe at the bottom of which he had hidden a can of Polyester Resin Body Filler that he had bought at Halfords. He had used it before for repairs on his van. He added the catalyst, mixed up the paste and then pushed it with his fingers into the mould in the bucket. It would, he knew, be ready in an hour.

He had saved the packet from some Carr's Table Water Biscuits that his mother liked to have with cheese in the evenings; it was about eight inches long and he filled it partially with cotton wool. Then he found a piece of paper and pondered over what he should write. He was competent at many jobs but putting words on paper wasn't one of them. It filled him with dread. An hour passed before he wrote anything at all, and then he laboriously inscribed in capital letters: THIS IS WHAT YOU DO TOO ME.

He bent over the bucket now and gently pulled the model from the rubber moulding. It was perfect. It looked bigger than he expected but he was seeing it from new angles.

He fetched his gold aerosol paint spray from the wardrobe and set to work, using a newspaper to catch the paint that missed.

Half an hour later he proudly packed the golden phallus and his note into the biscuit carton and wrapped it up in brown paper. He could hardly deliver it so he decided to send it in the post. He wrote Cathy Gray and her address on the outside and headed for the post office.

People called him an odd job man, he thought, as if he was only capable of simple work for a simple mind, but he didn't know anybody who could have produced the extraordinary gift that he had just manufactured.

The whole creative endeavour had stretched his mental capacity to its outer limit and so he didn't notice that he had forgotten to put his name to the message.

Duncan Baxter had been in England for a week when he decided that he could prevaricate no longer. He had used the Ford Sierra to see a little of the country that his mother had left when she was carrying him. He had been to London and sat in traffic jams that had immobilized him for most of the day, and he had driven to the coast to see the sea that he had seen only once before. At home he had to go to Lake Michigan to see water that stretched to the horizon, and standing on the seafront in Weymouth he caught a sense of Britain's smallness and insularity.

But after seven days he thought that he could detect a streak of cowardice in himself; it wasn't an attribute that he could permit. He got the Sierra out of the Kennedys' garage and cruised round to the green. He had discovered quite early in the week where Barnaby Barton lived and had driven past his gloomy bungalow several times out of curiosity. He turned left at the bottom of the green and drove along the lane until he came to the newly-painted sign that said SOUTHFORK. Two lapwings flapped across the road towards the river.

A muddy path led across the small, neglected front garden to a front door that needed paint. He banged the knocker a couple of times and felt his heart beating. He had been in some difficult situations in his life, both socially and in business, but he had never felt as nervous as this. From inside the bungalow there came the sound of a bolt being loosened on the front door.

It was cautiously opened to reveal no more than was

necessary, but it revealed Barnaby Barton in an old green cardigan over a grey shirt, a pair of baggy worn trousers and some frayed slippers.

'Yes?' he said.

'Mr Barton?' said Duncan Baxter.

'You from the oil company? They said they couldn't find any.'

'The oil company? No, no. I wonder whether I could come in?'

'Are you an American gentleman?' Barnaby Barton asked, diverted by the accent. 'I saw you in the Ferret.'

'That's right,' said Duncan Baxter, trying a smile. 'I'm from the States.'

'What do you want?'

'I have a message for you. May I come in?'

Barnaby Barton didn't move. He did not like visitors in his house. They made critical remarks about his standards of cleanliness, and then tried to interfere with the way he ran his life.

'A message?' he said. 'Who from?'

'Lydia Baxter.'

Barnaby Barton froze and his eyes, focused on Duncan Baxter's face, grew bigger as if some awful physical calamity was about to grip his heart.

'Lydia Baxter?' he repeated, and relinquished his grip on the door. 'Come in.'

Duncan Baxter never forgot the room that he now entered. Occasionally, in later years, the memory of it would prompt him to take a shower. The décor defied classification. The wallpaper had peeled off parts of the wall and not been replaced. The carpet, threadbare in parts, had never been cleaned. The furniture seemed to be a job lot from a sale in a car park, and the curtains that hung on either side of the greasy French windows did not match, green check on one side and a dirty brown on the other.

He gazed stonily at a dog turd in the hearth. He had been told that the British were odd but nobody had prepared him for eccentricity on this scale.

'Lydia Baxter sends her love,' he said, finding his voice. This wasn't entirely true but it seemed appropriate to the moment. What she had actually said was 'Give Barney my regards, if he remembers me'.

Barnaby Barton stood by the mantelpiece, a faraway look in his eye. Judging by the smell which clung to his cardigan, he had recently cooked a large fried breakfast.

'Her love?' he said. 'Where is she?'

'She lives in Miami.'

Barnaby Barton turned, plucked a picture from the mantelpiece, went over to his rocking chair and sat down. For some time he looked at the picture without speaking and then he handed it to Duncan Baxter.

'Does she still look like that?'

Duncan Baxter was both stunned and moved by the discovery that after forty-eight years his mother's picture was still displayed in this house. He looked at the photograph and saw a pretty young girl with a central parting smiling shyly at what must have been a very basic camera.

'A little,' he said gently.

'She left me,' Barnaby said, as if this information would be news to his visitor. 'She went to a place called Halifax, Nova Scotia.' He pulled a tin from his pocket and began to roll a cigarette. 'Why don't you sit down?'

Duncan Baxter looked round and found an armchair with straw spilling from one arm. He sat down and watched Barnaby Barton making his cigarette. The first inch seemed to disappear directly he applied the match.

It was difficult to accept that this short, bald man with his red nose, his dirty cardigan, his humble shoulders and his pinched-up underprivileged face was his father. Duncan Baxter had fought his way to considerable prosperity, fixing deals, creating jobs and destroying rivals on the way. The timid creature in the rocking chair would be lost in a crowd of three.

Was this a triumph of environment over heredity? He had read that intelligence was determined by genetic rather than cultural factors but he could hardly believe that his own case supported the theory. He sat in his uncomfortable seat thinking about the impact of environment on genes and chromosomes, of random genetic mixes and hereditary patterns, and wondered what had made him the man he was.

'Have you any pictures of yourself with her?' he asked. He was curious about how his father looked when he was courting the young Lydia Baxter, what sort of young man it was his mother had succumbed to.

'She didn't want any pictures of me. I wanted pictures of her. I suppose she married some Yank who sells blue-chip stocks?'

Duncan Baxter looked at him. 'How do you know about blue-chip stocks?' he asked.

'I read a lot.' He waved an arm towards the crowded shelves of a bookcase in the corner of the room.

'Really? What do you read?'

'Anything I can get my hands on. Trash from the mobile library mostly. But I prefer my own books. I read a lot of classical mythology. I'm reading about Helen at the moment.'

'Whose face launched a thousand ships?'

'Everybody knows that bit. She was the cause of the Trojan War. When Menelaus chased her with a sword she calmed him down by baring her breast. I like that.'

Duncan Baxter felt that he had discovered a patch of light amid the gloom. Was it possible to describe as completely moronic a man who found his pornography in classical mythology?

He said: 'Lydia never married. Did you?'

'Me? No.' He made a strange noise which Duncan Baxter took to be a laugh.

'You mean you've lived alone for nearly fifty years?'

'Since my parents died.'

'Girl friends?'

'Only Lydia.'

Duncan Baxter found something strangely repellent about a man living in such sexual isolation for so long. It wasn't healthy. Baboons locked up in a zoo without female company – he had once read – could be turned on by their zoo-keeper's gumboot. The human equivalent didn't bear thinking about.

His own bachelorhood was a quite different matter, with a team of adoring ladies on hand, all of them anxious to become legally entangled with the rising fortunes of Baxter's Tires.

'That's very sad,' he said.

'I expected her to come back,' Barnaby told him, rubbing dropped cigarette ash into the carpet with his slipper. 'I suppose I've been waiting.'

'For forty-eight years,' Duncan Baxter said, more to himself than to the old man in the rocking chair. 'What do you do to pass the time, Mr Barton? How do you occupy yourself?'

'There's my potato patch. It keeps me busy.'

'It's a lot of land. Do you earn much from it?'

'Beer money. It's more than an acre.' He stared out of the window for a while and then turned back to his guest. There was something on his mind and it had nothing to do with the potato patch.

'Tell me, sir,' he said, suddenly according a new respect to his mysterious guest, 'when did you last see Lydia?'

'Couple of weeks ago.'

'The thing is this. I hardly like to mention it. She was expecting my baby. When she went to Halifax, Nova Scotia. You don't know what happened to it?'

'Indeed I do. That's one of the reasons I'm here.'

Barnaby Barton gaped at him.

'I am that baby. I'm your son.'

Duncan Baxter didn't know whether he had expected embarrassment or the wildest delight and celebration when he broke this news, but what actually confronted him was an old man crying. A grimy handkerchief was pulled from his trouser pocket and held to his eyes, but all power of speech seemed to have deserted him.

Duncan Baxter went over and patted him reassuringly on the shoulder. It was a long time before either of them spoke and it was Barnaby Barton who finally broke the silence.

'I want to see Lydia,' he said.

Harry Grant sat in his potting shed with an undiluted gin and wondered whether his not getting married was a sign of weakness or of strength. He was beginning to believe that for men marriage was a kind of abdication which seemed to reduce them in stature. He had noticed how, when a married couple were interviewed together on television, it was always the woman who did the talking.

At the same time he could not deceive himself about the difficulties he was experiencing in finding sensual young ladies now that he had, at a speed that surprised and depressed him, reached forty. There were still women who seemed unable to keep their hands off him but this was not a temptation that even occurred to the lovely ones he really wanted.

He heard the phone ringing in the cottage and picked up the extension in the potting shed. It was Dakers, his news editor.

'Got a little story for you, Harry,' he said. 'I like to make your life easy. Do you know a girl called Rachel Kirby?'

'Yes,' said Harry. 'What's happened to her?'

Immediately he saw his daughter dead, the victim of a road accident or worse. A lot of Dakers' calls concerned distant road accidents with local victims.

'According to a Press release I have here she's won £100 in an essay competition. Pretty bright, is she?'

'Well,' said Harry, 'her father's pretty bright.'

'They've sent us a picture so you needn't fix that.'

When Dakers had rung off with his usual regrets about not having a quiet life in the country instead of the tension-filled drama of the news desk – a distinction that Harry knew to be wholly bogus as the most dramatic thing likely to hit the news desk was a drop in cattle prices – he rang the Kirbys.

Nadine answered.

'Harry Grant,' he said.

'I remember you.'

'My news editor tells me that Rachel has won a prize for an essay. He wants me to write about her in the public prints.'

'Your newspaper is on the ball. She only heard this morning.'

'People who give away £100 prizes are apt to tell newspapers. They don't hide their light under a bushel, whatever that means. Keep forgetting to look it up.'

'I'll send her to the Refectory. You can interview her over a cup of tea.'

'You don't want me in your house, do you?'

'Best not.'

'How are you, anyway?' he asked. 'I got quizzed by your husband.'

'You did a good job there, Harry. How are you? Keeping busy?'

'I work until the early hours,' he told her, 'of the afternoon.'

The Refectory was a café next to the bank on the other side of the green. Lights hung in baskets on chains from the ceiling, and elegant rococo furniture had succeeded in creating a curiously genteel atmosphere in what was, after all, only a tea room.

Harry Grant, one of its most regular customers, took his usual seat in the window. From here he looked out in a fruitless search for news and saw only moorhens on the duck pond at the top of the green and, occasionally, a wagtail alighting on the leaf of a water lily. In other less ordered parts of the world his professional colleagues watched guns blaze, governments topple, revolutions explode. He ordered a pot of tea for two.

The waitress, he noticed rather late, was a new girl with the face of an angel. When she returned with the tea, he said: 'Who might you be?'

'I might be Cathy,' she said.

'I'm definitely Harry,' he told her. 'Are you new here?'

'In the job and in the village. We've moved up from Cornwall.'

'Who is we?'

'My mother and me,' she said, smiling down at him. Her eyes seemed to be full of secrets, and her Cornish accent made him think of sex in fields. But before he could pursue this welcome possibility Rachel Kirby came in wearing a red polo-neck sweater and jeans. She had none of the shyness which afflicts ten-year-old girls: she exuded a weary self-confidence which was the envy of girls twice her age.

'You wanted to see me, Mr Grant?' she said, sitting opposite him before he could suggest it. It was not surprising that they had met so seldom when they lived opposite each other on the green. From guilt or embarrassment or just a buried sadness he made conscious efforts to avoid this girl.

'You've won a prize,' he told her. 'Congratulations. The *County Gazette* wants to know all about it. You see, I write too.'

'I read your "Village Notes" column every Friday. One day I'd like to be able to write like that.'

'What was your essay about?'

'My father.'

He poured her a cup of tea and eased the sugar in her direction. He would have hoped for any essay subject but this one.

'Your father?' he said, imagining for one wild moment that she was about to reveal that she knew who her father was.

'I don't really know anyone else well enough to write about them, do I?'

Harry Grant admired this conscientious approach which would have found little enough sympathy in the *Gazette* office where ignorance of a subject was not accepted as an adequate excuse for not writing about it. He asked: 'What did you say about him?'

'I said that he was a sad and angry man,' she said calmly, as if this was quite normal.

'Sad and angry?' asked Harry, astonished.

'Oh, yes. He's seething with anger. It never quite boils over, but it's there all right.'

'Why do you think that is?'

'I don't know,' she said, shrugging. 'I suppose that he wishes he was somebody else. A lot of people do.'

He stared at this bright girl and wondered how much he had missed by not being involved in her upbringing. But the subject was one that he had avoided before; it gave the sort of tug on your heart, he had found, that murders happiness.

'Has your father read it?' he asked.

'He only reads balance sheets.'

'It sounds just as well to me. What are you going to do with the money?' She didn't seem to have told him much that he could publish.

'Oh, I'll save it. I want to travel one day. How can I become a journalist?'

He smiled at her. 'Why on earth would you want to do that?'

'It's the best first job, isn't it? Playwrights, film producers, even Chancellors of the Exchequer – they all begin as journalists and find out how the world works.'

'Come and see me when you're ready,' he said.

She smiled at that and stood up. 'Thank you very much.' She turned to go and stopped. 'You didn't ask how old I was. Newspapers always put ages in, don't they? Sometimes quite irrelevantly, in my opinion.'

'I know your age, Rachel.'

When she had gone Harry Grant scribbled some notes in his pad. That's a wise child who doesn't know her own father, he thought.

Cathy the waitress came over to his table. He smiled up at her. There was a gap in his life that this exquisite new arrival could fill.

'Are you a reporter?' she asked.

'That sort of thing,' he agreed. 'Why do you ask?'

What he saw best and most enjoyably from his seated position were her long brown legs. It was a sight that he needed; in his latest sexual fantasy he had been playing strip poker with the Queen.

'You seemed to be interviewing that girl. I thought you could interview me. You know, write about me.'

'Why would I do that, Cathy?'

'I'm a model. At least, I've done a bit of modelling in Cornwall. If you wrote about me I might get work round here.'

'Have you any pictures?' he asked. Lubricious snaps were not exactly a *Gazette* speciality, but Harry liked them; and illustrations that came free were always popular with the editor.

'Lots,' said Cathy. 'Would you like to see them?'

'Why don't you bring them over to my cottage some time? I live across the green.'

He produced his card from a very old wallet and handed it to her.

'I'll drop in,' she said.

The village store was a small supermarket although its prices were rather above the normal supermarket level. It was the last shop at the top of the green, next to the post office. Duncan Baxter was shopping for two.

He pushed his trolley down the narrow aisles, trying to identify food items that his father would enjoy but could not afford. It was difficult. Barnaby Barton was probably too set in his ways now to welcome food that he didn't recognize and had probably never heard of. Even the lasagne that Duncan Baxter could see in the cold compartment would seem exotic and fill him with alarm. He picked up two steaks and dropped them in his trolley. There was a very good butcher at the bottom of the green along from the Flatulent Ferret and run by a cheerful young man called Michael but Duncan Baxter didn't know that. He decided to play safe and go for quantity rather than quality; his trolley was soon full of potatoes, lettuces, tins of beans, sausages, soups, sardines, peas and a dozen cans of minced beef.

Two days earlier he had rung Lydia Baxter in Miami.

'I have just been talking to the remains of my father,' he said.

His mother's voice came back loud and clear as if she was in the next town. 'How is he?' she asked.

'A sad, lonely man living in a bungalow that needs fumigating.'

'What does he do?'

'Reads classical mythology.'

'No job?'

'Odd jobs, I gather. But he has your picture over the fireplace.'

'My God,' said Lydia Baxter.

'He wants to see you.'

'My God,' said Lydia Baxter. 'He's not coming over here, is he?'

'I think a ten-mile trip would stretch his powers of organization.'

'What did he say when you told him who you were?'

'He burst into tears.'

'Poor man. What are you going to do?'

'Make him rich. Everyone else round here is.'

Thinking about it in the supermarket, Duncan Baxter wondered whether his mother would consider flying to England. She had talked often enough of seeing the country before she died. On the other hand, the Barnaby Barton she would meet today would bear so little resemblance to the youthful lover in the haystack in 1942 that the resultant shock and depression might prove damaging.

At the end of the aisle he bumped trolleys with Toby Beauchamp.

'Some people have got wives to do this,' Toby said, looking slightly uneasy at being discovered in this domesticated role. 'How are you liking living in Sin?'

'I don't think the pastoral life is my bag,' said Duncan Baxter. 'My engine likes high revs.'

'Slow revving engines last longer,' said Toby. 'Do you fancy a coffee when you've done your shopping?'

When they were sitting in the Refectory he asked: 'Have you been to see Barney yet?'

Duncan Baxter nodded grimly. 'What a disaster that man is.' He was about to tell Toby about the dog turd in the hearth but a newly surfaced fragment of filial loyalty stopped him.

'I was afraid you were due for a shock. There wasn't much I could do to help you.'

'Has he always been like that?'

'Ever since I've known him. People are nice to him, buy him the odd drink, offer him the odd job, but he doesn't seek company. He is, as you say, a disaster.'

They were distracted by the pretty blonde waitress who

brought their coffee. She was wearing a tailored white skirt that stopped three inches above her knees, and a green silk blouse.

'Cute broad,' said Duncan Baxter. 'Who is she?'

'Never seen her before,' said Toby. 'You have pretty girls in St Louis, I take it?'

'Got pretty ones of sixteen. Something happens to them after that.'

'It's the high-rev environment.'

Duncan Baxter drank some coffee. 'I've had an idea, Toby. As one businessman to another.'

'Is this a business idea? I like them.'

'Barnaby Barton, or my father as I must learn to call him, has no money.'

'I noticed that.'

'But what he has got is over an acre of land which must be worth something in the crowded south of England.'

'They talk about the crowded south of England,' said Toby, 'but if you fly over it in a helicopter, as I occasionally do, it's practically empty.'

'Why do you fly over it in a helicopter?'

'Looking for sites. Looking for places to build.'

'That's what I'm talking about,' said Duncan Baxter. 'He's got an acre or more and he grows potatoes on it, for Christ's sake. How many houses could you build there?'

'Ten good ones.'

'What would they sell at?'

'A hundred and fifty thousand round here.'

'A million and a half. What do they cost to build?'

'About eighty.'

'I make that £200,000 for my old man and half a million profit for you.'

'For me?'

Duncan Baxter put his hand on Toby's arm.

'What about it, Toby, old man? Do us all a favour.'

'I must admit I'd never thought of Barney's potato patch as a possible development site, but I could build a very classy close of up-market houses there.'

'Would you get permission? You've got some tight planning laws over here, haven't you?'

'I'd get permission,' said Toby Beauchamp. 'But would Barney want to sell? I had the impression that he was rather attached to his potato patch.'

'For £200,000 he'll sell. He can buy himself a dozen potato patches afterwards if he wants to.'

On the other side of the world the Kennedy family had decided to eat out. Staying in and cooking their own food, they were beginning to find, was a bit like being at home; only the 36-channel giant projection television hinted at the miles they had covered.

They had taken the hire car downtown and turned into the riverfront at Laclede's Landing. An arch loomed high above them as the car rattled over cobbled streets.

'How quaint,' said Gwenda. 'Do you think they imported them?'

The Robert E. Lee was the most impressive of the riverboats and one of the finer restaurants. It was an old white showboat, with freshly painted, curlicued circus lettering, massive grey funnels and multi-levelled wooden railings. They parked and walked up the wooden ramp. The river was ablaze with sunset.

Neil Kennedy was a great disciple of the sun, and there had been plenty of it here. It reduced blood pressure, improved oxygenation of the blood, reduced cholesterol levels, prevented brittle bones, warded off depression and stimulated his libido. But it was not an enthusiasm his wife shared. She said the sun aged her skin, hurt her eyes, reddened her nose, spoilt her hair and rumpled her clothes. And he wasn't entirely convinced that she welcomed its effect on his libido.

An unresolved question in their marriage touched on this delicate subject: whether a baby brother (or sister) would be a beneficial influence on the indefatigable Lindy. Neil Kennedy had always imagined himself having two children, as his parents had (there was an elder sister he never saw whose engineer husband had taken her to Monrovia), but the tireless infant that he had now sired seemed to have discouraged his wife from further visits to the maternity ward.

Even in St Louis her presence had proved disruptive so that what had been intended as a rest was proving to be the same old obstacle course, with father striving to entertain daughter for a couple of hours while mother lay down, before the roles were reversed. The only one who didn't lie down was Lindy.

The restaurant – brass fixtures, fresh roses and fine white linen – was surprisingly tasteful, which might have been why it was not as crowded as the McDonalds riverboat further along the waterfront. They were shown to a booth which curved to show the river.

Beautiful waitresses, who had evidently been cloistered for hours with their orthodontists, moved among them in saloon-gal dresses.

'What do you think surf 'n' turf means?' Gwenda asked.

'Daddy, can you whistle with two fingers in your mouth?' asked Lindy.

As usual, Neil Kennedy, in a new cane-cutter shirt and more interested in the waitresses than the menu, found himself dragged between two conversations.

'No, I can't,' he told his daughter, and felt that he had let her down. Perhaps he could go away and learn the trick before Lindy decided that her daddy wasn't good at anything very much.

'I think it's lobster and steak,' he said.

'Really? Why is steak turf?'

'I've no idea.'

He was mystified by much of the menu: Louisiana Riverboats ($5.50), Pecan-fried catfish fillets ($11.95), Cajun Dixieland feast ($14.95). They ordered lobster.

The waitress brought the salad before the main course and waited until they had finished before serving the lobster.

'Are you folks English?' she asked when they complained. 'I must be the only American in the place tonight.'

Neil Kennedy, who had become romantically convinced that the Clark Gable look-alike at a nearby table had just breezed in from a Nevada love nest, was mortified to find that he was surrounded by tourists.

'I bet fortunes were lost when they shunted gamblers down the river to New Orleans in this old tub,' he said, looking elsewhere for the glamour. But this was wrong, too.

'We don't discuss gambling, dear. Remember?'

'We wouldn't be here without it,' he said, and tried to whistle with two fingers in his mouth.

11

HARRY GRANT was being massaged by an entire girls' school, but his latest sexual fantasy refused to take off. There were too many characters for even his inflamed imagination to handle. They kept wandering away and refusing to enter into the spirit of things.

He was trying to write his 'Village Notes' column for the *Gazette* and, as he spent so much time looking at it, had chosen as his subject the village green. It was a topic that seemed to induce constipation in his ancient typewriter.

'The village green,' he wrote, 'once the home of the horse pond, the maypole, the pump and the stocks, has a mysterious history. Although ours in Compton Sinbury is oblong, many village greens are triangular and their shape is a clue to their uncertain origins.'

Harry Grant wasn't sure whether this was true but he vaguely remembered reading a book about the subject.

'A piece of land for common use in the centre of the community is thought by some people to have been created for reasons of defence more than a thousand years ago.'

A horde of unruly schoolgirls who wouldn't bend to his will disturbed the tenor of his thoughts. He sat poised over the typewriter like a pianist who has just had his music stolen.

'Villagers could bring their cattle into the safety of the village centre to protect them from thieves – or even wolves which were once common in Britain – and a triangular green gave the locals only three entrances to defend.'

He thought of African tribesmen making a square compound with their huts to keep out lions, of circles of covered wagons in a Hollywood Western, of circles of schoolgirls attending to his prostrate form. His confusion was ended by the ringing of his doorbell.

Cathy Gray stood on the step in a short red dress. She was holding a large brown envelope.

'I've brought the pictures,' she said. The rustic overtones of her Cornish accent made him think of fields again.

'Come in, come in,' he said, relieved at the interruption which, counting as work, would produce no feelings of guilt. He showed her into his front room where his stalled typewriter sat thoughtfully on a desk in the window.

'I like your Mustang,' she said, sitting down.

He had forgotten all about the single girl's obsession with cars. 'It's like me,' he said. 'All torque and no action.' He realized that this was the wrong audience for his puns and said: 'Let's see the pictures.'

She handed him the envelope and he pulled out more than twenty black and white photographs. In the first she was modelling an overcoat with a high collar that was turned up so that only her profile was revealed. In the next one she was wearing a two-piece suit. He was surprised at the pictures' professional quality.

'Where were they used?' he asked.

'In brochures and catalogues.'

The third one showed her in blouse and slacks; next she was in shorts. It dawned on him suddenly that the pictures had been placed in a certain order, like a frame-by-frame strip. Four pictures later she was in bra and pants, smiling happily at the camera with one elegant hand on a studio palm tree.

'They're nice,' he said.

'They get nicer,' she told him.

In the next she was bikini clad beside a pool, not smiling now but wearing a sultry expression as her eyes avoided the camera's lens. Some women looked as if it was only sex that kept them going, while others made it seem as if they would prefer any alternative. Cathy Gray was definitely in the first category.

Triumphantly topless in the last half-dozen pictures, she

shed her pants for the final two, revealing a trim bottom that made Harry's eyes pop. He looked at the owner of this alluring posterior. There was surely a sexual motivation in the order in which the pictures had been arranged?

'Would you like to see my potting shed?' he asked.

She laughed loudly. 'I've never heard it called that before,' she said. 'A bachelor like you must have lots of women.'

'They can be counted on the fingers of one leper,' he told her. 'And the potting shed is a drinks bar in my garden.'

Finding a picture that would not affront the chaste readers of the *County Gazette* was an enjoyable challenge that involved studying each of them several times. When he had selected a demure number in blouse and skirt he took her out to the potting shed where she asked for white wine.

His questions, designed to elicit sufficient information to provide a caption for the photograph, produced, with the help of the wine, a hand on his knee and a cosy proximity which the tall shaky stools and the potting shed's somewhat austere ambience didn't really encourage. Was this slip of a girl trying to seduce him? And, if so, why wasn't she succeeding?

Most women were attractive for the first hour. The flaws emerged slowly. But beguiled by her siren song and encouraged by the gin, he confessed: 'You mentioned other women. There are none. I'm the only man I know who can get a hard-on looking at tailors' dummies in Marks and Spencer.'

The sparkling white teeth at the top of her mouth covered her bottom lip. 'My, that's sad,' she said. 'Can I help you?'

He refilled his glass and considered this, uncertain what form her offered help would take. And he wasn't so drunk or desperate that he could overlook other considerations: in these days of proliferating sexual diseases, for instance, it was as well to know where your partner had been.

'You're much too young,' he suggested, 'to give me what I need. I seem to be forty and you're an innocent young thing.'

Her reply, directed at his accusation that she was innocent, astonished him and reinforced the mild alarm he had experienced at her too obvious willingness.

'Between my fifteenth and sixteenth birthdays,' she said, both elbows resting now on his tiny bar, 'there was hardly a day when my brother Owen didn't make love to me.'

He nearly dropped his glass. 'You were in love with your brother?' he asked, trying to grasp what she was telling him.

She laughed. 'I wasn't in love with him, silly. I just liked it and there wasn't anyone else around to do it with.'

'Where is he now?' he asked incredulously.

'He went into the church.'

Both professionally and privately Harry Grant had heard some odd stories, but none had thrown him into a panic like this. He couldn't have felt more alarmed if Cathy Gray had told him that she did it with her dog.

'Wasn't he prosecuted?' he asked. 'There are laws about that sort of thing.'

'Well, of course, nobody ever knew. We had an agreement and he is my brother.'

'And now he's in the church.'

'He's a curate, actually.'

'The incestuous curate,' he said, thinking in headlines. 'He ought to write his story, chuck his cassock and clean up.'

Cathy Gray picked up her wine, not liking this tone. 'It was very beautiful while it was happening, as a matter of fact.'

'Poignant, I should think.' The moment had passed for Harry now. He felt like a man who had been in a near miss.

'If I drive the picture over to the office tonight it will be in Friday's paper,' he said. 'I ought to do it. They're short of good pictures this week.'

Cathy Gray could see that this visit to the potting shed was not going to end in the way she had expected. She was confident that she could still turn him round, but she wanted her picture in the paper quickly and was prepared to wait for Harry Grant.

No single event in Compton Sinbury's year received as enthusiastic a welcome as the start of cricket on the green. Even people who found the game too tedious to discuss were cheered by the sight of men in white flannels dotted round the freshly mowed grass: it meant that another winter had been defeated, that summer was on the way.

Duncan Baxter was drawn to this ritual one Saturday afternoon, curious about a game that was quintessentially English and quite unlike the aggressive sporting events that he attended at home. It was some time before he began to understand what the players were trying to achieve.

Felix Kirby had brought a deck-chair across the road from his house and installed himself on the boundary to watch the game, and when Duncan Baxter wandered up he went back and fetched another chair. Now he was trying to explain the game's intricacies to the American visitor.

'That chap who's throwing the ball –' said Duncan Baxter.

'Bowling,' said Felix Kirby. 'He's bowling the ball.'

'Okay, bowling. It's Paul Vanner, isn't it?'

'Yes, it's Paul.'

'Anyway, he's bowling so slowly that the man with the bat could hit him into the road, couldn't he?'

'Paul's bowling his leg breaks. The ball isn't travelling in a predictable straight line. It's spinning and changing direction when it hits the ground. It makes it difficult for the batsman to hit, never mind smash out of the ground.'

Duncan Baxter had once talked to the pitcher for the New York Mets. The only leg break he worried about was the one he might inflict on the man with the bat. 'How long do these games last?' he asked, noticing the unhurried pace.

'This will last till seven. When England play Australia it lasts five days.'

'Five *days*?' said Duncan Baxter. 'How can a game last five days?'

'Very easily. Half of them are drawn then because they run out of time.'

'They play for five days and still don't get a result?'

'Often,' said Felix Kirby.

'I think it would take more than a month to understand this country.'

'You could go and see this game in the West Indies. That's on your doorstep. Of course they don't have our skill at bowling, with leg breaks and off breaks and so on. With them it's just brute force and speed.'

'So you trash 'em?'

'No,' said Felix Kirby irritably. 'They invariably beat us.'

Paul Vanner was finding the first game of the season as hard as usual. Tomorrow he would ache in several places. At one time he had been a fast bowler, swinging the ball down at a fearful rate, but he was too old or too unfit now for that sort of activity. He had slowed to medium pace but found his deliveries too easy to hit, so now he was dispatching slow and deceptive balls that were beating not only the batsman but also the wicket-keeper.

The wicket-keeper was Harry Grant who had been keeping wicket on this green for fifteen years. But the crouching position demanded by the job was proving a bit of a strain. The knees no longer enjoyed the summer exercise, or not the first few weeks of it when he always announced that this would be his last season. But by July the muscles had adapted to the strain; when he put his gloves and pads away in September he was already looking forward to next summer.

Today was the difficult day when it was agony to crouch and purgatory to stand up again. His gait as he walked between wickets at the end of each over made it look as if he had recently lost control of his bladder.

'What the hell are you bowling, Paul?' he asked. 'I'm not reading them at all.'

'They're called leg breaks, Harry.'

'They're turning a yard. Perhaps the pitch needs rolling.'

For more than a hundred years the first game of the season had been against the next village whose team today had an unexpectedly international flavour. It was quite against the spirit and tradition of the fixture to recruit outsiders, but the visitors claimed that their Indian spinner was the new owner of the local corner shop, the Australian had recently married a local girl and moved into the village during the winter, and the black giant who had hit the ball into the duck pond at the top of the green was a West Indian poet in search of rural solitude. Paul Vanner was all for demanding some documentary proof that this providential piece of team strengthening was genuine, but the home umpire, who was Colonel Arbuthnott, the chairman of the council, told him that away from the brutal realities of the money market some principles still survived in the country, where a man's word was accepted until there was compelling evidence that he was a liar. The visiting team declared at 200 for three.

'It looks as if we are going to lose our unbeaten record,' said Felix Kirby from the depths of his deck-chair.

'I thought this was the first match?'

'It is.'

Duncan Baxter was beginning to see the attraction of sitting in the sun and watching such leisurely activity. It didn't demand total attention like the Cardinals at home, and he was able to study the spectators who drifted round the perimeter in shirts and slacks and summer frocks, while still managing to retain an intelligent interest in the complicated ceremony on the pitch.

He could see the blonde waitress from the Refectory with several admirers on the opposite side of the ground. At the top of the green near the duck pond, a couple were watching the game from horseback. From a bench outside the pub Suzanne Vanner was sitting watching her husband play, and other people who had become familiar faces to him during his visit strolled past his chair without nodding. You would have to live here a long time, he thought, before anybody said hallo.

'Did my father ever play this game?' he asked. The idea evoked a pleasant picture of a young man in white flannels extracting some enjoyment from life, but Felix Kirby's reply was not encouraging.

'Not in my time,' he said. 'Barney playing cricket is a bit hard to imagine. Your father's a one-off. He hasn't even got a bank account.'

'What does he do with his money – hide it in a mattress?'

'I asked him that once. It's my business, after all, to find new customers. It turned out that he didn't have any. He leads a hand-to-mouth existence.'

Duncan Baxter found this information strangely embarrassing. Of course, his father was embarrassment incarnate, but in these thrusting times there was still nothing quite as embarrassing as failure.

He shook off the embarrassment by announcing proudly: 'My father's fortunes are about to improve, Felix. I'd be grateful if you would open an account in his name and then keep an eye on it.'

'I'd be glad to. Tell him to come and see me. How much do you think he'll be depositing?'

'About £200,000.'

'Jesus,' said Felix Kirby, impressed. 'That's a lot of Guinness.'

He wanted to ask where this money was going to come from, but the professional etiquette of his job demanded that he wait until he was told. Duncan Baxter, however, had nothing more to say.

The Compton Sinbury team were now batting and the black man, it could now be seen, was not only a powerful batsman but a lethal fast bowler too. He came in on a long run scarcely panting, and sent the ball hurtling past the batsmen's ears at a speed which thoroughly unnerved them. When he kept it lower the batsmen were relieved to discover their stumps spreadeagled, their ordeal over, and they headed happily for the security of the pavilion.

'He must be one of those West Indians you were talking about,' said Duncan Baxter, laughing. 'No skill, no subtlety.'

'That's right,' said Felix Kirby, ignoring the American's joke. 'He'd be better off playing a simple man's game, like baseball.

Even among those residents of Compton Sinbury who had created a life of leisure for themselves champagne was not the normal Monday morning refreshment. But the opening of Suzanne's, a new boutique for the discerning woman, was an occasion for breaking with tradition.

Suzanne Vanner had compiled a guest list for the opening party, drawn partly from those she judged to be potential customers, but also from those who might, in one way or another, be useful to her future fortunes. Colonel Arbuthnott boomed loudly at the centre of the celebration, and Daisy Balcombe, a woman of surprising influence who sat on the parish council with him, was also invited. Dr Frost, with whom Suzanne was trying to pluck up the courage to discuss the possibility that she might be pregnant, was invited because of his wife's expensive taste in clothes. Michael, the butcher from the bottom of the green, was asked along as a fellow trader. Felix Kirby and Nadine were present because it was the bank's loan, negotiated by Paul Vanner, that had enabled Suzanne to fill the vacuum in her life with this venture.

The Arts and Craft shop had moved out rapidly with its bread dolls and lace toilet-roll holders, and dresses, skirts, blouses, trousers and shorts had now replaced its odd collection of goods. On several trips to London Suzanne had discovered that, in the fashion business these days, you are almost too late to order in May the clothes that you want to stock next winter, but an agent for three French houses found her some summer stock once she had given him a hefty order for the autumn.

Harry Grant was invited in the hope of publicity and Toby Beauchamp was invited by Paul Vanner when he was drunk. Vanner had taken the day off work to witness the launching of his wife's business career. He secretly hoped that it would spread from town to town like a Wimpy Bar and remove the need for him to get up at five o'clock every morning. He drank champagne and beamed at faces he hardly knew.

'Who are all these people?' asked Toby Beauchamp as he threaded his way through scarves and belts towards the champagne.

'They're rented,' said Harry Grant.

Suzanne Vanner moved among her guests, sipping champagne and accepting messages of good luck. Felix Kirby held a glass that he barely drank from as he tried to gauge whether the bank's capital had been wisely lent. There was enough money round here to support this shop and, if the population of Compton Sinbury hardly merited such a classy boutique, the surrounding villages provided a catchment area that would bring in customers if Suzanne got it right. He took a tiny sip of his champagne – he had to return to his office soon – and crossed his fingers.

His wife was wearing a creation that could have come out of this shop: a yellow two-piece with a tight skirt. She had been slimming and her clothes lately had become brighter. She stood talking to her husband and Dr Frost who kept banging glasses and saying 'Cheers! I never say good health. It's bad for business.' But neither of them was interested in what she had to say, preferring to discuss the new community charge. When Nadine Kirby saw that someone had stopped listening to her she regarded it as her failure and not theirs; she wasn't interesting enough. Suzanne Vanner would react quite differently and kick the leg of the person whose attention had strayed.

Nadine left her husband's side and moved in the direction of Harry Grant who, in the fantasy he needed to sustain himself in these alien surroundings, was wrapped round Corazon Aquino on a yacht in Manila Bay. He couldn't understand the attraction that powerful women had for him. None of them was young and few of them were pretty but he was challenged and aroused by their lofty status. Kissinger had said that power was an aphrodisiac but Harry doubted whether he had ever thought about this.

'That was a nice story that you wrote about Rachel,' Nadine Kirby said.

Harry disembarked from the yacht in Manila Bay. 'She's a good girl,' he said. It was unusual for Nadine to approach him in public. 'She's a credit to you.'

'She seems more interested in journalism than banks. I wonder why that is?'

'Shush,' he said nervously, glancing across at Felix Kirby. He was scared that Nadine, having enjoyed the champagne, was on the verge of another indiscretion. He diverted her. 'You look very beautiful today, Mrs Kirby,' he said. 'Yellow suits you.'

She smiled, genuinely pleased. 'Thank you, Harry. You're wearing pretty well yourself. Better than some people I could mention.' She looked across at her husband who was consulting his watch.

A few feet away Toby Beauchamp had been cornered by Daisy Balcombe whose concession to this morning of fashion was a batik sarong, which hung like a tent from her angular frame. Daisy's life had recently settled into a series of misfortunes, and Toby Beauchamp, having uttered the innocuous 'How's life?' was dismayed to discover that he was going to be told. Fleas were breeding in her rush matting, and she had lost her budgie in the extractor fan. And then she had wasted weeks trying to persuade the parish council that the village should twin with Condom in France, an idea which to her continuing bewilderment had found no support at all.

It crossed Toby Beauchamp's mind, as he stood glassy-eyed before this catalogue of disaster, that the seventy-year-old spinster was after more than his sympathy; she was making a move on him as a romantic playmate. He pictured himself incarcerated in her thatched cottage, trapped in games of bridge or enigmatic conversations over the coffee and Amaretto, and he started to edge slowly backwards until his retreat was halted by a rigid tray of costume jewellery.

Suzanne Vanner was experiencing the wave of nausea which came to her often now. She put her arm in her husband's and smiled round the room.

'It's going well,' she said.

'They'll drink your champagne, but will they buy your clothes?' he muttered. 'What you need is publicity.'

'Harry!' she called, and Harry Grant made his way through the crowded shop with Nadine.

'Are you going to give Suzanne some publicity?' Paul asked.

'It's difficult to plug one shop. They'll all want a write-up.'

'What do I have to do?' asked Suzanne. 'Streak across the green?'

'I'm not the man to discourage you. Of course, it might attract the wrong sort of customer.'

'You've got to let the world know this shop is open for business,' Paul Vanner told him. 'That's why you're drinking champagne. You're not here for your talent behind the stumps, pal.'

'Place an advertisement in the *Gazette*,' Harry told them. 'Then it will be in order for me to write an exciting account about you and the shop.'

'Is that how it works? Give me the phone number of your advertising department. You've got a lot of readers, have you?'

'Ninety per cent penetration in the county.'

Nadine Kirby laughed. 'Harry can even make sales figures sound like sex.'

Two men who were not invited to the opening of Suzanne's sat in the Flatulent Ferret at a table in the corner. Duncan Baxter was drinking whisky, his father Guinness.

'I've been talking to Toby Beauchamp about your garden, Barney.'

There had been some initial embarrassment about what they should call each other. Barnaby Barton had not helped matters by trying to address his son as 'sir'. When he was dissuaded from this he started to use 'Mr Baxter'. Duncan Baxter could not bring himself to call this sad old figure 'dad' and they had agreed on Christian names although Barney somehow managed to avoid using it.

'You don't really need the garden, do you?' Duncan Baxter asked.

'It's the potatoes,' said Barney. 'They pay for a trip to Brighton.' He said Brighton in the way that another man might refer to Montego Bay.

Duncan Baxter didn't know what to say. Growing and selling potatoes didn't sound like the sure route to riches to him, particularly if you only had an acre, but he wasn't anxious to block this isolated example of enterprise by his father, or what seemed to be his rare moments of fulfilment.

'I want you to have a lot of money, Barney,' he said. 'So you can enjoy your old age. Everybody else round here seems to be loaded. Why not you?'

'I've worked myself up from nothing to a state of extreme poverty. Groucho Marx said that. It's in one of my books.'

'I know he did. But you don't have to settle for poverty.'

Barney shook his head. 'It's too late for me now. I missed my chance. I reckon I lost my drive when Lydia Baxter left.'

'But you've got an acre of land in the south of England. That's money, Barney, and you need money more than you need land.'

Barney's mind groped for the one essential fact about his land's importance. 'It's the potatoes,' he said again.

'Fuck the potatoes,' said Duncan Baxter in a momentary flash of anger. He couldn't decide whether the man was indifferent to money or too stupid to see that he could make some.

'Do you want a lot of money?' he asked in an attempt to clarify this.

'I've got my old-age pension and my £10 on Monday. And I do jobs for Terry Wallace.'

'Ten pounds on Monday? What's that?'

'Somebody sends me a £10 note every Monday.'

'Who?'

'I don't know. There's nothing in the envelope except the £10 note.'

'Good God,' said Duncan Baxter. He felt an awful sense of shame that some anonymous do-gooder, probably in this village, was helping to support his father. Colour my face red, he thought. 'You've no idea who's sending it?'

Barney shook his head and picked up his Guinness. He had long since ceased to wonder about the identity of his benefactor; even in the beginning his curiosity hadn't been exactly rampant. 'It arrives. That's all I care about.'

'But don't you want more? Don't you *need* more?'

It was axiomatic in the last decade of the twentieth century that it was not possible to have too much money, and certainly nobody he dealt with in America had ever expressed so heinous a thought. 'Wouldn't more be fun?'

Barney looked at him. This conversation, like so many before it, had moved beyond his range, leaving him confused and monosyllabic.

'What?' he asked.

'More money. Jesus, that's what most people want. Why should you be different? I told you, I've been talking to Toby Beauchamp. He would like to buy your land and build houses on it. He'd pay you about £200,000.' Duncan Baxter looked at his father in the hope that some sign would reveal how much of this had been taken in. 'Two hundred thousand pounds,' he spelt out, in case the words had confused him.

'I suppose I could grow potatoes somewhere else,' said Barney. The mention of a sum of money didn't seem to move him one way or the other.

'That's right,' said Duncan Baxter, encouraged. 'You could. On the other hand you might not want to grow potatoes any more. You could get to Brighton without it. Or Hawaii, come to that.'

'I've never fancied Hawaii,' said Barney as if this were an option he had seriously considered and rejected on aesthetic grounds. 'I'd keep the bungalow?'

'Oh, yes. They'd build a road up the side of it. There's plenty of room.'

'Tell Mr Beauchamp I agree,' said Barney very formally. It was as if, after a lifetime of disappointment, he didn't believe in the money but wanted to be polite.

'I'll get you a lawyer. What do you call it? Solicitor,' said Duncan Baxter. 'He'll come and see you and act on your behalf. Just do what he says and sign where he tells you. And one other thing you have to do is go round to Felix Kirby's bank and open an account.'

Barney looked at his Guinness. He never seemed to look at his son, not wanting, for some reason, to meet his eyes.

'When are you going back?' he asked.

'Couple of days.'

'Will I see you again?'

'I expect I'll be over.'

'Bring your mother next time, will you? Tell her I'm rich.'

12

THE DIFFERENCE between a theatre audience and a television audience was something that Neil Kennedy had learned about early in his career. A theatre audience, only too conscious of the high price of their tickets, listened with rapt attention and were open-minded, sympathetic and responsive. Television viewers, who had usually alighted on his work by accident, were talkative, distracted and impatient. They chewed food and slurped beer, constantly consulting newspapers for other options – or these days, more likely, banged a new film from the video rental shop into their Panasonic VCRs.

This battle to grip the viewing audience's attention produced an atmosphere of near hysteria in the tower block in North Acton where he was to rehearse some location shots for *Hot Air Rises*. One of these days they would actually go out and shoot the location shots and after that they would find themselves in the controlled pandemonium of the studio.

The Kennedys had flown back from America feeling more tired than when they left. Travelling thousands of miles had not separated them from the hyperactive problem in their midst. She ran, she shouted, she sang, and she demanded diversion, entertainment and instruction.

'What does denigrate mean?' she had asked, picking up a word she had just heard on the plane. 'No, don't tell me. Give me a clue.'

'Are you sure she's only three?' he asked his wife.

'It feels as if she had been around for years,' Gwenda said and fell asleep.

'So,' he said when she woke up, 'no more kids?'

'Could you go through it all again?' She looked at him as if he were mad. 'I always imagined that after a month or two I'd be back at work making an office hum, but I'm too tired to iron clothes. Did you ever notice the mountain of unironed clothes in the utility room? We can't get any sleep at night and we can rarely have a rational conversation during the day. If we can find a babysitter with enough energy to handle her we're too tired to enjoy ourselves when we escape. There isn't a single job I can do at home without being interrupted ten times, and when there is the chance of relaxing in front of a good programme on the television in the evening she will be sure to ruin it. And you want more?'

'Other people seem to handle two or three kids,' he said, but he knew her answer already.

'Not kids like this,' she said. 'Other people's kids are asleep by seven. Most parents get twelve clear hours a day without a sound from their children. It's hell's own job to get this one to doze off for an hour or two at midnight.'

While the tedium of a transatlantic flight had sent many passengers to sleep, Lindy sat on the floor of the plane making a coastguard's boat with her Playmobil. They did not arrive at Heathrow in the refreshed condition their holiday was intended to produce, and a day or two later, Neil Kennedy, scared of not giving his best in *Hot Air Rises* on the interrupted sleep that had become the norm, moved into a separate bedroom before his career was destroyed.

Now, four floors up in a glass box with dry air and subsidized cholesterol dispensed by a canteen staff of Afro-Caribbean immigrants, he reflected that St Louis to North Acton was not a journey that anybody in their right mind would make.

Actors he had known when they were pretty, young and exciting fell gushingly upon him, volunteering unasked an update on their careers while looking over his shoulder to see who it would be advantageous to fawn over next. The writers, two spotty 45-year-olds wearing 1950s' clothing from Oxfam, appeared and hovered on the periphery of this reunion.

His escape came with a call on the PA to go to rehearsal room 401 where a menopausal drunk with hennaed hair, who was trapped in a moment of prolonged decay that she had decided could only be preserved by dressing like a brick-layer's hod-carrier, whispered effusively: 'Neil . . . wonderful . . . Denis was so thrilled that you could join us on this one.'

Denis, the director, arrived to greet him with exaggerated enthusiasm. He was clearly in some stage of Aids but everyone was rallying round and being brave and normal.

Neil Kennedy was used to this, as indeed to every other type of horror that could emerge on a film set which he had decided a long time ago attracted the most flawed bunch of people you would find outside a funny farm. Thin skins, prodigious egos, latent bile and flabbergasting mendacity were what they brought to work with them. Professional smilers with knives up their sleeves, they learned quickly to despise each other whilst waging a constant battle with the producer about their 'standing' – which could involve anything from whether they had their own driver on location to whether or not wardrobe or make-up was responsible for emptying their colostomy bag.

The leading lady, who was to play his wife, was called Beatrix. She probably had as many talents as any woman but acting, unfortunately, was not one of them. This was a considerable drawback on stage, which she had now learned to avoid, but on television the camera could make the actress. In fact the camera had fallen in love with this one, highlighting her fine bone structure and fascinating the viewer for long enough for some words to come out, before hurrying away to another angle. Keeping the lines short, and making sure that her eyes didn't look as if there was absolute brain death, directors had created a star from the unlikeliest material. Indeed, in the age of Rambos and bimbos she had once been described as a Garbo.

'Hallo, Neil,' she said. 'Isn't it a wonderful script?'

'Magical,' he told her. Enthusiasm was the single most important commodity in this environment. When enthusiasm faded, things started to come apart at the seams.

'What have you been doing lately, anyway? I haven't seen you around.'

She meant that she hadn't seen him on television. If you weren't seen on television you were dead.

'I've moved to the country,' he said, pretending that he thought she meant he hadn't been seen in London.

She was a tall, slim blonde with icy blue eyes, and he wondered whether the romantic scenes were going to be a problem. He could imagine her castrating a bull without thinking about it, but perhaps now that he slept alone he would find the amorous reserves that would make the scene come alive.

The read-through was played to a nodded satisfaction from Denis, the director, and produced a surprising number of laughs from the cast itself. For the first time Neil Kennedy began to wonder whether *Hot Air Rises* might, after all, not be the débâcle he had imagined; there was a certain brittle cleverness that could impress the critics.

This glimpse of hope, however, did little to alleviate his low spirits. Talking to people he didn't know and saying things he barely understood while wearing clothes that didn't fit and being told what to do by a dozen minions he didn't care for, seemed a strange way to earn a living. The problem was that he was so good at it.

'Brilliant, Neil,' said the ailing Denis. 'I knew directly I read it that the role of Julian was you.'

Neil Kennedy didn't say anything. His attitude to jobs like this was to turn up on time, stay buttoned, deliver the goods and ignore the bloody shambles all round him. That way you went home with your sanity intact.

He knew that this was just the sort of drivel that might catch on with the warm British public and put his name up in lights again. He knew that *Hot Air Rises* would mean that he made far more money this year than he did last.

But most of all he knew that by next week he would be getting up at five o'clock so that he could be on location in a suburb of Pevensey by half past six, when he would walk up a drive a dozen times, stopping on each occasion to ask Festino the gardener how the apples were coming along, and the entire crew would address itself to the really important problem of how to shoot the dog mess on his suede shoe.

*

Harry Grant sat in his potting shed trying to earn some money. It was so easy if you were a writer. There were no tedious journeys to unpleasant appointments, no stress-filled meetings where you attempted to impose your will on others, no complicated deals that involved an irascible managing director, two solicitors and three accountants. All you needed was a pen and a few sheets of paper and the next thing you knew, there was a cheque in the post.

That was the theory, anyway, but it was some time since the postman had brought him anything but bills. Today's little extramural activity was to compile a list of Sod's Laws. There was a mania for lists in the land and magazines paid for them. Ten things you bought and never used, ten people to avoid at parties, ten left-wingers who went to Eton.

Life brought a new Sod's Law every day and if he could rake together ten of them somebody would send him £20. He poured himself a gin, stared at the blank sheet of paper, and then he wrote down the Sod's Law that had started him off on this quest: *You will always want to go to the lavatory when the window cleaner is doing your house.* He added a second immediately: *You will always return from the laundrette with an odd number of socks.*

The gin was supposed to help him, to stimulate his mind, but his mind had a mind of its own. To his astonishment today's sexual fantasy involved Nadine Kirby. At the opening of Suzanne Vanner's shop she seemed to have shed a few pounds and a few years with them. When he had glanced at her, she had glanced at him. Now, in her absence, the relationship had raced ahead. Sexual intercourse standing up in a haycart was only the beginning. They had rolled naked into a swimming pool in Capri, made furtive love on an airliner, and performed on stage for money in a seedy Soho strip club. After that he had become seriously sexy. He had masturbated in her armpit, sucked dollops of fragrant turd from her beautiful bottom and got his tongue so far up her vagina that it had knocked her hat off. Her fervent enthusiasm for sudden, unexpected copulation made his head spin.

He wrote: *At a temporary set of traffic lights, more cars will always get through from the opposite direction.* And, thinking of cars, he added: *You will only get a puncture when it's raining.*

But his picture of Nadine Kirby, and the memory of the things they had once done together, was so intense that he put his pen down until he could control his thoughts. She had shunned him for a decade like a dutiful wife, but suddenly the possibility of actually making love to her seemed real again. He couldn't imagine why or what had happened in the Kirby household to bring about this change of heart. But he could feel it in the air.

The ringing phone in the cottage dragged him back from his blissful reverie. He wrote: *The phone will always ring when you're washing your hair.*

He picked up the extension in the potting shed. It was Dakers, the news editor.

'Your copy's lovely, but you didn't do the vicar,' he said.

'The vicar? We don't have a vicar at the moment. We've got a late vicar.'

'You've got a new vicar. I thought I sent you a note so you could interview him.'

'I didn't get it. What's his name? I'll go and see him.'

'I've got it here somewhere. Yes, Owen Gray.'

'Owen Gray?' said Harry. 'I think I know about him.'

'What do you know about him?'

'He used to make love to his sister.'

'An incestuous vicar? I'd better check our libel insurance.'

'I think we should ignore that aspect of his rise to fame, don't you?'

'Yes, I do, Harry,' said Dakers firmly. 'I'd be most grateful if you forgot to mention that.'

Harry put down the phone and drank some more gin. He wrote: *The best stories a reporter gets are the very ones he can't publish.*

Owen Gray sat at his new desk in a vicarage built of knapped flint and stone dressings, and wondered whether he was the only vicar in Britain who didn't believe in God. He decided that he probably wasn't and that a loss of faith was only to be expected among vicars as among others as the world lurched uncertainly towards the millennium.

He didn't see that it mattered. Did a politician always believe in the policies he was obliged to espouse? Did a salesman always have faith in the product? The life of a vicar had appealed to him ever since a harassed careers master had pointed him in the direction of the church on the basis of some extraordinary marks in a religious-knowledge exam.

Of course, in those days he believed, or thought he did. But the seeds of his doubt had been sowed years earlier, when he was nine years old and a man had walked on the moon. His interest in space had grown alongside his interest in God and at some period, which he couldn't quite pinpoint now, had overtaken it.

Owen Gray was a tall thin man of thirty with wild fair hair that always needed brushing. His arrival in Compton Sinbury was a promotion that was thoroughly deserved.

He opened the magazine on his desk and read: 'Andromeda lies 13 quintillion miles away from earth. It takes 2.25 million years for light to travel this enormous distance.'

As far as Owen Gray was concerned, science had not merely nibbled at the edges of religious belief, but gobbled it up and spat it out. If you left the earth in a spacecraft that travelled at 10 million miles a second, where would you be in a month, in a year? Not in the Kingdom of God. If you left the earth in the best spacecraft yet built 11,000 years ago at the beginning of our civilization, you would still have not reached the nearest galaxy.

All this lent a somewhat parochial air to St John's Gospel which he was supposed to be reading this morning. Other duties were listed on a piece of paper which had been pushed to one side in favour of the magazine. The names of several of the most devout parishioners, who would welcome a visit from him, had been provided by one of the church wardens but he knew only too well what that would involve in this prosperous neighbourhood. He would be invited to watch a video they had made of their grandchildren or their dog or their holiday. The video camera had provided new horrors for the casual visitor: at least he could flip through holiday snaps at his own fast pace.

There was a knock on the front door and he went out. The vicarage was sparsely furnished and poorly heated, but it had huge rooms and a large garden and was the best home he had ever had.

The man at the front door said: 'Harry Grant of the *County Gazette*. I wondered if I could . . .'

'Come in,' said the new vicar of Sin. His visitor was an untidy-looking man of about forty with big round glasses and a boyish face, as if life hadn't touched him very much. 'You want copy.'

Harry Grant followed him into his study. He had sat here before with Owen Gray's predecessor, discussing one financial appeal or another, and nothing had changed. The desk, the bookcase, the red carpet that didn't really fit, clearly survived each incumbent and gave the vicarage a curiously timeless character.

'You're thirty years old and you were born in Cornwall,' he said when he had sat down and produced a notebook from one of his rumpled pockets. And you used to have intercourse with your teenage sister, he wanted to add.

'You're well informed,' said the vicar.

'I know Cathy,' Harry told him.

'Ah, Cathy,' Owen Gray said, looking only slightly uneasy. 'Of course, I wanted this job to be nearer our mother. Are you a religious man, Mr Grant? Shall I see you when I'm in church?'

'Only if you stand on a ladder and look across the green at the pub, I'm afraid.'

'The Commandments don't hold much sway with you then?'

'I wouldn't say that. I'm all in favour of loving my neighbours – there are some very attractive women round here.'

The vicar looked at him across the spartan room. The phrase 'bibulous hack' came into his mind.

'How is Cathy settling down here?' he asked.

'Cathy is the village pin-up.'

'I'm worried about that girl.'

It was difficult to see this solemn, even ascetic, young man as the brother of a sex siren, Harry thought, and even harder to take him seriously when you knew that he had enjoyed her first. But journalists knew too many unprintable things about people to take anybody very seriously. Owen Gray's projected image of the celibate celebrity, however, was going to look particularly fraudulent, given Harry's knowledge of his unpromising start in the world of sexual relations.

'Can you tell me a little,' he asked, 'about your career in the church, and how you came to enter it in the first place?'

Owen Gray recited a list of curacies which seemed to run in a horizontal line from Hereford to Cambridge and had delivered him, after an appropriate period of apprenticeship, to his present eminence.

'I went into the church almost by accident,' he confessed. 'I'm afraid that being a vicar these days is a job like any other. All that pastor of the flock nonsense, adorned in the panoply of the Lord, is out of the window in today's secular climate. You are part social worker, part salesman, part politician.'

'I suppose it is this modern approach that has made you one of the youngest vicars in England.'

'Am I really? The thought had not crossed my mind.'

'But what about belief?' Harry asked. 'When did this conviction that life doesn't end in the crematorium first grip you?'

The vicar turned a page of the space magazine that lay on the desk in front of him. 'Do you know,' he said, 'I can't remember.'

He began to wonder now what sort of congregation awaited him in Compton Sinbury. Another fifty miles from London and he would have expected a peaceful, slow-moving calm, and a quiet relaxed population. But this place was in reach of the capital. Its ancient cottages and modern houses were presumably filled with an unusually disparate flock: underpaid villagers, overpaid commuters, sleepy rustics and city slickers, the gullible and the cynical. He imagined luxurious people with swimming pools in their gardens and poorer ones with chicken runs. He imagined grand ladies with famous relatives living in stately homes, retired army officers, television producers, lawyers and business tycoons who hid in the country at weekends, all of them having the sort of quick-witted conversation that could disconcert him, and all of them living alongside the rural poor, the labourers and the frequently unemployed whose taciturnity he found equally difficult to handle. And, in all probability, there would be a noisy cluster of dedicated environmentalists who had abandoned life's conventional struggles to return to nature and live on what they could grow. They referred to 'the planet' not 'the world', talked of denuded forests and poisoned lakes and behaved as if God had nothing to do with it.

'I think I first believed in God when I was a small boy and prayed for a bicycle at Christmas,' he said.

'And the bike duly arrived?'

'Yes, it did.'

'I wonder what path your career would have taken if the bike hadn't shown up?'

But speculation on this hypothetical matter was prevented by a knock on the door. Owen Gray didn't move and presently Harry saw why. The new arrival had her own key and the knock was no more than an announcement that she was here.

Cathy Gray was wearing another knee-revealing skirt, grey this time with a blue woollen top. She carried a large blue handbag which she dumped on the vicar's desk before giving him a long affectionate kiss. When she turned eventually to his visitor, she said, 'Hallo, Harry' and gave him a formal peck on the cheek.

'Are you interviewing my brother?' she asked. 'Isn't he clever? A vicar at thirty!'

Side by side he could see this pair as brother and sister now, the tall, slim build, the identical fair hair. In their eyes, too, he detected a shared knowingness, a common reaction to a world of secrets.

'What have you been up to?' Owen Gray asked warily. 'You have my good name to think about round here now.'

'I've been looking after old ladies in the Refectory. Tea and cakes, tea and cakes. Look at this!' She picked up her handbag from the desk and opened it. 'It arrived the other day.'

From her capacious bag she produced the gold phallus and held it up for inspection.

'What on earth is that?' Harry asked.

'I think we can see what it is,' said the vicar primly. 'Where did it come from?'

'The postman gave it to me.'

'*Gave* it to you?'

'Not personally. He delivered it in the line of duty.'

'Who on earth would send you that?' asked the vicar.

'There was a note,' said Cathy, producing it from the bag.

'"This is what you do to me",' read Harry. 'To with two o's.'

'It looks home-made to me,' said the vicar.

'Well, I didn't imagine that he bought it in Woolworth,' said Cathy gaily.

'We've got to find out who sent it,' her brother said.

'We're looking for a well-endowed, semi-literate handyman with a dirty mind,' said Harry. 'That should narrow it down to about two hundred people.'

'Do you mean you think it's a model of himself?' the vicar asked dubiously.

'It looks that way to me,' Harry said. 'It's polyester resin, isn't it? It wouldn't be hard to do.'

'But he'd have to be hard to do it,' Cathy said, laughing. 'He's big, isn't he?'

'Is he?' said Harry. 'Only a woman would know.'

'I've never seen anything like it in my life,' said Owen Gray.

'Well, I should hope not,' said his sister. 'There've been more than enough queer vicars.'

The golden model lay on the desk in the vicarage while all three gazed at it with varying feelings of disquiet.

'Dear God,' said the new vicar. 'No wonder they call this place Sin.'

Somewhat to her surprise Nadine Kirby found herself alone for a week. She had known that her husband was to attend a bankers' conference in Harrogate, and she knew that Rachel's school had organized an educational week in Brittany, but it was only when the time arrived for them to leave that she realized that it was the same week.

At first she welcomed the peace of it, the sheer selfish pleasure of doing exactly as she pleased. On the Bank Holiday Monday she settled down to read all the Sunday newspapers that she never seemed to have time to look at properly, and caught up with fashionable obsessions like global warming, contaminated food, vanishing elephants and diminishing rain-forests and felt helpless before the growing list of humanity's problems. She read about cruelty to children and cruelty to animals and realized that she was sharing the earth with a crowd of maniacs and could do nothing about it. She remembered now why she had never been too meticulous about monitoring the news. The previous year on television she had watched a Romanian family in Sibiu putting the dead body of a relative into a makeshift coffin and strapping it to the roof of a very old car like holiday luggage: it was an image that returned to haunt her.

She switched on the television now. Grown men were trying to hit tiny balls into small holes; it seemed an odd way to pass the time. She stood up and saw through the front window that it was the day of the May Fayre. She had forgotten. The green was covered with stalls and roundabouts and bouncy castles. At one end children were riding ponies, at the other adults were engaged in a slow bicycle race. At the side there were train rides for children; from somewhere else helium-filled balloons were rising into the air with labels bearing the names and addresses of the people who had released them.

She went out and was immediately in a carnival atmosphere with children shouting and laughing, and their parents, just this once, making fools of themselves. It was much more cheerful than the newspapers.

She looked round for familiar faces. Everybody turned up at the May Fayre and within half an hour she had seen them all. Paul Vanner was running a coconut shy in aid of the cricket club, the Kennedys were giving their daughter a ride on the train, Harry Grant was strolling down past the duckpond that was now surrounded by daffodils, in the company of what looked like a Press photographer. The new vicar, whose picture had appeared in the *Gazette* that week, was wandering around with the waitress from the Refectory. Distrait was the word for him, she decided.

She watched Harry Grant arrive at Paul Vanner's coconut shy and headed in that direction.

'I'd pay £50 to fondle that girl's breasts,' Paul Vanner was saying.

'She'd take it,' said Harry whose latest sexual fantasy, coincidentally, had been playing topless snooker with Mrs Thatcher.

Nadine Kirby looked round and saw that they were talking about the girl with the new vicar.

'How do you know, Harry?' she asked.

'I've met her. I've looked into her eyes.'

'But you haven't fondled her breasts?'

'I didn't have £50 on me.'

The Kennedys came up with their daughter, who was clutching a ball of pink candyfloss on a stick. The candyfloss was slightly bigger than her head.

'A news item for you, Harry,' said Gwenda Kennedy. 'The odd-pets contest has been won by a green salamander.'

'I'll tell them to hold the front page.'

'How was America?' Nadine asked.

'I've seen the future and it's wonderful,' said Neil Kennedy.

'It would have been better still if we had left Lindy at home,' said his wife.

'Is she a strain?' Nadine asked.

Gwenda Kennedy's eyes rolled skywards in a woman-to-woman gesture. 'When I look at today's dissolute teenagers with their holed jeans and their funny haircuts I think about the poor bitch who spent two or three years of sleepless nights and dirty nappies rearing them. I wonder if they feel it was all worthwhile when the child grows up and they see what a monstrosity they have lovingly produced?'

'We're not producing a monstrosity,' said Kennedy, taking his daughter's hand. 'Let's go and have a glass of something that will make me feel optimistic.'

'I think Lindy's more interested in popcorn and hot dogs.'

'We'll get both.'

The three of them strolled away and, when a customer arrived for Paul Vanner's coconut shy, Nadine Kirby and Harry Grant found themselves together. All round them parents with impatient children were being dragged from one queue to the next, several of them carrying video cameras.

'There's progress,' said Nadine. 'What happened to the Box Brownie?'

'It went the same way as shelling peas,' said Harry. 'Let's walk. I don't see Felix about.'

'He's away for a week at a conference.'

'How is he?'

'Too selfish to commit suicide, I'm afraid.'

'Perhaps,' he suggested, 'I could take you and Rachel out to dinner?'

'Rachel's away too. School trip to France.' She looked at him. 'I'm all on my own.'

There was a silence while Harry Grant considered this.

'Well, fancy that,' he said. 'I've got a week's holiday due myself, as a matter of fact. Why don't we –?' He stopped. The idea was not only absurd, it was dangerous.

'Why don't we what, Harry?'

'No, forget it,' he said. 'Silly of me.'

'Try it. I'm bored.'

'Have you got a passport?' he asked.

13

THEY FLEW OUT in a sort of panic, convinced that somebody would spot them. How many thousands of pairs of eyes swept the concourse at Heathrow, and wouldn't there, somewhere among that number, be a pair that knew one of them? They pretended that they weren't together and then communicated with several feet between them. They moved anxiously from counter to counter in search of a flight, any flight. The plan was to get out of the country as soon as possible, regardless of destination, and merge into a foreign crowd a thousand miles away.

The popular flights were predictably booked but there were two seats on a plane to Bordeaux. Harry Grant steeled himself during the flight for a horrendous taxi bill, and two hours after landing they were admiring the Atlantic from a bedroom in a hotel in Biarritz, awe-stricken at what they had done. The hotel was the Hôtel du Palais, which had originally been built as a palace for Emperor Napoleon III; for Harry Grant this burst of extravagance was almost as daunting as the thought that he had decamped with another man's wife. Two credit cards took it in turns to satisfy the demand for francs and, after a while, he ceased to care. Clifftop walks on tamarisk headlands, seafood meals in fishing-port restaurants, scented pinewoods and golden sand dunes: it wasn't something to add up on a credit-card bill.

There was also bed which, in the case of one of the few great palace hotels remaining in Europe, was a luxurious, sprawling affair in which a couple who had fallen out could sleep in absolute solitude. Nadine Kirby came to its ample dimensions with an attack of nerves. For Harry Grant, whose fevered imagination had transported him to erotic heights that few had experienced or even contemplated, a de luxe bedroom in Biarritz with Nadine Kirby was like an everyday event.

'It's been a long time,' he said when he reached the bed and found her naked, waiting for him.

'I've been punishing myself,' she whispered. 'I felt so guilty. He doesn't know to this day.'

'Why don't we tell him?' he asked, taking her in his arms.

She ran her hands down his body. 'You haven't changed much,' she said.

'Celibacy keeps you young. You seem to be getting younger yourself.'

'I'm more celibate than you are.'

It was as if nothing had changed – her firm, sexy body was just as he always remembered it. He spent some time kissing it. They made love with a kind of fury at the years they had wasted.

'Why don't we tell him?' he repeated as they lay in each other's arms afterwards.

'Because of Rachel.'

Harry thought of little Rachel with her bright face and bright mind, then he thought of Nadine with her sad face and sad mind, and then he thought of Felix Kirby with his angry face and angry mind, and he wondered how much sacrifice you were supposed to make for other people during your own brief stay on this earth. Nadine's life was slipping past in a glut of misery, frustration and guilt, and who was the beneficiary of all this pitiful self-denial?

'Rachel will be all right,' he said. 'Kids are more resilient than you know.'

'Not at her impressionable age they're not. The truth would knock her for a loop.'

'She must be told one day who her father is.'

'One day.'

'In the meantime?'

'Ring me.'

'Or, in these liberated days, you could always ring me.'

'Liberated is what I'm not.' She pulled herself closer to him. 'It's only in the last six months that I've realized what a dreadful mess I've made of it all. I should have left Felix when I was pregnant. God knows, he wouldn't have missed me, and there would be no big shock waiting for Rachel.'

'Also, you'd have got laid.'

'That, too. Are you ready to do it again?'

'I thought you'd never ask.'

A cloud that seemed to sit permanently over the Bay of Biscay gave them uncertain weather. They got taxis to Anglet and Bayonne, and then spent a day in the beautiful Basque fishing town of St Jean de Luz where they watched the trawlers unload their catch for auction.

Wearing a dazed smile of satiation, they checked out of the Hôtel du Palais after four days. Harry Grant doubted whether he would ever manage another sexual fantasy.

They discovered that the taxi from Bordeaux had been an unnecessary waste and that they could make the return journey by train.

'Fingers crossed there haven't been any phone calls,' said Nadine as they flew up the French coast.

'No problem,' said Harry. 'Say you were in and the phone never rang. There are compensations with our dreadful telephone service.'

He had learned long ago to be a master of duplicity. At Heathrow Nadine got a taxi and he waited a couple of hours before driving home alone in his Mustang.

Suzanne Vanner was sitting at the back of her shop ironing new stock when Cathy Gray came in. They had met in the Refectory when Suzanne occasionally shut the shop and slipped out for a coffee.

'I've been thinking, Mrs Vanner,' Cathy said brightly. 'What you need is an assistant, then you won't have to shut the shop when you want to go out.'

Suzanne Vanner had already decided that she wanted an assistant so that she would have more freedom of movement and would be able to visit the suppliers in London without closing up, but she wasn't sure that she could afford one on the takings so far. The message from the till was that she was neither getting rich nor going broke, but another wage would affect the balance.

'Are you applying for a job, Cathy?' she asked.

'Yes, I am. I was never meant to be a waitress. I used to be a model and I know about clothes.'

Suzanne Vanner looked at the thick blue jumper and short red skirt and suppressed a shudder. It was not an outfit that would inspire confidence in somebody who was being asked to pay a couple of hundred pounds for a blouse. Still, if Cathy worked here she could buy her clothes at cost and look quite dazzling.

'I wonder what sort of money you're thinking about?' she asked. 'This isn't exactly a city centre.'

'I'd work cheap in the village. If I had to travel ten miles to work I'd need more. If I built up business perhaps I could have a small share of the profit?'

Suzanne Vanner decided to brush this idea aside for the time being. The idea of Cathy as her assistant had its attractions. Delegation had always been her forte. What she wanted, if she was to leave this girl in charge of her till, was some reassurance about her honesty.

'Have you any references, Cathy?' she asked.

'Yes, I have.'

She put her blue handbag on the counter and opened it up. The golden phallus fell out, rolled across the counter and clattered against the till.

'Jesus Christ,' said Suzanne Vanner. 'What the hell's that?'

'Well, you can see what it is, can't you?' said Cathy Gray, laughing. 'I think it's cute.'

'Cute isn't the word I'd have chosen,' said Suzanne Vanner, picking it up. 'My God, I think I recognize this.'

She remembered an afternoon in the conservatory with One-cell Tel, and then realized that she had made a terrible mistake. Luckily for her, Cathy misunderstood.

'Of course you do,' she said. 'You're a married woman.'

'Where the devil did you get it from?'

'It arrived one morning in the post. No name but a local postmark.'

'Do you mean there's some crackpot round here sending anonymous willies to people?'

'I'm afraid so, Mrs Vanner. I don't really know what to do with it.'

Suzanne Vanner was absently running her tape measure along its side.

'I thought so,' she said distractedly. 'It's huge.'

'I wish I could find the rest of him,' said Cathy Gray, laughing again.

'Perhaps he'll post you a bit more soon.'

'My brother was shocked. Well, he would be in his job.'

'Why? What's his job?'

'He's the new vicar here. You must have seen him.'

'I have. I didn't know he was your brother. If your brother is the vicar I don't think I need ask for references.'

The following morning before opening the shop she went to see Dr Frost. She knew very well what the news would be but she needed to hear it. She had no idea what would happen after that. The part of her brain that came up with ideas had been fully occupied with creating the boutique and she even managed to forget for quite long periods the problem that she was going to have to face now.

'You're pregnant all right,' said Dr Frost. He was a big man with lots of black hair, and his manner was perpetually jolly as if he didn't really take medicine seriously. His test had involved no more than placing a stethoscope on her stomach. 'Your husband will be pleased,' he said.

'Not necessarily,' said Suzanne Vanner. At one time she had nurtured the fanciful hope that she could delude her husband into believing that he was the father of this microbiological compound, but her failure to engage him in anything that even remotely resembled sexual intercourse made this a difficult idea to float.

'Oh?' said Dr Frost. 'He doesn't want children? Isn't that something he should have thought about?' He was like an actor who was giving a rather unconvincing performance as a medical practitioner.

'It's a question of paternity,' said Suzanne Vanner from behind the screen where she was dressing.

'Ah,' said Dr Frost. 'I catch your drift.'

His patient emerged, looking only slightly embarrassed. 'I'm afraid our sex life at home would make a Trappist monastery seem like a hotbed of debauchery.'

'A Trappist monastery probably *is* a hotbed of debauchery,' said Dr Frost. 'A thousand jokes suggest it. Still, I can see your problem.'

She sat down. 'Is there anything you can do about it?'

Dr Frost said that there was always something that could be done but it cost money and took a little time to arrange.

When she reached the shop half an hour late Terry Wallace, in his usual jeans and yellow T-shirt, was waiting outside with a bag of tools. She had forgotten sending him a note more than a week ago, asking if his talents ran to putting up shelves. He gave her the sort of look that she imagined a small rabbit would extend to a petulant snake.

'You want some shelves done,' he suggested.

'I do, Terry. Come in,' she said, unlocking the door. 'I'll show you where.'

One-cell Tel carried his bag of tools into the shop. He felt safe in here. It wasn't like being cornered in someone's house. Soon he was drilling the necessary holes in the wall at the back of the shop.

Suzanne Vanner sat at the till counting change. The idea that a man with a puréed brain, who was still struggling to master his mother tongue at twenty-five, was the father of her unborn child made her feel queasy.

'Do you know Cathy Gray, Terry?' she asked.

'Who?' He stopped drilling.

'I have both your addresses here. She seems to live next door to you.'

'Cathy Gray,' he said. 'Well, not as such.'

'What do you mean? You know her or you don't know her?'

'Put it like this. I know who you mean. Never spoken to her.'

She shut the till. 'You've got a beautiful girl like that next door to you and you've never spoken to her? Terry, you're slipping.'

He was still young enough to blush. 'She don't know me,' he said.

'But you sent her a present, a golden phallus.'

One-cell Tel stopped work again. 'Golden what?'

'Willy. Penis. Chopper. Schlong. There are lots of words for it.'

'Yes, I did,' he said, proud that his handiwork was at last in the public domain. 'And she never even said thank you.'

'She doesn't know it was from you. You didn't put your name to it. But I recognized it, Terry.'

One-cell Tel looked at her, puzzled. 'I never put my name in?'

'Nope.'

'Bloody hell. I wondered why she hadn't answered. I thought she didn't like it.'

'She thinks it's cute. She carries it around with her. How did you make it?'

One-cell Tel laughed. 'With great bloody difficulty. I had to lie down over a bucket.'

'And you managed to maintain your – you managed to do it like that?'

'What?'

'I see.'

The idea that a man would not only do it, but freely discuss it afterwards struck Suzanne Vanner as positively weird. One-cell Tel was obviously a lot more simple than she had given him credit for.

To her relief a customer came in.

When June's heat had produced the temperatures that gave the tabloid newspapers their annual HOTTER THAN THE MED! headlines, Neil Kennedy decided that some of his television money should be used to return such hospitality as he had received since arriving in Sin. He threw a barbecue.

He spent the morning ferrying steaks, beer, champagne and wine to his house and then he went out again and hired boxes of glasses. He was determined to enjoy himself. The previous day, given a break from filming, he had been asked by his tired wife to deliver Lindy to the playgroup that Gwenda had now enrolled her in at the village hall in a new attempt to find three hours' peace somewhere. It had been a peculiarly depressing experience. He was shocked to see the young mothers who brought in their children. Only four years ago they had presumably been carefree, single girls laughing in a disco and now, as if hardened by some battle, they were assertive, humourless creatures he would not care to live with. They had aged fourteen years in only four and he wondered what their husbands made of this dreadful transformation. It was only when he was walking home that he realized that Gwenda must have changed too – and perhaps he had. Was that what growing up meant? That you stopped laughing?

He drank half a bottle of wine in an attempt to stem the years, then set about arranging the Sure Glow charcoal briquettes on his barbecue at the end of the patio. He hoped that Mrs Crosby from next door was going to enter into the spirit of this informal feast; a lady of delicate tastes, she was alleged to top and tail whitebait.

The people seemed to arrive all at once, as if they had been waiting in the drive for the clock to strike seven; suddenly the back garden and patio were crowded with people in colourful summer dress, some of whom he didn't know. His wife had obviously been drawing on a quite different segment of the population with her invitations.

Prominent among the guests in an orange shirt and pale blue slacks was Toby Beauchamp who announced that he was wearing his barbecue gear. He fussed around Gwenda Kennedy as she laid steaks on the grill as if he was anxious to demonstrate that this was not Men's Hour.

'I must say you've taken to the country life,' he said. 'I thought when you came down from Islington you'd find it too quiet.'

'My doubts about the country seem to have been unfounded. I expected crafty rustics with a streak of violence, snobs in the mansions, rapists in the hedgerows. I also expected a lot of promiscuity now that villages are full of the idle rich rather than the exhausted poor. You know, the lazy days and the wicked nights.'

'Ah, there you're nearer the mark, my dear. I always wanted to be promiscuous myself, but I could never find a woman to be unfaithful to.'

'And now you're too old for it.'

'The older the vine, the finer the wine.'

Neil Kennedy came over with a bottle of champagne.

'Are you chatting up my chattel?' he asked.

'Certainly not, old son. As a midshipman I was told: never touch a man's pocket, his stomach or his woman.'

'I didn't know you were in the Navy, Toby?'

'There used to be a thing called National Service. Two compulsory years in the forces. Nobody seems to have heard of it now.'

'I should hope not,' said Gwenda Kennedy. 'Fighting is for the simpler races.'

Harry Grant was standing in some discomfort on the lawn. He had just noticed to his horror that the tan he had collected in Biarritz matched exactly the tan on Nadine's face and both stood out as being quite different from other sunburnt faces at the Kennedys'. The wind off the Atlantic had produced a reddish-brown colouring that sunbathing in Compton Sinbury never supplied. He stood in anguish, wondering whether what seemed so conspicuous to him would be noticed by anybody else.

Newly enriched by £20 for his Sod's Laws list, he was also wondering what else he might do to compensate for his extravagant dash to France. There were ways that he could make money if he could stay out of the potting shed for long enough: brochures, free newspapers, features that a syndication agency could sell to English language papers abroad.

Nadine was suddenly beside him.

'Hallo, Harry,' she said in a casual way that could be overheard without danger.

'Our tans match,' he whispered. 'We look like bloody twins.'

'But nobody will notice. Self-obsessed, that's Compton Sinbury.'

He glanced across to the patio where Felix Kirby was talking to Colonel Arbuthnott, the council chairman, who was wearing, incredibly in this heat, brown brogues and lovat tweed.

'Didn't Felix notice?' he asked. 'He could hardly have thought you picked up that tan in the kitchen.'

'I told him I spent a day at the sea. It could have been Benghazi for all he cares. He's become obsessed with squash. He picked it up at this conference he was at and now sees it as the secret of eternal life.'

'A serious mistake, I should have thought. The squash courts of this country are littered with middle-aged corpses.'

'Let's not tell him.'

Neil Kennedy appeared through the crowd carrying paper plates. 'Get your mandibles round this,' he said. On each plate was a fillet steak and salad. He moved among the assorted neighbours, followed everywhere by Lindy who carried the cutlery.

Suzanne Vanner was watching Lindy thoughtfully, marvelling at the maturity of one so young. She saw the delight of the girl in acting as her father's assistant and thought about the abortion that she had now arranged for the following week.

Paul Vanner, ignoring the steak and concentrating on the champagne, said: 'That kid should be in bed.'

'Children are people, too,' said Suzanne.

'That doesn't endear them to me. I can't stand people.'

'Don't be silly, Paul.' Nervous about the abortion, and worried about how she was to explain a two-day absence to her husband, she was in no mood for his misanthropic humour.

He put his arm round her shoulder in a public display of affection, and realized that she actually wanted children and he had let her down. Not that he saw it entirely as his fault. She had often been so drunk that making love to her was not an attractive proposition. But since she opened the shop the drinking seemed to have stopped. Her eyes were brighter and her personality was more agreeable.

Perhaps the fresh air, and the sun and champagne, would revive the rake he had once been and he would be triumphant again in his own bedroom. He strolled across the patio in search of the last of these ingredients.

'Where are the Nebuchadnezzars of champagne?' he asked.

'We only have magnums here,' Neil Kennedy told him, 'not being unabashed monetarists.'

'That will do nicely, Neil. Do you happen to know whether champagne is an aphrodisiac?'

'All alcohol is up to a point. Then it isn't.'

He took the bottle back to his wife, who was standing alone on the lawn and looking almost sadly at this cross-section of apparently contented villagers. He put his arm round her again and filled her glass.

'Look, I know we haven't made love much lately,' he began. He had already drunk quite enough to raise the subject.

'Much?' she said.

'Okay, I know. But let's get started again tonight.'

'Tonight?'

She recoiled with horror. It was only because her husband had ignored her that he had failed to notice her gently swelling stomach. If he got near her tonight he would make a discovery that would wreck their marriage. Not that she was in the mood for it at all until her present problem had been cleared up.

'Not tonight, Paul,' she said. 'I don't feel too good. Let's wait until the right moment, shall we?'

'My God!' he said angrily. 'And I thought you were screaming out for it.'

A few yards away Harry Grant and Toby Beauchamp were talking to Colonel Arbuthnott who, despite his wife's strident remonstrations, was pouring himself more champagne. His wife harangued him steadily, but he behaved as if she wasn't there.

'So where's the new plot, Toby?' asked Colonel Arbuthnott.

'Barnaby Barton's place in the lane. He's got an acre at the back and I'm hoping to get planning permission any day now.'

'You'll regret this drinking tomorrow,' said Mrs Arbuthnott. Her bulk seemed to be slowly slipping earthwards and it was easy to imagine that her bottom would soon be resting on her heels.

'Barney's going to be rich, is he?' Harry asked.

'Harry Grant, quidnunc *extraordinaire*,' said the colonel.

'It's what I'm paid for, Colonel. I've got gossip I haven't even printed yet.'

Felix Kirby had lost his wife but found a chair. He sat on the patio with his drink and wondered where Nadine had got to. Her behaviour had been strange ever since he returned from his conference. She had taken to singing round the house in a way that he found worrying. Even Rachel had noticed it.

'Mummy seems very cheerful these days,' she had whispered to him the previous evening.

'She isn't drinking, is she?' he had asked.

Alcoholism among wives was on the increase, he had read. While men were to be found in pubs drinking a steady pint or two, the women were secretly demolishing a bottle of vodka before breakfast. Far more women died of cirrhosis of the liver than men, and people stood around at the funerals and explained in genuine bewilderment that they had never even seen the women drink. Some people hinted that Suzanne Vanner was a bit of a lush. He decided to check a few cupboards when he got home.

Daisy Balcombe, whose attendance here owed something to her role in Lindy's playgroup, had suddenly spotted Toby Beauchamp. She had spotted him only a few seconds before he spotted her and now he stood, nailed to the spot, wondering how he could extricate himself from her coquettish onslaught. Most women had only to start talking to plummet dramatically in his esteem, and this one never stopped.

He looked at his watch. 'I have to get home to take a phone call,' he said desperately.

Gwenda and Neil Kennedy were discovering at last the benefit of having a tireless daughter. While they sat on the patio with their drinks, Lindy collected empty plates and carried them to the kitchen.

'Toby's legging it,' said Gwenda. 'It's the only way he can escape from Daisy.'

And across the garden they could see Toby Beauchamp escaping into the road through a side gate, looking like a prisoner whose cell door has accidentally been left open.

He was watching World Cup football from Rome on his Bang and Olufsen the following day when his phone rang. It was Brynwyn Rolfe.

'I've got to talk to you, Toby,' he said. 'Can I come round?'

'I'll get a bottle out, old son.'

'A cutthroat razor might be handier.'

Toby Beauchamp replaced the phone and lit a small cigar. He was becoming accustomed to the strange mixture of pessimism and exuberance that dwelt uneasily in Rolfe's Celtic soul. Bureaucrats, anyway, thrived on drama, artificially created, childishly magnified; it was what they needed to enliven their dreary existences.

He settled down again to watch the football. It must have been his hangover, he thought, that had dumped him in front of this boring spectacle. There was nothing about modern football that made it worth watching. All the players seemed to be part of the defence except for two forlorn 'strikers' up front who got flattened, without the referee appearing to notice, every time they got near the ball. He switched it off and fetched himself a brandy.

Brynwyn Rolfe arrived in a state of suppressed agitation half an hour later. He slumped in an armchair and accepted a brandy himself.

'The game's up, boyo,' he said. 'They're coming at us from my end now as well as yours.'

Toby sat down in an armchair opposite him.

'Tell me what's happening, Brynwyn. And for Christ's sake calm down.'

Brynwyn Rolfe emptied his glass. 'This Southfork place. Why the fuck's it called Southfork, anyway?'

'The man's a nutter.'

'Well, I've got it through. You can build ten up-market homes, so long as the design's okay, and a road to the lane.'

'That's terrific,' said Toby, but his mind was already running through the figures. The homes, at £150,000 each, were a million and a half. Eight hundred thousand for costs, £200,000 for Barney and half a million for Toby. He could afford to be generous, and Brynwyn Rolfe seemed in need of assuagement. He went across to a picture on the wall, a Hockney print, and removed it. From the safe that had been concealed behind it he took a pile of plastic envelopes, each packed with £50 notes.

'I thought we would get round the cheque problem if I paid you cash,' he said. 'You ought to get yourself a safe like this.'

'I'm going to the Isle of Man next week so I can take it. How much is here?'

'Fifty thousand.'

This was rather more than Toby was accustomed to paying the planning officer, but it sounded as if Rolfe was in need of a judicious reminder about where his pension was coming from.

Brynwyn Rolfe stacked the envelopes into a neat pile on his lap. 'That's very generous, Toby,' he said. 'Very generous indeed.'

'Just remember, old son, there's more where that came from.' He took his guest's empty glass and refilled it.

Brynwyn Rolfe took the drink but shook his head. 'I'm afraid not, Toby. I told you, the game's up.'

Toby sat down again. 'Why?'

'Do you remember old Faulkner died and there was a by-election? The new man, Armstrong, is a sort of Dennis Skinner, with teeth. Suspicious, awkward questions, incessant phone calls. He came in and checked on the outgoing post last week to make sure it was all council business. He thought the postal bill was too high.'

'He sounds crazy.'

'He sounds dangerous. And he brought you up at the planning meeting.'

'Brought me up?'

'"Has Mr Beauchamp ever had a planning application turned down?" was his question.'

'Jesus. What was the answer?'

'Nobody knew offhand, but the damage was done. You could see it on the faces round the room. They'll turn down your next ten applications whatever I recommend, just to feel good. In fact, I'll have to recommend that they turn them down to cover my back.'

'Couldn't I have this man buried in the foundations at Southfork?'

'Too late. He could drop dead today and it wouldn't make any difference. The poison has been put in. You're bloody lucky that he didn't bring it up until after the council had approved Southfork, but of course it was that vote that put the idea in his evil head. Now they're all wondering why Toby Beauchamp has been so lucky with his building applications. I tell you, I've got to tread very carefully now or I'll be wearing one of those funny suits with arrows on.'

'I don't think they have them any more, Brynwyn.'

'Small consolation, boyo. Have you got another of these?'

Toby Beauchamp went over to his drinks cabinet to fetch the brandy bottle and contemplated a drop in his income. The income had been considerable for a long time and if everything stopped now he wasn't going to end up drinking meths in a public lavatory and pleading for a bed. But there had been a satisfaction in what he did, a sense of achievement, and he was no longer motivated entirely by money. The houses that he would build at Southfork would be a stylish addition to Compton Sinbury. Scores of families were the proud owners of tasteful homes, or the worried owners of hulking mortgages on tasteful homes, and they owed it all to him. If all this was going to stop there would be nothing for him to do but sit around and grow old.

14

Relieved as he was to be earning money again, and delighted that his half-forgotten face would be leading the autumn schedules on the nation's television screens, Neil Kennedy nevertheless bitterly resented the way that his heady days in front of the camera ended with him being herded into the commuters' cattle-truck, packed with half-drunk office workers and knackered civil servants.

He travelled first class and read a book, but even in these expensive cubicles his peace was disturbed by yuppies with cans of beer hitting each other with newspapers, and idiots with portable phones who never stopped discussing share prices with another workaholic twenty miles away. It was a world that was alien to him.

One evening he found himself sitting opposite a sleeping Paul Vanner who was slumped in a corner with his outstretched legs invading Kennedy's floor space. He too was clutching a can of beer that was now presumably empty; an evening newspaper, open at the city pages, was sprawled on his lap like a napkin.

Neil Kennedy could not imagine somebody going through this routine every day, five days a week, forty-eight weeks a year. Two hundred and forty times a year? There and back it would be nearly a thousand hours of travelling every year. That was more than a hundred working days! The sheer horror of such a lifestyle made him screw up his face.

And yet . . . and yet. Paul Vanner had the Manor House with swimming pool and tennis court. He had a car in the garage that was reputed to be worth more than £300,000. He didn't have to be pathetically grateful for such crumbs as his agent threw him. He didn't feel a cold chill when his bank statement dropped on the doormat. It looked as if financial reward in this world was not related to your skill or your talent, or the sacrifice that you made for your art, but to the amount of agony and inconvenience that you were prepared to endure.

Neil Kennedy opened his book and shut his mind to the misery of commuting. The book was the novel on which *Hot Air Rises* had been based and it was interesting for him now to see what the original story had been before its mangling by a pair of television script-writers. With any luck the book would be reissued in the autumn with his picture on the cover. A red flash in one corner would proclaim: NOW A MAJOR TELEVISION SERIES. There was no such thing as a minor television series.

When the train pulled in to Compton Sinbury, Paul Vanner, who had slept soundly through a dozen stations, woke up.

'Hallo, Neil,' he said.

'It must take a lot of practice to wake up at the right moment like that.'

'I'm not a man. I'm a machine. Let's go and have a drink.'

Only Barnaby Barton and One-cell Tel were in the Flatulent Ferret, enjoying their usual conversational silence in the corner. Sylvia, behind the bar, explained that her husband was watching sport on television.

'A pint of lager and a gin for Neil,' Paul Vanner said. 'Am I right?'

Neil Kennedy nodded and took the drink.

'Why do you do it every day, Paul?' he asked. 'I was looking at you on the train. With your rumpled clothes and your worn-out face you looked like a dosser who had just crawled out of a cardboard box under Waterloo Bridge.'

'For a fat salary is why I do it.' He drank half of his pint very quickly and sat on a stool at the bar.

'You don't need a salary that fat,' Neil Kennedy said, sitting next to him. 'According to this thing I'm in on television, there's a place in Japan where there are three fountains. One is health, one is wealth, and the third is happiness. You can throw coins in only two of them. Do you imagine anyone chooses wealth?'

'Japs? You bet, pal. They're cornering the world market in money. Soon nobody else will have any.'

'Okay, forget the Japs. I'm talking about money generally. Once you've got enough to cover your needs, making more is boring, isn't it?'

'Boring?' said Paul Vanner. Didn't Kennedy understand the buzz of the market, the thrill of the deal?

'It's like being obsessed with food or cars.'

'I am.'

'They're things you need to be able to do the real things. They're not an end in themselves.'

'What is this, Neil? Are you trying to make me as poor as you are?'

'You're missing so much in life. In fact, you're missing the point.'

Vanner finished his drink and ordered more. 'When you were born in a council house in Stepney it provides wonderful motivation.'

'I'm sure it does. The house and the cars are an affirmation of your arrival. But you don't have to go on leading such a god-awful life, do you?'

'Yes, I do. I haven't paid for them yet.'

'You're affluent on borrowed money? I never did understand finance. I think money should be a by-product of what you do. Just to make money itself is cutting something out of life.'

'The nearer you get to it the more you make. That's my experience.'

Neil Kennedy paid for the drinks. He had a £5 note but he paid with a £20 note. Paul Vanner's remarks about him being poor had got to him a little. Was that how people saw him?

'People are quite shameless about self-indulgence these days,' he said. 'I blame Thatcher. But the novelty of consumption is going to wear off when people discover there's no lasting satisfaction.'

Paul Vanner attacked his second pint with the same urgency that he had destroyed the first. 'Consumption is for idiots. A fool and his money and all that. What I'm into is investment. My house and my Ferrari are making me thousands of pounds every week, way over the interest on the debt. You're an actor, Neil. Your choice. But actors don't understand money.'

'You're dead right. When I was in America I discovered that it was the world's largest creditor at the beginning of the eighties, and the world's largest debtor at the end. It consumed a trillion dollars more than it produced in those ten years. America in debt! Every country's in debt. Who the hell is lending this money? Where's it coming from if nobody's earning it?'

'Why don't you go to evening classes and study economics? Put yourself out of your misery.'

Neil Kennedy drinking his second gin began to feel light-headed. The filming schedule today had not allowed for lunch and he had settled for a packet of crisps.

'I was trying to put you out of yours,' he said. 'Your life looks like all stress and no fun.'

'Today's stress is tomorrow's fun, pal. I'm setting myself up for early retirement. When you're playing in a pier theatre's summer season, I shall be fishing for marlin from a boat off Cuba.'

This precise glimpse of the future gave Neil Kennedy a jolt. He had in his lower moments envisaged just such a fate for himself. There was no one big pay day in the career of an actor, no one huge cheque that removed all problems. You went on acting until you dropped – or were carted off to the Sunset Home for Demented Thespians, mumbling snatches of Hamlet to an audience that never appeared. When Neil Kennedy thought about his future his blood ran cold.

He looked at Paul Vanner with his tired eyes and his hangdog expression and wondered whether he really would escape to a brighter world or whether, shackled by debt, he was on a conveyor belt that he could never get off. The way that he drank there was a good chance that he would never live long enough to enjoy the fruits of his effort. Already he was standing up and pushing his empty glass across the bar in search of a refill.

'Another gin?' he asked.

'Not for me. Gwenda's cooking dinner.'

'I wish my wife cooked dinner.'

Neil Kennedy emptied his glass. 'Thanks for the financial lesson. I see where I went wrong now.'

'You've got it, have you? I owe more than you. So I am extremely rich and you are a pauper.'

Neil Kennedy stood up. 'Could you ease off on the poverty line?' he said. 'I might not own the Manor House but I'm not exactly bankrupt and for a few weeks I'm probably earning as much as you.'

'Of course. Sorry. But it was only the other day that you couldn't afford to play poker. Well, I could afford to play poker.'

'I played poker,' said Neil Kennedy, now thoroughly riled. 'In fact I won £29,000 playing it.'

'Not when I was there, you didn't.'

'Oh, you were there, Paul. We were all there together.'

'And you won £29,000? You're dreaming. You lost £5,000 one night and couldn't afford to play again.'

'Well, you might not have recognized me. I'm an actor, remember?'

Paul Vanner stared into his drink. 'Just a minute,' he said. 'Were you the sheikh?'

Neil Kennedy nodded. 'One of my better performances.'

'I thought there was something fishy about that bastard. His hands didn't look right.'

'His hands?'

'They didn't look as if they had ever seen a desert.'

'What did you want? Sand under the nails?'

Neil Kennedy was laughing, but Paul Vanner was wearing a quite different expression. 'Just a minute, pal,' he said. 'You conned us. I lost ten grand that night. Toby lost seven.'

'Oh, come on. Other people won pots that night. It was a long game. Who can tell where your money ended up?'

'My recollection is that all the money ended up with you.'

'That doesn't mean I won it from you. I might have won it from somebody who won it from you.'

Paul Vanner sat down. 'I don't believe I'm hearing this. You took seventeen grand off your friends by deception and you're laughing about it?'

'You lost a game of poker,' said Neil Kennedy. 'I can't see it makes much difference whether I was dressed up as a sheikh or Good Queen Bess.'

Paul Vanner was calmer now. 'If you believed that, Neil, you wouldn't have dressed up as an Arab. It was a brilliant idea. Joke over. I want my money back.'

'You want what?'

'I want the money you conned me out of. Of course I do. Do you take me for a sucker?'

'No, I took you for ten grand. It seemed quite legitimate to me. The money was there for anybody to win. Blame the cards. Blame the dealer. Don't blame me.'

Paul Vanner looked at him. 'I don't think I'm making myself clear. I want my money back.' He looked so angry that Neil Kennedy wondered whether violence was about to break out. Well, he would drop this windbag with two hits.

'All's fair in love, war and poker,' he said. 'And I can't stay here drinking all night. You're rich and I'm poor. Remember?'

Paul Vanner sat at the counter looking at his hands. He didn't know whether his anger stemmed from the loss of the money or the fact that Kennedy had taken him for a fool. What he was certain about was that he had to get the money back.

He turned to tell Kennedy this but he had already gone.

In the room that he called his office at the vicarage, Owen Gray pondered the nature of celibacy, its attractions and its discomforts. What Owen Gray knew about celibacy was that it was palpably unnatural, but in his position singularly difficult to avoid. He had once listened to an eminent theologian – a Regius Professor of Divinity, no less – extolling its virtues when the man had six children and a seventh on the way. The golden period of Owen Gray's sex life could now be seen to have been concentrated into several magical months when he was in his teens and it was followed immediately by a shocked withdrawal from such things. And the abstinence went on and on. Go forth and multiply was a difficult instruction to follow when you were the vicar of Compton Sinbury. Perhaps the typically contradictory injunction to avoid the sins of the flesh was intended for him.

He went to the window and looked at the dark outline of St Thomas's. Losing his faith, he still loved the church, its lavish size, its elegant nooks and crannies, its wonderful theatre. The spectacle on Sunday mornings, flowery, impressive and steeped in history, was the equal of anything on Broadway or Shaftesbury Avenue, and it demanded and received a more passionate involvement from the audience. The music was better, too, having stood the withering test of time. When he walked up the dimly lit nave he felt a power and an influence which evaporated when he stepped out of the porch into the real world; on Sunday mornings, reciting the Creed, leading the hymn singing or delivering one of his increasingly ambivalent sermons, he would feel an approbation that few men experienced in their work.

He shuffled through the papers and magazines on his desk. They arrived uninvited: copious quantities of reading matter were sent as a matter of course to men of the church in the vain belief that they were uniquely placed to give some obscure campaign a helpful push.

Compton Sinbury was the 'parish of the month' in the *Diocesan News*. He supposed he ought to read it.

> With just 500 houses and 1,200 inhabitants Compton Sinbury is the smallest parish in the diocese. It must also enjoy one of its most idyllic settings. It is approached over a five-arch bridge fording the river, and dominated by its village green where cricket has been played for over a century.
>
> Today it is still an important focus for local cricket and attracts crowds of sightseers in the summer, drawn as much by the picture postcard setting as the cricket.

Compton Sinbury Parish Church, St Thomas's, was built in the fifteenth century. The view from the church and nearby vicarage looks out over the green and down to the river.

The church has an average congregation of 43 each Sunday, with two services, Holy Communion at 8 a.m. and Choral Communion at 10 a.m. There is also a family service once a month: a recent introduction and an indication of how things are changing in Compton Sinbury.

The Revd Owen Gray said: 'Until recently our congregation was made up mainly of retired people. We simply did not have any young families, but now they are beginning to come back to the village and we are delighted to see some of them at St Thomas's. We hope that this is a trend that we can build on.'

Life is constant change, and nowhere is this more marked than in a village which used to be a centre of work and is now largely an escape from it.

Twenty years ago many of its inhabitants were local workers, on the farm and in rural industries, and this was reflected in the congregation.

Now, though, Compton Sinbury is proving popular with busy executives, many of whom commute to London each day, and find the village's quiet setting a tranquil contrast from their high-pressure working environment.

The Revd Owen Gray said: 'The executives, particularly those who are self-employed, live in a competitive world where it is very much the survival of the fittest and most able. They must not put off until tomorrow what can be done today. These are all qualities which we can learn from.'

It was astonishing the drivel that you were expected to spout if you were a vicar, he thought. On the other hand there were several little jobs that were waiting for him here that should not be put off until tomorrow.

The church electoral roll had to be revised every six years

and this was the year. There was a World Day of Prayer planned. More urgently he had to write his monthly letter for the parish magazine.

He picked up a newly sharpened pencil and wrote quickly: 'Much has been written in the newspapers about the 1990s and what will happen in the new decade.' It was a little late to discuss such things but he hadn't been in Compton Sinbury at the start of the year. 'The church has called it the decade of evangelism. In an article in the Church of England newspaper, the Bishop of Taunton makes the point that the decade of evangelism means changing the priorities of congregations.'

Changing the what? And what did it mean alongside such incontestable facts as that Saturn had 1,000-mile-per-hour winds, or that a year on Venus lasted only 224 days? If he ever left the church his capacity for inconsequential waffle would dump him straight into politics. Celibacy was not a problem in that preening world.

He heard the front door slam and realized that his sister was paying him a visit. She had taken it upon herself to drop in regularly since he moved to Compton Sinbury, perhaps to check that he was looking after himself.

'Good morning, vicar,' she said, bursting in. 'I've brought you some sandwiches for your lunch, made by your mother's own fair hand.'

'Thank you, Cathy,' he said, laying down his pencil. His interpretation of what the Bishop of Taunton was trying to say would have to wait. 'How is the new job going?'

'Wonderful, thanks. Beautiful clothes are much more interesting than bread rolls.'

He looked at the yellow jeans she was wearing with a mauve blouse and reflected that the new position had certainly improved her appearance. She looked like a seductress in search of a victim.

'Did you find out who sent you that pagan ornament?' he asked.

Cathy Gray laughed. 'The willy? Yes, I did. It came from my next-door neighbour, a young man called Terry Wallace. He secretly lusts after me, I gather.'

'Have you spoken to him about it?'

'Certainly not. He's not my type.'

'Perhaps I should?'

'He's not one of your flock, is he? I can't see him in church.'

Owen Gray wanted to say that he didn't see her in church either, but he was afraid of creating a rift. He was frightened by his sister's sexuality and its potent appeal, and could imagine the emotional turmoil she caused as she sauntered round the village, whetting appetites that were better ignored.

'You ought to get married, Cathy,' he said. 'Find yourself a nice man.'

'I do – often. Tonight I shall meet a wealthy young man called Paul Vanner. It's his wife who owns the shop and she's away.'

'But that's outrageous.'

'You used to be outrageous, Owen.'

It was the first time that she had referred to it.

'My God, I go through hell whenever I think of it,' he said. 'But we're grown up now.'

'You were pretty grown up then from what I recall.'

'Only physically, Cathy. God forgives the sins of our youth, but I did you a great wrong. I know that now.'

'Don't feel too guilty. You showed me a good game.'

'You make me feel even more responsible for your moral welfare than I did before. What can I do for you, Cathy? How can I make amends?'

But he realized that what was to him a festering source of guilt was no more than a half-remembered bit of fun to his amoral sister. He could almost detect, hanging in the air, an implicit willingness on her part to do it again if life failed to deliver her quota of excitement.

'No amends,' she said and bent to pick up her bag. He stared at the perfect circle of her bottom in its tight jeans and realized that she was wearing nothing underneath. He found himself reciting the seven deadly sins to himself: anger, avarice, envy, gluttony, lust, pride, sloth.

At least I've avoided six of them, he thought.

*

In the seclusion of the potting shed Harry Grant and Nadine Kirby were embracing among bottles of wine.

'Tell him. Leave him,' said Harry. 'He couldn't be any more miserable than he is now.'

'As long as I didn't take his Guy Mitchell records he probably wouldn't notice.' She kissed his mouth and spilt some wine.

'Well, then.'

'It's not Felix that I'm worried about. It's your talented daughter.'

'She's going to know one day,' he said, 'about her talented father.'

'She's too young for the shock.'

The memory of their trip to Biarritz served to remind Harry now of what his life could be like. He imagined them on the Piazza di Trevi, or weekending in Venice. Their togetherness in his mind always involved a journey of many miles to separate her from the family ties. Felix Kirby's new-found addiction to squash provided Nadine with the opportunity to skip across the green, but these snatched moments of privacy, which had once seemed so exciting, were no longer enough for Harry Grant.

'Supposing I talk to Rachel?' he suggested.

'And tell her she's your daughter? Please don't. Kids aren't equipped to handle that stuff. I can barely handle it myself.'

'She could handle it.'

'I don't want to take the risk of producing a disturbed child.'

He poured them more wine and changed the subject. 'I love the new slim you.'

'Sadness makes you hungry. That's why the miserable are usually fat.'

'They're fat because they're miserable? I always thought they were miserable because they were fat.'

The shrill blast of the telephone in the cottage interrupted this conundrum and he picked up the extension.

'Satellite dishes,' said Dakers, the news editor.

'What?'

'We're talking trash from outer space here.'

'We are?'

'Have you got any?'

'Trash from outer space?'

'Satellite dishes. In Compton Sinbury. I know it's a bit of a modern concept for your little time warp. I don't suppose Sin has seen the rotary washing-line yet.'

'No, we use those old spin-driers.'

'Jump into your Mustang and do a little check in the village, will you? We're doing a survey across the county and want to know how many you have there.'

'Spin-driers?'

'No, satellite dishes. They don't do anything there except watch television, do they? You should be sprouting dishes like flowers in the spring.'

'Hard up for news, are you?'

'Not a bit of it, Harry. We've got a real sensation this week. It's going to make the nationals.'

Despite his resentment at the interruption, Harry Grant had to ask what it was. He couldn't remember the last time that Dakers had described a *Gazette* story as a sensation.

'What happened? You buy a round of drinks?'

'Bribes, Harry. Backhanders, graft, kickbacks, palm-greasing. An everyday story of planning folk.'

'Who says so? The *Gazette*?'

'We're not that brave. The police say so. They've arrested the chief planning officer.'

When Harry Grant eventually replaced the phone, Nadine was preparing to leave.

'Same time tomorrow?' she said.

'Be here. And be sure to bring your body with you. I've got to go out now and count satellite dishes. It's a perilous business being a fearless investigative reporter.'

Paul Vanner left the London train in a worse mood than usual. It had been a difficult day at work where the money market was behaving strangely, and it was a long time since life at home had been enjoyable. Neil Kennedy was showing no inclination to return the money he had won so dishonestly at the casino, and now Suzanne, after behaving coolly for days, had gone to visit her mother without giving any good reason.

He had believed once, when he viewed the world through a dirty council-house window in Stepney, that if he could leave his unpromising beginnings behind and get for himself one of those city jobs where the salary made the neighbours gasp, all the other things that made up a man's life would fall into place. But now that he had achieved the impossible targets he had set for himself, his life was riddled with the same problems that beset everybody else.

He climbed into his Ferrari – his *second* Ferrari, as he now called it – and drove out of the station car-park. He had left work early because Suzanne had asked him to check the shop. She had left the new girl running it but wanted her husband to count the takings and lock up the money at the end of the day. After that, a few pints of lager in the Flatulent Ferret might lift his depression.

Suzanne's, he was pleased to see, still had customers, although he had gathered that customers in a shop like this didn't necessarily mean sales. They picked their way through the very best clothes, occasionally removing them from the hanger and holding them up to the mirror or sometimes disappearing with them into the small changing cubicle. And then they emerged and said 'I'll have to ask my husband' or 'Have you got it in another colour?' and disappeared back into the street.

He went in and tried to decide which of these women was the hired help. A girl with long blonde hair and an extraordinarily sexy face came over to him. He recognized her as the girl he had seen walking with the vicar at the May Fayre. She was wearing a mauve blouse and yellow jeans.

'Can I help you?' she said.

He looked at her and knew immediately that she would let him make love to her. The look that she gave him conveyed a message that was quite beyond the constraints of language.

'You must be Cathy,' he said. 'I'm Paul, Suzanne's husband.'

'The Ferrari man,' she said. 'Would you like to sit down? I'll be closing in a minute.'

He liked her voice with its echoes of the West Country, and the graceful way she moved about the shop. Her patience with the customers appealed to a different part of his brain: he wanted this business to make money. He sat down and waited while she discussed the virtues of an iridescent sarong with a young lady who was looking for something to wear on a Sardinian beach, and he felt his sexual appetite return.

He had never understood the public taste for sex last thing at night. He always arrived in bed exhausted and thought it the worst possible time to make love. Sex during the day when you were still fresh, preferably outdoors in the cool, fresh air, was a much better choice. He wondered where he could take her.

In the event, she made the decision for him. When the last customer had left the shop, and the day's meagre takings duly recorded, they arrived together at the door.

'You're all on your own,' she said.

'Utterly.'

'Do you fancy a walk? Get some fresh air in your lungs after the dirt of London.'

It was a long time since he had heard anyone suggest a walk as an end in itself. It made him feel quite young again.

'Okay,' he said. 'Then I'll take you for a drink.'

'You drink a lot, Paul, don't you?'

'Boatloads.'

'I think that's rather sad.'

'After two or three pints it gets quite cheerful.'

At the top of the green a path took them between the church and the village hall and out into the fields which rose in a sharp incline until they were looking down on Compton Sinbury. The gradient here meant that the grass had never been ploughed or sprayed with strange substances, and sheep who could handle the angle grazed free from the hazards of chemical fertilizers.

Cathy Gray strode ahead during this hill climb as if she had a destination in view, while Paul Vanner, unused to such exertion, struggled to keep up, scared that he was dissipating his finite energy on the journey itself.

'Don't you love the country, the fresh air and the fields?' she called. 'Away from all that modern pollution?'

With a superhuman effort he caught her up. He was glad that he had left his jacket in the car.

'Flatulent herbivores are the new pollutant,' he said.

'What are?'

'Farting cows. Too much methane gas going into the atmosphere.'

He followed her tinkling laugh as she strode ahead again and his face was level with a slim bottom in yellow jeans, his mind filled with erotic possibilities that a few hours ago seemed to be already in the past. He had not struggled to this unlikely spot to discuss environmental hazards or bovine bowel problems.

Cathy Gray's interest in Paul Vanner was not sexual although she was thoroughly prepared for sex to come into it. It usually did and she sometimes feared that sex was all she had to offer. But what interested her was that Paul Vanner had money. She didn't want his money but she wanted to be *near* it. She wanted to mix with people who had it instead of the no-hopers who hadn't, and find out how they got it. Life on a council estate had given her a yearning for something better. The council estates had been filled with dim women dominated in a strangely regimented life by even dimmer men, without money, drive, dreams or hope. Her brother's escape from the same bleak background was the example that gave her confidence, the proof that success was impartial. Cathy Gray's only real success, she knew, was that during a thrusting, sexually ambitious spell in her teens she had done the best blow-job in the Royal Duchy of Cornwall, but it wasn't enough for her simmering ego which craved public prosperity rather than private gratitude.

'We could rest here,' she said.

They had come to a flat golden field of corn, a plateau at the top of their climb where the possibility of lying down without being seen was embarrassingly obvious. More than a hundred yards away a young couple were not concerned about seclusion. A young boy, discovering an appetite that would engross him for years, was attempting to tug the knickers off a protesting nymphet. Was this, Paul Vanner wondered, where the young came for their fun? He looked at the corn, waving very gently in the mildest of winds, and then lay down in it.

'I'm not used to walking,' he said. 'I use cars.'

'Would you like me to lie down with you?' she asked.

'What a wonderful person you are.'

As he lay on his back in the corn and gazed up at her she gave him a look and then undid and removed both the blouse and the jeans with a speed that frightened him. The girls of his youth, whose pants had central locking, could have learned a lot from Cathy Gray, he thought. He had never seen a woman discard clothes so quickly – it had the professional efficiency of a stage act. What was even more exciting was that she was wearing nothing else: she had gone out into the world today wearing only blouse and jeans. Was this tryst in the cornfield already on her itinerary?

Her beautiful breasts, healthily tanned, were suddenly coming towards him and one of them landed in his mouth.

'What would Suzanne say?' she whispered.

He wanted to answer 'She'd be well put out' but he had been told not to talk with his mouth full. Her hands had undone his trousers now and were pulling them down. It was like being processed by a combine harvester: all she had to do now was separate the seed from the stem. Rolling in the corn in a mist of lust he found himself on top of her and then, a little later, in her, listening to her grateful murmurs at his desperate pounding. A piece of corn had got up his nose but he was too far gone to notice it as the excitement reached an almost unbearable pitch. He ejaculated with a relief that he could scarcely believe and thought for a moment that his balls had come off.

'Jesus Christ Almighty,' he said.

'I don't know why Suzanne looks so miserable all the time if that's what you do to her.'

'I know,' he said, recovering quickly. 'Some women have got no gratitude.'

They lay there for a couple of minutes and then heard somebody approaching. Vanner leapt up to hoist his crumpled trousers and found himself staring at One-cell Tel.

Terry Wallace, unlike many residents of Compton Sinbury, was a genuine country boy who spent many happy hours wandering through the fields. The memories of his boyhood – a field mouse in a tin, hide and seek in the cornfields, rabbit shooting at harvest – were more important to him than anything he ever saw on television. Today's walk in the warm evening sunshine had been particularly enjoyable – and now he was confronted by this terrible sight: Cathy Gray, stark naked again but with Suzanne Vanner's husband who seemed to have lost his sleek city trousers. He had no right to be with her. She was his, or she was going to be his.

He launched himself into the air and punched Paul Vanner heavily on the nose.

'Have some of that,' he said.

But Vanner was not the effete city clerk that One-cell Tel had evidently taken him for. The playing fields of Stepney equipped a boy for life's vicissitudes just as much in their own way as the playing fields of Eton. He had learned to punch, kick, butt and gouge before he knew the capital of France and when he had recalled a couple of these rusty talents One-cell Tel was lying in the corn, twitching slightly.

'Somebody has done a number on your olfactory organ,' said Toby Beauchamp in the Flatulent Ferret. 'The city must be getting rough.'

'Time I've finished with the bastard they'll need dental records to identify him,' Vanner told him.

Beside Toby Beauchamp, his face the colour of a brick, was Felix Kirby in a white shirt and white shorts. 'Did you irritate an overpaid yuppie?' he asked.

Vanner struggled for landlord Barry's attention. He didn't want the conversation to settle on his fracas in the cornfield.

'Some of these money dealers aren't as civilized as you'd imagine,' he said.

'I never imagined they were *civilized*,' Felix Kirby said. 'Ruthlessly efficient and disgustingly greedy, but not civilized.'

'What on earth have you been doing, Felix?' Vanner asked to get the subject off his swelling nose. 'Your face is the colour of a pillar box.'

'I've taken up squash.'

'And that's good for you, is it?'

'It's supposed to be, although I must admit I feel a bit rocky.'

'Your mistake,' said Toby Beauchamp, 'was to come to the pub. You should go home and lie down.'

'My mistake isn't coming to the pub. It's going home from the pub.'

'Another story of domestic bliss,' said Vanner. He was glad now that he had persuaded Cathy Gray to head for home.

'You promised me a drink,' she had reminded him as they walked hand in hand from the cornfield that they had so enjoyably flattened.

'I think it would be unwise,' he said. 'People talk, is my experience.'

'I work for your wife. It would be quite natural.'

He wavered at that. There was a perfectly legitimate reason for him to buy her a drink in the Flatulent Ferret: she was minding the shop while his wife was away. But he could imagine what the malicious tongues would make of it in the pub and his face wouldn't provide a very convincing rebuttal. After all, they *had* made love and people could always tell.

They sat on a stile and waited to see whether One-cell Tel would recover enough to make his way home.

'What had it got to do with him, anyway?' he asked.

'I don't know. I've never spoken to him. But he sent me this.'

She produced the phallus from her handbag.

'What on earth?' he said.

'It's my lucky charm.'

'It doesn't look very charming to me. Did he make it?'

'Suzanne thinks he did.'
'Suzanne? How the hell would she know?'
'One-cell Tel does odd jobs for her. Look, there he goes.'
The bruised prototype of this priapic trinket was limping into the sunset like the hero in a Western.
Standing in the Flatulent Ferret and thinking of the immense golden organ that Cathy kept in her handbag, Paul Vanner delicately felt his nose which was twice its usual size and of a strange bluish hue.
'Don't talk to me about domestic bliss,' said Felix Kirby. 'God release me from that frigid cow.'
At that moment Harry Grant came into the bar looking mildly dishevelled.
'Harry's been hanging out of some woman by his willy by the look of it,' said Toby.
Harry Grant ignored the cackles and ordered a Bell's.
'Why is there always a hosepipe ban the only month you need to use them?' Barry asked him as he served the drink.
'And what do all the other countries that aren't surrounded by water do?' asked Harry. 'Don't ask me. I'm a humble hack. What happened to your nose, Paul? It seems to have been in some sort of collision.'
'My nose doesn't want publicity. I'll give you another story. Did you know that a young man who uses this establishment has sent a golden replica of his erect organ to a spinster of this parish? What is occurring?'
'I've seen Cathy's little bauble. I wanted to write a story about it but it wouldn't sit too comfortably in the pages of a family newspaper.'
'Or anywhere else for that matter.'
'All right, I'll give you another story,' said Paul Vanner. 'Anything to keep my nose out of the paper. Did you know that the sheikh who took all our money in the casino was Neil Kennedy in disguise?'
'I don't believe it,' said Toby Beauchamp.
'He admitted it. I don't know why we didn't think of it. He *is* an actor. Personally I think it's disgraceful. We should get our money back.'

But Toby Beauchamp found that he couldn't share Paul Vanner's outrage at this coup. He had sailed pretty close to the wind himself in his financial arrangements and was left now with a reluctant admiration for Kennedy's nerve.

Felix Kirby, standing and listening in mute astonishment, saw the awful risk that Neil Kennedy had been prepared to take with his bank loan. He made a mental note to look very carefully at any further requests for credit from that particular customer.

Harry Grant said: 'It sounds like a masterful deception to me. But where's the story? I don't imagine the man is about to call a Press conference.'

'It's deceit,' said Vanner. 'It's a swindle, it's fraud, it's imposture. It's a con.'

'It's neat,' said Toby Beauchamp. 'I think a man with a half-million-pound mortgage can stand the joke.'

'I lost ten grand, pal. Please explain the joke.'

'A lot of humour depends on somebody's misfortune. In fact most of it does. You're the sacrificial victim, old son.'

'You lost a few grand yourself.'

'Easy come, easy go.'

'It doesn't come so easily in my case.' He glowered at the others and reached for a glass that was already empty.

'Let me fill that for you,' said Harry Grant. 'I don't want your poverty to embarrass you.'

'You don't want my stories either, by the sound of it.'

'As it happens we're up to here with stories this week. The *Gazette* lead will be an absolute lulu.'

'What is it?' Toby asked. 'Whet our appetites. We may even buy your paper.'

'Do you know who Brynwyn Rolfe is?'

'Of course. He's the man who – what's happened to him?'

'He's been arrested. As of now he's incarcerated in the pokey.'

'What for?'

'It's a story of bribery and corruption, the biggest scandal to hit the town for years.'

'Who's Brynwyn Rolfe?' Paul Vanner asked.

'He's the chief planning officer over at the council, the guy who recommends planning permission to build. Apparently he's been doing some building of his own. He's built a bloody great offshore nest egg, or so they say.'

'Where did you get this from, Harry?' asked Toby Beauchamp. He sat looking at Harry Grant and feeling a bit sick.

'The office. They're full of it. It's the biggest thing since the floods of '67.'

'When did it happen?'

'I believe the police lifted Mr Rolfe this morning. He'll probably come up in court tomorrow and be remanded for a few weeks. Is he a pal of yours, Toby?'

'Well . . . I wouldn't say pal. Naturally I've met him a few times. I've put in a few planning applications myself.'

'I hope you didn't give him any presents,' said Felix Kirby, smiling.

Toby looked at him. Kirby was remembering the cheques that had gone through his account. A small feeling of panic began to rise in Toby Beauchamp's chest.

'Do you know any more, Harry?' he asked.

'I gather it all began with some new Labour councillor who started to dig around. It seems he struck gold. Not so much a can of worms, more a nest of vipers. Illegal payments going back years. I must say Brynwyn Rolfe disguised it well. From his clothes and his car I always thought he was rather hard up.'

'You look quite shaken, Toby,' said Paul Vanner. 'And your glass is empty. Let me get you another.'

'I don't feel that good,' said Toby. 'I must be getting along.'

'I've never seen him leave this early before,' said Harry Grant when Toby Beauchamp had gone. 'He didn't even say goodbye.'

In his dust-caked bungalow Barnaby Barton was in a familiar position: behind the curtain, watching the road. But the postman never appeared when he waited for him. What was it his mother used to say? A watched kettle never boils. He stood in the hall and looked at his face in a cheap, wood-framed mirror from which the metal coating on the back of the glass had been peeling off for a long time.

He had spent the first twenty years of his life dreading appendicitis, the next twenty fearing cancer, and the last twenty fretting over his imminent heart attack. He was now a fairly fit sixty-six, but a lifetime of worrying about his health showed on his face.

He turned to go back to the curtain but the post hit the mat. It was as if the postman hid somewhere until Barney abandoned his vigil, and then darted in to deliver it when he wasn't being watched.

The familiar envelope lay on top of another and he picked it up and tore it open. But inside there was no £10 note, only a message. Typed and unsigned, it said: 'You won't need my £10 note any more.'

For a moment Barney looked as if he might cry. He might not need the £10 note any more soon, but he needed it now. There wasn't enough in his pocket to buy a pint of Guinness, and Terry Wallace had come up with very little work since the man from the oil company had filled his head with false hopes and wild dreams.

And perhaps his son had filled his head with false hopes too. Toby Beauchamp had been round to look at the land and promised to buy it, and then some council official had called in to check the boundaries. The solicitor that his son had mentioned had come round with some documents for Barney to sign, but that was weeks ago, and the subject now seemed to have been forgotten by everybody.

He let the unsigned note slip from his fingers and then he remembered the other letter. This was typed too, on bank notepaper, and it was signed by Felix Kirby.

Dear Mr Barton, it began formally. It was funny to think of Mr Kirby, who called him Barney in the pub when he spoke to him at all, addressing him in this way.

> This is to tell you that your new account has today been credited in the sum of two hundred thousand

pounds (£200,000) upon receipt of a cheque from Beauchamp Developments Ltd. If you would like to call in to the bank I will give you a cheque-book which will enable you to draw on these monies, and, at the same time, if you so wish, we could discuss the best way for you to invest it.

Barnaby Barton felt slightly intimidated by the prospect of owning a cheque-book. He had never had or needed one. People gave him money, he gave it to Barry in the pub and Barry turned it into pints of Guinness. This was the way it worked and a cheque-book sounded like an unwelcome hindrance in what had always been a fairly painless series of transactions.

He sat in his rocking chair and read Felix Kirby's letter again. Money had always been a mystery to him and this money didn't mean very much to him now. There was nothing that he wanted, no possessions that he craved. He was suited to the simple life that he had created, and feared disruption. The money, he realized finally, would only have some point if he had Lydia Baxter with him.

He was suddenly consumed with the idea that he should write to her. He could explain that there had been a change in his situation. It was a very long time since he had written a letter, but there was an old pile of notepaper in one of his drawers – he had noticed it often. Soon he was sitting at the kitchen table, struggling with words.

'Good fortune has come my way,' he began, 'and I can now write and ask you to join me. Duncan gave me your address when he was in England. I could hardly believe that he was my son! It has been a hard life and I hope that times have been kinder to you.'

At this stage the old Biro gave out, perhaps from surprise at being used. He scoured the bungalow for another, but when he sat down again he discovered that the sudden flood of inspiration that had produced those words so quickly had dried up and he had nothing further to write.

The thought that this message might appear on the brief

side after a forty-eight year silence never occurred to him. 'Love from Barney' he wrote with a valedictory flourish, and went out to search his old drawers for an envelope.

15

FELIX KIRBY strode across the green in a hurry. He had a call to make before his game of squash, and the adrenalin and the venom began to build up as he walked swiftly across the green. Felix Kirby was going to have to go through hell but he could see a sort of bliss at the end of it – a life of peace in which other people's moods happened in other people's houses.

Harry Grant was sitting at his typewriter in his shirt sleeves, trying to write his weekly 'Village Notes' column. It was a feature which melded fact with opinion and was the only place in the paper where he was allowed to ramble. Freed from the restrictions of news reporting, he could be as outrageous as he liked so long as a writ for libel did not come winging into the office and frighten the editor.

A satirical look at the stocks was what he had in mind today, along with the suggestion that it was time to re-introduce them. He had dug out all the facts: in 1376 Edward III ordered every village to maintain a set of stocks for the punishment of offenders, and they remained in business for nearly five hundred years. Stocks were last used in 1865, and the ones in Compton Sinbury had remained in position for another hundred years, no doubt to amuse visiting foreigners who had a quirky eye for that sort of thing.

But in a part of the world where old fogies were to be heard demanding the restoration of capital punishment, not to mention the birch-rod, the cat-o'-nine-tails, the treadmill and the ducking-stool, there was a risk that Harry's light-hearted call for the return of the stocks would be greeted by howls of acclaim. It was a risk that he was going to have to take.

He stared at the empty sheet of paper and waited for the first sentence to arrive from he knew not where. The doorbell chimed. An interruption at this crucial moment of creation was as welcome as a gas bill.

Felix Kirby stood on the step in his squash kit. His sandy hair was all over the place.

'You lied to me, Harry,' he said, marching uninvited into the cottage. Harry Grant shut the door and followed him in.

'No, I didn't,' he said.

'I've seen the passport. Bordeaux. You came back separately but you left together.'

Harry Grant had no way of knowing whether this was a guess. Felix Kirby sounded so confident that he had probably prised the information from Nadine.

'I didn't lie to you, Felix,' he repeated.

'She's been over here. She's been seen. Not everyone in the village is blind. You think I'm going to let you make me look an idiot? I'm going to take you, Harry, for every penny you've got.'

Harry Grant sat down, but his guest stood over him, white-faced and shaking.

'What I told you was true at the time, Felix. However, I can't deny that things have moved on since then.'

'And you're going to move on with them. There's no room for you in the village.'

Felix Kirby was in a state of nervous agitation that worried Harry. He looked as if he was about to implode.

'Take your glasses off,' he said now. 'I want to hit you.'

Harry Grant sighed. 'Save your energy for the squash court, Felix. Why don't you sit down? Either that or piss off.' There was a lot he would like to say to his unwelcome visitor about the lovely Nadine and Felix's treatment of her. Most of all he had a powerful desire to tell him who Rachel's father was. But for Nadine's sake he felt that he could hardly say anything at all.

Felix Kirby was not bound by such constraints.

'Here's the way it's going to be,' he said. 'You made a fool of me. Fair enough. Now it's my turn. I'll sue the whore for divorce, and then I'll sue you for alienating my wife's affection. You can then try to survive together without food.'

Harry Grant turned in his seat. 'Felix, if you don't shut your teeth you won't have any tomorrow,' he said wearily.

'Teeth are what you won't be needing. You're going to starve, boy.'

Suddenly, as if the conversation had taken a turn that displeased him, Felix Kirby walked out of the room. A moment later Harry heard the front door slam.

He sat at his typewriter, his concentration destroyed, and wondered what happened next. He picked up the phone and dialled Nadine's number.

'Five-o-four,' she said.

'He knows.'

'I know he knows.'

'I didn't know you knew he knew.'

'I didn't know *you* knew he knew.'

'Do you know how he knows?'

'Somebody saw me visit you and mentioned it to him. Then you rather carelessly mentioned Bordeaux in the pub and he found my passport and had a look. Then he remembered our tans. Two and two are four, particularly if you work in a bank.'

'Would you like a drink?'

'Not at your place.'

'I'll see you in the pub.'

'Being rich is a great strain,' pronounced Barnaby Barton in the Flatulent Ferret. 'You don't have the freedom of a poorer man.'

'What do you mean, Barney?' asked One-cell Tel.

'You take yourself. Do you have to worry about interest rates?'

'Give over, Barney. You sound like the Chancellor of the Exchequer.'

'That's what I'm saying, Terry. It's a strain. You don't have strain.'

'The only strain I have is waiting for you to spend some of

this money. I thought you'd throw it around, but you're like a bloody miser.'

'That's another problem,' said Barney, fiddling with a new pipe. 'If you've got money, how do you know that people really like you? How do you know they're not after your money? If you start spending it like a drunken sailor you won't know who your real friends are. You get hangers-on.'

One-cell Tel did not like the sound of this. His first reaction to the news of Barney's windfall had been a strange whooping noise followed by a little dance of excitement. He couldn't see how some of this money could fail to reach his pocket as he had, over the years, been instrumental in putting plenty into Barney's. But this *quid pro quo* hadn't even occurred to the older man. The money that had come his way as a result of his association with One-cell Tel had arrived by dint of long and arduous activity. He had held ladders, carried ladders and climbed ladders; he had hung doors, planed doors and painted doors; he had raked gardens, mowed gardens and dug gardens. He had sweated long hours with One-cell Tel's imperfectly articulated injunction ringing in his ears: 'Nothin' is for nothin'.'

'If you don't throw it about a bit you won't have any friends,' said One-cell Tel.

'Nothing is for nothing,' said Barney, finally igniting his pipe. 'If you need money I'll find you work.'

'I do need it. I had a ton on the nose of a donkey that fell over last week.'

This oblique account of a gambling loss on a horse meant nothing to Barney who said: 'Do you want to work for me?'

One-cell Tel's need for money was considerable, but the prospect of having Barnaby Barton as his employer seemed to suck the zeal out of him.

He leaned forward and wrapped a fat hand round his chosen refreshment, a bottle of Newcastle Brown. With a contemptuous and violent inhalation of air, he hoisted about two fluid ounces of mucus up his nasal passages and, after some facial distortion, swallowed hard.

'What I really want,' he said, after this protracted exercise had been satisfactorily completed, 'is to get my head up a lady's skirt.'

'I've got some new fences,' Barney said. 'They need painting.'

'You do it, Barney. You was always good with a brush.'

'It's what I said. Being rich is a strain. You can't get staff.'

One-cell Tel drank from his bottle of Newcastle Brown. For some reason it was a drink that seldom arrived with a glass. 'What have you got new fences for, anyway?' he asked. 'You getting flash? The old ones not good enough for you?'

'The old ones have gone, haven't they? They're building houses on my potato patch.'

The rural calm at the back of Barnaby Barton's bungalow had been replaced by a noisy building site. Saxon village communities might have had to rely on local materials to build their homes, but today's developers brought it in by the lorry-load. Every morning he looked out at the turmoil and wondered whether he had done the right thing. He seemed to have replaced his beloved hobby with money that he didn't really need.

The door opened and Harry Grant came in.

'Bell's,' he said, grabbing a stool at the bar.

'You look a bit harassed,' Barry told him as he offered him the whisky. 'Not enough happening?'

'Plenty happening, Barry. Too much, since you ask.'

The whisky disappeared very quickly; soon the empty glass was travelling back across the counter for a refill.

'How's Mrs Kirby?' asked Barry with a wink.

'I don't know what you mean, Barry.'

'Oh, I've seen her drop over your place a couple of times.'

'You didn't happen to pass this nugget on to Felix, I suppose?'

'Certainly not. I'm a publican, not a marriage-guidance counsellor.'

Nadine Kirby came in with a rush. She was wearing a blue blouse and white skirt and looked fairly chirpy, Harry thought, in the circumstances.

'Hallo, lover,' she said.

Harry Grant grimaced as Barry watched from behind the bar.

'Well, it's not a secret any more, is it?' she said. 'Now I shout it from the highest hill. Don't pretend you can't remember Doris Day.'

'You're pretty cheerful.'

'A weight has been lifted, Harry. Also I had two glasses of wine. We'd had a rather distressing scene.'

'Was Rachel there?' he asked anxiously.

'Luckily, no. She had a dancing class at the village hall.'

'Have another wine.'

'What a splendid idea.'

'Then you can tell me what happens next.'

'I was rather hoping that you would tell me.'

Felix Kirby felt bad even before he went out on the squash court. The row with Harry Grant had upset him more than he had expected. He had handled some fairly heated discussions in the inner sanctum of the bank with an icy control that had demoralized many an excitable customer, but his personal involvement in this latest row made it quite different.

His opponent, as usual, was Tadley, a bigger and younger man who coached newcomers to the game at the sports club and let them buy his drinks afterwards. As the new player improved, he increased the power of his own game so that the learner was continually stretched. Although he was trying to provide encouragement now, Tadley won the first set 9–0. Felix tried to slow the game down with some lobs, but he was moving too slowly to make it a game.

'Are you okay, Felix?' he asked. 'You don't look too good.'

'I'm fine.'

But he began to feel terrible. A central pain had gathered across the sternum in his chest: he felt as if a man in large boots was standing on him. Already sweating from his exertions, he began to sweat more.

Tadley's drives, volleys and drop shots were defeating him so easily that it was becoming embarrassing. He stopped playing.

'I think I'll have to go and lie down,' he said. 'I'm sorry.'

'Good idea,' Tadley said. 'Take it easy, Felix. You're not twenty-five any more.'

Felix Kirby left the court and picked up his jacket but felt too ill to put it on. He went out of the club and started to walk across the green to his house but the pressure on his chest was so intense that he had to stop every few yards and wait for it to ease. Then he walked again. Then the pain returned.

He was now seriously frightened. What was happening? Was this a heart attack? But the pain wasn't where his heart was, or where he had always imagined it to be. If he could get home and lie down, he told himself, the pain would go away. It was just a question of getting across the green.

He walked a few yards and the pain became intolerable. He stopped and waited, and then moved on again. The short walk from the sports club to his house began to seem like a feat of endurance. And the fear was almost as bad as the pain.

There were people out here leading a normal life, doing normal things, all of them unaware of the nightmare journey he was making. Boys played cricket on the green, others fished off the bridge at the bottom. A woman in a blue canvas chair painted a water-colour of the duck pond. A youth cycled up to the post office next to the supermarket and posted a letter. Beneath the tree on the green a couple sat kissing. Nobody noticed his fitful, agonizing progress from one side of the green to the other and, if they had, would probably have been too polite to interfere.

To the pain and the cold sweating had now been added a feeling of nausea, and he began to dread that he was going to throw up in public like the drunken teenagers he despised. He moved, he stopped, he waited and wondered, and then he moved on again.

He reached his house, a sixty-second walk, in twenty minutes. There was some relief in his achievement as he stopped and opened the door, but inside he felt worse again. He was going to be sick. He started to climb the stairs to the bathroom but the pain in his chest forced him to wait on every other stair. He climbed two steps and waited, but he wasn't sick.

He reached the bathroom in a ferment of fear. The fear had grown and enveloped the pain. He looked in the mirror and saw his contorted white face – that was the last thing he did see. He blacked out while standing up, and was dead before he hit the floor.

'Divorce,' said Harry Grant. 'It's becoming terribly popular. If it were mathematically possible, it would be more popular than marriage. There were only 27,000 in 1961, but by 1985 there were 175,000. Get fashionable. Dump him.'

'I read the same article,' said Nadine Kirby, picking up her wine. 'It contained another little statistic. Two-thirds of second marriages end in divorce.'

'Well, some people are just bad at marriage. It wouldn't apply to us.'

He ordered another Bell's and was about to pay when Rachel Kirby rushed in. He had never seen her in the Flatulent Ferret before. She was wearing a white leotard from her dancing class and looked frantic.

'It's daddy,' she said, deathly pale. 'He's on the floor.'

Nadine Kirby put down her drink and wheeled round on her stool. 'Rachel – what do you mean?'

'I found him on the floor. Dr Frost is there. You'd better come.'

'Stay here,' Nadine said to Harry. 'Who phoned Dr Frost?' she asked her daughter.

'I did. Quickly.' She pulled her mother's hand and the two of them left the bar. When they arrived breathlessly at the house a minute later Dr Frost was waiting for them at the front door.

'I'm afraid he's dead,' he said, 'Clearly a heart attack.'

Rachel began to cry.

Nadine said: 'Dear God!'

'I've rung the ambulance. It'll be here in a minute. I gather from his clothes that he had been playing squash?'

Nadine nodded. 'He'd just taken it up.'

'Ill-advised at his age, I'm afraid, Mrs Kirby. I told him so myself but he was convinced that the exercise was good for him. Let's go in and sit down.'

The three of them walked slowly into the empty house. Only Rachel's quiet sobbing broke the silence.

'There was nothing I could do, I'm afraid,' said Dr Frost, sitting down. 'It was too late.'

Nadine sat down too. Distraught and confused, her mind had settled on one fact; the bank owned this house.

'What would have happened?' she asked. 'What does a heart attack actually mean?'

'The strenuous exercise caused an increased demand for blood to the heart, but the narrowing arteries couldn't deliver it.'

'He was ill then?'

'Not necessarily. The post-mortem will tell us, but the likelihood is that if he'd stayed off the squash court he could have lived for years.'

From the window of the Flatulent Ferret Harry Grant saw an ambulance outside the Kirbys' house. The vehicle of doom. A body covered by a sheet was carried out on a stretcher by two men in uniform. There was no sign of Nadine.

He went back to the counter and picked up his whisky. He would have to go and see her now. All he had to decide was what he was going to say, what note he should strike. The situation was a nasty compound of tragedy and joy, of calamity and relief, and he was uncertain what mood he should arrive in. Even more unsettling was the fact that he had no idea what mood Nadine would receive him in. He finished his drink and went out.

She opened the door, pale-faced and dry-eyed, and then she threw her arms round his neck and said: 'Oh Harry, he's dead.'

He held her tightly and looked for the right line. 'How awful,' he said.

'You'd better come in.'

Rachel Kirby was sitting on the stairs, her elbows on her knees and her hands covering her face. Harry looked up to her to speak but her face did not appear.

'Leave her,' said Nadine. 'She wants to be alone.'

'Is she very upset?'

'Very.'

They went into the sitting room and flopped on the sofa.

'I'm truly sorry, Nadine,' Harry said. 'You know that if there's anything I can do . . .' Like marry you and take you away from all this, he thought, but it wasn't the right moment.

'There's nothing anyone can do,' she said vaguely.

He wondered if she would be better if she cried.

'Dr Frost said that he could have lived for years if he hadn't taken up squash.'

Harry Grant found that there was no reply that he could make to that. He took her hand and squeezed it. Presently she got up and fetched them both drinks.

'I suppose I've got to set about arranging a funeral,' she said.

'I think the undertakers do it.'

'Relatives to tell, letters to write, his papers to sort out.'

'Don't worry about all that now. Why don't you take a sleeping pill and go to bed?'

'I've got to look after Rachel.'

She drank her wine and stared at the floor. Suddenly she seemed to pull herself together.

'You'd better go. I must phone his sisters.'

'Of course. If you need me, phone me too.'

He had some things to do himself, he thought. His 'Village Notes' column was still unwritten, and now there was another story he would have to deliver to the office before the morning. BANK MANAGER FOUND DEAD.

'There's one thing I'm glad about,' said Nadine, putting down her glass. 'He never found out that he wasn't Rachel's father.'

Sitting on the stairs and listening to this with horror, Rachel Kirby felt the security and certainties in her young life being brutally kicked from under her.

It seemed entirely appropriate to the Revd Owen Gray that his church was named after the doubter Thomas, and that a man whose faith had been shot to ribbons should be the custodian of the creed today. The church of St Thomas could name every church warden back to Thomas Peyto in 1581, and it was a consolation to Owen Gray that four hundred years of church servants had begun with a man who had the same doubtful name.

On a hot day in August he got into his Morris Minor and went to see Mrs Harwood about her old age and its concomitant ills.

Odd things were going on. A concentration of carbon dioxide, sent into the atmosphere from factories and cars and the burning of forests, was going to trap the sun's heat like a greenhouse and raise temperatures, create deserts, melt ice packs and swell oceans.

It had been the warmest March for twenty-two years and the hottest April since records began. In May, instead of gentle spring days, the temperature had reached the eighties and now, in August, a British record temperature of 99°F had been recorded in Cheltenham. Trains and planes had been delayed as rails buckled and runways melted. And yet, in January, vicious winds had hit Britain for the second time in eighteen months, killing 45 people. Was this the first sinister manifestation of a fundamental change in the world's climatic conditions?

And where was God in all this?

Even more remarkable – and much more intriguing to Owen Gray – was the fact that flattened circles of corn, like those which had been discovered in southern England for nearly twenty years, had begun to appear in Farmer Garrity's fields, and Owen Gray was going to have a look at them.

But first he had to drop in on Mrs Harwood, whose health had recently interrupted a record of church attendance in Compton Sinbury that few people could equal. It was her birthday and he was taking her some fruit. She opened the door with an old grey shawl round her shoulders; it was a month since he had seen her and she seemed to have aged years in that short time.

'Come in, vicar,' she said. 'It was kind of you to call.'

'Mrs Harwood,' he said. 'Happy birthday. Which one is it?'

'I'm eighty-five,' said the old woman, shuffling back into the house ahead of him.

In the unseasonal darkness of her living room he was confronted by an impressive array of birthday cards which stretched the length of the mantelpiece, obscuring ornaments and vases. As he picked them up to read them, an awful truth dawned on him. The cards had been saved over many years. Several were from the same person, one was from a woman he knew had died years ago. Another was 'To Mother' although Mrs Harwood had no children. He emerged half an hour later, shaken at the secret tragedy of people's lives and oppressed by his responsibility to alleviate it.

It was a relief to head for the bright open spaces of Farmer Garrity's fields.

Owen Gray hoped that the mysterious circles of flattened crops that were appearing in ever-increasing numbers in the corn fields of the south were trailers for the coming evidence that earth was a very small place in the general scheme of things and other creatures – other much brighter intelligences – were thriving in huge numbers elsewhere. This development would, presumably, kill a dozen assorted religions stone-dead and put his mind at rest even if it put his body in the dole queue.

Farmer Garrity, a big perspiring man in a straw hat, was standing with the reporter Harry Grant in the middle of one of these flattened circles that was nearly seventy feet in diameter. The corn had all been flattened one way as if it had been the victim of a gigantic rotating comb.

'Good morning, vicar,' said the farmer. 'Something extraordinary is happening here.'

'The corn is as flat as an elephant's mat,' said Harry Grant.

Owen Gray acknowledged the two men and stood for a moment wiping his brow. I'm not a hot-weather person, he thought. I've got the wrong thermostat.

'Do you believe it's extraterrestrial activity?' he asked hopefully.

'There are a lot of possible explanations,' Harry Grant said, 'most of which have been eliminated, I gather. I'm trying to write a story about it all.' The heat was getting to him, too. He was wearing a white short-sleeve shirt and cotton slacks.

'It's another planet talking to us,' said Owen Gray. 'I'm speaking off the record, Mr Grant, of course.'

'Pity. That's a fine quote from a vicar. Some people think it's this planet talking to us about the way that we mistreat it. Some people think it's chemicals applied by farmers.'

'Not in this case it's not,' said Farmer Garrity. 'It's not the downwash of a helicopter, either. I'd have heard it. What about a hoax?'

'Two hundred and thirty in four months?' asked Harry Grant. 'Some hoax. And now they're appearing in Japan and Canada and America, so either somebody is spending a fortune on air tickets or there's an international federation of hoaxers. Amorous hedgehogs is another theory, but the favourite at the moment is stationary whirlwinds: rapidly spinning air caused by a mini frontal-pressure system passing over a hill and flattening the corn with a corkscrewing motion.'

Owen Gray wondered why everybody was so anxious to find a mundane explanation for something that promised the exciting possibility of life-changing revelations.

'I doubt whether such perfect circles could be created by random vortices,' he said. 'It's the same round pattern every time, and look at the smooth edges of the circle. Wind couldn't do that.'

'I had a man out here this morning with a dowsing rod,' said Farmer Garrity. 'He was talking about high-energy force lines.'

'Medieval rubbish,' said Owen Gray. 'There's somebody out there watching us. What do you believe, Mr Grant?'

'Reporters don't believe in anything, vicar. It's an article of faith. We're always interested in what other people believe, though. Somebody out there watching us, you said. Do you mean the second coming?'

'Small creatures with thin green bodies and three eyes. Antennae coming out of their ears.'

'Sounds more Hollywood than Church of England.'

'Did you know, Mr Grant, that the Andromeda Galaxy contains three hundred million stars, and beyond it there are billions more galaxies? I mean, what's really out there?'

'No *Gazette* readers, that's for sure.' He looked at his watch. 'I've got to go to a funeral. I believe that you're conducting the service.'

'So I am. What sort of man was Felix Kirby?'

'He was a wonderful fellow.'

Neil Kennedy was in bed with the ice maiden, Beatrix. The degree of romantic fervour which this proximity was intended to generate was not being helped by the focus puller who was holding a measuring tape from beside the lens to the tip of his nose, a make-up girl who was pressing chamois leather dowsed in eau-de-Cologne against his brow, and the gaffer who was shouting at the sparks to 'put in a blue gel'. Despite these bothering ministrations, Neil Kennedy was being helped to produce the right expression by the ice maiden herself who had buried her hand in his boxer shorts.

They were lying under one white sheet, stripped to the waist but both wearing pants, and she had got her hand right down into his and showed no sign of ever removing it. Although Kennedy found this as enjoyable as anything that had happened to him recently, there was something nagging at the back of his mind which told him it was odd.

'We're ready to go,' said Denis the director.

'Quieten down now, please, we're going for a take,' said the assistant. 'Roll camera!'

'Camera rolling,' somebody said.

'Roll sound.'

'Sound.'

'Mark it!'

At this point the clapper boy held up a board in front of Neil Kennedy's face. It said 'HOT AIR RISES. Scene 23. Take 1.'

JULIAN: You don't know what you are doing to me, Wyn.

WYN: Yes, I do.

JULIAN: And you don't care? You're going to go on doing it?

WYN: I don't see why not.

JULIAN: Some women see men as toys that they can play with when they feel like it.

WYN: And put back in a box when they're bored. What a lovely idea.

'Cut!' shouted Denis. 'Wonderful!' He turned to continuity. 'Print it.'

'Check the gate,' shouted the first assistant.

Hearing this Neil Kennedy knew that the take was a good one; it was now a question of waiting while they checked that a hair that would look like a tree-trunk on screen had not got into the gate and on to the camera's lens. What they dreaded to hear now was 'Hair in the gate, sir' which would mean that they would have to shoot the whole scene again.

Not that Neil Kennedy was in a hurry to move. Lying in bed and being caressed by the ice maiden's delicate fingers seemed as good a way as any to earn a living, but then he heard the camera team shout 'Gate clear' and her hand had gone. He waited for the detumescence that would make his appearance acceptable when he emerged from the sheet. It was a long time coming, or going.

He was handed a dressing-gown when he left the bed: the next scene would find him in the bathroom examining his face in a mirror. It was a difficult shot because the camera wanted to show his face and his face in the mirror without showing the camera in the mirror. To achieve it he had to stand slightly to one side of the mirror so that he couldn't see his own face at all. Staring at the wall, but appearing to the viewer to be studying his own reflection in the mirror, he had to mutter: 'To this am I reduced.' And then, turning his head slightly, he had to call over his shoulder: 'I thought women stopped riding horses when they had a satisfactory sex life?'

One day, he assumed, the combined efforts of the director,

the producer, the direction assistant, the production assistant, the designer, the art department, the construction team, the sparks, the grips, the make-up artists and God knew who else, would pull these meaningless fragments into a coherent story which would glue a nation to its sofa.

He went over to the chuck wagon for a coffee. He could have done with a drink but, although the meal provisions on these occasions were generous, the one thing you could never get from film catering was alcohol. Trusted people and accepted alcoholics made their own arrangements.

Beatrix had discovered a need for coffee, too. She stood, alone and ignored, in a pink robe.

'That was nice,' he said.

She turned, appreciably cooler than she had been in bed. 'What was?'

'Oh, lying in bed with you.'

'Don't get carried away by it.'

'Never fear,' he said. 'Old Neil never gets carried away by anything.'

He remembered then what he had forgotten in bed, when there had been something worrying away at the back of his mind which was already heavily occupied with remembering his lines while it fought the distraction of her wandering hand. She was, against all appearances, a militant lesbian who didn't mind discussing the shortcomings of men in some of the more esoteric women's magazines.

'Why did you do it?' he asked.

'In the interests of art, darling,' she said with a strange smile. 'It improved the scene.'

It was a subdued group who gathered that weekend by the Vanner pool. The invitation to the Manor House to swim, sunbathe and drink champagne had been passed around before the death of Felix Kirby and now people were not quite sure how much enjoyment it was proper to display.

The previous afternoon, some of them had congregated sedately in the gloomy and unfamiliar setting of the parish church to witness the departure of Felix Kirby. Harry Grant, who had placed himself a discreet two rows behind the widow and her daughter, thought that the late bank manager, surly in life, would have been gratified by the way that the ceremony correctly evoked his own joyless disposition.

Toby Beauchamp found that he could best produce the appropriate expression of pain and sorrow by concentrating his attention on Brynwyn Rolfe rather than Felix Kirby. Contemplating a future that was already destroying his sleep transformed him into an authentically lugubrious funeral guest. His attitude to the death itself was idiosyncratic. He always took it personally when friends died: it showed such a disinterest in *him*.

Suzanne Vanner arrived in a fetching black outfit that she had borrowed from her own shop. She saw herself now as a model, a one-woman publicity campaign for the clothes that were available from her boutique that too few people were patronizing. With her was Gwenda Kennedy, no great fan of Felix Kirby but on this occasion representing her husband. Neil Kennedy felt a debt of gratitude to the bank manager, but filming a scene in bed with a woman for *Hot Air Rises* prevented him from attending. Also not there was Paul Vanner. It would have to be the funeral of a very close relative to keep him away from work.

Nadine Kirby sat in the front pew with Rachel and other members of the family. In this tableau of grief, Rachel stood out as being particularly stricken. White-faced and hollow-eyed, with her long black hair tied severely behind with a black bow, she seemed, to those guests who noticed, to be a peculiarly tragic figure, alone, shattered and lost.

Owen Gray presided over the obsequies with a histrionic flair that sprang from his growing conviction that church was theatre, and that in the television age it took more than an old man mumbling into his missal to get people out of the house. It was only after a lengthy period of consideration that he had recently decided against using the phrase 'bums on pews' in the parish magazine.

And now, a day later, it was champagne round the pool. Life went on, and Paul Vanner wasn't going to allow a funereal mood to infect his poolside party, particularly as his wife had been kind enough to invite her new assistant. In his younger days, before the feelings of insecurity had been swept away by a tide of money, he might have worried about how his white, fat body was going to look to the svelte, tanned Cathy Gray, but today, with the confidence of conquest, the thought never occurred to him. She was his, or she had been his. Even a blind pig found the occasional acorn.

Cathy Gray, feeling over-dressed in a yellow bikini, was flattered to have been invited. A swimming pool in your back garden was a bit of a novelty if you lived on the Colemore Estate, although she secretly believed that the ultimate luxury was an *indoor* pool. She stood waist-deep in the water, watching Paul Vanner drink champagne. Perhaps when he had drunk a bit he would loosen up and come over, even if his wife was watching.

Paul Vanner's problem today was not his wife but Saddam Hussein. The Iraqi dictator had sent his army into Kuwait and announced to an enraged world that the tiny country now belonged to Iraq. His invasion, and the subsequent arrival in the Middle East of American tanks and planes and ships, not to mention nuclear submarines, guided missile cruisers and an army in gas-proof clothing, was having an unsatisfactory effect on the money market. The dollar was losing cents against the pound and had dropped to an all-time low against the mark. Vanner's talent was dealing with the dollar on an hour-to-hour basis. When politics, about which he knew nothing, intervened, and people started killing each other, the situation became difficult for him to read.

Other people round the pool – framed by pink camellias and blue hydrangeas almost as big as footballs – had preoccupations of their own.

Suzanne Vanner, in a white bikini and a new pair of Rayban sunglasses, both from her shop, lay on a sunbed wrestling with feelings of guilt and fear about the abortion. After years of imagining herself as a mother, it had been more traumatic than she had expected. Now she was scared that her husband would find out, and even more scared that permanent damage might have been done to her delicate insides.

Toby Beauchamp, sprawled on a sun lounger and wearing a blue silk shirt and white shorts, was watching the girl who worked for Suzanne bouncing in the pool and hoping that she could take his mind off Brynwyn Rolfe. It seemed inconceivable now that his name was not going to surface during the police investigations into the backhanders that Rolfe had eagerly accepted over the years. He felt like a clay pigeon that was about to be propelled into the air in front of the waiting guns.

Neil Kennedy, who lay apart from the others as if he wasn't really a guest, was worried about his sister in Monrovia. A battle to oust the Liberian president, Samuel Doe, was raging in the streets there and 5,000 people had died in the fighting. When he got his mind away from that there were other things to fret about. He thought about the four acres that the Vanners had here, the paddock, the tennis court and the swimming pool, and wondered why a man who had so much could get het up over a loss at a game of cards. Lying there and being ignored by the host was an embarrassment that his wife had inflicted on him. At first he had refused to come along, and the ensuing row meant that his wife wasn't talking to him either. So he lay in the sun with his eyes shut, present only physically, pretending to be asleep.

The conspicuous absentee was Nadine Kirby. While everybody was anxious to cheer her up there was some uncertainty about whether inviting her to a drinks party on the day after her husband's funeral was a bit of a social gaffe, and she had been left out.

So Harry Grant sat alone on the edge of the pool, his feet trailing in the water, wondering what the future held for him and Mrs Kirby.

Only Gwenda Kennedy and Lindy were taking full advantage of the facilities. Lindy, with a water wing on each arm, was crossing the pool on her own while her mother hovered within reach in case they deflated.

'I'm like Winnie the whale,' said Lindy, remembering a visit to Windsor Safari Park.

Paul Vanner joined them in the water, his eyes sliding towards Cathy Gray.

'Paul is *much* more like Winnie the whale,' said Gwenda, 'except that he's white like Moby Dick.'

'I'm a beached whale,' Vanner said, and began a laborious backstroke that eventually brought him to Cathy Gray's end of the pool.

'Well, hallo,' he said. 'You look stunning.'

'You look pretty husky yourself. How's your nose?'

'Nearly back to normal. I suppose if this was the south of France you'd be topless.'

Without a word she removed her bikini top and let it float on the water. The sudden appearance of naked breasts here was doubly startling to Vanner. In the sudorific heat the magic of sex had seemed to be receding, and the knowledge that his wife was within sight provided an extra frisson.

The unveiling was enough to lure Harry Grant into the water, but he had to leave his glasses by the side of the pool.

'I can't help noticing that your breasts are as brown as the rest of you,' he said when he arrived at their sides. 'We reporters are observant like that.'

'Even without your glasses,' said Cathy Gray, glowing with confidence. 'I'm brown all over, actually, probably because I mow the lawn in the nude.'

Harry Grant wondered whether he had the raw material of a new sexual fantasy here and, as Vanner and Cathy Gray started to play ball in the water, he tried to prod it into action but nothing would come. Where the Queen and Mrs Thatcher would gladly leap into action on his command, Cathy Gray stuck fast. Perhaps she lacked the necessary *gravitas*.

He headed for the side of the pool as Suzanne Vanner came out of the Manor House with a tray of ice-cream – pink, white, yellow, brown and green. She stopped alongside Toby Beauchamp's sun lounger.

Toby Beauchamp was thinking now about his teddy bear. It was a very old teddy bear with one eye and a torn ear and he had been given it when he was two. In the early days it had shared his bed and then it was relegated to a cupboard. But he had never been able to bring himself to throw it out.

'I'm still faithful to my teddy bear,' he said. 'He's the only bastard who hasn't double-crossed me.'

Suzanne Vanner looked at him and moved on with her tray.

'Is Toby worried about something?' she asked Harry who was climbing out of the pool. 'He's talking about his teddy bear.'

'He's got a big problem and the prognosis isn't good.'

Suzanne allowed herself a disbelieving stare at Toby's prostrate form. That *would* be the day when the world was allowed to harm the urbane Mr Beauchamp. She carried the ice-cream tray along the water's edge to where her husband was playing ball with a topless Cathy. Her big brown breasts, half in and half out of the water, seemed to be floating like marker buoys. Her husband was so absorbed in this spectacle that he didn't notice her arrival.

'Ice-cream, anyone?' she called.

'Please,' her husband shouted.

Suzanne Vanner's despondent mood was not helped by the discovery that her assistant was flashing her boobs at her gaping husband. With the action of a shot-putter, she pushed the tray of ice-cream into the air and watched as it curved and then splashed upside down beside them.

PART THREE

• Hot News •

I don't pretend to understand the Universe – it's a great deal bigger than I am. People ought to be modester.

Thomas Carlyle

Crime is a logical extension of the sort of behaviour that is often considered perfectly respectable in legitimate business.

Robert Rice
The Business of Crime

16

TOBY BEAUCHAMP waited for the police in his gazebo. He felt like a gunman holed up in the last redoubt before being swamped by the furious forces of law and order. He lit a small cigar and looked at the garden that he had created.

Below the terrace with its potted plants was a lawn that looked like the centre court at Wimbledon before the first match had damaged the grass; then, with hedges of yew, there was an avenue of neatly clipped beeches which led down to the decorative white gazebo which he used as a summer house. On one side of that avenue, tulips sprang from a sea of forget-me-nots; on the other, roses bloomed round an old stone pool. In a corner of the garden what had once been a Victorian shrubbery was now the home of rhododendrons and magnolias.

Toby Beauchamp looked at all this and thought of the effort that he had put into its development. It was something that he loved. He had no use for the modern accoutrements with which people adorned their gardens: swimming pools, fish ponds, tennis courts. To him a garden was a place where beautiful things grew, and as he looked at it now he wondered whether he was going to lose it.

The police had rung an hour ago and asked, very politely, whether he would be in this morning. He had intended to visit the Southfork site to check on progress but, anxious not to offend, he told them that he would be at home until lunch.

Now he sat in the gazebo and tried to guess the reason for their visit. Were they making a few innocent inquiries about the world of planning applications, or was he to be subpoena'd as a witness in the case against Brynwyn Rolfe? He didn't allow his mind to dwell on the third possibility, that he was about to be arrested himself.

He hadn't known, until the police rang, whether they even knew of his existence. If Rolfe was taking bribes from Toby, he could be accepting them from a dozen other developers, and the case against him could involve furtive deals that Toby knew nothing about. Until the phone rang, this thought had sustained him through a difficult period.

A few days earlier he had driven into town and buried himself in legal books at the public library. He wanted to talk to his solicitor but didn't want to blacken his name unnecessarily in front of the man who handled all his land contracts and never tried to conceal his admiration for Toby's extraordinary financial success.

In the library he pored over the three relevant Acts: the *Public Bodies Corrupt Practices Act 1889*, the *Prevention of Corruption Act 1906* and the *Prevention of Corruption Act 1916*. He skipped through the arcane legal jargon with a heavy heart: it seemed that all or any of these ancient pieces of legislation could skewer him to the wall. By the time he got back in his car he discovered that he had, quite accidentally, memorized whole slabs of the stuff: 'If any person corruptly gives or agrees to give or offers any gift or consideration to any agent as an inducement or reward for doing or forbearing to do, or for having after the passing of this Act done or forborne to do, any act in relation to his principal's affairs or business, or for showing or forbearing to show favour or disfavour to any person in relation to his principal's affairs or business; or if any person knowingly . . .'

The man Toby wanted to talk to was Brynwyn Rolfe but it would be a dangerous mistake to contact him; his phone was probably bugged. Brynwyn Rolfe was in purdah. His brief appearance before the magistrates produced only a few lines in the *Gazette*: reporting restrictions had not been lifted. He had been charged with corruptly receiving money 'for assisting in or procuring the grant of planning permission'. He had been remanded on bail and sent for trial at the Crown Court which might not take place for months.

Toby stubbed out his cigar and decided to abandon his vigil in the gazebo in favour of a drink. The more he thought about the situation the more he wanted a drink. He found the vodka, half-filled a glass and took up a new watching position by the front window.

The white police car pulled up at his gate almost immediately. Two uniformed policemen, a constable who had been driving and a sergeant who was in the front passenger seat, climbed out. They looked at some papers in their hand, then at the name on the gate, and then they pushed it open and walked slowly up the drive.

Toby Beauchamp thought it only amiable to greet them with a glass in his hand.

He opened the door and said: 'Good morning.'

'Mr Beauchamp?' asked the sergeant, referring again to the papers in his hand.

'That's me.'

'Mr Toby *Alfred* Beauchamp?'

The question arrived with a piercing gaze and a strange emphasis as if the world was full of Toby Beauchamps and the problem here was finding the right one. Toby disliked both the gaze and the stark formality of the question. It lifted the conversation far away from the friendly atmosphere that he had planned for it.

'Would you like to come in?' he asked.

'That might be best, sir,' said the sergeant.

The two men followed him into the front room and declined seats. The nature of the papers in the sergeant's hand now became clear.

'I have a warrant here for your arrest, Mr Beauchamp,' he said. 'I must ask you to accompany me to the police station. You can ring your solicitor from there.'

Toby found, to his surprise, that he could only smile. 'Have I jumped a red light, sergeant?' he asked.

'I'm about to read the charges, sir. And I must warn you –'

'Bit late for that, old son. May I get a coat?'

'I'll go with him,' said the constable.

When Toby returned with his coat the sergeant insisted on

reading out the charges. After the sojourn in the public library, they had a familiar ring.

'How many charges was that altogether?'

'Six, sir.'

'Jesus!' said Toby Beauchamp.

The split-screen Morris Minor edged its way on to the Colemore Estate. Here, at least, it didn't stand out as the inferior vehicle of a poor man.

The Revd Owen Gray pulled up outside his mother's shabby home and for a while he just sat in the car. It was at this stage in a man's life that he might have been expected to provide his mother with some of the comforts that she had missed while raising a family, but Owen Gray had thrown his lot in with God, that celestial Thatcherite whose attitude to pay indicated a divine disapproval of inflationary wage settlements.

And so Owen Gray arrived at his mother's house with his customary feeling of inadequacy and his sense of guilt at how little he had been able to give her. He got out of his old car and walked up the footpath to the door.

She was working as usual, carrying a vacuum cleaner from one room to another. She had a pleasant face that had once been beautiful. You could see where Cathy's looks came from.

'Come in, dear,' she said. 'It's nice of you to drop in.'

He climbed over the discarded vacuum cleaner and went into the sitting room.

'How are you, mother?' he asked, sitting down.

'We're fine. How are the crop circles?'

'It's a mystery nobody can solve.'

'Do you think it's funny people from outer space?'

'I don't see why not. If the earth's gravity is no longer a restriction for us, why shouldn't somebody else be out there travelling too?'

'What does the Bible say?'

Mrs Gray, who never went to church, derived a mild pleasure from teasing her son; it was something he was used to.

'It's not exactly specific on interplanetary travel.'

She offered him a chewy meringue which carried the lingering aroma of mouse droppings. Outside there was the sound of a lawn being mowed.

'It's not specific about anything very much, is it, except turning the other cheek?'

'It's even ambiguous on that, I'm afraid. God wanted to smite his enemies with scab, itch, piles, mildew and a sore botch that could not be healed, according to Deuteronomy. So much for turning the other cheek.'

'How difficult for you, dear,' said Mrs Gray. 'Still, if you believe in the incarnation I suppose you're lumbered.'

He finished his meringue and wiped his fingers on his handkerchief. 'You never believed in anything, did you, mother?'

She laughed. 'I used to believe in Harold Wilson. It was a phase we all went through.'

'I meant God.'

'Oh, no. But I think it's wonderful that you do. You've no idea how proud I feel when I tell people that the new vicar is my son.'

He listened glumly. The idea of his mother getting satisfaction from such small fragments of reflected glory depressed him. How much better it would be if he could buy her a house, a car, a holiday.

The sound of the lawn mower grew louder, and he looked out of the window and saw a naked woman. Long brown legs and a lovely bottom were going away from him and the shoulders that were pushing the mower were covered by long blonde hair.

He said: 'Did you know you've got a naked woman on your lawn?'

'It's only your sister. She always cuts the grass like that. She says it keeps her cool.'

'My God! What do the neighbours say?'

'They'd have to climb on the roof to see her.'

Unable to resist, he got up and went to the window. Her body had filled out since he last saw it. Statuesque, he thought. Junoesque. Voluptuous. Curvaceous. Provocative. Exciting.

'You don't have to stare, dear,' said his mother doubtfully.

But if he turned now she would see how he had reacted to this unexpected sight.

'Yes, I do,' he said. 'We don't get a lot of naked woman on the lawn at the vicarage.'

'It must be a bit of a downer having the chairman of Men's Hour arrested for corruption,' said Gwenda Kennedy. 'Will you have to impeach him?'

'He never was "chairman" of Men's Hour. That was just you being sexist.'

'*Me* being sexist! You gather together like naughty boys, desperate to keep women away, and you call me sexist?'

'Listen. Felix is dead, Toby's arrested and Paul Vanner isn't talking to me. The battalion's decimated. Don't dance on our grave.'

Neil Kennedy was trying to dig a sandpit for Lindy. He had written to a firm that specialized in that sort of thing, but didn't care for the numbers on their quotation. He wrote back: 'Dear Sir (in this context, dear means expensive) . . .' Now he was trying to do the job himself.

In the old days, before he was pauperized by domestic bliss, he didn't have to learn anything very much except how to leave a bar before it closed, but now he had to learn how to dig a sandpit. It seemed to him, glancing round the lawn, that he had a horde of helpers right on the scene if only he could mobilize them. The grass was infested with moles and, reading up on the problem, he had discovered that a four-ounce mole could shift ten pounds of earth in twenty minutes. He could poison them, trap them, shoot them or drive them away with sonic vibrations, but what really appealed to him was training them to dig his sandpit.

'I always thought he was a pain in the fundament, anyway,' said Gwenda Kennedy. She was sitting in a deck-chair on the patio watching her husband's efforts with a spade.

'Who was?'

'Mr Beauchamp.'

'There's nothing wrong with Toby.'

'Nothing that a four-stretch won't put right.'
'What on earth's a four-stretch?'
'It's a line from one of your old films, darling. In fact you said it. I gathered it meant four years in prison.'
'He won't go to prison, will he?'
He found her enthusiasm for kicking a man when he was down distasteful.
'Suzanne Vanner says he will.'
'My God, you women don't even wait for the jury to come back.'
The filming schedule of *Hot Air Rises* had given the over-worked cast a day off today and so last night the Kennedys had slept together. The occasion had not been a total success. Gwenda, having become used to the space and peace of her own double bed, seemed to resent his intrusion, and either the sexual innuendo in his conversation was so subtle that she missed it, or he was talking to deaf ears. Eventually, feeling pressured, she submitted, but it wasn't the excited, pleasurable coupling of a year ago.
'I sometimes wonder,' she said with chilling disdain after-wards, 'whether what men do in their brief moments of enthusiasm between the sheets is entirely adequate.'
And he lay awake for a long time remembering other sexual experiences, in fields, on beaches, in cars and trains, at parties and once, memorably, in a telephone kiosk at Kensal Green. As a young actor of twenty, ten years ago, he found that girls seemed to appear uninvited like nuts in May with voracious but easily satisfied appetites. But he knew what Gwenda would say should he be foolish enough to parade this teeming segment of his past before her: That was before enough women learned to complain.
Lindy, bored suddenly with her umpteenth Rainbow video, rushed into the garden to see what progress he was making with the sandpit. A black plastic policeman's helmet concealed her curls.
'Where's the sand?' she asked, disappointed.
'I have to dig the pit first, then I'll go and buy the sand,' he told her. The way that toys had developed he was surprised

that she wanted one. Stone Age children had probably played in sandpits. Today's children might have been expected to ask for more. After all, in another thirty years or so she would probably be holidaying in a Japanese-owned hotel in outer space.

'That's big enough,' she said.

'Is it?' he asked, relieved. He scraped out the loose soil and filled the wheelbarrow. Lindy jumped into the pit, delighted.

'I'm off to the garden centre to get some sand then,' he told his wife.

'You're off to the pub to get some beer.'

'That, too. Is the venison casserole in the Aga?'

'We have corned beef.'

In the Flatulent Ferret Toby Beauchamp was sitting on his stool like a waxwork effigy of himself. Even the vodka on the bar in front of him failed to induce movement.

Neil Kennedy, sweating from the effort of carrying sacks of sand, was delighted to see him.

'Toby, me old mate, me old mucker, me old jailbird. What did you use – a tunnel or a helicopter?'

But this chirpy approach, it was clear, leaned towards the malapropos.

'I was just wondering,' Toby said, without even looking at the new arrival, 'how many of those tablets you have to take with a glass of whisky.'

'What are you talking about, Toby?'

'The long goodbye, the big sleep, goodbye cruel world, I've gone to join the circus.'

'What is this? Some sort of quiz?'

Toby Beauchamp looked at his vodka but didn't pick it up. 'I sometimes wish my life had been unhappier. It wouldn't have gone so quickly.'

'I've seen plays like this at the National,' said Neil Kennedy. 'In fact I was in one once. They miss out every other line and call it cerebral.'

'This might be an amusing diversion for you, Neil, but it's

the end of the road for me.' Toby turned to him now but still ignored his drink. 'Three to seven years, that's what my lawyer says.'

Sylvia appeared from a back room, having heard Kennedy come in. He drank quite a lot of his pint of lager before sitting on a stool next to Toby.

'You did bung him money then?' he said.

'One oils the works, Neil. It's the way the game is played. Why should I make half a million because a piece of land is suddenly designated fit for building when the man who has decided it gets fourpence a week? It wouldn't be fair. It wouldn't make sense.'

'Three to seven years?'

'That's what he said.'

'I'd have thought the stigma of conviction and a big fine would have dealt with it.'

'That doesn't seem to be the popular view. I've made too much money for a fine to hurt. I'm on bail and I had to surrender my passport.'

He finally picked up his vodka, drank it in two gulps and then held up the empty glass as if he could hardly believe what he had just done.

'All that planning, all that work and it ends like this,' he muttered.

Sylvia reappeared, hearing a glass on the counter, and Kennedy handed her two empty glasses.

'Same again,' he said.

She looked at Toby and, knowing that he had been arrested, wasn't quite sure what to say.

'I'm a pariah already,' he said when she had gone. 'I'm the invisible man. Disgrace, ostracism, prison – that's what I've got to look forward to.'

Compiling so precisely this inventory of his expectations produced an even darker mood.

'What are the tablets called, Neil? Para-something.'

'The para you've got is paranoia. Delusions of persecution. Why don't you plead not guilty and spend some of your mazuma on getting the best barrister in Britain? That's what famous people do and much to everybody's surprise they're always acquitted.'

'It would take Marshall Hall to get me out of this.'

'Hire him.'

'He died sixty years ago, unfortunately.'

How do you stop somebody from committing suicide? Neil Kennedy wondered. He could hardly go home with him and follow him round the house until his mood changed, and yet Toby's dystopian view of the world today produced a depressingly real picture in his listener's mind of whisky and pill bottles, of razor blades and opened arteries, of rubber tubing from the exhaust pipe of a blue Porsche, of a single muffled shot from the privacy of a gazebo.

He said: 'Come round to lunch. I've got to build a sandpit.'

Toby produced a weak smile. 'Very kind, but I've got a couple of sites I have to visit. I've got to earn some – what was your word? – mazuma.'

He finished his drink and stood up. He no longer looked like a debonair matinée idol from the day before yesterday. Today he looked more like a man who had forgotten how to sleep. But up on his feet and glancing at his watch he looked like a man who would still be here tomorrow.

Neil Kennedy attributed this to the curative powers of alcohol.

The telephone dragged Harry Grant from the deepest sleep. He had taken a few glasses of Scotch in the potting shed in the hope that they would provide him with the right topic for his 'Village Notes' column which was showing a perceptible reluctance to materialize. As usual, he had a list of possible subjects beside his typewriter, ancient and modern: witchcraft, the poll tax, antique auction rings, something amusing about compost heaps. But none of these ideas had the impetus to carry him to the next stage of the exercise: getting words on paper.

The whisky had let him down as well, producing oblivion instead of inspiration, and he was slumped fully dressed in a chair dreaming of a flight from New Zealand to Australia which only cost five pounds, when the jangling of the phone hauled him to a sort of consciousness.

'Harry?' Nadine sounded petrified. 'I've rung and rung. Are you ill?'

'I think I was asleep.'

There was a sob and a gasp at the other end of the line as if she was having difficulty talking.

'It's Rachel,' she said. 'She's disappeared.'

'Disappeared?' His head was too fuzzy for him to be sure that he was understanding her.

'Oh, Harry. Please come over.'

'I'm coming.'

He put down the phone and went out and rinsed his face. By the time he had crossed the green he almost felt normal. Nadine was waiting by an open front door, tears running down her pale face.

'She's been murdered,' she said. 'I know it.'

He put his arm round her and ushered her indoors.

'Tell me what's happened. How long has she been gone?'

'She went out to play at seven. She's always back within an hour. What's the time?'

'Ten o'clock.'

'Oh, my God.' Her hands covered her face. 'I was watching television.'

'We must phone the police,' he told her. The word police frightened her: it was an admission that something serious was happening. She looked at Harry but he was already picking up the phone. Soon he was talking to a policeman he evidently knew.

'They're coming round,' he said, leading her to the sofa. Nadine had found a handkerchief now but instead of drying her eyes she twisted it backwards and forwards nervously in her hand.

'I thought she must be with a friend. I just sat here expecting her to appear. And then suddenly it was so late that I knew something was wrong.'

'Had she seemed all right?'

'I don't know. She's been strange ever since Felix died.'

'Well, she was upset. Naturally.'

'It's more than that. Her attitude to me has changed. She's been aloof, withdrawn.'

'Has her bike gone?'

Nadine nodded silently.

'Perhaps she's got a puncture.'

'She would never go far enough away for that to matter. My God, what can have happened to her?'

'She's not the runaway sort,' Harry said, standing up.

'Then somebody's got her. I'm being punished for my sins.'

'I'm going to make you a cup of tea.'

He went out to the kitchen, feeling a chill in his stomach. He wasn't sure that he was equipped at the moment to deal with a crisis, let alone a tragedy. He tried to imagine what had happened to his daughter. She was upset and disturbed and she had run away. But that didn't mean that she hadn't fallen into the hands of some homicidal pervert who, according to the news stories, were in plentiful supply these days particularly, for some reason, in rural areas. It was the girls who had run away from home that these people preyed on, posing initially as friends before the time came for the obscene assault and the bludgeon to the skull. He saw a frail body covered with leaves in a wood, a bloodstained figure, bound with cords, in the boot of a car.

'She'll be all right,' he said when he took the tea in. 'Rachel is much too sensible to let anything silly happen.'

But when he sat down a dark mood gripped him, and he was glad when two policemen arrived at the door. They looked grim. Missing children was their least favourite investigation. Drunken drivers and large thefts were what gave life a lift, but lost children could involve thousands of hours of work with nothing but misery at the end of it, and not only for the family. By the time they found the tiny body buried on the scrubland, the villain was light years away.

'We'd like a photograph of Rachel,' said the sergeant when he had filled his notebook. Nadine removed the most recent one from a frame on the television.

'What did they say?' she asked when Harry had shown them out.

'They'll search the fields at dawn.'

17

THE MEN who were truly interested in money were never any good at sex, thought Suzanne Vanner as she sat at the back of her shop. A more potent obsession had taken over their minds and it seemed to occupy the same part of their brain that had once been filled with thoughts of bed. The great unquenchable love found a more enticing object of desire: the lust became a lust for money.

The conclusions were based on her own experiences but when she looked further afield they still seemed to stand up. Toby Beauchamp was accumulating a small fortune but had no time for women. One-cell Tel was so busy looking for women he had no time to earn money. The randy poor and the preoccupied rich.

Suzanne Vanner was interested in both sex and money and she wasn't getting enough of either. The account sheets in front of her proclaimed an unpleasant truth: the boutique was not attracting enough customers. She knew it already. In two hours the only caller had been the postman with a fistful of bills, and when he appeared tomorrow he would only bring more.

If this enterprise was going to collapse it would put her in a humiliating situation with her friends and an impossible one with her husband. It would not be a subject that he would relinquish easily. I earn it, you lose it. What *is* occurring?

She looked at Cathy Gray arranging some new stock on hangers in the window and realized that there was one economy she could make now. It didn't worry her – cavorting topless with the boss's husband had been a bad career move.

'This isn't working,' she said.

Cathy Gray stopped what she was doing. 'What isn't, Mrs Vanner?'

'The shop. The business. I can't afford you.'

'Do you mean you want me to leave?' Cathy Gray asked. She had been nervous of Suzanne Vanner ever since the ice-cream landed in the swimming pool.

'I'm afraid so, Cathy. You can see for yourself. There just isn't the business.'

'I know it's been bad. I thought it would improve.'

'So did I, but there's no sign of it. I'll give you a month's money.'

Cathy Gray stepped out of the window. She had felt uneasy on these premises since her walk with Paul Vanner. A month's paid holiday was an unexpected gift.

'Okay,' she said.

But when she had gone Suzanne Vanner began to feel worse. Problems seemed larger when you were on your own, and with no one to talk to there was nothing for her to do but stare at the depressing message of the figures. They told of steady losses with no reason to hope for a turn.

She sat for an hour without a single customer or telephoned inquiry. It had always been her ambition to own her own shop; it was something that she was quite capable of handling successfully. But opening it here had been an act of folly.

When she tried to think about something else her mind turned to the abortion. It had only taken fifteen minutes with a light general anaesthetic but the after-effects were more mental than physical. Dilation and evacuation, they called it. Nearly two hundred thousand women in Britain did it every year, and it had left her with an urgent desire to do the job properly and have a baby.

Bouncing between two unwelcome trains of thought she saw an escape. She would shut up the shop, just for today, and go and have a drink. The clothes on the racks – immaculate, expensive, unsold – seemed to be pressing in on her, chiding her for her poor judgement. She locked the door and stepped out into the sun with a feeling of relief.

The heatwave had continued and people who in the depths

of winter had cheered themselves up by booking summer holidays in the sun were now flying off reluctantly to places that were cooler than Britain.

Air-conditioning had not reached the Flatulent Ferret but a fan on the counter was doing its best. Sitting near it was Harry Grant, nursing a whisky. He looked up but didn't smile.

'Rachel's gone missing,' he said.

'Missing?'

'She disappeared last night and hasn't been seen since.'

'Oh, my God. Where's Nadine?'

'She won't leave home. She's hoping for a phone call.'

Suzanne Vanner sat down. 'How awful,' she said, feeling guilty at the comfort that came with the news that other people had problems too.

'I think she's waiting for a ransom demand,' said Harry Grant.

Suzanne Vanner looked at his whisky and decided to order one for herself. The turning fan sent cool air in her direction.

'You can't be serious,' she said.

Harry Grant looked like a man in need of sleep. 'Well,' he said, 'she's been gone seventeen hours.'

'What are the police doing?'

'Hunting. But they don't know where to look. Give me another Bell's, Barry.'

Barry produced another whisky and then went off to answer the phone on the wall. 'It's for you, Harry,' he called.

Suzanne Vanner was surprised at how quickly her first whisky had gone and decided to have another. She had made some progress with the second when Harry came back.

'That was Nadine. They've found Rachel's bike in a ditch by the side of the motorway.'

'What does that mean?'

'Damned if I know. Kidnapped, do you think?'

'Oh, surely not. Poor Nadine. First her husband and now this.'

A thoughtful silence filled the bar.

'Perhaps she hitched a lift?' said Barry.

There was no consolation in this suggestion. What sort of

person picked up a ten-year-old girl and drove off with her? And would a girl willingly leave her beloved bicycle lying in a ditch?

'The police, apparently, are going to issue her picture at three o'clock if she hasn't been found,' Harry said.

'It'll be on television then?' said Barry.

This prospect seemed to make the situation even more ominous.

'Have a drink on me,' said Barry. 'You two don't look that cheerful.'

Harry Grant wondered how he was going to handle the story. Nadine's hatred of publicity was known to him even before Rachel disappeared, and now she felt that stories in the newspaper would reflect badly on both her and her daughter.

'Publicity will help find her,' Harry told her, but Nadine couldn't see it. He had stayed with her until four o'clock when she had fallen asleep on the sofa, and crept back to his cottage to write his 'Village Notes' column – on the birds that came to Sin in the summer – which he had driven in to the office at six. At seven he went back to Nadine who, by this time, was making tea.

Now he felt dreadful with a head full of sawdust. He looked at the new whisky and thought that, at the very moment when he was going to be able to introduce himself to his daughter, and start to make up for all the sad, lost years, she had disappeared and could very well be dead.

He wanted to tell people that he was the father of the missing girl and not a disinterested observer of this appalling episode, but it was a revelation that would betray Nadine's biggest secret.

Suzanne Vanner, feeling her own miseries thoroughly eclipsed, decided that three whiskies had restored her sense of hope, and that four would probably make an even better job of it.

'Have one, Harry,' she said.

He covered his drink with his hand. 'Better not. I need a clear head. Give me a sandwich, Barry. This might be a long day.'

Suzanne drank the fourth whisky slowly and wished that she could show similar restraint. Before she opened the shop her drinking had begun to frighten her. Sometimes, when she ran out of alcohol, she was quite prepared to pour anything down her throat: Chinese tea, Coca-Cola, even cough mixture. And after a spell of solitary drinking she was at her most stupid. She remembered a crazy burst of expenditure in a department store, a carload of goods none of which she really wanted. She remembered One-cell Tel in the conservatory.

This wretched memory straightened her up, but then she looked at her nearly empty glass and decided that one more wouldn't hurt. She had better make it last.

'If there's anything I can do for Nadine,' she said. 'Tell her, will you?'

'Thanks,' said Harry. He was thinking that the motorway meant London. Nobody on earth knew how many children were murdered *there* every week. Many were not only never found, they were never missed.

Outside the sun beat down on the green where other children, now in the middle of their school holidays, were playing a game of rounders. Rachel should have been among them.

He turned to Suzanne Vanner but she was getting off her stool. It was just as well. He had never seen five whiskies disappear so quickly.

'I'm off,' she said. She didn't even seem tipsy. 'Give my love to Nadine.'

Suzanne Vanner had decided that she did want another drink but that any further drinking was best done at home. Outside she wobbled slightly in the bright sunshine and found that walking in a way that would not attract attention needed concentration. She walked past the car park and up the lane that led to the Manor House.

Men made money, she thought. Why should it be easier for them? They lolled about and got drunk and behaved like children for much of the time and yet the money rolled towards them in waves. They didn't know what to do with it. They bought clothes they never wore, books they never read, cars they never drove.

The Ferrari Daytona, all £300,000-worth of it, was ignored in the garage, silent testimony to her husband's earning power. It was never even discussed but just sat there, a huge and daring investment that nobody was allowed to touch.

When she had walked up the long drive she opened the garage door and had a look at it. Its shiny red chassis gleamed in the sun. She opened the driver's door and got in. She sat in it for a while and then she knew she had to drive it.

The keys were in the drawer by the side of Paul's bed; she went upstairs and found them, and then she changed her shoes and went down. If she drove it up to the motorway she could put her foot down and find out what was so special about this expensive machine, and she would have it back before he got home.

The engine started with a roar that would have alarmed her had she been sober, and the car came out of the garage more quickly than she had expected. She drove slowly down the drive, trying to get used to the controls, and then turned into the road. There was power in this car that only a motorway could satisfy. She drove past the Flatulent Ferret and imagined Harry Grant hearing the throaty roar outside.

She moved to brake as the car turned on to the bridge but the vehicle suddenly shot forward with terrifying power and hit the low balustrade with a force that lifted the back wheels off the ground. Suddenly she was in the air and going upwards and then she felt the car turn in the air and start to fall and she knew that they were both going to land in the river.

Flossing his teeth and snipping at pieces of hair with a pair of nail scissors, Neil Kennedy studied his tired face in the mirror. At thirty he still thought of himself as young but that wasn't the verdict of the mirror. His black curls, he fancied, were receding a little, and there were lines round his eyes that depressed him. In another, less stressful, job, where he didn't have to worry about where his next pay cheque was coming from, the years would probably have been easier on him, but then he wouldn't have got the part of a middle-aged husband in *Hot Air Rises*.

He was beginning to think that the series was exceptional after all. Millions of people who were addicted to those substitutes for real life, soap operas, would be hit between the eyes in the autumn by something more abrasive than their usual bland pap. As it gradually came together it seemed to be saying something original and provocative about marriage today. Denis had started to talk about winning awards.

Neil Kennedy could see himself granting interviews on the programme's message, expatiating knowingly to countless hacks on matrimony, 1990. Who was the woman writer who said that an actor without a script was like a dummy without a ventriloquist? Not this one, Julie Burchill.

He shaved with his new Grundig and applied some aftershave. He had changed from Chanel to Armani and felt that this had helped his image, although it was an improvement that would pass unnoticed by 10 million viewers. On the shelf in front of him were several empty tinfoil sheets that had recently held the headache tablets that Gwenda increasingly relied upon.

The cause of her demoralized state came into the bathroom.

'I had a dream,' she said.

'Did you, Martin Luther King? What about?'

'Dogs. Nasty dogs.'

'Why were they nasty?'

'They could talk. They said nasty things.'

'Oh, my goodness. What an awful dream.'

'No,' she said impatiently. 'That wasn't all of it.'

'What else happened, Lindy?'

'They had string.'

'String? What did they do with it?'

'Tied people up.'

They went downstairs. After much weekend filming this was a day off.

'Why don't we eat an Indian tonight?' he suggested.

'Are you talking about cannibalism or curries?' Gwenda asked from the coffee machine.

'I thought curries.'

'I don't like Indian food,' Gwenda said, offering him a

coffee. 'They only cover the meat with all that stuff because the meat is so awful, and it's awful because they haven't got decent grazing. Well, we have and we've got decent meat.'

'Got it. Anyone for fish and chips tonight?' He drank his coffee.

'The sandpit is a disaster,' said Gwenda, pouring a coffee for herself. 'Every cat in the village is using it as a lavatory. It's a danger to Lindy's health.'

He looked at his wife and wondered how different she would be if there was no Lindy to drain her vitality. When he had met her in the advertising agency one sunny spring morning she had been a sensible contrast to the flibbertigibbets he met in the theatre, a cheerful, admiring and sexy lady. They were not adjectives that anybody could use today.

'I'll fill it in,' he said. 'Or should I make a cover?'

'It's too late for a cover. It's already a lavatory.'

He finished his coffee and went out to find the spade. Marriage, he decided, was a question of hanging on. A plump PA on the set had evidently fallen in love with him, but to surrender to her malodorous embrace would require a desperation that he had not quite reached.

Lindy regarded the disappearance of the sandpit with equanimity; she was a girl of short-lived enthusiasms.

A long time afterwards, when the sand had been sprinkled round the edge of the garden and the pit was filled with soil again, she said: 'Take me for a walk, daddy. I want to look for fish in the river.'

As usual, she insisted on bringing a doll. She held it firmly in one hand while gripping his hand with the other. He loved the confident way that she now walked. He wondered what she was going to be when she grew up. He wondered what he was going to be when he grew up.

They came round from the Meadow Estate to the top of the green and walked down the side of it, past the supermarket, the post office, Suzanne's and the Refectory, the newsagent and the bank. On the green children were playing rounders.

'I'm going to have a baby,' said Lindy, withdrawing her hand from his to pat her stomach. 'I felt it move.'

'What are you going to call it?' he asked, wondering what post-modernist children's television programme had planted this idea in her head.

'Trimpy Doodle,' she replied immediately.

They heard the roar of the car as they stepped on to the bridge and then there was a red blur in front of them as the huge machine hurtled into the wall. He bent to scoop up his daughter, but the car was already past them and rearing into the air. She could have been killed, he thought, hugging her roughly as she stared wide-eyed at the cartwheeling Ferrari. And he still stood there, frozen by fear or relief, as the car vanished over the bridge.

'There's a woman in that car!' an old lady shouted.

He turned and saw Daisy Balcombe exercising a small white creature that was presumably some sort of dog. All he could see when he looked over the bridge was the bottom of the upside-down car with two of its wheels still spinning. He rushed to Daisy Balcombe and planted Lindy in her arms.

'Don't let go of her,' he shouted.

Then he got up on the bridge's low wall and jumped. It was only a 10-foot drop and the river was no more than 3 feet deep, but he stumbled and, for a moment, was totally submerged himself.

He dragged himself up and tried to open the driver's door, but it refused to move against the weight of the water. The window was open, though. Suzanne Vanner, her face registering pure pain, was struggling under the water with her seat belt. She succeeded in undoing it, and he took a deep breath and ducked under the water. He leaned in the window and got a hand in each armpit. At first he couldn't move her because her leg was caught but then she suddenly came with him and he had her standing up in the water beside him. She gasped and spluttered but couldn't speak. When he went to release his grip on her to wipe his own face she began to sink back into the water. Eventually he managed to lift her up and carry her to the river bank. She seemed to have lost consciousness and he laid her on the grass.

People had gathered on the bridge now to look down at this unexpected piece of drama.

'An ambulance is on the way,' somebody shouted, but Neil Kennedy was too busy checking on Suzanne Vanner's breathing to hear. He sat on the grass beside her feeling fairly ill himself. The taste of river water in his mouth was acrid. He probably needed a stomach pump.

Eventually people came down from the bridge to where he was sitting. Among them was Harry Grant, who had heard the noise from his bar stool.

'Jesus,' he said. 'That's the Daytona. What happened?'

Daisy Balcombe arrived, anxious to return the restless Lindy.

'Daddy jumped in the river with his clothes on,' said Lindy. 'What a silly billy.'

Suzanne Vanner opened her eyes. 'It's my back,' she said.

'You jumped in and got her out?' Harry asked.

Neil Kennedy nodded. Like Suzanne, he was soaked from head to foot and the riverside trees were keeping the sun from drying him.

'Just lie there, dear,' said Daisy Balcombe. It was quite clear to everybody else that no other option was being considered. She lay on her back with her eyes closed, her bedraggled hair spread across her forehead and her face a mask of pain. Daisy Balcombe's dog looked at her quizzically.

'Phone Paul,' she said without bothering to open her eyes.

'The car thought it was a plane,' said Lindy. 'It wanted to fly.'

Neil Kennedy looked at it in the river. It was obviously a write-off.

An ambulance arrived and parked on the bridge. Two men began to clamber down the river bank with a stretcher.

'"Actor Saves Woman In River",' said Harry Grant. 'I can't believe what's happening in this village.'

On the fourth floor of his London bank, Paul Vanner was staring at his three green screens and trying to work out what was happening to the dollar. There was a stand-off in the desert where the military forces of America and Britain were looking at the Iraqi army across the Saudi Arabian border. Soldiers who had flown half-way round the world were finding that their only battle was with the heat.

All this had depressed the dollar, but one news flash from the Middle East could shift it either way and the news was being monitored at least as tensely as in the Pentagon.

One of his number crunchers called: 'Watch it, the Fed's in!'

The Federal Reserve Bank of America moved in quickly when dollar dealing moved the price. It sold if the price was too high and bought if it was too low.

He punched up figures on his screen and was leaning forward to extract some conclusion from them when a female voice some yards away shouted 'Call, Paul.' A personal telephone call at work was discouraged and rare, and he picked the phone up almost guiltily.

'Neil Kennedy, Paul,' said the voice.

If he thought that he could heal their split with a call during working hours he had made a serious mistake, Vanner thought.

He said: 'I can't talk now.'

'This is serious, Paul,' said a very weary voice. 'It's Suzanne. She's had an accident.'

The dreaded word pulled him up.

'What sort of accident?'

'A car accident. She's in hospital.'

'How bad?' he asked quickly.

'She's damaged her spine.'

He pictured her in hospital. 'What the hell happened?'

'She crashed on the bridge and both she and the car landed in the river.'

'Oh my God! Was she drunk?'

'I've no idea, Paul. But she asked that I ring you. I think you ought to come.'

Vanner looked at the clock on the wall, the one that told the time in London.

'I suppose the Mercedes was a write-off?' he said.

There was a pause and he wondered if the connection had been broken. But then Kennedy's voice came back at him with its terrible news.

'She wasn't in her Mercedes, Paul. She was in your Daytona. And, yes, it is a write-off.'

'She was *what?*'

The scream rang round the bank floor, disturbing obsessed young men who were constructing huge dollar–mark and dollar–yen deals in the most difficult circumstances. Angry faces turned in his direction.

'It wasn't insured,' he shouted.

'Not insured?'

'Only fire and theft. I wasn't going to risk it on the road.'

'I'm sorry, Paul,' said Neil Kennedy, but this time the line had gone dead.

Paul Vanner was banging his head on his desk with such force that somebody jumped up to restrain him. There was blood on his nose and tears in his eyes.

'The bitch has written off my Daytona,' he said, when they could get some sense out of him. 'I've got a three-hundred-grand debt and no asset.'

18

Men's Hour that Sunday in the Flatulent Ferret was a solemn occasion.

Men who habitually used the event to assert, if only to themselves, their robust untrammelled masculinity, looked for the most part like victims of a pack-rape or, at the very least, martyrs to post-partum depression.

Toby Beauchamp sat on his stool in jeans and a matching denim shirt looking like an out-of-work film director who had just heard that the money had run out.

His enthusiasm for a lethal cocktail of whisky and tablets had waned a little as the days passed, but the thought still crossed his mind over breakfast. Suicide was an early morning activity. The will strengthened as the grey day lengthened. By evening it was even possible to nurture hopes about tomorrow. But in the morning the bleak reality was overwhelming again, as he imagined himself locked up in a small room for several years with two violent and unwashed degenerates.

He knew now how wise the police had been to demand his passport as a condition of bail. If that priceless little document was still in his possession both he and it would already be in Rio de Janeiro. But the world was playing cat and mouse with him and all he could do was wait.

Paul Vanner looked like a man who had been hit on the back of the head by a falling oak but had pluckily refused to go down. He stared glassily in front of him, reluctant to meet anybody's gaze, and thought about money and how to get it.

He was committed now to paying £20,000 every year for the next ten years, plus an agreed and preferential 10 per cent interest which lifted his total debt from £200,000 to

£310,000 – all for the privilege of being the former owner of some Italian scrap metal. The £100,000 of his own money that he had put into the car purchase was gone for ever.

He had tried to tell Suzanne this when he had arrived at the hospital in a cold sweat, but it had been a serious error of judgement. Strapped into some sort of frame while doctors examined her twisted spine, she whispered: 'Are you talking about *money?*' The frowns from the men in white coats conveyed the depth of their contempt for him and he left the hospital in a hurry to buy his wife a bouquet of flowers.

Initially anxious to talk, to unburden himself temporarily of the worries created by his disaster, he had opened Men's Hour by delivering a compendious account of his woes which would have brought tears to a glass eye; but in a bar where misfortune had sought out most of them with the diligence of a Silkworm missile, there was only Neil Kennedy to console him.

He discovered that there were few things more depressing than somebody determined to cheer you up.

Harry Grant sat on his stool as tense as a hunted cat. The previous evening he had turned on the television and seen his daughter's face. It was the photograph that Nadine had given the police, and now the police were appealing for the public's help. Rachel Kirby, aged ten, still missing. She was wearing . . .

It had made unbearably real something that still had the gauze-like quality of a nightmare. Nadine had become a prisoner in her own house, refusing to move for reasons that multiplied daily. Originally they had been that Rachel might appear – or phone. Then she thought a kidnapper might phone. After that she couldn't face the neighbours with their implied criticism of her carelessness. Now she was just too tired to go out.

Harry did her shopping and sat with her during the lonely vigil, trying occasionally to cheer her up with his jokes. When she complained about lying awake all night he told her that insomnia was not worth losing sleep over but she was in no mood to laugh.

He had hidden from her the copy of Friday's *County Gazette* that carried Rachel's two-column picture on the front page, just inches away from another picture of a Ferrari in a river. He didn't tell her what people had said.

What people had said was that if the story was to have a happy ending Rachel would have to turn up within forty-eight hours of her disappearance. Forty-eight hours was the popular time limit for her safe return. After that period the chances that something terrible had happened increased exponentially and hope diminished on a balancing scale. Today was Day Five.

And so he sat in the bar, his stomach in a knot, waiting for the news to hit him, waiting for the telephone call that he dreaded more than he had ever dreaded anything in his life.

Neil Kennedy, who did not regard his life as problem-free, was, in this company, beginning to see it as unbroken euphoria. And in the autumn he would be famous again.

Paul Vanner emerged from his reverie to tell him: 'I owe you, pal. You saved her life.'

Kennedy laughed. 'I thought I owed you?'

'Forget it. Forget what I said about the poker. We're square. I don't think Daisy Balcombe could have done what you did. She'd have drowned in the car.'

'How is she?'

'She's going to be all right. She thought she was going to end up in a wheelchair at first, but the back's only twisted and what she needs is rest.'

'Well, cheer up then. Life goes on.'

'So does death,' said Harry Grant. 'Did any of you see Rachel's picture on television?'

They had all seen it and reached their own conclusions about how it was going to end. Nobody had any hope to offer and were uncomfortable at the subject being discussed.

Barry, the landlord, who was accustomed to ribald jokes on a Sunday morning, felt as if his premises had been hired for a wake. When One-cell Tel and Barney wandered in he greeted them like long-lost friends, confident that here at least was normality and the possibility of a smile.

'Buy 'em all drinks,' said Barnaby Barton. 'I'm not having people calling me a miser.'

Barry, relieved, filled everybody's glass to muffled murmurs of 'Cheers, Barney'.

'It's not drinks this lot need,' said Neil Kennedy. 'It's electro-convulsive therapy.'

'I can remember when Men's Hour used to be fun,' said Toby Beauchamp, gripping his new vodka.

'You'll find prison a bag of laughs in comparison,' Vanner told him. The idea knocked Toby back in his shell and half-remembered television pictures of three men in a cell returned to haunt him.

'My God, you people think you've got problems,' said Harry Grant suddenly from the gloomy isolation of his stool. 'Well, let me tell you something.' He turned to face them. 'Rachel is *my* daughter. I'm her father. It was supposed to be a secret but it doesn't look as if it matters now.'

When they all stared at him in disbelief they saw that he had tears in his eyes.

On Wednesday evening Paul Vanner and Harry Grant sat side by side in ancient deck-chairs at the front of the cricket pavilion. It was Compton Sinbury's annual match with the council.

Vanner was on a week's holiday, his first of the year. He should by now have been comfortably ensconced with Suzanne in a quiet hotel in Lamorna Cove, not far from Land's End, but the business on the bridge had changed all that. Now he was spending a week on his own and rediscovering the pleasures of selfishness.

The previous evening he had invited Toby Beauchamp round for a game of snooker. Toby's situation seemed to be even worse than his own and he hoped that mixing with a man who was on the edge of an abyss might make his own predicament seem less grim. It had worked for a while. Toby had talked dismally about his forthcoming appearance in court, when he expected to be sent for trial, and Vanner had contrasted this with his own little difficulties which only involved money. But their respective concerns produced an uncontrollable thirst; by the third frame they were both so drunk that they could scarcely remember what it was that they were worrying about in the first place.

Now, sitting in the sun and watching cricket on the green, it was hard to believe that anything could interfere with such an idyllic existence. No doubt somewhere to the south, where the eastern Mediterranean washed up against the shores of half-a-dozen unhappy countries, there were corpses in the street, paramilitary repression, tracer fire and tanks – in fact, by now there could be H-bombs over Baghdad – but that wasn't what life was supposed to be about.

This was what life was supposed to be about.

He looked at Harry Grant, padded up and ready to bat, and asked: 'How did you manage to keep a secret like that for ten years, Harry?'

'With great difficulty. Journalists are great blabbermouths. Their instinct is to spill beans.'

'And Rachel still doesn't know?'

Harry Grant shook his head. He was grateful to hear Vanner refer to her as if she was still alive: the police were now giving the impression that they were looking for a body and not a girl.

'It's exactly a week,' he said. 'Wednesday evening last week was when she went.'

He was prevented from conducting a maudlin discussion about the significance of this period by a shout from the wicket and the sight of an incoming batsman. He stood up and picked up his bat.

'Put your best foot forward,' said Paul Vanner.

'Better foot,' said Harry. 'Only two feet.'

He walked out to the wicket for what turned out to be a brief stay. A new councillor, Armstrong, was sending down some lethal stuff. His first ball reared and knocked Harry's cap off; his second removed two stumps.

'That's the bastard who got Toby into trouble,' he said as he met Paul Vanner on the way out.

'He didn't do you much good, either.'

'Hammer the sod.'

Paul Vanner's approach to batting owed more to baseball than to cricket; it made his innings a popular spectacle. He lifted the first ball into the duck pond and put the second through the post-office window which carried a police poster showing Rachel's face. Armstrong glowered and remeasured his run. It was the last ball of his over and Vanner hooked it on to the pavilion roof. When he faced the bowling again, after a quick run by his partner, he was delivered a very slow ball by a bald, middle-aged spinner. It travelled so slowly that he was having his second attempt to hit it when it dislodged his bail.

He reached the pavilion to find that his deck-chair had been taken by Cathy Gray.

'How's Suzanne?' she asked.

'Hallo,' he said. 'She's coming along okay.'

Cathy Gray was wearing very short white shorts and a man's shirt with a lot of buttons undone. He took off his pads, found another deck-chair and pulled it as close to her as he dared.

On her other side Harry Grant was scribbling in a note-book.

'"A bright and breezy 18 runs off three balls by city executive Paul Vanner was the highlight of the Compton Sinbury innings. He lofted new Labour councillor Darren Armstrong into the village duck pond off the first ball and then hit him through the post-office window. Back in the pavilion afterwards, canoodling with sultry village sexpot Cathy Gray, 25, he said –"'

'I could utilize a bonk tonight.'

'"Cathy, who is reputed to strip naked when she mows the lawn at her home on the Colemore Estate, said –"'

'I like the way you wield that thing.'

'"It is understood that she was referring to Mr Vanner's expertise with a cricket bat, although, as usual with the delightful Miss Gray, the remark was freighted with ambiguity."'

'You earn a living writing like that?' Vanner asked.

'It beats going to work,' Harry told him.

The captain of the council team, discouraged by the treatment Armstrong had received from Paul Vanner, had replaced him with a gentler bowler and now the village batsmen were steadily accumulating the runs they needed to win. When it was over Harry Grant left immediately to see Nadine, and Vanner found himself alone with Cathy.

'Do you fancy a game of tennis?' he suggested.

'Your place or your place?'

'My place.'

'Sock it to me.'

He didn't really want to play tennis but it gave his invitation a respectability that it wouldn't otherwise have had. And when they reached the Manor House he duly found the rackets and balls.

'Your wife sacked me,' she said as they walked on to the court.

'It's very sad, but the shop isn't taking the money.'

'It's too up-market. Her stuff is too expensive.'

Interested as he was in this diagnosis of the shop's problems, Paul Vanner had more pressing things on his mind.

'I suppose with a chest like that topless tennis is out of the question?'

Cathy Gray laughed. It wasn't going to be just tennis after all. Suzanne Vanner could sack her, but seducing her husband was adequate revenge.

'We could always swim afterwards,' she said.

The following day Paul Vanner drove his remaining Ferrari into the hospital car park and felt a resurgence of hope. A week off work had given him time to think and he wasn't a man to waste time when money was involved. He had a plan. He could get his money back if he had the nerve! He could get his money back if he was prepared to take a risk!

He parked the Ferrari next to a grey Japanese answer to the Range Rover and climbed out whistling.

Suzanne was sitting up in bed in a blue nightdress.

'I walked today,' she said.

The big open-plan ward was a surprisingly cheerful place with large windows offering views of green fields. The patients had not been immobilized by anything serious, but were all making steady recoveries from physical injuries brought about, in most cases, by their own carelessness.

'You walked? Wonderful. When are you coming home?'

'The doctor says Monday. The back needs a bit more rest.'

'That's terrific. You look good.'

She was surprised at how cheerful he was. There was enough about, God knew, to produce one of his sourest moods – the fate of the Daytona, the failure of the shop, the debts they both faced over these two calamities – but instead he had the easy-going attitude of a man who had lost a pound bet.

'I saw Rachel on television again last night,' she said. 'There's no news then?'

He sat on the edge of her bed, plotting his financial recovery. He could hardly concentrate on what she was saying.

'No news is bad news,' he replied eventually.

'Poor Nadine.'

'Poor Harry. He's Rachel's father.'

'Her father?'

'Apparently. Harry and Nadine used to be close.'

'And Felix never knew?'

'A village called Sin.'

A small Irish nurse appeared with a cup of tea.

'All right, Mrs Vanner?' she asked.

'Fine, Terry,' Suzanne told her, taking the tea. Her husband seemed distracted and she wondered what was on his mind. The deliberate avoidance of the Daytona gave their conversation an unreal air. 'How have you been spending your holiday?' she asked.

'I've been very sporty. Cricket last night against the council, tennis and snooker with Toby.' He wanted it to sound as if the tennis had been with Toby, too, but she didn't pick it up.

'It's done you good,' she said. 'You're losing your city pallor.'

It hadn't been his complexion he was thinking of when he made love to Cathy in the pool last night, but it was good to know that he looked better for it. He handed his wife some magazines he had bought that concentrated on homes and gardens, her favourite reading. When he left with a kiss on the forehead she settled down to study them, but couldn't stop thinking about Harry Grant being Rachel Kirby's father. The duplicity of people who had seemed so straightforward always came as a surprise to her.

Paul Vanner walked out of the ward thinking about money. He had decided after his first visit not to mention the ruined Ferrari as long as she was in hospital, and now he scarcely wanted to. A loss today, a gain tomorrow. In the money market you didn't waste time thinking about the past.

He strolled down the hospital's long corridor planning a financial coup that would solve all his problems. He would go outside his limits, spend far more than he was supposed to, make a fortune and his reward would come with his bonus. It was against the rules, but it wasn't dishonest.

He could see it all so vividly that he was slow to realize that he was following a pair of legs. They belonged to Terry the nurse, and although her uniform concealed most of them, the part that he could see looked most promising. The face was arresting, too. There really was something about Irish eyes.

He began to wonder what stifled passions Cathy Gray had released. He hadn't been distracted by young girls like this since – well, since he got married.

He caught her up and she turned and smiled at him.

'Your wife's coming along well,' she said.

'Coming out Monday, she tells me.'

'That's right. But I expect she'll be back soon. She seems to like it here.'

'Does she?' he asked, surprised. He couldn't imagine Suzanne enjoying the restrictions and regulations of life in a hospital ward.

'Well,' said Terry, with a smile and a shrug, 'she keeps coming back.'

Paul Vanner was quite used to oblique conversations with people from Ireland in which intentions were deduced and meanings grabbed hopefully from thin air but this time he was stymied. He smiled at the pretty nurse in a way that he hoped would invite clarification.

'You know,' she said shyly. 'The abortion.'

'The abortion,' he said neutrally.

'That was only about six weeks ago. She's becoming quite a regular customer.'

'You'd better keep her bed aired,' said Vanner and walked out to his car.

19

ONE-CELL TEL had done many foolish things in his life, most of them related to women. As a Wolf Cub he had rolled round on the floor in the hope of looking up Akela's skirt. As a teenager, unsure of what to expect on his first momentous date, he had put aftershave on his testicles before dancing a tarantella of agony in the steamy privacy of his bathroom. As an adult he had stripped naked on a girlfriend's front doorstep only to have the door opened by her father who was supposed to be in Germany.

But nothing now in retrospect quite matched the lunacy of the golden phallus. The thought of it preyed on his mind. The plan had misfired – or not fired at all – for instead of arousing the carnal appetite of a beautiful woman who was desperate to be introduced to the functioning prototype, its dispatch had been met by a wall of apathy.

Now, finally convinced that it was not going to achieve its ambitious objective, he worried about where it might appear. He imagined angry women brandishing it in the street, policemen at his front door and, worst of all, the ownership passing to his furious mother.

He had to get it back.

Cathy Gray no longer worked in Suzanne's and didn't seem to have found another job. He had heard her playing records and watched her strolling aimlessly down the road.

Often, with a frontal façade that exactly matched the golden model, he watched open-mouthed as she mowed the lawn, before masturbating ferociously into a voluminous bath towel that was now as stiff as a barrister's collar and could be leant against the wall like a piece of plasterboard.

On Monday morning when Mrs Gray had departed for the

shops with a basket on her arm, he stepped over the low wooden fence that separated their front gardens and knocked on her front door.

Cathy Gray had been washing her hair and was about to dry it in the garden. This involved sunbathing, and all she was wearing when she opened the door was a pink towel. She was surprised to see her next-door neighbour standing on the step: they had still managed not to speak.

'Hallo, Terry,' she said.

One-cell Tel stared at the cleavage which the towel couldn't conceal, and emitted a guttural yowl which he hoped would be construed as a greeting.

'Sent you something,' he said eventually.

Cathy Gray was feeling playful. When you spent your time hanging around at home any distraction was welcome, even daytime television.

'What was that, Terry?' she asked.

One-cell Tel remembered a John Wayne film. 'I've come to fetch my toy,' he told her.

Cathy Gray gave her towel a little pull. 'I think you'd better come in. I can't stand at the door dressed like this.'

One-cell Tel followed her into the house, a mirror image of his own. The towel rode up as she walked, revealing an inch of bottom, and his jeans began to feel uncomfortable. She led him into the dining room which seemed to be the living room as well with two armchairs and a television, and a table and chairs where she ate with her mother.

She sat on the table and his view now was of brown thighs vanishing into a pink towel.

'What was it that you sent, Terry?' she asked innocently.

One-cell Tel's life was a constant search for words but in this context they proved particularly elusive. He looked at her and he looked at the floor and he tried to remember the word that people had come to use these days.

'My willy,' he said triumphantly.

Cathy Gray's eyebrows rose. 'Your willy? You sent me your willy? That was bloody sporting of you.'

'It was golden,' he said. 'I made it myself.'

'Ah, yes. I remember. You didn't put your name to it.'

'I forgot.'

'So how do I know that it's yours?'

'I made it for you. I laid in a bucket.'

Cathy Gray looked at him. 'You laid in a bucket? Do you mean it's an exact replica of you?'

One-cell Tel thought that he understood this and nodded, smiling broadly.

'I can hardly believe that, Terry. I don't know much about these things but it seemed awfully big to me.'

'It's me,' he said, faintly aggrieved. Suddenly he was tugging at the zip on his jeans and the next moment a protuberant penis was produced for her appraisal. She stared at it fascinated, and it grew larger as she looked.

'I've seen smaller ones on a horse,' she admitted.

Her thoughtful manner as she studied the exhibit reminded One-cell Tel of an expert on the Antiques Roadshow television programme. He moved towards her and got hold of her towel which he pulled down to reveal her breasts.

'Stop that, Terry,' she said, jumping up. 'And you can put that thing away now. It got 9.8 from the Romanian judge.'

One-cell Tel could not believe that he was being dismissed. This was a girl who had seemed to advertise her availability. He looked at her uncertainly, but her expression did not encourage him. Perhaps, like many girls, she needed persuading, but he could not forget that his mother was on the other side of this thin wall, and persuasion was never peaceful. He looked down at his proudest possession which, not knowing that it had been rejected, was still rampantly enthusiastic about the way that things were going.

'It's definitely a match,' said Cathy Gray. 'Do I gather you want to take my present back?'

He nodded, not trusting himself to speak.

She left the room and went to find her blue handbag where she had kept the golden phallus ever since it arrived.

But when she opened the bag it had gone. She had lost it. It had rolled out of the bag once too often and she hadn't even noticed.

She hurried back to give her visitor this bad news. He was trying to stuff the bloated original back in his jeans before dashing home to the tacit acquiescence of his bath towel.

On that Monday morning Paul Vanner returned to work from his holiday with a plan clearly formed in his head. Huge amounts of money were made in this office and today some of it would be his. There was a bonus coming up and if he could pull off one very big deal the extra money would get him out of his financial quagmire.

For some time there was nothing he could do. In New York it was the middle of the night. He wrote a reference for a dealer who was leaving. You will be a lucky man if he agrees to work for you, he wrote. He never did a stroke for me, he wanted to add.

At eleven thirty he went out. There was a lull in trading because it was lunchtime on the continent and the Americans wouldn't start work until one o'clock, London time. He went into the City Circle for some red wine. He was normally careful about his lunchtime drinking but today a certain nervousness increased his thirst. He didn't bother to check where the wine had come from but there was no question about where it was going. Soon the bottle was almost empty.

He felt slightly drunk and decided to get out. He needed a clear head today: he was working for himself. He dropped into a hamburger bar for something to soak up the wine. Suzanne was endlessly critical of his affection for junk food but he told her that he was interested in salaries not calories, deals not meals.

The deal today involved buying far more dollars than he was allowed to, because every available source of information – and he relied on many – told him that the dollar, hit by the American intervention in the Gulf, was going to start going up again. By the time he had sold them at an enormous profit nobody was going to be too upset that he had strayed beyond his limit, and the profit would be reflected in his bonus.

He sat at his screen. All round him people were communicating through phone, telex or voice box and nobody was interested in what he was up to. In a matter of minutes he had bought 60 million dollars at 1.55. His limit was 20 million dollars. In exchange for the dollars he had sold 93 million marks. He sat back tensely and waited. The wine made him feel dreadfully sleepy.

Williams said: 'The Dow's opened a hundred points down and is sliding.'

Paul Vanner looked across at Williams, another number cruncher from the East End who actually wore red braces and white socks. A tendency to believe the last thing he had heard made Williams an unreliable source of news, but looking at the screens in front of him Vanner saw that it was true. Now he had to wait to see whether, if the Dow Jones was going down, the dollar would follow.

Players in the forex market have nerves of steel, he told himself. In spot trading there was no room for hedging risks. At the same time he was aware that, although he had endured some alarming moments in the past, nothing equalled this. He wanted to turn this money round quickly, not sit here all afternoon with 60 million dollars exposed.

When the dollar dropped to 1.54 he began to feel slightly sick. When it reached 1.53 his hands began to shake and he had to sit on them so that no one would notice. Should he sell and take the loss, or wait for a revival in the fortunes of the dollar and risk a bigger one? Whatever he did he had to behave normally and not attract attention to what he was doing.

He went over to the coffee machine and wondered whether his gait betrayed the wine. The coffee tasted dreadful, but his body desperately needed fluids. When he got back to his desk the dollar stood at 1.52.

This time he knew he had to act. The dollar was on a one-way journey today and the experts, not for the first time, had been proved wrong.

He checked to see whether there were any international economic statistics that were due to be released today which might arrest its decline, but there was nothing. He was a master of misjudgement and he was looking at a disaster that could only get worse.

He plunged in and discovered that the dollar had dropped another cent even while he was thinking. He sold with professional coolness at 1.51 and picked up his pocket calculator. He had sold the dollars for 90,600,000 marks, a loss of 2.4 million marks!

He had lost 1,550,000 dollars!

His future was no longer in doubt. He sat and stared at one of the computer terminals as if it were a soap on television. The shouting and the feverish activity that were going on all round him were no longer his concern. There was a hallucinatory quality about the artificial excitement – the shouts, the gestures, the expletives and the groans which were what passed for normal behaviour in this office and were now another world. They had a phrase, as tortured as many of their other phrases, for the situation that he was in: negative employee retention.

It had been a hard journey from the council house in Stepney to this temple of greed and ambition, and the years of effort that had brought him to this pinnacle had been wasted in a few minutes of madness. But he wasn't as surprised as he might have been. Spot dealers walked a tightrope every working minute and the possibility of a fall from grace was always at the back of their minds. The shock was smaller, too, because his head was anaesthetized by the wine.

'Are you okay, Paul?' somebody asked, noticing his lack of activity.

'Stomach,' he said. He would have to go to the toilet now to give his complaint some credibility. The toilet was just about the only acceptable reason for leaving the floor. As he walked across the room he stumbled and began to wonder whether he really was drunk.

He locked himself in a cubicle and then leaned against the wall. He didn't even want to go to the toilet, but the peace out here was a welcome relief from the strange glances and little green screens. He tried to think clearly about his desperate situation and whether there was a way out of it but the wine did not help clear thinking. For a while he sat on the toilet, fully dressed and head in hands, but then realized that he was dangerously close to falling asleep. A faulty fluorescent light flickered on and off above his head. He went out and threw cold water over his face.

When he got back to his desk there was a yellow note asking him to see the Treasurer.

Arnold Schnabel was a mature family man who disproved the media myth that this was a world where participants burned out early. He had spent ten years as a dealer before reaching his present position, but he was still a dealer at heart. Every night he took home with him the small Reuters machine which gave him the latest news on major exchange rates, and he was in his office at seven o'clock like everybody else. He had grey hair brushed back over his ears and the clipped accent of an army officer. His obsession was owls on postage stamps, and he was reputed to have three hundred of them.

When Vanner entered his office he waved at the seat in front of his desk with a gesture that meant 'sit down'.

He said: 'Your wastepaper basket costs the bank £50 a year.' He was referring to the square-foot rental of the space it occupied.

'I know,' said Vanner.

'Employing you is an expensive business and we expect a return. Are you drunk?'

Vanner shook his head in case his speech was slurred.

'Your eyes say you are. Why did you do it, Mr Vanner?'

'Why did I do what?'

'Take a large position outside your limits.'

'I took a punt.'

'Outside your limits.'

'I'm afraid so.'

Arnold Schnabel leaned back and folded his arms, and then, as if he was in a corner from which there was no escape, he raised his eyebrows and shrugged.

'Well, I have to sack you, Mr Vanner, as you well know,' he said. 'I'm not sacking you because you lost 1.5 million dollars. I'm sacking you because, one, you were outside your limits and, two, you're drunk.'

Vanner stood up. There was no point in prolonging the conversation, particularly as he had nothing to say. He had known half an hour ago that he would have to endure this little ritual, and all he wanted now was to get out without the embarrassment of talking to his colleagues.

Luckily they were far too busy to say goodbye. He slipped into the street with his briefcase, glad to have escaped without fuss. In Moorgate it was another sunny day.

Arnold Schnabel would go home to his wife and family, his job secure, his huge salary still pouring into a provincial bank account. The Arnold Schnabels of this world never took a large position outside their limits. They cruised through the day like a robot and then went home to look at the owls on their postage stamps.

Vanner had managed to develop a considerable antipathy towards Arnold Schnabel by the time he caught his train. What sort of name was Schnabel, anyway?

But on the train he began to feel frightened. The soothing effects of the wine were beginning to recede and reality was poking its head in again. The future that he now faced was too horrifying to contemplate for long, however: the mortgage, the debt on the car, the secret abortion, the failed shop. The prospect of greeting Suzanne with his fresh bad news when she came home from hospital this evening meant that his terrible future was going to start quite soon.

He picked up his evening newspaper to take his mind off it. A headline on the front page said RACHEL: DAY 12.

Toby Beauchamp knew he was getting old: he bought shoes that you could slip on without having to bend to tie up. He knew, moreover, that he was getting old quickly: his mirror told him so.

On the Tuesday morning that he was to appear in the magistrates' court he spent more time than usual on his appearance, brushing his hair, combing his moustache, burnishing his rural gentleman image. It might not impress the magistrates but he would probably be mistaken for one of them by everybody else when he arrived at court.

He left his cleaning lady Mrs Hockley with Hoover at full blast and went out to his Porsche. Driving along the country lanes he couldn't bear to think about the day that lay before him, and he thought instead about his lost love, Miranda. She was such a fiercely ambitious lady that she would probably turn out to be one of the magistrates. A pretty young woman on horseback waved gratefully as he slowed down; he wondered whether she would have behaved differently had she known his destination.

The court-house was a new redbrick building on the edge of the town. Britain was packed with new court-house buildings when all the evidence suggested that what it actually needed was new prisons; but, of course, magistrates sat in court-houses and only prisoners sat in prisons.

Toby went into the courtroom and slipped unobtrusively into an empty public seat. At one end of the room three magistrates, none of them Miranda, sat at a table on a platform that placed them several feet higher than anyone else. The message on the wall behind them said DIEU ET MON DROIT. To Toby, it sounded like an expletive.

Down among the lawyers he could see his young smoothie solicitor Gavin Riley, newly browned by a fortnight on the Istrian peninsula.

The case in progress concerned a young man who was accused of being drunk in charge of a motorbike. A policeman had found him sound asleep on his bike in a hedge with the engine still running.

'When I woke him he said "What's that up there?" I told him it was the main road, and he said "Just what I was looking for" and roared off,' said the policeman. 'He was later arrested in a ditch.'

He was followed into the dock by a wretched old pseud who was striving to be recognized at his own inflated valuation of himself but who was handicapped in this objective by the fact that he was accused of indecent exposure. Tears rolled down his cheeks as the court listened to his story.

The chairman of the magistrates was a woman who, it seemed to Toby, had a face like a bucket. Impossibly, her mouth seemed to be wider than her head. She took what

Toby regarded as an unnecessarily prurient interest in whether the man had an erection but then he gathered that it was an intrinsic part of the case. Without one, it was a much milder charge, insulting behaviour rather than indecent exposure. On the evidence of a bird-like schoolteacher, the magistrates decided that neither the defendant nor the indecency case stood up which somehow made his situation doubly galling. He was fined on the lesser charge.

As an amused constable shepherded the whimpering flasher to the cash department, Gavin Riley made his way down the court towards Toby.

'I'm going out for a fag and a fart,' he whispered. 'Your case won't be up yet.'

'I'll come with you,' said Toby.

Outside in the sunshine Gavin Riley lit a cigarette but did not, so far as Toby could tell, break wind.

'I spend my life looking into the black heart of man,' he said cheerfully.

'Flashers and burglars and drunks,' said Toby. 'Very edifying.'

'And then there are people like you which raises the tone of the whole business.' He tapped a gold ring on Toby's finger. 'In this violent age an expensive ring on your finger could result in the painful loss of a finger.' It was as if Gavin Riley would talk about anything rather than the important matter in hand. Toby wondered whether he was embarrassed by the hopeless nature of his case. Well, he could remedy that.

'Where do we stand, Gavin?' he asked.

Gavin Riley exhaled cigarette smoke thoughtfully through his nose. He didn't look a day over thirty.

'I'm going to argue that this was the way it worked and if you didn't play ball you'd be left behind by the others and never get permission to build anything.'

'That should go down like a cup of cold vomit.'

'It's the only mitigating plea we have.'

'Said Riley wryly.'

'I'm glad you can joke, Toby. Frankly, I think you're in a dire position.'

'I know it.'
'But you'll have the best defence that money can buy.'
'We couldn't bribe anyone, I suppose?'
Gavin Riley gave a dutiful laugh and threw his cigarette on the ground.
'We'd better get back in. Of course nothing is going to happen today. The prosecution will outline the case and then ask for it to be sent to the Crown Court for trial, and the magistrates will agree.'
'Is that what we want?'
'It's what everybody wants. The prosecution want it because the maximum sentence the magistrates can impose is six months and the Crown Court can give seven years. And we want it because a jury of twelve good men and true is more amenable to reason than three reactionary, boneheaded magistrates.'
They went back into court just in time.
'Toby Alfred Beauchamp,' the clerk called.
Toby rose and was beckoned forward. Six charges were read out. The prosecuting lawyer stood up and talked a lot about the *Prevention of Corruption Act 1906*. Gavin Riley scribbled notes. The woman chairman sat, chin in hand, gazing at the prosecuting counsel as if she would like to provide him with some sexual service. Toby Beauchamp sat on a chair in the dock feeling ignored.
Half an hour later, bail renewed but passport refused, he was driving home – a man awaiting trial.

20

The apostasy of Owen Gray was an idea that had yet to crystallize when he sat at his desk in the vicarage the following morning reading a magazine article about the celestial sphere. The burden of an apathetic parish was only made tolerable by these regular appointments with outer space.

There were more missionaries with more money than ever before, but who today was motivated by a fear of God? Some villagers still sought solace in religion, but another far larger contingent looked for it in the Flatulent Ferret.

The thought was no sooner formed than it was followed by another: he must go down to the pub with the funny nickname and meet some of the parishioners who preferred the sustenance that it provided. If it wasn't exactly Jesus mingling with the sinners, it would at least provide him with the chance to meet some non-churchgoers. And who knows? Perhaps next week, or the week after, there would be fresh faces gazing up at him as he stood in the pulpit.

He left the vicarage and walked down the green past the duck pond, not knowing quite what to expect. Respectful neighbours and their Chardonnay-drinking wives? Lost souls in need of redemption? Ungodly whispers about combinatorial coupling? Hostility?

In the event there was only one person in the bar at this early hour, and for a moment he hesitated at the door, wondering whether his mission was worthwhile. But the man behind the counter was already saying good morning and a departure now would be even more embarrassing than his arrival. He asked the barman for a whisky, a drink he often had one of at the end of the day.

The solitary customer was a big man with a heavy face and short black hair. He was wearing old paint-flecked trousers and a short-sleeved red shirt, and he was drinking whisky rather quickly. Astonishingly, for the hour of day, he already looked drunk.

'Another,' he said to the barman without bothering to look in his direction. 'Are you here to make money or what?' He took the drink and turned on his stool to face the only company he had. 'A vicar in the Flatulent Ferret! What *is* occurring?'

'It's all part of my parish,' said Owen Gray with a nervous smile. 'And you are?'

'Paul Vanner. I know your sister.'

Carnally, I expect, thought Owen Gray, but he felt it best not to discuss Cathy.

'I decided it was time I met a few people,' he said. 'And more of them seem to come in the building at the bottom of the green than the one at the top.'

Vanner believed that all churchmen were mad – lights on, but nobody at home.

'I've never really discovered what vicars are for,' he told the new arrival amiably.

'They're here to help people with their problems,' said Owen Gray with a smile. This was a mistake.

Vanner drank some more whisky and his face lost a little of its colour. 'Problems?' he snarled. 'Well, cop hold of this lot. I've got a half-million-pound mortgage and I've lost my job. My wife has just written off my £300,000 car which wasn't insured. Her business is going bust, and she's just had an abortion I knew nothing about. If you're going to tell me that God moves in a mysterious way, I'll move you in a mysterious way.'

This was not the sort of conversation that Owen Gray had expected at all and he licked his lips nervously. Retracting his tongue, he suggested: 'You've been dealt an awful hand.'

'After you with the platitudes, vicar,' Vanner said, emptying his glass.

'Can I buy you a drink?'

'Why don't you turn the water into whisky and save us all a few bob?'

Owen Gray had hoped for something less contentious. Where was the traditional village gaiety? Where was the bucolic bliss? He ordered two whiskies and felt like an ice-cream salesman in January.

The previous evening he had called on Mrs Kirby to sympathize with her over her missing daughter but Harry Grant had appeared at the door to say that she didn't want to see him. His new drunken friend was obviously the man from the Manor House whose Ferrari went over the bridge. Terrible things were happening in the village and the church was no help.

He said: 'You have to look at your problems in a larger context. A fifth of the world is suffering from malnutrition, thousands are locked up without hope of release and hundreds are bombed, shelled or shot every day. If you live in the Manor House in Compton Sinbury you've got a lot to be grateful for.'

'What a lucky little bugger I am,' said Paul Vanner. 'I can't think what I'm complaining about. I'll sell the house and get a tepee, replace the Ferrari with a yak-skin coracle and live on nuts.'

'Weeping may endure for a night, but joy cometh in the morning. Psalms. But I don't suppose you read the book.'

'Leave it out, pal, I saw the movie. Charlton Heston, wasn't it?' Vanner picked up the whisky that Owen Gray had bought him. 'What cometh in the morning is hangovers in my experience.'

Owen Gray picked up his own drink. It was strange how one whisky on its own was quite sufficient, but if you had two you wanted a third. He supposed that if he were any good at his job he could bring comfort to this man and give him the strength to overcome his misfortunes. It was often a series of disasters that drove people into the church, but Owen Gray's subversive opinion on this well-documented phenomenon was that it was only because they had been mildly unhinged by their wretched experiences.

'Cheers, vic,' said Vanner and emptied his glass. 'Take me to your leader. I want to nut him.'

'Do I detect a scintilla of belief?'

'You'd need an ultramicroscope. Why don't I buy you a drink? I've never got pissed with a theological gentleman before.'

'Well, perhaps just one more,' said Owen Gray. 'What do you do for a living, Mr Vanner? Or rather,' he corrected himself, 'what did you do?'

'Spot dealer,' Vanner said, pulling a £20 note from his shirt pocket. 'You've heard of the money market?'

'Ah, that. The Eurobond dealer in his Docklands duplex. The money broker with his trendy and impenetrable vocabulary.'

'That's me, pal.'

'The money changers in the Temple.'

'I think it was them that fired my imagination. They were the ones who didn't get crucified. Landlord, sherbet.'

The whisky seemed to have mellowed Vanner, thought Owen Gray. He wasn't so angry now. Perhaps soon, before unconsciousness overtook him, he would actually laugh.

'You are not a religious man, Mr Vanner,' he said, and realized from the difficulty he had in pronouncing 'religious' that he was fairly drunk himself. He took the new glass of whisky that Vanner had bought him and sipped it gingerly.

Vanner picked up his own glass with more enthusiasm. 'No, but I drink religiously,' he said. 'I went to church a couple of times as a kid but the second time I realized that I'd seen it.'

The final whisky had a peculiar effect on Owen Gray. Images of lust exploded in his head. Pictures of his sister mowing the lawn came back so vividly that he felt he could smell the grass. He looked round hoping that a woman – any woman – would come in. He swayed slightly at the bar and tried to think of something other than sex.

'I think I'd better go,' he mumbled. 'Be about my father's business.'

'Some business,' Vanner said. 'The shares are on the floor.'

But when the vicar had made a surprisingly unsteady exit, he remembered that his shares, too, were on the floor. He had never been a defeatist, all problems were there to be solved, but when he tried to apply the thought-producing qualities of whisky to his present problems they seemed so numerous that he didn't know where to start. The shop? The Daytona? The mortgage? The need to find a job? The abortion hung over all his thoughts, removing the possibility of concentration.

It had festered in his mind all weekend, but when Suzanne was driven home in an ambulance on Monday, still in some discomfort, he was so agitated by the loss of his job that afternoon that he was in no mood to address other issues. Suzanne, stretched out on the sofa and needing waiter service, was hardly in the mood to discuss either subject. She seemed incapable of comprehending the enormity of his disaster. They were staring at debts they couldn't possibly repay; the Manor House was about to be lost; the official receiver would soon be opening a file with his name on; and she was too weak to even rebuke him, let alone defend her own behaviour. He fetched her supper while an uneasy truce prevailed.

Now, in the Flatulent Ferret, released from the interference of a drunken vicar, he could see that the one problem he had to concentrate on was the servicing of his debts or else they'd bankrupt him. If he could pay the interest he could keep his head above water and perhaps one day reach the shore. His capital had gone on the Daytona, but he must know somebody who could help him keep the sharks at bay while he was struggling in the water.

Who had money? He didn't care whether it was Albanian leks, Panamanian balboas or gourdes from Haiti as long as it was currency that a bank would recognize as loot. The city was full of stories of men who had gone bust and then clambered back to the top.

The obvious candidate to ask for a loan was Toby Beauchamp but there was an element of financial rivalry in their relationship that made it too humiliating to approach him. He also had the impression, from Toby's reluctance to discuss money, that the Beauchamp hoard was stashed offshore in Jersey or Switzerland or the Cayman Islands, and its return to this country would bring the tax man running.

And then, suddenly, as his mind ran through the population of Compton Sinbury, he remembered who it was who had the money these days – Barnaby Barton! And the man was in his debt!

When Owen Gray left the Flatulent Ferret the walk back up the green to the vicarage looked marginally more difficult than climbing Everest in gumboots. His legs had developed a mind of their own, and severed all connection with his. His head, which had felt confused in the pub, now seemed with the onslaught of fresh air to have stopped working altogether. He looked at the physical challenge that confronted him and wondered who would notice his unsteady progress. He stepped forward and fell on his face.

Paradoxically, this unpromising start was a helpful experience: it sobered him a little and increased his concentration. His gait was unusual but the distance between himself and the vicarage dwindled. After ten minutes of struggle, he reached the vicarage gate.

Cathy was waiting for him with a cake that their mother had made.

'I wondered where you were,' she said. 'Listen, I've got my job back. I'm working in the Refectory again. My life among the unemployed is over. The cake's chocolate, by the way . . .'

She realized that her brother was listening to none of this. He was preoccupied with removing his trousers.

'Owen!' she said. 'What *are* you doing?'

Holding a chair to steady himself, Owen Gray had got rid of his shoes and was now trying to kick his way out of his trousers which were round his ankles.

'Get your blouse off, sister,' he said. 'I need the warmth of your bosom.'

'Owen, have you been drinking?' she asked incredulously.

Owen Gray was now naked from the waist down. 'And the Lord God said, it is not good that the man should be alone,' he said.

He caught hold of her blouse and tore it open. 'Wonderful, no bra,' he muttered. 'Let brotherly love continue.'

Cathy Gray, retreating across the room in disbelief, felt his hand caressing her breast.

'I have chosen thee in the furnace of affliction,' he said, trying with one hand to undo her skirt.

'Let go, you mad bastard,' she shouted, frightened now. 'Sober up, you daft sod.'

Owen Gray's hand plunged down the skirt it had failed to undo. 'Thy belly is like a heap of wheat set about with lilies,' he said. The smell of whisky seemed to fill the room. 'Thy two breasts are like two young roes that are twins.'

'You're pissed witless,' said Cathy Gray, as he finally tore her skirt open.

'A faithful friend is the medicine of life,' said Owen Gray, trying now to wrestle her to the floor. She held on to a sideboard with one hand and tried to hit him with the other, but he was so close that she could only hit his back.

She still thought that the moment would pass, that he would abandon this attempt or perhaps just collapse. His speech was slurred and his eyes unfocused but his strength was greater than hers.

He tried to pull her hand from the sideboard so that she would have no support but at the same time he was busy rubbing himself against her thigh.

She looked desperately round and then saw, on the sideboard, a brass candlestick that had probably once done duty on an altar. Letting go of the sideboard, she grabbed hold of it.

'Let go,' she said, giving him one last chance, but he wasn't listening.

'Some seed fell by the wayside,' said Owen Gray as the candlestick crashed down on his skull.

Most women believe their own sex lives to be uniquely jinxed by the ineptitude of their partners, but they accept it and wonder enviously about their friends, thought Gwenda Kennedy as she cleaned the carpet.

She had developed a passion for cleanliness which her husband regarded as an obsession that verged on sickness. She waged war on dust but they were always running out of sugar; the vacuum cleaner droned on but there were often no toilet rolls in the lavatory. Neil Kennedy's bachelor flat had much in common with Miss Havisham's decaying mansion, but at least he never ran out of toilet rolls. He found the sound of the Hoover depressing, particularly as in a matter of hours she would have to do the same job again.

It was Lindy's fourth birthday party, and twenty children were about to invade the spotless home. Birthday parties had come on a bit, Kennedy discovered, since he was a kid. First, he was delegated to tie balloons on the gate to let the guests know where the party was. They hadn't thought of that twenty-five years ago. Next, and much more sinister if you were financing the occasion, the hostess bought all the guests presents. Twenty 'party bags' containing balloons, sweets, crayons and God-knew-what, were stacked in the kitchen waiting to be pressed into tiny hands. Who, he wondered, dreamed up this unhealthy practice?

'Do you think most women are unhappy with their men?' Gwenda asked when the cleaner had been switched off. 'You know, in bed?'

'I expect so,' he told her. 'It's the impression one gets these days, isn't it?'

'But why? Why are men so bad at it?'

'Thank you, darling. It probably isn't natural for a man to keep doing it to the same woman. A little variety would improve his performance.'

'Don't you try it,' said Gwenda Kennedy, picking up the cleaner. 'You've got responsibilities.'

He went out to the kitchen and looked at the feast which his wife had prepared for twenty small guests: a birthday cake with ballerinas on, jellies in the shape of My Little Pony, sausages on sticks, tiny cakes and sandwiches, quiches and crisps, and home-made biscuits with the name of each guest piped on in icing. It wasn't only parties that had changed since he was a boy. Names had changed too. Tiffany, Petra, Kerry and Saskia. Saskia had learned the alphabet at two, an effort that may have been responsible for her prematurely haggard appearance. Neil Kennedy remembered a wonderful fragment of conversation he had overheard in the post office when Daisy Balcombe had bumped into Saskia and her mother. 'What a hideous child!' said Daisy. 'Is it yours?'

The party itself was going to be easy because Gwenda had had a good idea. His heart had sunk when she announced the fact. When Gwenda had a good idea it meant that she had just worked out how to spend another £100. She never had a good idea about how to bring money in, but it wasn't a subject he cared to discuss with her because when she was working she earned a high salary, and she was not working now only because she was bringing up his daughter.

The good idea was to hire a conjurer and his wife. For £75 they were going to organize games for the children during the first part of the party, and provide a conjuring show for the last part. This meant that, apart from when they were eating, the Kennedys wouldn't see the kids at all.

The hostess took some time to get ready, picking her way through her growing collection of dresses in search of the appropriate ensemble. She selected a black taffeta dress that had a big white collar edged in lace with green and red embroidery. There was a sash with a bow at the back, and a black net petticoat. She came proudly downstairs and announced: 'You've got to keep out of the way, daddy. This is for children.'

'Really? Who's coming?'

'Christopher Lillywhite,' she told him.

'And plenty of others, I hope.'

'Christopher Lillywhite is my favourite. He's the best boy.'

Neil Kennedy found it slightly disturbing that his four-year-old daughter was already caught in the biological trap that would, a couple of decades later, have her asking: 'Why are men so bad at it?'

The previous week at the children's pool she had seen her first naked male and told her father when she got home: 'I saw James with no clothes on. He had something up his bottom.' It seemed an unpropitious start to a life of romance.

When the children had been delivered by their parents, grateful to be presented with two hours of peace, and passed on without a beat to the visiting conjurer and his wife, Neil Kennedy took a can of beer out to the patio. He was supposed to be celebrating himself.

Work on *Hot Air Rises* had been completed yesterday and a buoyant mood had infected everyone involved with its production. The director talked of huge viewing figures, pictures on the cover of *Radio Times*, appearances on Wogan. All previous looks at marriage were going to seem jaded or blurred alongside this pellucid glimpse at modern matrimony.

In the meantime he was out of work again. He phoned Howard, his agent.

'I'm available for work,' he said. 'You know – the stuff you are supposed to find for me.'

'Neil! How's the Talking Bus?'

'The what?'

'Your daughter's toy.'

'It's like me. It needs new batteries.'

Howard's cackle came down the line.

'I hear good things about *Hot Air Rises*,' he said. 'You could be big again.'

'That's what my wife says.'

More cackle. 'Did I mention *Be Rude* to you?'

'Yes, an offbeat panel game.'

'You're on. They're going ahead with a pilot show and have accepted my assurance that you're amazingly rude. I don't see it getting on the screen myself, but they'll pay for the try-out.'

'I'll be as offensive as I can manage. Anything else?'

'Be patient. When *Hot Air Rises* hits the screens you'll be swamped by offers.'

Sitting on the patio, Neil Kennedy considered this possibility. His career had been in the doldrums for long enough. Other noisier, younger men had usurped the nation's attention. They couldn't act as well as he could but they had a quality, noisiness, which the programme makers had come to value. Well, he would edge them out. Kennedy was coming back from the dead. Hallo, Lazarus! How have you been?

Gwenda Kennedy came out to join him on the swing hammock as he was picturing a glorious future.

'It's bedlam in there,' she said.

'But so peaceful out here.'

'Well, don't get too settled. You've got to help me serve teas to twenty tiny people in a minute.'

'Don't *you* get too settled. Now the telly's over I'm moving back into our own bed. Sleep? Who needs it?'

'Oh, good. I shall be able to continue research on my book *Men Are A Soft Option.*'

'Will this be before or after *My Love Affair With a Vacuum Cleaner?*'

'Some women think a vacuum cleaner is the answer.'

A door opened inside and suddenly the kitchen was filled with hungry children.

'Hoover you with last night?' he asked.

'"Vicar Tries To Rape His Sister"?' said Harry Grant, thinking in headlines. 'I can't handle it.'

'He came very close,' said Cathy Gray. 'In fact, he came over my shoe.'

Harry Grant recoiled with distaste from this unpublishable information. He had come to the Refectory in search of printable news. The vicar was in hospital but nobody knew why, although everybody had seen the ambulance an hour ago outside the vicarage. Now that his sister was a waitress again the truth would be easy to find. A broken leg? A heart attack? An appendicectomy? No, a skull fracture. 'Vicar tries to rape his sister.'

'Of course,' he said, 'a precedent was created.'

'We were kids, for God's sake,' said Cathy Gray. 'It didn't give him an open ticket.'

'It evidently gave him the taste.'

Cathy Gray looked round the Refectory. There were no customers waiting for her so she sat down.

'The thing is, Harry, I could be in the dock on an assault charge. People want to know what's happened. The doctors are curious. Apparently they are supposed to notify the police if they think a crime has been committed.'

'What has Owen told them?'

'He hasn't said anything yet. I'm not sure he knows where he is.'

Harry couldn't imagine what sort of statement the vicar could issue when the power of speech returned. VICAR INCEST BID SETBACK was not the sort of headline one expected to see in the *Gazette*. RECORD ENTRY AT FLOWER SHOW was more their line of country.

'So what are you going to tell them?' he asked.

'I expect they can tell by the wound that he didn't hit his head on a chair.'

'"Candlestick Fells Sex-Starved Vicar",' said Harry. He couldn't get away from headlines today. 'Never mind the police – *I've* got to write some sort of story today. I can't just say that the vicar of Compton Sinbury was detained in hospital with head injuries. It leaves more questions than it answers.'

'Well, I mind the police,' said Cathy Gray. 'And I don't want to put my brother in the dock either.'

A customer called for her bill and she left him to ponder the problem on his own. He wasn't in favour of violence of any kind, but he knew what a provocative number Cathy Gray could be, and she was probably the only woman that the vicar had made love to. And so the odour of sanctity was replaced by a whiff of lechery as an abortive and farcical attempt at sexual gratification was played out in the vicarage.

Not many villages were given a scandal on this scale. The tragedy was that he couldn't use the story. A newspaper couldn't say that a vicar tried to rape his sister unless the police alleged it and a jury agreed with them. There was libel as well as contempt of court to consider. When Dakers received a letter from a solicitor he developed a nervous tic in his cheek.

He finished a cup of tea that Cathy had brought him and wondered what to do. The subject would certainly lift his 'Village Notes' column from its matrix of normality, but some fare was too rich for the paper's good.

Cathy came over.

'Why don't you go and see him?' she asked. 'Tell him to be careful what he says. Tell him I won't report him to the police. You could sort out a story between you about how he hurt his head.'

'Will they let me see him?'

'Creep in. You're a reporter, Harry. He's in ward 6.'

Cathy Gray was much too bright to be a waitress, he thought half an hour later as he drove into town in his Mustang. She was a girl who had never found her niche. He parked next to an Alfa Romeo Spider and wondered whether it was time to change his Ford. Its purchase had been an entirely uncharacteristic piece of flashiness which he was convinced, some years ago, would enhance the quality of his sex life.

Owen Gray lay in bed in ward 6, looking like a man who was enjoying a Sunday morning lie-in. Harry had expected to find him with his head encased in plaster and tubes coming out of his nose, but he looked no different from any other man who is reluctant to throw off the sheets as dawn hits the bedroom windows. It was a small ward with only four beds and the other three patients were asleep too.

Having crept into the room without permission, Harry was alarmed to hear footsteps behind him but, when he turned, it was only a young doctor called Bridson who played with him in the cricket team.

'Hallo, Harry,' he said. 'Worried about the vicar?'

'That's why I'm here. How is he?'

'Fine.'

'He's got a fractured skull, for God's sake.'

'A fractured skull is nothing,' said Bridson cheerfully. 'Quite insignificant. It's what happened underneath that matters – torn blood vessels, that sort of thing. In his case there's no bleeding. All he's got is concussion and a headache. He could be walking by the end of the day.'

'Do you know how it happened?'

'He hasn't told us. But I can tell you one thing. He stinks of whisky.'

'So he probably fell?'

'That's my guess.'

An urgent noise jumped out of Dr Bridson's pocket.

'Excuse me,' he said. 'I've been bleeped.'

When he had gone Harry went over to Owen Gray's bed.

He lay on his back with his eyes firmly shut and his hands joined together on his chest as if in prayer.

'Hallo, vicar,' said Harry.

Owen Gray opened two bloodshot eyes and looked up at him.

'Mr Grant,' he muttered.

'What happened?'

'God knows.'

Coming from a vicar this sounded like a promise of sensational disclosures rather than a confession of ignorance, but Owen Gray had nothing to add.

Harry sat on the bed. 'What do you remember?'

'Cathy was there.'

'She was and you tried to rape her.'

Owen Gray closed his eyes.

'But don't worry. She's not going to tell anybody. She wants you to tell people that you fell over.'

'Is that what you'll put in your paper?'

'Yes. You fell over.'

'I fell over.'

'Good.' Harry stood up. 'I'd better go. I'm not supposed to be here.'

Owen Gray opened his eyes again and managed a weak smile. 'Thanks,' he said. 'I didn't know whisky gave you a headache like this.'

'You'll be out in no time, apparently,' Harry told him, but no answer floated up from the bed.

He went out of the ward and walked furtively down the corridor, writing a story in his head. *The vicar of Compton Sinbury, the Revd Owen Gray, was taken to hospital with a fractured skull after a fall at the vicarage on Wednesday. His condition is satisfactory and he is expected to be released in a few days.* He added for his own amusement: *He is not thought to have been trying to rape his sister when the accident happened.*

Compton Sinbury, which had once seemed to be a sleepy little sinecure in which a row over the whist drive results represented the peak of local excitement, had suddenly become the news capital of the county. Perhaps the *Gazette* would offer him more money.

He stepped out of the hospital's big front doors and narrowly avoided being hit by an arriving ambulance. It juddered to a halt three inches from his foot and three men jumped out to open its back doors.

They pulled out a stretcher and Harry saw Nadine.

Nadine Kirby had got up that morning feeling worse than ever. It was exactly two weeks since Rachel had disappeared, and the arrival of this milestone seemed to put a seal on her fading hopes.

She believed now that she was being punished for her unfaithfulness, that there was a perfect balance in the world and the good were rewarded while the bad suffered. In her calmer moments she wondered whether embracing such primitive notions meant that she was going mad. For fourteen days she had mooched around the house, refusing to go out, waiting for the phone that never rang, snapping unreasonably at Harry Grant on his frequent visits, dusting furniture and rearranging it.

From the record player came the sound of one of Felix Kirby's favourite Guy Mitchell records, 'The Roving Kind', with Mitch Miller and the French horn. It wasn't that she wanted music; the record reminded her of her husband because now that Rachel had gone she needed him here.

For a moment, yesterday or the day before, hope had invaded her misery. She convinced herself briefly that if Rachel had met her death her body would by now have been found, and that in the absence of such a discovery she must still be alive somewhere. But this heartening reflection did not survive for very long. Some bodies were never found.

She had lost a stone. The slimming process that earlier this year had been a struggle of discipline and self-denial, was now a simple matter. She hardly ate and each meal was harder to face than the last.

She sat alone, turning the pages of old photograph albums, watching Rachel grow up. The pretty girl who made her laugh a lot at six. The more serious girl of eight, coming to terms with the discovery that the world wasn't entirely a comedy. And the bright girl of ten who was learning to control and develop her talents and could write an essay that won £100. These excursions into the past always ended in tears if she wasn't crying already, but she was drawn back to the photographs time and again.

Rachel's bedroom had been cleaned and polished, curtains washed, drawers tidied, shoes brushed. In fact all these jobs had been done twice. At the same time, bills – including one for the funeral – had been left unopened, and letters – including one from the bank about her widow's pension – left unread. Only the newspapers were studied regularly for their frequent references to the missing girl.

A television man had arrived at her door after a week with a request for an interview on film. He had tried to persuade her that Nadine's tearful appeal on the nation's screens would somehow help to find her daughter. She could see how it would add piquancy to their television news programme, but she couldn't see how it would help Rachel and she turned him away. Instead the cameraman stood on the green and took some footage of the house which appeared on television that evening with the caption A MOTHER WAITS.

The village had responded to her tragedy with a discreet silence. It was understood that visitors were not welcome at her door and the more sensitive of her neighbours suffered a helpless anguish at her plight. Notes and cards were dropped on her mat. 'Our thoughts are with you' was the most common message, but three people sent her flowers.

None of these communications received a reply. Nadine Kirby was moving in a world where little was real, and normal behaviour had been suspended. After two weeks she was beginning to drift around the house in a sort of trance. She had no energy and was having difficulty in concentrating on anything.

What she needed that morning was a black coffee. She went out to the kitchen and took down the coffee tin. It was empty. She couldn't believe it. Harry had been doing her shopping with tremendous efficiency and in two weeks she had not run out of anything. She picked up the last list she had given him. Coffee wasn't on it.

She sat down, balancing her need for a black coffee with her reluctance to go out. It wasn't only the possibility of a missed phone call that made her unwilling to leave the house. She dreaded the conversations that might be inflicted on her. She rang Harry Grant but there was no reply. After ten minutes she knew she had to go herself.

The supermarket at the top of the green was only a few yards away but the journey seemed like an ordeal. She felt weak when she left the house and weaker when she got to the shop. At the far end she could see Daisy Balcombe fingering the potatoes, and she made for the coffee shelf in the hope of a quick exit. As she reached up for the tin she was overcome by a dreadful dizziness and then she hit the floor.

'Mrs Kirby's fainted,' said someone.

'She looks terrible,' said somebody else. 'I think we should phone for an ambulance.'

21

Barnaby Barton had abandoned his furtive surveillance of the postman's movements after the typed message had told him that there would be no more £10 notes, and so he didn't see the letter from America land on his mat. He was engrossed instead in a novel from the mobile library. He laid the book on his lap to roll himself a cigarette and there was a knock on his door. He finished making the cigarette, then lit it before creeping quietly up to the window to see who was there. To his surprise it was Paul Vanner. Mr Vanner was something big in the city and had never come within a hundred yards of Barney's home.

As he reached the front door he saw the airmail letter on the mat. Had his son written to him, or was this the answer he had been waiting for from Lydia Baxter? He picked it up and opened the door.

Paul Vanner looked dreadful. His face was blotchy, his eyes were red with tiredness, and his hair needed a comb.

'Hallo, Barney,' he said. 'May I come in?'

'Mr Vanner,' said Barney. 'Have you come to visit my humble abode?'

'As it happens, Barney, I've come to ask a favour,' said Vanner, walking past him. Once in the living room he felt as if he had stumbled into a bus shelter that was frequented by dossers. The mess on the floor – mud, cigarette ash, drink cartons, animal fur – was so extensive that a normal person would dispense with cleaning, burn the carpet and start again.

He walked to the window, hoping for fresh air, but they were all shut. On the patio was a steamer chair: Barney was obviously becoming accustomed to leisure. Beyond, on the other side of a new fence, builders were at work on what had once been his land.

'I'm behind the eight ball, Barney,' Vanner said, turning to face his host, but this meant nothing to the small man who stood in the middle of the room holding an airmail letter and smelling like a wet dog. 'I've got a financial problem,' he added, wondering whether this clarified things.

'Money?' said Barney. 'What you have to do is sell a bit of your garden and let them build houses on it.'

'If I don't get hold of some money soon it won't be my garden to sell,' Vanner told him. 'I've got a mortgage to pay.'

'I never had a mortgage,' said Barney. 'I don't agree with them. They take too much back in interest.'

The last thing Paul Vanner had come here for was a lecture on financial prudence from a man who had difficulty in telling a £5 note from a luncheon voucher. He sat down in a deep armchair which carried the lingering aroma of kippers.

'I've got this letter,' said Barney, holding up his post. 'From America.'

Vanner wasn't sure whether he was trying to change the subject or was merely certifiably insane.

'Good,' he said. 'Is it from Duncan?'

'I don't know. I haven't opened it yet.'

'Duncan made you all that money from Beauchamp Developments Limited,' said Vanner. 'You're a rich man, Barney.'

'It's in the bank,' said Barney. 'I'm getting fourteen per cent.'

The remark suggested a financial understanding that alarmed Vanner. What had happened to the innumerate Guinness drinker who was grateful to work for £20 a day? In his waking hours – an ever-increasing number – Vanner had spent much time contemplating this visit to Barnaby Barton. Separating him temporarily from some of his Toby money, he had decided, would be easier than confiscating a baby's rattle. And now the man was talking about percentages and interest rates.

'The thing is, Barney, I need a loan,' he said. There was no room here for anything less than a direct approach. 'I thought you might be able to help me.'

Barney looked at him as if he had switched to a foreign language.

'It could be from Lydia Baxter,' he said, holding up the letter again. 'I wrote to her.'

'Good,' said Vanner. 'That's good. I hope she's answered.' It would obviously require a crane to keep this conversational ball in the air, but he had to try. 'You got two hundred thousand for your land, didn't you?' he asked.

He had always regarded Barnaby Barton as a man who was simple to the point of imbecility, but the money seemed to have provided him with a glimmer of brains. There was an artful, crafty look about him as he considered Vanner's question.

'Got a few bob,' he said. 'Going to spend it on Lydia Baxter.' A dry piece of something fell out of his nose.

'She's in America?'

'She is now, but she's going to live with me.'

'Well, how about lending me some money until she gets here?'

'Neither a borrower nor a lender be, Mr Vanner,' said Barney. 'That's what my mother used to say.' With no discernible embarrassment, he released a volley of farts which made Vanner wish he were anywhere but here.

'Don't give me grief, Barney,' he said. 'You've lent money to the bank. That's why you're getting interest. Why not lend it to me?'

'Security,' said Barney with a smile.

Vanner looked at him with a feeling that was indistinguishable from hate. He imagined a humane killer pressed against the old man's temple. He was as much use as a car with no windows and he was the only hope Vanner had.

'Suppose I provided security?' he asked.

'If you had security you could borrow from the bank. They've got a lot of money they want to lend. I read it in the paper. Interest rates are so high that they can't find any takers.'

This last contribution to the conversation made Vanner think seriously about beating Barnaby Barton unconscious. If he wasn't going to get the loan that he desperately needed he could at least leave with some feeling of satisfaction if Barney was reduced to a few bloodstains on his own filthy carpet.

The urge to resort to violence became so strong that he thought he should leave. He had enough problems without adding manslaughter to the list. But if this bloody simpleton couldn't see that he stood between Vanner and the scrap heap he was no use to anybody and ought to be dead, leaving space, food and fresh air for somebody more worthwhile. The fury that swelled inside him was almost frightening.

'That's it then?' he said. 'You won't lend me what I need?'

'It wouldn't be good for you,' Barney said, sucking at a cigarette that was no longer alight. 'Money has to be earned or it's not appreciated.'

Vanner shot out of his seat, unable to believe what he was hearing.

He knew that he was in serious trouble, but if he was reduced to listening to Barnaby Barton deliver a lecture on the psychology of money he might as well cut his throat.

He walked quickly across to the front door, dimly aware that he was taking the smell of kippers with him. He left so quickly that it was only when he was walking back down the road that he remembered that he had not played what he thought would be his trump card.

One night in the Flatulent Ferret, when the conversation had turned to his inflated salary, he had noticed that Barnaby Barton could not afford to buy himself a drink, and Vanner thought back to the poverty he had seen in Stepney as a child.

To make himself feel better – and Vanner had no illusions about the fact that he was doing it for himself as much as anybody else – he had sent a £10 note to Barney every week for more than a year.

When Vanner had gone, Barnaby Barton settled into the chair that he had vacated and tore open his letter. It had arrived from an address in Miami.

'My dear Barney,' he read. 'It was lovely to hear from you after all this time, and I am glad to hear of your good fortune. It was kind of you to ask me to join you but I am settled here in Miami and have everything I need. I bet it was a surprise to you when Dunc appeared! He told me all about you. He is doing very well in his business and I am very proud of him. We have discussed the possibility of spending Christmas in England. I would like to see the place before I go. What I would love you to do is send me a photograph of yourself. Dunc forgot to do it. Love, Lydia (Baxter).'

Barnaby Barton got up and went out to the old mirror by the front door. He studied his features for some time and then started to comb his hair.

On Thursday evening, when the *Gazette* presses had begun to roll and Harry Grant usually adjourned to the potting shed for a little reward after the week's events, he sat instead in front of the television in his cottage wondering what fresh calamities could hit the village. The amount of activity was beginning to make him nervous: for years he had been able to cover the news round here without breaking into a trot.

He switched on the six o'clock news. Mikhail Sergeyevich Gorbachev's single-handed attempts to end the cold war were causing discomfort in some unexpected places. Mrs Thatcher was becoming twitchy about the prospect of a united Germany, Poland was getting worried about its borders, and Israel, which had once begged Russia to release her Jews, was now begging her to hang on to them as Israel ran out of space and jobs. But the big news was still in the Middle East where scores of Britons were being held hostage in Iraq as the world waited for a war.

Alarming as it was, his mind switched off to it. He had enough to worry about here. Normally on a Thursday he began to worry about where he was going to find the several thousand words he needed for next week's paper but the challenge didn't seem as daunting as it once had: these days the news arrived unbidden.

He was just thinking that a short visit to the potting shed

was the least that he deserved when Rachel's picture came up on the screen. The news froze him to his chair.

'Hope is fading for Rachel Kirby, the ten-year-old schoolgirl who vanished from her home fifteen days ago,' said the voice behind the picture. 'Police announced today that they were scaling down the search for Rachel, whose bicycle was found beside the M3 the day after she disappeared . . .'

He flicked the remote control and hoped that there was no television on in the hospital ward where Nadine was now lying. For twelve hours she had been under sedation and doctors had expressed concern at her poor condition.

Dr Bridson, surprised to see Harry back at the hospital so quickly, had told him: 'She's hardly eaten or slept for a fortnight. That can make you seriously ill. She'll need a week of careful looking after before we can let her out.'

That afternoon Harry had sat by her bedside for two hours, but she had shown no interest in whether she stayed in hospital or not. It almost seemed to him that she was losing the will to live.

Thinking about it in front of his television, he remembered now that he had promised her during the visit that he would check her house. She had fears about birds coming down the chimney and wreaking havoc in the sitting room, power cuts causing the fridge to flood the kitchen, and unsolicited circulars remaining in the front door and telling everybody that the house was empty. He also had to water her plants.

It seemed a good idea to do all these things before whisky confused his brain, and soon he was walking across the green. To his right was the five-arch bridge where Suzanne had crashed, to his left the vicarage where Owen Gray had been overcome by a wayward libido, and ahead of him was the house from which, fifteen days ago, Rachel Kirby had vanished. Gilbert White may have devoted his time to studying the feeding habits of the bat, or the history of the red deer, but here in Sin there were other things to think about.

He went into the Kirby house, pulling from the letter box an invitation to invest in double glazing, a cut-price offer to clean carpets and a catalogue of garden furniture. The empty home depressed him. Only weeks ago a normal, or fairly normal, family of three was living here; now the daughter had disappeared, the mother was in hospital and the father was dead. He went out to the kitchen, filled a jug with water and began a tour of the begonias and fuchsia and other plants with which Nadine liked to decorate her house. He was finishing the job by watering her weeping fig-tree when the telephone rang. He hesitated for a moment and then picked it up.

'Compton Sinbury 504,' he said.

A cockney voice asked: 'Is Mrs Kirby there?'

'Not at the moment.'

There was a pause at the other end of the line and he stood and waited. In other circumstances he might have wondered whether Nadine had a boyfriend who was surprised to hear a man's voice answering the phone.

'We have her daughter,' the man said eventually.

Oh my God, thought Harry. This is the kidnappers' call that Nadine had always feared.

'You have Rachel?' he asked nervously. 'Is she all right?'

'She's fine. She's sitting here with me now.'

'Where are you?'

He waited for the evasive reply and the demand for money.

'Sorry. This is Hounslow police station. We picked Rachel up an hour ago. She was recognized in a deli.'

'A what?'

'A delicatessen. Who am I talking to?'

'A friend of the family. Rachel's mother is in hospital. The worry's made her ill.'

'Ah,' said the cockney voice. 'That's awkward. Rachel wants to come home.'

'Keep an eye on her. I'll be there within an hour.'

He slammed the phone down and ran out of the house. Tears filled his eyes as he tore across the green towards his car. He threw himself into it and treated the neighbours to a Grand Prix-like start, then he roared round the green and over the bridge and put his foot down.

It was only when he reached the motorway that he

wondered whether he should have phoned Nadine, but then he was glad that he hadn't. How did he know that it was Hounslow police who had rung? Why hadn't he asked to speak to Rachel? The world was full of nutcases who would make a call like that. Rachel's disappearance was hardly a secret.

He had been in a daze ever since he had heard that Rachel was alive, but now a nasty chill of reality crept into his thoughts. The news had knocked him sideways and he had reacted like an idiot. He thought it all through again as he cruised up the fast lane at 90 miles an hour and realized that he had to stop at the first service station and phone Hounslow police. A sign said that the next service station was twenty miles away.

He thought he could do it in a quarter of an hour, but these days the motorways could be as jammed with traffic as the minor roads they were built to relieve. Soon they were all moving nose to tail at less than forty miles an hour, wondering what the obstruction was that held them up. Eight miles later they saw it: a lorry embedded in a car, an ambulance and a police car which between them blocked two of the three lanes. The motorway traffic crept single file through the bottle-neck and accelerated away. Harry Grant reached the service station some twenty minutes later than he had expected.

He found a phone kiosk, a plastic balloon on a wall outside the restaurant, and dialled inquiries. By now he half-expected to hear that there was no police station in Hounslow, but a bright girl came back with a number very quickly: 577–1212. He dialled it.

'Hounslow nick,' said a cheerful young man.

'Somebody there rang Rachel Kirby's home half an hour ago to say you'd found her,' Harry told him.

'Who am I talking to?' the policeman asked.

'I'm the friend of the family who answered the phone. I'm driving up to fetch her and I suddenly had the awful thought that it was a hoax.'

He waited for bad news.

'No hoax. Would you like to talk to her?'

'I'd love to.'

There was a long delay and Harry Grant started to feed coins into the box. In the restaurant people were queuing with trays for food that he wouldn't care to eat.

'Hallo,' a shy voice said on the phone.

'Rachel? Hallo. This is Harry Grant. Are you okay?'

'I'm all right. How is mum?'

'She'll be okay. But she's in hospital at the moment. Will you come home with me and we'll go and see her?'

'I'd like that. Thank you.'

'I'll see you in half an hour. Don't run away!'

'I don't think they'd let me.'

She hung up then and he immediately rang the hospital.

'Is Dr Bridson on duty?' he asked. Dr Bridson was the only person in the hospital who could identify him and would believe what he was saying.

'He's here somewhere,' said a bored male voice.

'Can you tell him it's Harry Grant and urgent? It's about Rachel Kirby'

There was another wait and he had to put what coins he had left into the box. He heard a shuffling at the other end, and then Dr Bridson's quiet, calm voice came on the line.

'Harry?' he said.

'I've found Rachel. She's safe. Can you tell Nadine? We'll be with her in an hour or so.'

'No kidding?'

'She's in Hounslow police station. I'm on my way there now.'

'That's wonderful, Harry. I'll go and break it to her gently. Drive carefully.'

Another hold-up on the motorway, which turned out after several slow miles to be roadworks, delayed him further and he used the time to consider what he was going to say to her. Was this the moment to admonish her for the worry she had caused? Was this the right occasion to tell her that he was her father?

He left the motorway at Sunbury, having answered neither question. Ten minutes later he pulled in to the police-station car park, wondering what to expect. He was glad that he had postponed his visit to the potting shed earlier in the evening; these days the breathalyser could condemn you on the morning after the night before.

The fresh-faced young policeman on the desk was expecting him.

'A man recognized her in the deli from Press pictures and she admitted who she was,' he said. 'He had the impression that she was glad it was over.'

'She only had to pick up a phone.'

'In that situation they find it difficult to do.'

'Do you know where she's been?'

'Living with an Asian woman in a block of flats round the corner. She's perfectly all right. The doctor's seen her.'

'She must have hitched a lift up the motorway and then walked.'

'One day she'll realize how lucky she was.'

'Didn't the Asian woman have a television, or read the papers?'

'No to both. We've checked her out. Rachel told her she was homeless. Come and see her.'

Nervously he followed the policeman down a shiny corridor. Hounslow police station did not appear to be overstaffed. Posters on the wall pictured middle-aged men whose antisocial behaviour had made the police eager for an introduction; all wore expressions of simmering resentment. They stopped at an open door and the policeman ushered Harry in first.

Rachel was sitting at a desk with a young policewoman, playing dominoes. She was wearing a new pink dress and white fabric shoes that Harry hadn't seen before.

'Hallo, Mr Grant,' she said.

'Rachel, what a relief to see you,' he said, going across. He wanted to kiss her but that was not what she would expect. Instead, she stood up politely. She looked, if anything, healthier than when he had last seen her. At home, perhaps, she spent too much time doing homework.

'Sit down,' said Harry, sitting down. 'Tell me what you've been up to.'

'We'll leave you for a few minutes if you like,' said the policewoman getting up. She went to the door with the young policeman.

'Once you've gone we'll be putting out a Press statement,' he said. 'It'll be up to you to dodge the photographers. Journalists are a bunch of jackals, I'd better warn you.'

'If it wasn't for journalists,' said Harry, 'she'd still be lost.'

They shut the door.

'Have you told mum?' Rachel asked.

'She'll know by now. I rang the hospital.'

'Is she very ill?'

'She'll be getting better quickly now. She was very worried, Rachel. She worried herself sick.'

Rachel stared guiltily at the floor.

Elated as he was to have found her, Harry didn't mind her feeling guilty.

'Why did you go?' he asked her.

'I don't want to tell you.'

'Well,' he said, putting his hand on her shoulder, 'you don't have to.'

'I heard mummy say that daddy wasn't my real father,' she answered promptly.

'She said that?'

'She was talking to you the night daddy died. I was sitting on the stairs.'

Harry remembered. He could imagine what a blow it would be to a sensitive ten-year-old. Suddenly the whole episode made sense. First she lost her father, then she learned that he wasn't her father and then, in confusion, she fled.

'Tell me about the lady you lived with,' he said, to get her away from it. 'How did you meet her?'

'Mrs Somayaha,' she said, brightening. 'She bought me this dress.'

'And those shoes?'

'Yes. Her son's a millionaire. He owns corner shops.'

Harry Grant dropped a tentative notion to find this woman and repay her. Instead he asked again: 'How did you meet her?'

Rachel sat straight-backed on her chair as if she was trying to remember how it happened. Her long, black hair looked greasy and needed washing. It emerged that she had met Mrs Somayaha within a couple of hours of leaving home. She had been picked up on the motorway by a soldier who was driving up from Dorset on a foreign posting. Having hidden her bike in a ditch, she told him that she was on an initiative test, an idea which evidently made sense to the soldier. He dropped her off when they reached the edge of London and she wandered round for an hour before arriving in Hounslow. She needed a bed and so she decided to wait outside a large block of flats. When Mrs Somayaha approached the building Rachel told her that she had nowhere to sleep because her father was dead and her mother had run off with a man.

'And by the time your picture appeared on television the soldier who gave you the lift was abroad?'

'He was going to Germany from Harwich.'

'Was Mrs Somayaha kind to you?'

'She was nice but the food was funny.' She thought for a moment and added: 'I picked her deliberately.'

'What do you mean?'

'An English woman would have told the police.'

'What did you do all day?'

'I kept a diary and did Mrs Somayaha's shopping.'

Harry marvelled at the adaptability of children. They accepted without question a change of lifestyle that would prove traumatic to an adult. He supposed that it was because they hadn't been around long enough to get into a congenial rut that tied a man, for instance, to the Flatulent Ferret.

'Are you ready to go home?' he asked.

She looked doubtful. Perhaps there was some trauma waiting for her after all.

'Is mum cross?' she asked in a quiet voice.

'Not cross, Rachel. Just sad. Very sad.'

Something seemed to have drained out of the child now and she sat very still, staring at the floor.

'And it's all my fault,' she said.

'Your mother isn't going to blame you. She'll probably blame herself.'

'But I shouldn't have run away.'

'You had your reasons.'

'Yes, I want to have a daddy,' Rachel said, and suddenly the pent-up tears burst forth. She cried so much that she shook and gasped, not bothering to wipe her face. Harry took her in his arms and tried to comfort her, but the tears continued to come, soaking his shirt.

'Rachel, Rachel, I have something to tell you,' he said, but nothing could halt her breathless sobbing.

The door opened and the policewoman looked in.

'Are you all right?' she asked.

Harry nodded and she closed the door.

He sat there holding her, waiting for the weeping to subside, and wondered how he could tell her. He began to fear more tears at the revelation that he was her father. Who knew what dreams she had about the man who was really her daddy? How far short of her ideal would he fall?

After a while she stopped crying but continued to hug him. I've had to wait years to hug my own daughter, he thought, but it was best not to entertain thoughts like that. He could almost cry himself.

Suddenly she came to life again, pulled herself away and stood up.

'What have you got to tell me?' she asked. 'Do you know who my real father is?'

He nodded. 'Yes, Rachel, I do.' He passed her a clean handkerchief and she began to wipe her face. When she had finished she returned the handkerchief and looked at Harry as if she didn't really believe him.

'What's he like?' she asked.

'He's a very nice man who loves you very much,' he told her.

She gave a short, bitter laugh. 'How can he love me if he doesn't know me?'

Harry stuffed the damp handkerchief in his pocket. 'Oh, he knows you, Rachel. He knows you very well. He's watched you grow up and thinks you're wonderful.'

She looked confused now. 'Do I know him?'

Harry nodded.

'What does he do?'

'For a living, do you mean?'

'Yes, what's his job? Is it interesting or boring?'

'Mostly, it's interesting. He's a journalist.'

'Like you?'

'Yes, like me.'

'I want to be a journalist. Would he teach me if I asked him?'

'What little he knows.'

She looked at him strangely then and saw the truth.

'It's you, isn't it?'

He nodded again, and his eyes filled with tears. She came to his side and put an arm round his shoulders. Now she seemed to be comforting him.

'Why didn't mum tell me?'

'She was married to Felix so I had to stay away. Because Felix didn't know that I was your father. I'm afraid it's rather complicated.'

'No, it's not. I understand.'

Harry felt as if he was being forgiven for something.

'I'm afraid it's all been rather a mess,' he said.

She looked at him thoughtfully. 'It must have been sad for you,' she said surprisingly.

'Dreadfully. But I used to watch you. I watched you riding your bike. I came to see you in the school play.'

'You called me talented in the paper.'

'Well, I could say that because nobody knew I was your father. Of course now I shall have to say that you were terrible.'

She laughed. Since he had come into the room she hadn't even smiled. When she stopped laughing she just stared at him as if she was seeing him for the first time.

'You,' she said. 'I remember wishing once that you were my father because you wrote things.'

'And all the time I was.'

'Shall we go and see mummy now?'

He got up and looked round the room. It was so bare that

he imagined it was used for interviews with short-tempered gentlemen who were not averse to throwing furniture if they didn't care for the drift of the conversation. He glanced in vain for bloodstains on the wall.

'Yes, let's,' he said.

As he opened the door, Rachel stopped. 'There's one thing,' she said.

'What's that?'

'I think you ought to marry mummy.'

'Okay,' he said.

'Do you think she'll marry you?'

'Let's go and ask her.'

There were still some formalities to be completed at the desk. The police preferred a missing child who had been found to be delivered by them to the family.

'We ought to phone Mrs Kirby at the hospital,' the policeman said. 'To check that this is all right.'

'Please do,' said Harry.

They waited while he went off to make the call. He came back smiling.

'I've talked to your mummy, Rachel,' he said.

'What did she say?'

'She said get a move on.'

As they went to the door, the policewoman came out.

'Are you going home now, Rachel?' she asked.

'Yes,' she said, taking Harry's hand. 'My father's taking me.'

PART FOUR

• Iced Drinks •

A sip of the country life of England
can be dangerously addictive.

Edwin Yoder

We are here and it is now. Further
than that all human knowledge is
moonshine.

H. L. Mencken

22

In a television studio in west London Neil Kennedy was trying to be rude. An industry that was desperate for new game shows, panel shows and chat shows – anything that did not involve the huge costs of rehearsing hundreds of people for weeks or sending camera teams to distant spots on the map – was testing the possibility of injecting a little venom into the familiar smoothness of studio games and experimenting with a trial programme of *Be Rude* which might – or might not – one day reach the nation's screens.

Neil Kennedy's agent, Howard, had fulfilled his promise to get him a chance on *Be Rude* on the strength of his forthcoming appearance on *Hot Air Rises*, and his own painful experience of the actor's mercurial talent for verbal abuse after a few drinks.

The format for *Be Rude*, as explained to them by the producer, a tall, willowy young man called Wendell, who had a habit of covering his worried face with a spreadeagled hand in moments of crisis, was for two people to talk to each other for two minutes, being as rude as they thought appropriate. The winner, as chosen by a studio audience, would subsequently be as offensive as possible to whoever had triumphed in a similar tête-à-tête on the same programme.

'We really don't know whether it's going to work,' said Wendell, 'but we're going to do a pilot, run it up the flagpole and see if anybody salutes it.' When he went out to give the same message to the studio audience, Neil Kennedy availed himself of the liquid hospitality which, unusually but necessarily, was waiting for the participants backstage.

There were eight of them and it was hard to guess where they had come from. They didn't look particularly aggressive.

Neil Kennedy had been paired with an MP who was known for his love of television. Even the arrival of cameras in the House of Commons had failed to quench his appetite. Kennedy thought that an MP was a soft target for vituperation, but Wendell explained that it had not been easy to find eight people who could deal with public unfriendliness and still show the necessary aplomb.

First on was an East End car dealer who slugged it out with a newspaper columnist beyond the hearing of the other six belligerents. The noise from the studio audience, who had never heard anything like it, suggested that *Be Rude* deserved a wider audience. There was not only the usual applause and laughter, with which studio audiences were notoriously generous, but a few bellowed contributions as well which, judging by the mirth they provoked, were quite as insulting as anything thought up by the two contestants.

A vote among the audience adjudged the car dealer to have won the first confrontation, and the recording was stopped while they were replaced by Neil Kennedy and the MP. They sat at two desks that were placed at right angles to each other so that each partially faced the audience. A space of several feet had been allowed between them, perhaps in case proximity led to violence.

A disembodied voice announced this new pairing. 'Vincent Protheroe, Member of Parliament, Neil Kennedy, actor,' and a bell like those used at boxing matches rang out. The politician, not unexpectedly, jumped in first.

'Mr Kennedy, I understand that you have recently left London to live in the depths of the country. Was this because the pace of London was too much for you?'

'Not at all . . .'

'What's the all-engrossing topic of conversation down there? Last night's television?'

'Schopenhauer.'

'I find that hard to believe, Mr Kennedy. Why haven't you got straw in your hair like a proper yokel?'

Neil Kennedy thought that this was in danger of becoming one-sided.

'Mr Protheroe, ten years in the House of Commons seems to have given you a somewhat deranged air,' he said, 'but you're a fine colour. Been to the Algarve or have you been hitting the port?'

Mr Protheroe did indeed have a very red face which contrasted spectacularly with what looked like a flaxen toupee. 'Port is not my tipple,' he said, and was about to go on but Neil Kennedy was now in full flow.

'I thought all MPs spent much of their time in an alcoholic haze with the bars open all day, and then hid from their visiting constituents? They wander through life nurturing the illusion that they're a bit alert but what they actually know about the real world could be written in headline type on a flea's nuts. I imagine that in Ulster, where you evidently came from –'

'I'm Scottish, you cabbage,' said the MP with a noticeable Glaswegian rawness, 'and your attempt to impugn my integrity and that of my colleagues does you no credit. Being an MP is an honourable job carried out by people of honour, whereas acting is an escape for people who can't face what they really are.'

Neil Kennedy sought to dent his impervious smirk while wondering, at the same time, whether this was a very bright way to earn a living.

'Mr Protheroe – a decade on the back benches. Why no promotion? The competition isn't too hot from what I've seen of it.'

'Mr Churchill was on the back benches for –'

'Well, I don't think we have to drag him in, do you? Churchill is Churchill, but you – well, when they circumcised you they threw away the wrong bit.'

'One of Lloyd George's better insults. Still, I don't expect original remarks from an actor.'

'Winston Churchill, Lloyd George, Vincent Protheroe. Spot the odd man out.'

Neil Kennedy reached for a glass of water and saw that the floor manager was silently doubled up behind one of the cameras. Vincent Protheroe's fingers tapped the desk in front of him.

'I had hoped that I would warm to you, Mr Kennedy,' he said, 'but I can see that it is going to be difficult. Your discourtesy I have to accept, but your ignorance is a terrible reflection on your pampered profession. Why did you decide to become an actor, anyway? Wasn't the real Neil Kennedy enough of a person? You needed nose paste, false hair and spirit gum to create a more acceptable version of yourself? Is it shyness or a feeling of inferiority that drives people to seek refuge in that sort of thing?'

'False hair? I should take care, Mr Protheroe, that the studio lights don't melt your toupee.'

'That's pretty rich coming from a man who spends most of his life putting make-up on his face.'

'You're a philistine, Mr Protheroe, like so many of your ilk.'

'And you, Mr Kennedy, are a poser, like so many of yours.'

The studio audience, displaying the customary prejudice, were noisily opposed to the politician and decided afterwards that he had lost. Neil Kennedy wasn't so sure but his conscience was eased later when he was badly mangled by the car dealer who thought, apparently, that all actors were sponging pansies, an opinion he expressed in the forceful dialect of the East End.

It was odd afterwards to see the warring couples shaking hands and congratulating each other as if they had all been involved in a Sunday afternoon tennis tournament. Wendell, the producer, moved among them, his face contorted by worry lines: 'I don't know, I don't know,' he kept saying. 'There's an old Gaelic proverb: If you want an audience start a fight. But I don't know.'

'It sounded like lively television to me,' Kennedy told him.

'Lively, yes. But is it a good example? Will it upset that bunch of loonies who seem to think that television is a sort of nanny?'

The answer to this came soon enough or, rather, never came at all, because *Be Rude* was never heard of again.

The Vanners lay in bed with a yard between them like two men who had been forced by circumstance to sleep together but were each determined that the other should not mistake him for a homosexual. The space between them and the silence dominated the room.

It was already nine o'clock but neither showed any inclination to get out of bed. Suzanne lay on her side and with her back to her husband and her eyes shut, trying to return to a sleep that was long over. He lay on his back with his eyes closed but his mind racing.

The dwindling money in the bank would pay the mortgage and the car loan for a couple of months. He had been told that he would never get another job in the city. He felt like a condemned man who knew that after a few weeks there wasn't going to be a lot to look forward to.

For all of these problems his wife was to blame, and he lay in bed having morbid fantasies about poisoned drinks, greased stairs and accidents in swimming pools.

He should never have married her in the first place, he told himself. She was very pretty, but why should the configuration of flesh on her skull mean that he would enjoy the things that she said or did? Her stupidity had ruined him – on his own he would now be rich and successful. Instead, after the recent holocaustal events in his life, he would soon be envying a blind beggar in Marrakesh.

The previous evening had been the big showdown, but now that it was over his situation didn't seem to be any clearer. He had held back for a week or two because she seemed to be in pain, but now her movements were almost normal again.

They were having a television dinner, each eating food off a small table in front of them. On the television a chef was cooking another meal which did not seem to Vanner to be large enough to satisfy a mouse.

He decided to soften his wife up with some body punches before administering the glorious knock-out. The trouble was that he did not enjoy having rows with her. She was slippery, elusive and clever. She was also an adroit counter-puncher.

'We'll have to move, you know,' he said, when the chef stopped talking.

'Why do you say it like that?' she asked. 'As if it's my fault?'

He looked, at her, surprised already. 'Who wrote off the Ferrari?' he asked.

'If we have to move it won't be because of the Ferrari. It'll be because you lost your job.'

'And why did I lose my job?'

'Because you were stupid enough to break the rules.'

She had changed already into an ankle-length white nightdress, and was obviously planning an early night. Since her return from hospital she had spent far more time asleep than she ever did before. He wondered whether it was a way of shutting him out.

He asked: 'How much do we owe the bank on the shop?'

'You don't owe anything, Paul.'

'Oh, really?'

'My father is sorting it out.'

'I thought he hadn't any money,' said Vanner suspiciously.

'His brother has left him some.'

'Well, good for him. That just leaves the mortgage and the Ferrari.'

Suzanne finished her meal and wiped her mouth. 'As far as the Ferrari is concerned, has it occurred to you that I was drinking too much because of my lousy life?'

'In your Manor House with your swimming pool, your tennis court and your Mercedes while I worked myself to death. A lot of women would like to have a lousy life like that.'

'A bird in a gilded cage! Jesus, you don't listen to women, do you?'

'The trouble is,' he said, 'it takes so much time.'

She got up, collected their plates, and went off to the kitchen. He shouldn't have married a clever woman, he thought. He needed a beautiful dunderhead who would be grateful that he had chosen her. There would be excitement in the bedroom, and freedom out of it.

She returned with a glass of water. This was the signal that she was going to bed. The water was placed beside it every night. She looked quite beautiful standing there in her long, white nightdress. He could remember when he would have followed her up the stairs, kissing her ankles on every step.

But there was no time to think about that now: this was the moment for the big punch.

'You're talking about sex, aren't you?' he said.

'Oh, you remember it, do you? It's what you used to do when you were young.'

'And what you still do,' he told her.

She looked at him. 'What do you mean by that?'

'I know about your abortion, Suzanne.'

Now he had her. She had walked right into it, reeled back and could feel the rope burns on her shoulders.

'How do you know?' she asked, confused.

'A nurse at the hospital. I even know who the father was.'

'You bloody well don't. Nobody knows.'

And he didn't, but he remembered Cathy telling him that Suzanne had identified the golden phallus, and it was worth a guess.

'One-cell Tel,' he said.

To his horror he saw that he was right.

She seemed to be close to tears, now, but she didn't cry. 'It wouldn't have happened if you . . . looked after me,' she said, and left the room.

'My God,' he said, 'even the abortion is my fault.'

But she had gone and he was left staring at the television screen and trying to believe that his wife had chosen, of all people, One-cell Tel.

And now they lay in bed, neither speaking nor moving, contemplating another bleak day.

He heard the chink of milk bottles outside. At least somebody was working. The telephone began to ring downstairs and he picked up the extension by the side of the bed. In the old days, calls taken here were usually about the nocturnal movements of the yen.

'Mr Vanner? It's Banks.'

Banks was his insurance broker.

'I've been waiting to hear from you.'

'Why?' Vanner asked. 'Do I owe you money as well?'

'Not at all. But I read about your wife's accident with the Ferrari, and I've been waiting for your claim.'

'Claim?' said Vanner, frowning to himself. 'It was only insured for fire and theft.'

'Quite so. But I rather got the impression that your wife took your car without your consent. What we call theft in the insurance business.'

Vanner was confused. 'She's my wife, for Christ's sake.'

'There's nothing in the policy that would exclude a member of the family.'

'Do you mean that I can get the three hundred thousand back?'

A small laugh came down the phone. 'Well, I don't think you would need that much. Do you know anything about classic cars or did you just bung it in the garage as an investment?'

'That's exactly what I did,' Vanner admitted.

'The only thing that can really destroy them is fire. Then the chassis melts and you've had it. It's the chassis number that counts. That's where the value is. They can rebuild the rest. New bodywork, panelling, this and that. I've been to the garage to look at your car in a professional capacity and I reckon it would take fifty thousand to put it right. Then I sat here waiting for your claim and nothing arrived.'

Vanner began to feel better than he had for some time.

'Are you telling me that the insurance will pay the fifty grand to make the Daytona sound again?'

'That's it, Mr Vanner. All we need is your claim.'

'But that's bloody wonderful. I thought I was ruined.'

'Of course there are a couple of conditions that the insurance company would insist upon.'

Vanner's elation vanished at once. Of course there would be conditions when such a wonderful prospect was dangled before him, and of course they would be conditions that it would be impossible to fulfil.

'Let's hear them,' he said.

'In the first place there would have to be a conviction.'

'A conviction?'

'Your wife would have to be convicted of the theft of the car. That shouldn't prove too difficult.'

'You don't think so?'

'Not if you co-operate with the police.'

'And what do you think my wife would say?'

'For £50,000 I don't think I'd listen.'

'What's the other condition?'

'After the claim's been settled the insurance company would naturally try to get its money back by suing your wife, and they'd expect your co-operation.'

'And who the hell do you think pays my wife's debts?' Vanner asked angrily. 'My God, for one moment I thought you were really going to help me.'

'They'd sue her, not you, Mr Vanner. She could go bankrupt.'

'So my wife is now a convicted thief and a bankrupt? Things are bad enough round here, Mr Banks, without your help.'

'Well, I'm just filling you in on the situation. It's your car.'

'Yeah, cheers, pal,' said Vanner and banged down the phone.

He turned over in bed and looked at his wife's back. He thought she must ask some questions about the phone call after listening to his end of the conversation, but her feeling of oppression was evidently stronger than her curiosity.

'How long is sex supposed to last?' asked One-cell Tel as he thoughtfully scratched an ear. Something that had recently been liberated from one of his nostrils was fixed like a wedge of cement to the nail of the finger that had been assigned ear-scratching duties.

Barnaby Barton, unaccustomed to being consulted about anything, least of all this recherché subject, stalled. 'Why do you want to know?' he asked.

'You're not supposed to come too quick,' One-cell Tel told him. 'I read it in a magazine.'

'I didn't know you read magazines,' said Barney accusingly.

'It was at the barbers,' said One-cell Tel as if this was both justification and excuse. 'It said you had to make it last. You know, for the girl. But how long are you supposed to make it last? That's what I want to know. You're a man of experience. You had a son.'

'It's called prejudicial ejection,' Barney told him. 'You have to think about something else that's got nothing to do with sex. Like Mrs Thatcher.'

'When I'm doing it, I like to think about it,' said One-cell Tel. 'I don't want to think about Mrs bloody Thatcher.'

'That's how you get your prejudicial ejection,' said Barney. 'You're supposed to think about the balance of payments and things like that.'

This sexual seminar was being conducted in the Flatulent Ferret where Barney, no longer suffering from the embarrassment of poverty, spent a lot of time investing in the health-giving properties of Guinness.

'A funny thing happened the other day,' he said.

He was happiest sitting here with One-cell Tel, chatting about nothing in particular and getting quietly squiffy. It meant that One-cell Tel wasn't out earning money so Barney had to buy the drinks. It was an arrangement that suited both of them. The only problem was that One-cell Tel's powers of concentration were not his most conspicuous asset and so Barney had to continue with his story without the expected request for details.

'Paul Vanner came round and asked me to lend him money,' he said, with a manic gleam in his eye.

'Paul Vanner?' said One-cell Tell. 'That bastard.'

'He's lost his job, according to Barry. And his wife smashed up his big car.'

'Good thing,' said One-cell Tel. 'The bastard had too much money anyway.'

Barney picked up his Guinness. 'Why do you keep calling him a bastard?' he asked.

'You remember. Him and Cathy. We had a fight. I'm going to get my own back one day.'

'I thought it was funny,' Barney said, not interested in this. '*Him* asking *me* for money.'

'You didn't give him any, I hope?'

'Not any. When did he ever give me anything?'

The door opened and Suzanne Vanner came in. She swept up to the bar in white jeans and a white shirt and sat on a stool at the counter.

'I'll try a Bacardi,' she said.

'You haven't got a Ferrari outside, I hope?' said Barry with a smile. 'How are you? Is your back okay now?'

'I'm fine, Barry. Put a tonic in it. The bubbles make the drink work quicker.'

Suzanne Vanner had walked into the village to do some shopping, but her head was filled with the row with her husband. She reached the pub before the shops and had come straight in without a second thought.

'It was some crash,' said Barry. 'We haven't seen you since.'

'I believe it was,' said Suzanne. 'I remember very little about it.'

She didn't want to talk, she wanted to think. For once she had put herself in the wrong with Paul and she needed time to work out what she should do. The failure of the shop was something a husband could overlook. The crashing of the car was something he might forgive. But the abortion? That had placed her in dangerous territory.

One-cell Tel had appeared at her elbow clutching two empty glasses. He was wearing his usual yellow T-shirt and jeans. If she needed company this wasn't it.

'Good morning, Mrs Vanner,' he said, and to Barry: 'Pint of bitter, pint of Guinness.'

'Hallo, Terry,' she said. He stood there with his mouth open. His mouth was open quite a lot, a sure sign, she thought, that his brain was in neutral.

'Fit now?' he asked politely.

She nodded and smiled and hoped that he would go away. Conversation at his level was intellectually inferior to the babbling communication in a zoo.

But One-cell Tel, usually untroubled by abstract thought, had had an idea. While Barney had rambled on, he had returned in his mind to the fight with Paul Vanner and his need for revenge, and now he saw a chance. Ignoring the full pints that Barry had pushed in his direction, he leaned against the bar to face Suzanne.

'Is your husband still knocking off Cathy Gray?' he asked.

Suzanne Vanner turned to him wearily. The man might have the brains of a lobotomized monkey and the morals of an African warthog, but he seemed to be saying something that she should listen to.

'Is he what?' she asked.

'Knocking off Cathy Gray. I caught them at it up on the hill.'

'At it?'

'Screwing.'

'I don't believe you, Terry,' she said.

'We had a fight over it. Do you remember his nose injury? I did that.'

Now she believed him.

'He said it happened at work.'

'Well, he would, wouldn't he?'

Satisfied that he had now caused maximum damage to Paul Vanner's prospects of a peaceful life, he picked up the glasses. 'He wants to keep away from Cathy,' he said. 'She's mine.'

'Not exclusively, apparently,' said Suzanne Vanner. She was remembering that her husband was sporting his swollen nose when she came out of hospital the first time. He had actually been making love to Cathy Gray while she was having the abortion.

'What does she see in him?' she asked. 'He's no oil painting. More an oil slick.'

'Money,' said One-cell Tel. 'That's what girls like. Dresses, cars and that.'

'Paul doesn't have any money,' she told him.

'So I hear. He's been round to Barney begging for a loan.'

'He tried to borrow money from Barnaby Barton?' She didn't know which of these news items horrified her most.

'He didn't get any,' said One-cell Tel, smiling. He picked up his glasses and change and made his way back to Barney's table.

'I've stitched Vanner up like a kipper,' he said proudly, but Barney was too preoccupied with breaking into his Guinness to reply. When he did speak it was about something else.

'I've got to get my picture taken this afternoon to send to Lydia. Do you think she'll say I've changed?'

'How long is it since she saw you?'

'Forty-eight years.' He pulled a pipe from his top pocket and started to fill it with dark brown tobacco.

'Not a bit, Barney,' said One-cell Tel. He didn't know very much, but he always knew the answer that Barney wanted. The subject was of no interest to him anyway. He looked across at Suzanne Vanner and wondered what she was going to say to her husband. She was ordering another Bacardi so it ought to be good.

Toby Beauchamp looked in the bathroom mirror. It was impossible to believe that the person he imagined himself to be inhabited these decrepit premises. The events of the last few weeks were certainly taking their toll.

He went downstairs, feeling as trapped as usual, and poured some Alpen on a plate. His morning newspaper had not yet arrived and so he switched on breakfast television, to see if the rest of the world felt any better than he did. The answer was it felt angrier. Banner wavers were out in force.

FREE THE BIRMINGHAM SIX
DOLPHIN-SAFE TUNA!
REPEAL CLAUSE 28
EARTH FIRST!
KILL THE POLL TAX

There was no end to the world's complaints, and no shortage of crowds to make them. Didn't these people have lives to live, and livings to earn? He made himself a coffee and wondered if they served coffee in prison.

Mrs Hockley, his cleaning lady, was due in this morning. It

was a good enough reason to go out. He decided to walk down to see how the Southfork development was coming along. The name Southfork seemed to have stuck and there was talk now of the finished homes being called the Southfork Estate.

He crossed the bridge and went down the lane to where the newly rich Barnaby Barton was no doubt having his peace disturbed by the team of builders who could never operate without the blare of at least two transistor radios.

The homes were half up. The sight which normally warmed his heart now filled him with a feeling of desolation. By the time the money rolled in he would presumably be slopping out in some Victorian dungeon. He had already discussed with his solicitor, Gavin Riley, the possibility of the lawyer handling Beauchamp Developments Ltd while he was away.

He couldn't see the foreman and so he stood in the sunshine watching men laying brick on brick. The buildings were growing before his eyes.

He heard footsteps behind him and turned to see Barnaby Barton approaching. He had spotted Toby from his window, and now Toby was cornered.

Barnaby Barton walked, he thought, as if his top half and his bottom half belonged to two different people. He waddled through the mud like a duck on speed.

'Good morning, Mr Beauchamp,' he said. 'It's coming on well, isn't it?' There was a bloodstain on his collar from a shaving mishap but he hadn't thought it necessary to change the shirt.

'It's fine, Barney. You'll soon have some new neighbours.'

'Of course, when Lydia Baxter gets here I may buy one of the new houses myself.'

Toby didn't like to tell him that this wouldn't leave him much change from the money he had received from Beauchamp Developments Ltd, nor that the imagined value of his bungalow had been sorely hit by the loss of its acre. Toby always proceeded on the basis that half the world was raving mad; it was an assumption that made things a lot easier to bear.

'Good idea,' he said.

'I've had some pictures taken for her,' Barney said, pulling an envelope from his pocket, along with some loose tobacco, a ring of keys, a toothpick, a very old toffee and what looked suspiciously like a pre-war condom.

Toby watched him restore some of these treasures to his pocket while trying to extract the pictures from the envelope. He decided that a new definition was required for human beings: there was a sub-species hanging on at the bottom who didn't quite qualify for inclusion but were still passing themselves off as people.

'I got them done in a booth,' said Barney. 'One of those quick passport places.'

Toby found himself looking at two identical pictures of Barney, grinning hideously in close-up. More than anything he looked like a dangerous sex maniac who had been unexpectedly paroled by a group of progressive magistrates, and was now delighted to discover that he was, after all, still in business.

'Quick what places?' Toby asked.

'Passport. You know, if you want a passport in a hurry.'

Toby's mind, which had foundered in the labyrinth of Barney's conversation, suddenly took off. Barney might have meant a passport that you wanted quickly, but there was such a thing as a quick passport, a one-year job that you could get in any post office. And who would know in some remote post office that the police had confiscated his real passport? In his head he could hear the sound of doors being unlocked.

'You look like Robert Redford,' he said cheerfully.

An hour later he was parking his Porsche in Winchester. He walked briskly to the main post office and went in to find the relevant form. It was headed 'Application for a British Visitor's Passport' which was valid for one year. He stood in the post office and studied the small print. All he needed was his birth certificate, two photographs and £7.50.

He put the form carefully in his pocket and went out whistling to look for a photo booth.

23

IN THE PRINTING WORKS at the *County Gazette* men stood around waiting to fix the final page to the Goss Community web-offset machine. At any given moment, it seemed, only a couple of them were ever working. They all had jobs to do, but no job ever coincided with another and so there were always men standing around and smoking or leaning against a wall reading some other newspaper.

Among them today was Harry Grant who had driven into town to collect an early copy of this particular issue. In the printing works he was something of a legend, the man from the backwoods who had a wonderful life falling out of pubs and yet managed to retain his place on the payroll. He had escaped the restraints which controlled the lives of the reporters upstairs and survived while leading a life of debauchery in the country. This wasn't quite how it was seen in the editorial offices on the floor above where the volume of his copy was weighed every week against his salary and expenses.

'Nice of you to drop in, Harry,' said one of the printers. 'Thought you'd retired years ago.'

'So have you lot, by the look of it. When are you going to print this paper?'

'As soon as we get the front.'

Dakers, the news editor, came into the works to collect a copy himself. He was a tall, thin man with horn-rim spectacles that made him look middle-aged although he was still in his twenties. Seeing Harry, he came over.

'When was the last bald Prime Minister, Harry?' he asked.

Harry Grant was quite used to the strange questions that

were asked in newspaper offices. Even a reader's letter could raise queries that a sub-editor had never imagined himself asking. In this case, it turned out, a local man had invented what he claimed was a cure for baldness and a list of bald and famous men in the article about him had raised some editorial doubts.

'Apart from Mrs Thatcher, do you mean?' Harry asked. 'Would you call Douglas-Home bald?'

'Not really,' said Dakers.

'It must be Churchill then,' said Harry. '1955.'

'We haven't had a bald Prime Minister for thirty-five years? That must prove something, but I'm not sure what.'

'You'll have Kinnock soon.'

'Who's Kinnock?' said Dakers.

The litho plate of the front page arrived suddenly in a rush and two men set about fixing it to the machine's cylinders. Soon the giant reels began to turn and copies of that week's paper emerged on a conveyor belt.

Dakers took the first. 'You've done us proud, Harry,' he said. 'How did you get them to pose? They refused the nationals.'

'They're friends of mine,' said Harry, picking up two papers himself.

The lead story was about how wheelie-bins were to replace the district's dustbins, but the main feature at the top of the front page was a five-column picture of Nadine with Rachel in her arms. The headline above it said: SO GLAD TO BE HOME! It was an unusually good picture because Harry had arranged for more than three dozen to be taken and had then chosen the best.

Driving back to Sin he wondered what Nadine would make of it. She loathed publicity and was suspicious of journalists. The Press publicity that followed Rachel's disappearance had added considerably to her misery, and Harry had explained in vain that without it the girl would still be missing.

The reunion in hospital had brought tears to everyone's eyes, including the nurses. Nadine's recovery had been swift from that moment. She left hospital two days later – two days in which Rachel lived in Harry's cottage. It was, it appeared, much more to her taste than the bank's house opposite.

She watched him writing stories for the paper and then read them, and afterwards joined him for a lemonade in the potting shed.

'I don't think I can call you daddy,' she said on their first evening in there. 'I've already used daddy.'

'Call me Harry,' he said.

Upstairs they converted the smallest room into her bedroom, fetching her things from across the green: duvet, pillows, books, a Walkman and some Jason Donovan tapes. But no sooner was she comfortably settled, than Harry had to move her out again. Nadine, on leaving hospital, wanted to return to her own home. Her objections to moving in with Harry were too numerous to argue about. It was 'too soon'; the neighbours 'would talk'; there were things that she had to 'sort out'; she had to talk to the bank. She had to talk to Harry.

So Harry dropped in to her house two or three times a day and waited until she was ready. He studied Rachel's homework, but never interfered. If the subject involved letters she led the class, but when there were figures on the page she was lost. He told her: 'There's an American lady called Fran Lebowitz who wrote to a teenager with your problem, "Stand firm in your refusal to remain conscious during algebra. In real life, I assure you, there is no such thing as algebra."'

'Is that the sort of advice you should give your daughter?' Nadine asked.

'It's the best,' said Harry.

He marvelled at her recovery and, even more, at the way that she avoided reproaching her daughter. Now that she knew why Rachel had run away she steered well clear of the subject and set about rebuilding their relationship.

They were watching television when Harry arrived with the papers, letting himself in with his own key. They were sitting side by side on the sofa with their feet up on a low table on which stood two empty coffee cups.

'Here comes a man,' said Nadine.

'Hallo, Harry,' said Rachel. 'Is that the *Gazette*?'

She took the paper and studied her photograph. Nadine barely glanced at it.

'Did they have to put it on the front page?' she asked.

'It's a very moving story.'

'Talking about moving,' she said, 'read this.'

She handed him a letter. It was from the bank and suggested that she should vacate the house within three months. The letter referred to details of her widow's pension on another sheet but Nadine did not pass him that.

'Come live with me,' he said. 'Come to the sunny side of the green and get a new perspective on Compton Sinbury.'

Nadine reduced the television's volume with the remote control and said: 'What about the neighbours?'

'There's not enough room for them,' said Harry sitting down beside her. 'Daughter, where's my coffee?'

'You don't drink coffee in the evenings,' said Rachel. 'You drink whisky.'

'We have an observant child, Mrs Kirby.'

'Let's go to the potting shed for a drink. You can show mummy where she's going to live.'

Nadine looked at Harry. She was almost as familiar with the cottage as he was. But she stood up and fetched her shoes.

They walked across the green in the evening sunshine. Four youths had erected a badminton net and were hitting a shuttlecock.

'I feel a bit like a shuttlecock myself,' said Nadine.

'Figuratively,' said Harry.

'I know what that means,' said Rachel. 'I know what a metaphor is, too.'

'The girl is going far,' said Harry.

'She's been quite far enough already.'

'I think you two ought to get married soon,' said Rachel. 'Otherwise I'm illegitimate.'

'But clever with it,' said Harry.

'I'm a clever bastard,' said Rachel.

'Rachel, that's enough of that,' said her mother. 'Harry and I will get married when we're ready.'

'I'm ready,' said Harry.
'I'm not,' said Nadine.

Strolling round his snooker table and practising his long pots, Paul Vanner began to feel that life still held something for him after all.

Encouraged by what his insurance broker had told him that morning, he had driven over to the garage to discuss the future of his battered Daytona with the garage owner in whose custody it had ended up. Soon after the accident Vanner had imagined that the car had been reduced to a square block and sent off somewhere else for recycling, possibly into bean cans, but the garage owner knew more about classic cars than he did, and he had kept the wrecked vehicle under lock and key and waited to see what happened.

'I couldn't bring myself to come and look at it,' Vanner told him. It was hard to see, now he was looking at it, how anybody could turn it back into a car.

'I understand,' said the garage owner. 'But I was going to have to ring you soon. It's using space. What are you going to do with it?'

'Sell it,' said Vanner. 'I can't afford to do anything else.'

'What were you thinking of asking?'

Vanner paused. The man sounded like a buyer. 'It's worth three hundred grand. The insurance people say the repairs will cost fifty grand. I suppose that makes it a quarter of a million.'

The garage owner shook his head. He was about forty and had the hard, well-fed face that seemed to come to men who spent their lives mixing with cars.

'They haven't held their value the way people hoped. The financial climate has brought prices down. Of course they may pick up again next year. Who knows?'

'Well, I know,' said Vanner. 'Interest rates come down to help the government win the election, and house prices and the prices of things like the Daytona go up. That's the way it's worked for thirty years. I don't see why it should stop now.'

'You're probably right, but we're talking about the situation today,' said the garage owner. 'I may be interested in buying this car.'

'Make me an offer, pal,' said Vanner.

The garage owner looked at the Daytona as if he had never seen it before.

'Two hundred, top whack,' he said.

Only a career in money dealing stopped Vanner from grabbing the man's hand and shaking it.

'I don't know,' he said.

'Top whack,' the garage owner repeated.

Vanner could see that although the repairs would have cost him fifty thousand, the bill would be only half that to a garage owner. This was a very good reason to sell the car to a garage owner. They were probably the only people who would find the idea of buying the wreck an attractive proposition.

'Done,' he said, and this time he did shake the man's hand.

Now, with his snooker cue in his hand and a cheque for £200,000 in his wallet, he began to believe that the future would not be all bad. He still faced a £20,000 annual bill on the car plus interest, and he still had a mortgage debt of £60,000 a year. But in his wallet he had a bit of breathing space.

He potted a red into a corner pocket, and walked round the table to take the blue.

Suzanne came in.

'You slimy toad,' she shouted.

'Don't give me grief,' he said. 'I'm having a good day.'

'That was then, this is now,' said Suzanne Vanner. 'You've been screwing Cathy Gray.'

'Suzanne, your language is fucking abysmal,' he told her, playing for time. 'Making love is the phrase that you're looking for.'

'I know all about you and her,' she said. 'You suddenly found a little sexual energy, did you?'

Vanner laid his cue on the snooker table. In some ways he was surprised that they were still together. Couples split today on far less provocation than he had suffered.

But divorce wasn't a family tradition. In the East End they

stuck it out whatever the cost, rather than give hard-earned money to lawyers. They also regarded divorce as a socially unacceptable personal failure. The sociological background was only part of it. He had too many other things to worry about without getting immersed in domestic upheaval. He was like an army that was already fighting battles on two fronts and was not anxious to open up on a third.

'This is the pot calling the kettle black,' he said. 'I think I need a holiday.'

'Why don't you go to Beirut?' his wife said. 'You could end up chained to a radiator with a blindfold on.'

'And no wife to nag me? How much are the tickets?'

'You hypocritical bastard,' she said, 'trying to make me feel guilty. Frankly, I think our marriage is beyond saving.'

He wondered whether she was talking seriously or just working off some ire over Cathy Gray. Despite its manifold deficiencies, Vanner still had the idea that marriage suited him, but two-thirds of divorces were on the demand of women.

'I've got enough on my plate at the moment without thinking about divorce,' he said. 'I think we should have what they call a cooling-off period.'

'You're entitled to your opinion, and I'm entitled to ignore it.'

'Okay,' he said, 'let's split up and you can have half my debts. The house is probably worth less than we paid for it, not that we've paid for it.'

The bleak financial prospect produced from his wife a thoughtful silence.

'We've both made mistakes,' he suggested when she didn't reply. 'We're human beings.'

'One of us is.'

'Yes, but you can pass as one when you're not tipping bottles of wine down your throat.'

She picked up the blue ball that Vanner had hoped to pot and rolled it down the table.

'Are you still seeing Cathy?' she asked.

'Not for ages.'

She rolled a red ball down after the blue.

'You're supposed to use a cue,' he said.

'Since when have you known what you're supposed to use?'

He wondered whether her talent for making painful remarks could be put to a commercial purpose.

'What are you going to do,' she asked, 'about work?'

He shrugged. 'Perhaps I'll end up as a rep in a Ford Sierra with my jacket on a hanger in the back. In the meantime, I'm going out for a drink.'

'No, you're not. You're having dinner at the Kennedys'.'

'Why would I want to do that?'

'Because we've been invited.'

Neil Kennedy had never known his father. It was a source of regret to him because they had lived together in the same house for twenty-two years. Now he was dead it was as if they had never met.

And so he worked at being a father himself, giving Lindy more of his time than she probably wanted, and more of his conversation. She latched magnetically on to any naughty words that escaped within her hearing and that week had strung most of them together. Tired of his company, she asked: 'Why don't you bugger off, you old sod?' Marvelling at her linguistic virtuosity, he buggered off.

But tonight the prospect of a dinner party had brought on her best behaviour. She helped to lay the table and then went upstairs on her own to choose a dress.

The Vanners arrived like two boxers who have climbed into the ring at the same time and now find themselves face to face after weeks of abusing each other in the Press. Opening the door for them, Neil Kennedy wished that he could produce a stopwatch and a bell.

'We don't get to dine with telly stars too often,' said Suzanne, looking grim. 'When's it on? I can't wait.'

'In a month,' said Kennedy. He was already beginning to resent the build-up of excitement for *Hot Air Rises*. It was as if all his previous work never existed.

'Bloody good of you to allow the unemployed in,' said Vanner, accepting a glass of champagne.

Gwenda Kennedy came in wearing a bright yellow dress. 'You forget that Neil is out of work, too,' she said. 'How's your back, Suzanne?'

They went into the dining room and sat down. Kennedy hated four at dinner. The table split into two conversations and you were always trying to hear the other one. But tonight both guests wanted to hear about the television serial and his life as an actor.

He told them how he had won a drama scholarship from school. He had been attracted to acting by Clint Eastwood rather than Laurence Olivier. Poncing around in tights while mouthing incomprehensible couplets had never seemed to him to be a manly way to earn a crust. He wanted to walk down mean streets with a fedora raked down over one eye and a cheroot in his mouth, and make women itch for his touch.

'And is that what you do in this new serial?' asked Suzanne Vanner. 'Make women itch for your touch?'

They were eating melon and Parma ham. There was red and white wine on the table, and champagne in an ice bucket at the side. Between Gwenda and Suzanne, Lindy sat in a high seat drinking lemonade and listening to every word.

'That will be the day,' said Gwenda dismissively. 'Or rather was the day. About 1979, wasn't it, Neil?'

'When the fan letters come in she'll stop grinning,' Kennedy suggested with a smile.

The previous afternoon, in a studio in London, he had posed endlessly for some colour pictures for *Radio Times*, one of which they were promising to use on the cover. His eye-to-camera expression had caught, he hoped, a quality of seductive sexual menace that women would find irresistible, but this was not something that he discussed with his wife.

'You Vanners are having a bad year,' she said now. 'Did you break a mirror or something?'

'It feels like it,' Suzanne said.

'Did you hear about the vicar?' Kennedy asked. 'Harry says

he sexually assaulted his sister and she hit him with a candlestick. I always wondered what the church meant when it talked of brotherly love.'

'And fancy Harry being Rachel's father,' said his wife. 'I must say that when we came to live in the country we didn't expect this much excitement. I thought it would be all bridge parties and car-boot sales.'

'It's probably no more exciting than anywhere else,' said Vanner. 'It's just that in a small community you hear everything.'

Gwenda rose to take their plates and returned a few moments later with a joint of roast beef. At the centre of the table was a flower arrangement of dried rosebuds in three shades of pink and reindeer moss, placed in a small terracotta pot that had been painted white.

'I'm worried about eating beef,' said Neil Kennedy. 'What about mad cow disease?'

'He worries about everything from arsenic in insecticides to radioactive seaweed,' said Gwenda. 'He'll end up living in a bubble.'

'Wash it down with wine,' said Vanner.

'And what about the additives they put in that?' Kennedy asked. 'Sulphur dioxide, benzoic acid. What about the insecticides they spray on the grapes?'

'We're all still alive, dear,' said Gwenda. 'Although it would be nice to see rather more evidence of it in your case.'

Kennedy poured them all wine.

'Does your wife have a pop at you, Paul?' he asked.

'Only all the time.'

'I've decided that all women are basically miserable. The single ones are miserable because they haven't found a husband, and the married ones are miserable because they have found a husband. This is what is known as the contrariness of women.'

'I think you could save this topic for Men's Hour,' said Suzanne Vanner. 'If we're going to discuss the inadequacy of the modern male we'll be here all night.'

'What does inadequacy mean, daddy?' Lindy asked.

'Not good enough,' Gwenda told her. 'Men are inadequate. You might as well find out now. It will save you a lot of *angst* later on.'

Behind her on the wall was a large colour picture of Lindy, sitting on a three-wheel bike, her face full of joy and hope. Vanner wondered what she would be saying when she reached her mother's age.

After dinner they moved into the sitting room with their drinks and played verbal games. Lindy's presence, the visitors gathered, made it impossible to play a game that needed cards or a board. She would want to take part.

Kennedy explained a game involving people's names.

'Tony Benn,' he said.

'Ben Elton.'

'Elton John.'

'John Laurie.'

'Laurie Lee.'

'Lee Marvin.'

'Marvin Hagler.'

'Hagler is nobody's Christian name,' complained Suzanne Vanner, whose turn it was. 'Trust my husband to bring things to a halt.'

'Why don't you bugger off, you old sod?' Lindy asked.

'Your daughter plays word games, too, I see,' said Suzanne.

Gwenda wondered whether she disapproved. She had noticed that Suzanne had not spoken to Lindy, nor betrayed the slightest hint of a maternal instinct.

'Have you ever thought of having children yourself?' she asked. She was always curious about other people's childlessness, whether it was intention or misfortune.

'We were going to try once but Paul fell asleep,' she said. 'What have I missed?'

'Not a lot. A moment's pleasure and sixteen years of slavery.'

'It's good to hear you owning up to a moment's pleasure,' said Kennedy.

'I was thinking, for once, of you, dear,' his wife told him. 'Have you noticed how many women of our age have taken up lesbianism? The male thing hasn't delivered the goods.'

'It's worn itself out delivering the money,' Vanner said.

'You wouldn't think we had two out-of-work men relaxing here, would you?' Gwenda asked. 'Gentlemen of leisure, shiftless, useless, pointless and sexless.'

'That's a bit harsh, isn't it?' asked Kennedy, but he could see what had happened. Guessing correctly that Suzanne Vanner was deeply unhappy with her husband, Gwenda had sought to cheer her up by attacking husbands herself. So other people were dragged innocently into their friends' misery and were soon in a similar position themselves.

'I think Men's Hour tomorrow will have to analyse the brutal assault that we've endured this evening, and decide whether our heroic efforts are being appreciated,' he said.

'Have you noticed any heroic efforts, Suzanne?' Gwenda asked.

'Only by me,' she replied.

'Where's Toby?' asked Harry Grant the following morning as he climbed on to his stool in the Flatulent Ferret. Toby Beauchamp's arrival at noon on Sundays was one of the few certainties left in an unpredictable world and this morning his stool was empty.

'He's gone away,' said Barry, wiping the counter. 'He left a note for Mrs Hockley, telling her not to clean the house until she heard from him.'

'Gone away?' said Harry. 'Man on bail flees country?'

'I didn't say that he'd left the country,' said Barry. 'The police took his passport, didn't they?'

'He'll end up on a wanted poster,' said Harry. 'It'll be very bad for his image.'

'Come to that,' said Barry. 'Where's the vicar?'

'In a home for the bewildered, I should think. There's a locum sky pilot looking after our spiritual welfare until he recovers. Any chance of a Bell's, or have you lost your licence?'

Barry went off to get the whisky. Paul Vanner came in. He looked no more than usually dismayed and hoisted himself on to his stool with only a nod.

'Where's Toby?' he asked when a lengthy period of orientation seemed to have been satisfactorily accomplished.

'We think he's done a runner,' Harry told him. 'We think he's in flight from the law.'

'On the other hand he may just be on holiday,' Barry said. 'You know how journalists like to dramatize things.'

'If he was on holiday he would have been able to tell Mrs Hockley when he was coming back,' Harry said. 'A pint of lager for the jobless money dealer, please.'

Neil Kennedy came in and wanted gin.

'What happened to Men's Hour?' Harry asked. 'Felix dead, Toby gone. We're an endangered species like the whale.'

'Just like the whale, pal,' Vanner said. 'We drift around not doing any harm, spout off occasionally and the next thing you know you've got a harpoon up your arse.'

'We certainly took some flak last night,' said Kennedy as he pulled up a stool. 'I sometimes think that women don't like men any more.'

'You're a disappointment to them,' Vanner told him. 'They've been reading magazines and think they ought to have multiple orgasms on the hour. Your attempts to satisfy their sexual needs are obviously laughable.'

'And this irritates them, you reckon?'

'It doesn't help. Who wants a drink?'

Harry Grant listened to this banter with some amusement. His sex life had never been better and it had been weeks since he had managed to muster up a sexual fantasy – which had collapsed like a house of cards when his drained energy failed to sustain the Rabelaisian scene that his imagination was struggling to create.

'In bed last night,' said Vanner – and they prepared themselves for an embarrassingly frank story of sexual humiliation – 'I was wondering whether to kill my wife. I have a feeling that it's a lot easier than people think. The important thing is for there to be no body that a pathologist can ponder over. You've got to bury her in small bits from Peterhead to Plymouth.'

'Is this off the record?' said Harry, pulling out a notebook.

'Journalists don't usually hear about murders until afterwards. "Compton Sinbury Man's Wife-Slaying Plans – Exclusive Interview".'

'The more I drink, the wittier you get, Harry,' Vanner said. 'It's people like you who have given murder a bad name.'

'What's wrong with divorce?' Kennedy asked.

'Divorce is expensive, murder is free,' said Vanner.

'Apart from train fares to Peterhead and Plymouth.'

'I'm sorry if the Press has given murder a bad name,' said Harry. 'It's always jumping in and taking sides. I remember that it got a bee in its bonnet about Mr Hitler. Never saw his side of the story at all.'

'Exactly. Crucified by the Press.'

'How were you proposing to kill your wife?'

'I'd bash her on the head with a spanner or something.'

'I'd pan her with a spanner, says Vanner. It's got headline potential.'

'Poison is too difficult, and you never know what they will trace.'

'I don't see that would matter very much,' said Kennedy, 'if her head's in Hay-on-Wye and her stomach's in Dumfries.'

'The amazing thing,' said Harry, 'is the way they keep replacing their stars. Keegan and Toshack and St John are long gone, but they're still the best team in the country.'

The reason for this abrupt change of subject became apparent to the others when they looked round and saw that their wives had joined them.

'How's Boys' Hour?' asked Gwenda. 'You ought to have a uniform – short trousers, badges, blazers and caps. You could get Barry to stock lager-flavoured lollies.'

'Any of you want a wee-wee?' Suzanne asked.

'If you hold it, I'll try,' said Harry. 'Can I buy you ladies something with my pocket money?'

'Like a double arsenic, do you mean? I'll have a wine, please, Harry. Dry white.'

'Me too,' said Suzanne. 'I think Lindy wants a lemonade.'

'How nice it is,' said Kennedy, 'to have the whole family together for a quiet drink on Sunday lunchtime.'

'I was just thinking the same thing, Neil,' said Vanner. 'A relaxing social occasion with the civilizing influence of the company of women.'

'Are these people growing up or are they genetically intolerant to alcohol?' Gwenda asked. 'And where's your chairman Mr Beauchamp?'

'If only we knew,' said Harry.

In a tatty *hamburgueseria* on the Costa del Sol Toby Beauchamp was drinking Coca-Cola and wondering what to do next. From an equally tatty juke box at his elbow came the mindless injunction to 'Twist and Shout'. In a corner a faded blonde who moved with all the elegance of a Mexican jumping bean was dancing to the music.

Toby stood at the counter and looked out of a menu-covered window at the sea. He had bolted here because he had read in the papers that this was where people bolted to when the police were snapping at your heels, and your nights were being disturbed by dreams of prison gates shutting. There were more than three hundred British fugitives on this coast, so the arrival of one more would not be noticed. They lived in Fort-Knox villas in the hills and were careful who they mixed with. Their windows were barred and their walls were high, not unlike the prisons that they were scheming so diligently to avoid.

But these were not the people Toby had seen in three lonely days on this coast. 'Howling proles' was the phrase that came into his mind as he studied the vulgar T-shirts, the execrable manners and the slovenly behaviour of the crowds who were making the most of their annual two weeks' escape from the factory. He did not relish the idea of sharing their company.

He finished his Coca-Cola and went out. The only rule he had made for himself was no alcohol before the evening, lest the days slip by in a blur, but the heat gave him a thirst which Coca-Cola did not begin to assuage.

On the beaches it seemed to be the age of the topless granny, while self-conscious teenagers, who hadn't endured forty years of sexual repression, concealed what they were not yet prepared to reveal.

They lay on their sunbeds, moving hardly at all. The heat seemed to have brought the whole world to a halt.

He walked along the front, with a road on one side of him and the beach on the other, and decided to buy a hat. He paused to watch a small funfair on the beach where families with children who wouldn't just lie in the sun were hurtling around in bumper cars. Beyond it was one of several stalls, and he bought himself a large straw hat and some dark glasses. These gave him, he imagined, a somewhat furtive air and he strolled on feeling more like the fugitive that he had now become.

The problem of what to do with his time seemed insoluble. He needed his books, his music, his television and his garden. He needed a drink in the Flatulent Ferret.

The heat now would take the skin off your nose, so he made his way up a narrow, shaded side street to the hotel where he had booked a room for a month. Nobody spoke to him when he went in. He got the lift to the third floor and walked along a bare linoleum-covered corridor to his room. It was a cheap but clean hotel and when he got into his small single bedroom he thought that a month would be a long time to live in it.

And after that, what? A villa in the hills with sinister neighbours who discussed marijuana smuggling and trafficking in cocaine? Life with a guard dog as his only company? Months of identical days with nothing to look forward to? Perhaps a life of saintly contemplation with a few uplifting books and the odd joss-stick was his route back to respectability.

He sat on his small bed and counted his money. On the *diez mil* note Juan Carlos looked like a man facing a firing squad. It was a depressing image. He had £5,000 in these strange foreign notes and two books of Eurocheques with which he could draw money from England unless they froze his bank account. Perhaps he should try to shift his money to Gibraltar. He had left Britain so quickly that he hadn't been able to organize his financial affairs.

He lay on the bed now and closed his eyes. What was he

doing in this tiny room in a second-rate hotel, cut off from his friends and home? He tried to dismiss the doubts that afflicted him by telling himself that this was only the third day and that life would improve when he had settled down. After all, thousands of people dreamed of moving here and starting a new life in the sun. It was the Mecca they yearned for.

He would have a rest and then walk along the seafront before an early evening drink. Then he would find one of the better restaurants and enjoy a good dinner.

But it seemed to him that he was almost inadvertently withdrawing from the real world. The withdrawal so far didn't involve much more than wearing dark glasses and a hat, but he could see the trend.

Owen Gray's estrangement from the world was no less profound. He had been dispatched by his bishop to a home for damaged clergy on the south coast and was now temporarily incarcerated in a clifftop mansion with a bunch of dribbling dotards who mostly moved with the aid of crutches, walking frames or wheelchairs while mumbling excerpts from the Bible in lieu of rational conversation. An upwardly mobile curate from Salisbury had been bussed in to Compton Sinbury to hold the line in the battle for the village's immortal soul.

Owen Gray found that this coastal prison nourished his scepticism to the point where he felt like taking flight. He read books, not all of them religious, and went on long walks on the cliff from where he could gaze down at wheeling seagulls and hovering gannets whose own urge to fly was unconstrained by thoughts of God.

'A claustrophobia of clerics,' he told the resident chaplain who presided over this convalescent home. The chaplain, a fat man of more than nineteen stone, was called Benedict Garfield, although he was predictably nicknamed Charlie by some of the younger patients.

Owen Gray was supposed to be resting, but there was something in the demeanour of this tall thin man with his wild hair that worried Benedict Garfield. A recusant vicar was not what he needed.

'A blow on the head can seriously damage your faith,' he said. It sounded like the health warning on a packet of cigarettes.

He had called Owen Gray in for a chat, and sat now on an outsize chair behind a black desk that his stomach prevented him from reaching. Owen Gray stared, fascinated by his girth. Was it metabolism or gluttony?

'It doesn't take a blow on the head,' he told the chaplain. 'Less than three per cent of the population are regular churchgoers. In the schools Buddhism is as important as Christianity. It's an uphill struggle hanging on to your own faith, let alone anybody else's.'

Benedict Garfield sighed. There was a whiff of garlic, a hint of whisky. Benedict Garfield was obviously a man who knew how to look after himself.

'I sometimes think that if suicide was easy it would be a lot more popular,' Owen Gray told him.

'The important thing about suicide,' said the chaplain, 'is that it is always premature.' He was quite accustomed to finding, among the neurasthenic collection of pastors who ended up at his door, one wild-eyed expert in heresy.

The bare maroon walls in this room gave the impression of a rather staid hotel that had been left behind by more thrusting competitors. Through the large French windows they could see a man in blue overalls supporting shrubs with some stakes.

'Moses the gardener,' said Benedict Garfield. 'He doesn't use fertilizer, he uses manna.' He smiled crookedly across the desk.

'Anyway,' said Owen Gray, ignoring this attempt at humour, 'why not Buddhism? Or Shintoism or Hinduism? Who was it who said that man wouldn't know how to create a maggot, but creates Gods by the dozen?'

'De Montaigne,' said the chaplain sniffily. 'He was a foreigner.'

'Well, Jesus didn't exactly come from Walton-on-Thames,' said Owen Gray, surprised by this insular trait in Benedict Garfield's thinking.

'No, but the great thing about Jesus is that he wasn't *French*!'

It took Owen Gray a few moments to absorb this idea. The history of the world would have been quite different if Jesus had been French. The history of Owen Gray would probably be a different story, too. He remembered that when St Denis brought Christianity to Paris he was decapitated on the hill of Montmartre. Owen Gray could easily be a bank clerk today, his only crisis of faith being in the pound.

He looked across the black desk at his interrogator. It was his crisis of faith that the fat man was refusing to take seriously.

He told him: 'I tried to rape my sister.'

Benedict Garfield's body shivered to a sort of attention.

'You tried to what?' he asked.

'Rape my sister.'

'Why?'

Owen Gray shrugged. 'Lust.'

'Lust is a sin.'

'Yes, I read that too.'

The chaplain sat silently for a moment, considering this new information.

'Does anybody know?' he asked.

'Well, she knows. She hit me. That's how I got the head wound.'

'I mean anybody else. The police, for instance.'

Owen Gray shook his head, very gently.

'Well, I think we want to forget about that . . . Owen. You have felt remorse? It isn't something that is likely to happen again?'

Benedict Garfield had dealt more often than he cared to remember with the sexual peccadilloes of the beneficed clergy, and his policy was always to hush it up if possible and protect the church's good name. Usually they involved red-lipped choirboys or tramps in lavatories, although it wasn't unknown for dogs or sheep to be the offended parties which was much better because they couldn't give evidence in court. A straightforward attempt at heterosexual gratification was a bit of a novelty, although it was a pity about the sister part.

'It won't happen again,' Owen Gray told him.

'Good. Well, that's fine. But there are a couple of books I would like you to read in the next few days. And when you've read them, we'll discuss them. What sort of books do you normally read?'

'I read quite a lot about space. I find it fascinating.'

'Space? I should have thought that space, by definition, couldn't help but be boring.'

'Anything but,' said Owen Gray standing up. The interview seemed to be over. 'Did you know that the nearest star to earth, Proxima Centauri, is 24 million, with another six noughts on the end, miles away? Where do you think God is in all that?'

'God is God,' said Benedict Garfield. 'He's not a ruddy astronaut.'

24

Cathy Gray awoke naked in bed and wished that a man was beside her. The pink sheets seemed wasted just on her. She wanted a warm, strong body that she could cling to before the day's realities intruded. As there was none, she ran her hands down her own body, pretending that they were masculine hands, strong, firm, inquisitive.

It was a surprise to her that she had reached this age without a man; there was a time when she had imagined her problem would be fending them off. But she had buried herself in this village, where the men were married, like Paul Vanner, or understandably single, like Terry Wallace, and had reduced almost to nothing her chances of finding a partner who would love her.

She lay in bed for a few more minutes contemplating another day as a waitress in the Refectory, when her mother came in with the usual cup of tea.

'A card from Owen,' she said. 'He seems to be on the mend.' She dropped the card and a letter on the bed and put the tea down on the small dressing-table, among brushes, tweezers, scissors and hair grips.

Cathy picked up the card. It was a picture of ponies in the New Forest. She read aloud the message on the back. '"Hope you are both well. Home Friday." That tells you a lot, doesn't it?'

'How did he manage to fall and hurt his head, anyway?' asked Mrs Gray. 'Does he drink?'

'Who knows?' said Cathy, swinging her brown legs out of the bed.

'I wish he'd never gone into the church. It seems such a sad and lonely life.'

Cathy picked up the letter that her mother had brought in. The address was typed and the postmark was London.

'Vicars can get married,' she said. 'They're not like monks.'

'Girls of twenty-five can get married, too,' said Mrs Gray. 'I don't know what's the matter with my children.'

She went out of the room, closing the door quietly behind her, and Cathy opened the letter. It was from one of the several magazines to which, over the months, she had sent her picture.

The magazine's editor wanted to know whether she would be prepared to pose for a series of pin-up pictures – he called them glamour pictures – in Compton Sinbury. The theme would be rustic, with backdrops of cornfields, farm animals and haystacks, and the feature would probably be called 'Country Girl' and run for five or six pages. There was a telephone number to ring if she was interested. The fee would be £500.

Cathy Gray gave herself a thumbs-up sign in her little pink-framed mirror; she had been waiting for an offer like this for a long time.

'What is it – boobs, as you call them these days?' her mother asked over breakfast. 'We used to call them something else.'

'And bums, I expect,' said Cathy.

She rang the magazine from the Refectory and was surprised at how civilized they sounded.

Three days later, having begged a day off work, she went to the Flatulent Ferret to meet the photographer who was driving down from London and had suggested a pub as the most suitable meeting place. She was wearing a yellow blouse and garish culottes; she didn't expect to be wearing them for long.

Paul Vanner was sitting alone at the bar. He stared at her floral culottes and said: 'What's mother doing for curtains today?'

'Hallo, Paul,' she said. 'How's Suzanne?'

'Suzanne is not a happy woman. What will you drink?'

Cathy put a little make-up bag she was carrying on the bar and wondered whether models drank alcohol before assignments. She thought they probably didn't.

'A fruit juice,' she said. 'Why is Suzanne unhappy? Because she's had to close the shop?'

'She's married to me,' Vanner said. 'It turns out not to be the secret of contentment.'

'I think I'd be contented,' she said.

Vanner perked up at this news. 'Would you? Do you really think you would be?'

'I'd love it,' said Cathy. 'I thought you were terrific.'

Vanner smiled. A little sunshine had fallen into his life. 'Why are you in here, anyway?' he asked.

Cathy told him.

'Will he photograph you with no clothes? Will he see your breasts and everything? Try to make your answer as arousing as possible.'

'He'll photograph what he wants to photograph. Then I'll get paid £500.'

'And where is this going to happen?'

'I thought I'd take him to one of Farmer Garrity's fields. They want cows and haystacks and things.'

'Boobs in the barnyard. What will they think of next?'

The door opened and a small man with a black beard came in. He didn't seem much more than twenty.

'Cathy Gray?' he said, coming over. 'I recognize you from the lovely pictures you sent. I'm Dave. All photographers are called Dave.' He smiled and shook hands. 'Is this your husband?'

'Not yet,' said Vanner. 'Do you want a drink?'

'Work first, drink later,' said Dave. 'Otherwise you get fuzzy and then the pictures do.'

They left Vanner with his pint of lager and went outside to Dave's small red Fiat. As they drove along the country lanes he complained that he had just flown in from Australia – 'wall-to-wall designer gum-trees' – and was severely jet-lagged. His meandering driving seemed to confirm a degree of tiredness that made motoring hazardous.

When they pulled up in the yard at the farm Cathy went to find Farmer Garrity.

'You can use the fields,' he said. 'If you want to use animals I want paying.'

Dave produced some new £5 notes on which the Queen looked like the woman who made her living impersonating her.

'Okay, let's go,' he said to Cathy. 'You can leave your clothes in my car.'

Cathy Gray took off her blouse and saw the two men looking at her breasts.

'They're terrific,' said Dave admiringly. 'I was afraid they were going to be white.'

She took off her culottes and stood there in a pair of pink pants.

'I don't have to take these off yet, do I?' she asked. Farmer Garrity, still perspiring under his straw hat, seemed to her to be getting more than his money's worth.

'Yeah, get 'em off,' said Dave. 'We don't want a mark round your waist from the elastic.'

She pulled them down reluctantly and saw their eyes drop to her pubic hair.

'It beats photographing kangaroos,' said Dave, hanging two cameras round his neck.

She walked naked across the yard with the two men in search of suitable locations. Farmer Garrity explained that he would have to come with them to see that the animals weren't upset.

'Are you the vicar's sister?' he asked.

She nodded.

'He was up here looking at the crop circles.'

Farmer Garrity liked talking to Cathy because a certain proximity was required for conversation. At one stage he seemed to be scratching his groin in a gesture indistinguishable from sexual stimulation. But Dave led her away from his unwelcome company and guided her through reels of film and dozens of pictures that would contrast her young beauty with an age-old pastoral setting.

Astride a farmhorse, stroking a cow, reclining in a haystack, peeping over a hedge, feeding a foal and strolling through a cornfield, she tried to produce the smouldering expression that Dave needed.

'What I want to do,' he explained, like a professor in a

laboratory, 'is maximize the impact of your magnificent breasts.'

'Golly,' said Cathy.

'It's all a question of angles.'

He finally settled on a stile between two fields on a hill. As she bent provocatively over it, Dave took a dozen pictures and promised that one would definitely be on the cover.

Cathy Gray, cover girl, peered sexily into the distance and saw Paul Vanner watching her from behind a hedge.

Harry Grant was undergoing a period of adjustment. When he woke up in the mornings now there seemed to be less room for him in the bed, and a trawl through the wavebands of his transistor radio was no longer an acceptable method of introducing himself to the new day. Nadine lay beside him and she hated getting up. She woke with a smile, said, 'Hallo, lover' and went straight back to sleep.

On Sunday mornings Harry was not anxious to get up himself and they lay in bed until Rachel brought them tea. The two of them had moved into the cottage with scarcely a hitch and now it was as if they had always been there.

The cottage changed, though. To Harry it seemed cleaner and brighter. The brightness baffled him for a time and then he saw that he had new, lighter curtains. Plants had begun to appear in various corners and there was new equipment in the kitchen: microwave, washing machine, toaster – even the kettle had been replaced. The only spot to remain untouched was the potting shed, a male domain that Nadine decided should escape her improvements.

The new ménage had settled down so well that as Nadine lay sleepily on her back he asked: 'Have you ever thought of having another child?'

'Don't you dare!' she told him. 'I couldn't go through all that again.'

Rachel came in with their tea and the papers.

'Oh well,' said Harry. 'Here's one I made earlier.'

'Good morning, parents,' said Rachel. 'You're missing Michael Jackson on television.'

'Thank God for that,' said Harry, picking up the Sunday papers. He read them dutifully because occasionally a local story leapt out at him – a village resident in an air crash on the other side of the world, a holiday accident in some sun-baked European resort. Today the paper was much occupied with the fact that the Kurfürstendamm had been reunited with the Unter den Linden after a 45-year tiff, but the *County Gazette* didn't cover Berlin.

As soon as he got out of bed the telephone rang and he went into his new office which Nadine had installed in the third and smallest bedroom and picked up the extension.

'Harry Grant?' said a voice that he knew.

'Yes.' He couldn't put a face to the voice but he knew that he knew the man.

'I think there is a little story that you might be interested in.'

On the whole Harry was not enthusiastic about news stories on Sunday morning, particularly before he had had his breakfast.

'I know your voice but I can't remember your name,' he said.

'It's Owen Gray here.'

'Of course it is. How's your head?'

'I'm okay now, thanks. I thought you might like to come to church this morning.'

'Really?' said Harry. 'What on earth gave you that extraordinary idea?'

'I'm not out to save your soul, Harry. Or mine, come to think of it. I thought you should attend in a professional capacity, in your lifelong pursuit of news.'

Harry Grant found this invitation highly unwelcome. His Sunday mornings, in the company of the newspapers, had always had a peaceful, undisturbed quality which delivered him tranquilly at noon to the relaxed grumbles of Men's Hour. To try to insert a church service into this agreeable schedule was to be unnecessarily disruptive, quite apart from the fact that to listen to a sinner like Owen Gray extolling the merits of God would be rather like hearing a tiger deliver a lecture on the virtues of vegetarianism.

'What are you going to do?' he asked. 'Rape Daisy Balcombe?'

'Yes, you journalists have got a dark sense of humour. But I'm just tipping you off, as a friend. I think you'll find that you were glad you were there.'

'I will be. What time do you open?'

'Open?'

'Sorry, I was thinking of pubs. What time does the service start?'

'It's the monthly family service and it starts at eleven.'

'Blimey, will it be over by twelve? I have a standing appointment in the institution at the other end of the green.'

'I think I can promise that,' said Owen Gray and hung up.

Harry went back into the bedroom.

'You'll never guess what I'm doing this morning,' he said.

Nadine was sitting in bed, as if it was now just possible that she would be getting up today. Harry thought she looked particularly nice in the morning, sleepy and relaxed, before the stresses of the day began to show.

'Paint the cottage?' she said. 'Fix the door on that cupboard?'

'I'm going to church,' he told her.

'Oh, don't get religion, Harry. I couldn't handle it. What is this, the male menopause?'

'Work. It's a story.'

'Who says?'

'Owen Gray. He just rang up and told me not to miss it. Pretty mysterious, eh?'

'He's going to slide down the pulpit banister in the nude. I'd better come with you.'

But later, as they walked towards the church with Rachel, she began to have doubts about whether it was such a good idea.

'They won't like it,' she said. 'We're living in sin. I bet we attract a few frowns of disapproval.'

'You could always get married,' said Rachel.

But when they went into church it was Harry Grant who attracted the odd glances. He was well known among the churchgoers as an *habitué* of the public house and not a man likely to turn up in a suit for family service on a Sunday morning. As he eased himself into the old brown scratched pew, he tried to look like a professional journalist who in the course of duty had found himself in many stranger places than this. He wondered what all these people did when they were not praying. At the back of the church an empty cardboard box had a notice on it which said: 'Your used stamps can help the church in Lesotho' so they evidently found something to fill their time. He took the pale blue hassock off a hook in front of him and laid it on the stone floor, and then he reached for the little red book on the shelf above it in the hope of finding some reading matter. It was *Hymns, ancient and modern, revised.* The only remotely modern artefact that he could see in the church was a brass fire extinguisher.

Michael the butcher was the organist and choirmaster and, as ten small boys in surplices and cassocks filed out of the vestry, he burst into a piece of solemn music on the huge organ behind the pulpit. The choir was followed by Owen Gray, who looked younger after his enforced absence, and seemed occasionally to be on the verge of smiling. He stepped up to the brass lectern and announced that the first hymn was written in 1864 by Mrs L. M. Willis. It was 'Father, hear the prayer we offer'.

Watching Owen Gray sing this, Harry decided that religion was a confidence trick, like gimcrack psychoanalysis or earning a living by pretending you knew what the weather would be like in a day or two. The words, which seemed particularly pertinent to his own situation, came out of Owen Gray's mouth as if they meant something quite different.

> Be our strength in hours of weakness,
> In our wanderings be our guide . . .

The congregation sang lustily, happily confident that there were no hours of weakness round here.

When they sat down for the sermon, Harry was beginning to ask himself why he was there. He looked up at the hammerbeam roof and wondered whether a thunderbolt from God was about to disperse this small throng of worshippers. After all, he had been promised a headline.

Owen Gray climbed the steps to the pulpit with fear in his heart. Since the blow on the head he seemed to lack the inner strength which a man needed to face life's little crises.

He looked down at his meagre congregation and wondered what they expected of him. They gazed back as if he was about to impart the secret of life.

Colonel Arbuthnott's interest in a Jew born 2,000 years ago was entirely out of character. He was suspicious of all foreigners, which included people who lived north of Reading. He was also, Owen Gray suspected, a proto-fascist who was, people said, even against ugly people breeding.

Daisy Balcombe, who was in charge of the church flowers, only wanted the customary assurance that life didn't end with death. At her age, it was a consideration.

Mrs Webberley had taken up coming to church when her husband died. She felt apparently that it helped her keep in touch with him as if the church was an unusually cheap sideline run by British Telecom.

The man in the yellow sweater whom Owen Gray had seen exercising a white poodle no doubt had his own problems. A craving for the choirboys, or a yearning for forgiveness? Owen Gray thought that he could bring this subject into his sermon.

Some couples arrived almost absentmindedly with their children, believing in nothing themselves except that the children should be exposed to a sniff of hellfire and damnation along with playgroup and the Brownies.

What a sad lot they all were; what awful voids must be lodged at the centre of their lives.

He placed his hands on the rim of the pulpit and began.

'Why do you good people who come to church every Sunday always look so miserable? It's not because the sinners are having all the fun, although you probably find that irksome. It's because you're worried about death, which is why you're here in the first place.'

He paused to glance at the expressions on the faces of his

congregation. The evidence that they were actually taking in what he was saying was not conclusive. Perhaps they never listened, but sank into their own dismal reveries until the next hymn. He decided that a more boisterous approach was needed.

'The idea that life terminates, as a reporter said to me the other day, in the crematorium, is a difficult concept for some people to accept. Man is the only animal who knows that he is going to die. And so some people sustain themselves with the notion that this short life is only a beginning, that there is an endless party afterwards with music and angels somewhere up there in the exosphere. The exosphere is the one above the thermosphere, which is itself above the mesosphere, the stratosphere and the troposphere, but none of the brave men who have plunged through this distant environment in their fragile spacecrafts has reported signs of a party.'

For the first time there was an audible laugh in the church. It came from Nadine Kirby who whispered: 'He's digging his own grave.' But Harry Grant was too busy scribbling in his notebook to reply.

'You're going to die,' said Owen Gray. 'There's nothing to it. You rehearse it every night when you go to sleep. And that, I'm afraid, is that. It is our deep psychological refusal to accept this simple truth which has kept the church alive – this church and hundreds of others – in all their panoply for thousands of years.' He looked out at the congregation. 'And who are these people who turn up every Sunday in the sublime belief that they are booking a seat at some future event?'

There was an uneasy shuffling of feet now as if some people in the church felt that something should be done about this scandalous outburst. Harry Grant looked round to see how the congregation were taking it. In the front pew, Daisy Balcombe's shiny, aquiline nose twitched ominously.

Owen Gray had raced on and was now saying: 'The high incidence of religious mania among practising homosexuals is a phenomenon that has received too little attention.'

Even those members of the congregation who regarded the

sermon as one of the *longueurs* that a Christian had to endure were aware now that something extraordinary was happening. The attention that was often so conspicuously lacking was bestowed on Owen Gray in full measure as the worshippers listened with an awful fascination.

'Next year we will have a new Archbishop of Canterbury. His successor, if the opinion polls are to be believed, will be chosen by an agnostic. In fact, by that time he may well be an agnostic himself. The game's up. The heavens are opening to us but they are revealing not God but a million scientific possibilities.'

He took his hands off the rim of the pulpit and it was clear that his valedictory sermon was drawing to a close.

'I'm off,' said Owen Gray. 'I'm off to write a book about space which is the past we know little about, and the future we don't yet understand. One infinitesimal step for mankind, but a giant leap for your former vicar. Good day to you.'

'You Judas!' shouted Daisy Balcombe, and she ripped open her handbag in search of something to throw.

As Owen Gray began to descend the pulpit steps, the golden phallus came hurtling across the nave and struck him on the forehead.

He pitched forward into the aisle and lay there with the giant organ just a few feet from his head.

'Morning service doesn't end with the sermon,' said Neil Kennedy.

'This one did,' said Harry Grant, drinking his Bell's.

The inquest in the Flatulent Ferret made even devout atheists wish they had been in church. Those who had, and had found it necessary afterwards to seek strong refreshment, found that their drinks were free as customers gathered round and begged them to tell the story again.

Harry Grant was agonizing once more over the thoroughly unsuitable nature of the headlines that his village was producing. GIANT PENIS FELLS ATHEIST VICAR was not at all what the *Gazette* editor wanted. Even the headline that was eventually used – FURY OVER VICAR'S LAST SERMON – was thought to be a bit strong for local tastes.

To write this story Harry had to spend his precious Sunday afternoon talking to people who had been in the congregation that morning, to gauge reaction to the last sermon of Owen Gray. He was not available for interview himself, being detained in hospital for X-rays.

Colonel Arbuthnott fulminated magnificently in his library.

'Ought to be sent to the Tar,' he said.

'The what, Colonel?' asked Harry.

'The Tar of London. Lock him up and throw away the key.'

He sat in a deep leather armchair, shaking his head in despair at the disgrace and, worse, notoriety that had been brought on Compton Sinbury by its erratic priest.

'What was that thing Daisy threw, anyway?' he asked. 'I didn't get a good look at it myself, but the wife said it looked like a chap's John Thomas.'

'It did a bit,' agreed Harry.

Trying to find an acceptable way of describing this missile to his readers was not the least of Harry's problems. The headline FLYING WILLY STUNS PRELATE kept jumping into his head. He decided that he would have to talk to Daisy Balcombe.

Her cottage on the edge of the village had roses over the door and a very old 'No hawkers, no circulars' metal notice fixed to the gate.

'Mr Grant,' she said, surprised. She was wearing a floral, ankle-length dress and held a sheaf of papers. 'I'm just organizing auditions for the village pantomime.'

'I won't be long,' said Harry, feeling that he was interrupting. 'I'm writing a story for the *Gazette* about our ex-vicar.'

'What he said was unforgivable,' said Daisy. 'You'd better come in. You're going to give the pantomime some publicity, I hope? We're doing *Cinderella* this year. I think that girl who works in the Refectory would be ideal in the lead.'

'Cathy Gray?'

'That's the girl.'

'Can she act?'

'Well, the standard isn't *that* high.'

She led him through the spotless cottage to a small

conservatory that had been built on the back. She settled into a wickerwork chair surrounded by scripts, costumes and sketches of sets, and waved Harry to sit in another.

'That thing you threw at the vicar,' he said. 'What the devil was it?'

'It's extremely valuable,' she said. 'It was stupid of me to throw it. Luckily it hasn't been damaged.'

'What is it exactly?'

'A fertility symbol,' she said instantly. 'I'd have thought you could see that.'

'May I ask where you got it? The thing is –'

'Kuala Lumpur,' said Daisy. 'Bought it on one of my trips. It was bloody expensive. It's fifteenth century, you know. Are you going to quote that blasphemous sermon? Do you think you should?'

'It's part of the story. It won't make a lot of sense unless we tell readers what he said.'

'The man's quite mad, you know. There were some strange stories going round about him before this morning's little contretemps.'

'I heard.'

'But his sister, apparently, is quite sane. She'd make a wonderful Cinderella.'

Harry Grant went back to his cottage and started to type. He always liked to write his stories while they were fresh in his mind. Before he began, he rang the hospital to check on Owen Gray's condition. They said that he had slight concussion and was being kept in overnight. Harry put down the phone, reeled some paper into his typewriter and began his story. The first sentence wrote itself.

> A sensational sermon that denied the existence of God brought morning service at St Thomas's parish church, Compton Sinbury, to a premature and chaotic conclusion on Sunday.

An hour later, as he typed ENDS at the bottom of the fourth sheet, Nadine came in.

'I don't approve of working on the Sabbath,' she said.

'We *are* getting religious after one brief trip to church.'

'You have a family now and the family wants you to take it out. Tea and cakes in an olde-worlde restaurant in the country is what we have in mind.'

'Good idea. I'll be with you in two minutes. We can drop the story in at the office.'

He got the pages together and read the story through. Parts of it weren't true, but the truth was unprintable.

> Miss Daisy Balcombe, 70, who is responsible for the church flowers, was so incensed by the vicar's remarks that she threw a small *objet d'art* at him as he left the pulpit.
>
> It hit the Revd Gray on the forehead and caused slight concussion only weeks after he suffered a fractured skull in a fall.
>
> 'What he said was unforgivable,' said Miss Balcombe, who added that the gold *objet d'art* was a fifteenth-century fertility symbol that she bought during a visit to Malaysia.

The sun-tanned man in dark glasses and a straw hat who strolled down the *paseo maritimo* didn't seem to belong to this raucous playground. He walked alone, pausing occasionally to look at the bodies on the beach, but he was never going to step down and join their world of sun, sea, sand, sloth, sangria and sex. Such distractions were clearly in his past.

In the fourth week of his exile Toby Beauchamp had developed a routine which carried him from one day to the next. In the morning, he walked two miles along the front and two miles back before stopping for coffee and a browse through a day-old British newspaper. In the afternoon, after a light lunch in the hotel, he rested. In the evening, he went out to the bars before moving on to a restaurant for dinner.

And one day a week, to break this routine, he went out for

a drive. He had driven in a hired car between pine and eucalyptus trees to white villages in the red-earth mountains to the north; he had visited Seville's Giralda, Granada's Alhambra and Córdoba's Mezquita. But what he could not do was adjust to the life of a fugitive. He saw himself as man on the run and found it impossible to relax. He caught himself looking over his shoulder and became paranoiac when people looked at him for more than a second or two. He found increasingly that he was constantly expecting a hand on his arm.

The bars in the evening, where he had hoped to find the most enjoyable moments of his day, filled him with unease. Conversations made him nervous because, sooner or later, people wanted to know something about you. He began to believe that they had seen his picture in an English newspaper that he had missed. He contrived to drink alone.

But it wasn't loneliness that was his problem; he was used to being alone. It was boredom that nagged him, the sheer emptiness of the days. He yearned to do a deal, watch builders at work, discuss plans with an architect. He wanted to drive round a greener land than this in his Porsche and look for sites.

Toby Beauchamp didn't know as he walked along the *paseo* that most of his fears were ill-founded. The police were not even aware of his absence and they wouldn't miss him until he failed to turn up for his trial. It wasn't a condition of bail that he report to them regularly, or at all. They would merely assume, as they held his passport, that he was in Britain.

What Toby did know this morning, however, was that he had to make a big decision about his future very quickly. His booking at the hotel expired in five days and he had to decide where he was going from there. For once, he broke off from his morning walk and went into a bar for a beer.

A man in a bow tie pushed a bottle of San Miguel towards him and he took it to a corner table. When you stood at the bar people talked to you.

A man with nothing to do is prey to worries that normally he would have no time for, and Toby Beauchamp was finding that fresh causes for concern alighted hourly on his shoulders.

The latest one, as he sat in the corner of the bar, seemed to have special qualities for disturbing him.

What was he to do when his one-year passport expired?

He wouldn't be able to replace it, and a man without a passport round here would soon find himself in trouble. If he was then sent back to England it would only mean that his prison sentence started – and ended – a year later than it would otherwise have done which, at his age, was a point to consider. It would also, thanks to his flight, be longer.

More importantly, the fact of his year's absence would be taken as an admission of guilt and considerably handicap Gavin Riley in his attempt to defend him.

He sipped his beer and ran through it all again. The problem was the passport. A postponed trial would give him less chance of acquittal and, on conviction, produce a longer jail sentence. And staying here for ever was beginning to seem almost as unenticing as a short stay in prison.

He looked out of the window at the crowds on the beach. They were only here for a couple of weeks. They all had their plane tickets home.

He finished his beer and went to the bar to pay. A group of noisy middle-aged Englishmen came in, all wearing identical blue sweaters; they were clearly on a golfing holiday.

Outside he walked briskly along the front looking for a travel agent. Fifteen minutes later he had a single ticket to Gatwick in his pocket for 5 November. He smiled to himself for the first time in a month.

25

It was only to be expected that as he trudged through the green channel at customs Toby Beauchamp would be called back by a small Customs official and asked to open his luggage. It was a vindication of his paranoia and at the same time a relief: he had expected to be greeted by a policeman.

Naturally there was nothing in his cases that would interest the expressionless official who worked his way through Toby's soiled shirts. He had enough problems without exposing himself to a charge of smuggling.

When he was allowed to go through he made his way to the newsagents, still expecting to find a story about himself. Instead he was confronted by dozens of copies of *Radio Times* with Neil Kennedy smiling seductively on the cover. He had barely recovered from the surprise when he noticed a naked Cathy Gray smiling even more seductively at him over a stile on the cover of another magazine.

What, as Paul Vanner would say, was occurring?

He bought both magazines and *The Times*, and went out to find a taxi that didn't mind travelling more than ten miles. As the old cab chugged west he read about Neil Kennedy and *Hot Air Rises*. On the cover he looked like the curly-headed lover wives left home for, but in the Flatulent Ferret it had never seemed as if his own wife found him particularly attractive. It was quite clear, though, that his role in this serial was regarded as something out of the ordinary by the BBC. It wasn't everybody who landed on the cover of *Radio Times*.

The other magazine was called *Crumpet*, and he was glad that he was able to look at it in the privacy of a taxi; it was not the sort of publication that he would brandish on a train.

'Cathy Gray is a country girl who is not interested in the high fashion of the city,' he read. 'In fact she is not interested in fashion at all. In the golden cornfields of her native Hampshire she sheds her worries and her clothes . . .'

Toby Beauchamp devoted rather more time to this piece of journalism than he had to Neil Kennedy, and then he put it aside reluctantly and picked up *The Times*.

The small headline at the bottom of the front page leapt out at him: PLANNING OFFICIAL JAILED. Brynwyn Rolfe had got five years.

In the Television Theatre at Shepherd's Bush Green, Neil Kennedy was drinking gin that evening. In dressing room number 1, not far away, Terry Wogan was drinking BBC coffee from a Styrofoam cup.

'He doesn't really like to meet people before the show,' said a production assistant. 'It spoils the spontaneity.' The production assistant, or probably one of several production assistants, was a pretty young girl who didn't look old enough for the job. She gripped the statutory clipboard.

'That's fine by me,' said Neil Kennedy, drinking more gin. 'I'm buggered if I know why I'm here.'

'You're here because the BBC likes to use this show to plug its new programmes,' said the girl briskly. 'Don't drink too much gin.'

Neil Kennedy took another look at her. Perhaps she wasn't as young as he had thought. He wondered whether she had seen a tape of *Hot Air Rises* and was now seething for him beneath her schoolgirl jeans.

'Have you seen *Hot Air Rises*?' he asked.

'Seen what?' she replied.

The technical rehearsal was going on out front and producing outbreaks of laughter from the crew. Neil Kennedy decided that it was time to stop drinking gin and go to make-up. He was the first guest which he took to mean that he was the least important.

He was ushered into the wings by the girl whose responsibility for him ended once he was delivered to the scrutiny of a live camera. The signature tune died down and was replaced by wild applause as Terry Wogan appeared and tried, as usual, to subdue their enthusiasm.

Kennedy wondered who was in the audience. The people who were let in free to watch a forty-minute television programme seemed to be quite different from the audience who paid to watch a two-hour play. Coachloads of semi-drunk shop assistants on a night out was the impression he had from the din. Then he wondered whether Gwenda would bother to watch. He knew that Lindy wouldn't. She had seen him on television before and thought that was what everybody's daddy did.

He heard Wogan saying '. . . another blistering look at modern marriage. The beleaguered husband in this domestic kerfuffle is played by everybody's favourite yesterday's man, Neil Kennedy, but before we meet him, let's have a look at a clip.'

On a monitor he saw himself in bed with the ice maiden, an occasion which brought back such memories that the production assistant was suddenly pushing him in the back and saying: 'Get on. He's announced you.'

Like all actors, he revived on stage. The music, the applause, the glow of approval all added inches to his stature. When he sat down and was confronted by the Irishman's famous charm, he felt able to ask: 'What do you mean, everybody's favourite yesterday's man, Terry?'

'Well, you used to be on everything, and now you're not.'

'It's the scripts, Terry. You have to wait for the good ones.'

'In this one you're a bit of a two-timer, aren't you? And you seem to believe that women should be shackled to the home?'

It seemed absurd that he should be asked to explain the writers' philosophy. Chat-show hosts loved to pretend that the actor was really the character he was playing. He remembered Larry Hagman being interviewed as if he really had been married to Sue Ellen. But Kennedy had no idea what effect the writers were aiming for, nor what their deepest feelings were about modern marriage. He had only met them twice and had been surprised that they could write a script. In conversation they seemed barely able to string a sentence together.

Luckily Wogan was so fond of talking that Kennedy's unnatural reticence was no obstacle to their instant rapport. Soon they were wandering back through the disordered career of Neil Kennedy – hot at twenty, frozen out at twenty-five and now back with a bang at thirty – and it emerged that Terry Wogan was a bit of a fan.

'I remember you as a teenage killer who went to the gallows in – what was it called?'

'*The Croydon Gun*.'

'I thought you were going to be the new James Dean.'

'I was a bit put off by the life-expectancy factor.'

Terry chatted on; the role of listener, oddly, was not one that he seemed to enjoy, and it was Terry who was talking when frantic hand signals from behind the camera told him to move on. A few yards to their left, a girl from the Welsh valleys was already in position to sing her new ballad, the haunting story of an unmarried mother whose child had been fathered by a terrorist. The next guest was a man called Ted Parratt who had written a book about the awful things that were put into your drinks to make them look nicer and last longer. It was called *Name Your Poison!*

As a grand finale Terry and his guests left the studio for a firework display on the green outside, a spectacle which the deserted studio audience was obliged to watch, like the viewer at home, on television.

The firework display on the green at Compton Sinbury produced the biggest crowd of the year because people drove in from other villages to enjoy the spectacle.

Neil Kennedy arrived in a BBC car that had been held up during the last mile of its journey by a London taxi that dawdled along the country lanes as if it couldn't understand where all the traffic jams had gone. When it stopped, just before the bridge, Toby Beauchamp got out, laden with cases.

Kennedy got the BBC car to stop there as well and jumped out.

'Toby!' he said. 'We'd thought you'd done a runner.'

'Just a holiday, Neil,' said Toby. 'I needed a break. There seems to be some sort of firework display on the green.'

'Dump your cases and we'll go and have a look.'

There were more than two thousand people milling about on the green. At their centre, where the Compton Sinbury Fireworks Committee were organizing things, a large bonfire burned. From its light Kennedy could see his wife and daughter standing in the front row enjoying the display. He worked his way through to them.

'Big bangs, daddy,' Lindy said.

'I don't know whether she's excited or frightened,' said Gwenda. 'Everybody saw you, by the way.'

'Did you?'

'Of course. I thought you were very good when you could get a word in. The rebirth of Neil Kennedy.'

He turned to pull Toby Beauchamp towards him through the crowd. 'Look who's here!'

'Toby! Hallo. We thought you'd gone into hiding.'

'Just a holiday, Gwenda,' Toby said. 'It could be some time before I get another.'

Harry Grant came up to them.

'Good God! Return of the fugitive,' he said. 'How are you, Toby?'

'I'm not a fugitive, Harry. I've been on vacation. How are things with you? I see Brynwyn Rolfe got five years.'

A huge bang a few feet away temporarily deafened them.

'He sure did,' said Harry. 'There'll be about six columns of it in Friday's paper if you want to know what happened.' Toby looked very brown and slightly thinner, but this year people were actually getting tanned in Britain. 'You didn't absquatulate, did you?' he asked.

'I've been no further than Devon,' said Toby. 'A dreadful little place called Clovelly. I don't have a passport, if you remember.'

A firework screamed into the air and burst into a multicoloured rainfall.

'Well, that's fine,' said Harry. 'You had us worried. We had visions of you skulking round some dusty *pueblo* with a bag over your head.'

'What have I missed?'

'Quite a lot, actually. My new family. The last sermon of Owen Gray. Neil on *Wogan*. Which reminds me – I ought to interview the man myself. "Local Star in Telly Shocker".'

'Terry Wogan and then Harry Grant,' said Neil Kennedy. 'Is my career on the way up or down?'

When *Hot Air Rises* reached the nation's television screens a few days later, the Vanners watched it in the Manor House, conscious that this was the first event to bring them together for some time. The Cathy disclosure had poisoned an atmosphere that was already toxic, and Paul Vanner, despairing of any improvement, was now allowing himself to imagine a new life: a new (lower paid) job, a new (smaller) house, a new (more amenable) wife.

Suzanne treated him like a lodger who had fallen behind with the rent; whatever little prestige he had ever had around here had vanished with his job. But the new financial stringency had not curtailed her drinking. More and more, it seemed, she needed a few glasses of wine to get her through the days. The wine made her careless, irritable or aggressive, depending on how much she had drunk.

Tonight she was aggressive, but their curiosity about Neil Kennedy's new television serial brought them together on the sofa where they were soon reminded, by the images on the screen, of what they were missing. The Neil Kennedy character was not only in bed with a blonde, but on top of her and making love. The script that accompanied this romantic fervour, however, had a biting, ironic quality that would eventually give the serial a cult status.

WYN: You're taking your time.
JULIAN: I can't think of anybody.

'This is degrading to women,' snarled Suzanne. 'Men's Hour – now a major movie!'

Harry and Nadine watched it in the potting shed. The

merged households had produced a surfeit of television sets and Harry had installed one of them in his bar. Tonight, this had the double advantage of keeping Rachel's innocent gaze away from one of television's raunchier romps while allowing her to get on with her homework without the distraction of background noise.

'If this is marriage, I'll have a gin and tonic,' said Nadine. 'Mr Kennedy was a bit of a surprise, though, I thought he was just another pub lush.'

'We all have our hidden sides,' said Harry.

'Oh, yeah? Where's yours?'

'I can't remember where I hid it.'

Toby Beauchamp watched it alone. He sat enthralled, wildly impressed with his friend's performance. In his younger days, when his good looks were frequently remarked upon, he had fancied a career as an actor himself. He had finally been deterred by his obvious lack of talent, and had been depressed since to see that this deficiency had not discouraged hundreds of others.

A slice of good television was one of the things that he had missed in Spain, and it was something he needed now with the fate of Brynwyn Rolfe hovering like a threat in his mind.

Neil Kennedy did not watch *Hot Air Rises*. He took Lindy into the toy room and played shops. Her latest toy was a Fisher–Price till with scales and a conveyor belt – a whole generation was now growing up with the dizzy ambition to be a check-out girl in a supermarket. The food that he was obliged to buy was plastic, but the money that Lindy stashed away in her till was real enough.

Gwenda was watching the programme on her own and recording it for him to watch later. To her it was just a story, a piece of escapism, but Kennedy would watch it alone from a quite different perspective. He would be studying the smallest detail of his own performance, and then he would watch the whole thing over again and look only at the other actors.

But as he sat on the toy-room floor he was curious about his wife's reaction to it. He respected her judgement, even if it veered occasionally towards the abrasive. He heard the signature tune, pinched from some half-remembered classic, and then she came out with a smile.

'What a schmuck, eh?' she said. 'But you were brilliant.' And she gave him a kiss.

'How do you think it's going to go down?' he asked her.

'It'll have the nation by the – what's the expression?'

'Ears? Nose?'

'Balls, I should think. Frankly, I thought it was the best thing you've ever done. You're a star. Why aren't we rich?'

The following morning he was up even before his restless daughter to visit the village newsagent. His wife was right. The chorus of acclaim was unanimous. 'Not since the welcome appearance of Sir John Gielgud in *Summer's Lease*,' said one critic, 'have we seen such classy acting on the box.' Another called it stunning, and couldn't wait for the second episode.

Kennedy made a pot of tea and took two cups upstairs.

That afternoon Cathy Gray and Daisy Balcombe were sitting in Daisy's conservatory reading the script for *Cinderella* when a man ducked below the roses to knock on the cottage's front door.

To Cathy, an appearance on stage was a logical progression from her début as a cover girl. And this was where she could learn the theatrical secrets. Like most girls, she didn't think it represented much of a challenge. She had spent many hours picturing herself in the spotlight with an adoring audience unseen out there in the darkness.

The problem was learning the words, and this read-through in the conservatory was to see whether she was capable of memorizing chunks of the script. Daisy Balcombe had been producing a pantomime in the village hall for thirty years and she knew that she could teach Cathy Gray how to deliver the lines later as long as the girl could remember them. She had seen too many young actresses signalling frantically to the prompter, and often they had strayed so far from the script by this time that the prompter was lost as well.

In fact, Cathy had spent so much time learning the words that she thought she could probably recite them backwards, and she was demonstrating her total command of this part of the enterprise when they heard the knock on the door.

'Blast,' said Daisy Balcombe, who did not like to be disturbed. 'I suppose I'd better see who it is.'

When she went through the cottage and opened the door, she found herself looking down at a small bald man with a black moustache who smiled up at her like a long-lost relative.

'Miss Balcombe?' he asked.

He was foreign, thought Daisy. Maybe Indian. But his voice suggested that he had spent most of his life here.

'I am Miss Balcombe,' she said formally. She had no idea what to expect.

'My name is Hummel. To put it briefly, I'm a collector and you have something I want to buy.'

Daisy Balcombe's finances were not so healthy that she could afford to dismiss this sort of overture.

'Really?' she said. 'Would you care to come in?'

The little man followed her through to the sitting-room which opened out on to the conservatory.

'Do sit down,' said Daisy, sitting down herself. 'What is it that you want?'

'A fertility symbol,' said Mr Hummel, lowering himself into a very old armchair. 'I have the biggest collection in Europe, maybe the world, and I understand you have one.'

'How did you know that?' asked Daisy uneasily.

'I'm registered with a Press cuttings agency. Anything published about fertility symbols reaches me eventually. I got a cutting from a newspaper called the *County Gazette* and found your address in the phone book. Was the story true? Often they aren't.'

'Oh, it's true,' said Daisy boldly. 'Would you like to see it?'

'I'd love to,' said Mr Hummel, smiling happily.

Daisy went to an old escritoire in the corner of the room and from one of its small drawers produced the golden phallus. Mr Hummel took it in his hands like a connoisseur and then held it up to study the lines.

'The paper said you bought it in Malaysia?'

'Kuala Lumpur.'

'It wouldn't have come from Kuala Lumpur,' said Mr Hummel, 'but it could have come from south of there. Sumatra, perhaps, or Java. It could even have come from one of the Polynesian islands. It's in remarkably good condition.'

'I've looked after it,' said Daisy. 'I don't really want to sell it.' She had heard that this was how you got the price up if you wanted to sell something.

'Everything in the world is for sale, Miss Balcombe,' said Mr Hummel calmly. 'It's just a question of price. For a billion billion pounds you could probably have Buckingham Palace.'

'Well, of course,' said Daisy thoughtfully. 'If the price is right.'

He twisted the golden phallus in his hand and studied it in silence for some time.

'I'd like to buy it,' he said. 'What price would you think *is* right?'

'It's very rare,' said Daisy.

'Don't I know it,' said Mr Hummel. 'It would be a prized addition to my collection.'

Daisy Balcombe wondered what figure she should suggest. She was loath to let her toy go, but £100 would be useful this month. There were bills in the kitchen that had arrived all at once, as if the telephone people and the gas board and the electricity board and the television-licence records office were all in a conspiracy to cause maximum discomfort to pensioners.

'Make me an offer,' she said. That was the phrase, she seemed to remember, that people used in this situation.

'I'll give you twenty,' said Mr Hummel.

'Twenty?' said Daisy.

'Twenty thousand pounds.'

'Twenty thousand pounds?'

'All right, twenty-five. But I couldn't go much higher than that.'

Daisy Balcombe sat down.

'You've got a deal,' she said. Her phrases today seemed to have been picked up from the bottom end of the television network's output. She was worried by the way her heart was pounding. It didn't do at her age to get excited.

'I can hardly expect you to trust my cheque,' said Mr Hummel standing up. 'I have cash in the car, if you'll excuse me.'

Cathy Gray's interest in the *Cinderella* script had vanished some time ago. She watched the negotiations in the sitting-room with disbelief. Nobody had told her that the mysterious object that Daisy had thrown at her brother in church was One-cell Tel's private gift to her. The one person who could have recognized it and told her was lying unconscious at the foot of the pulpit. Harry Grant must have known but she hadn't seen him since the unfortunate business in church.

When Mr Hummel went out to his car, she jumped up and rushed into the sitting-room.

'Now look here, Miss Balcombe,' she said. 'That golden willy is mine.'

'Yours?' said Miss Balcombe, feeling a rare flush of embarrassment.

'It fell out of my bag somewhere and you must have picked it up. I'm pretty sure I lost it in the post office.'

Daisy Balcombe nodded sadly. 'Yes, the post office.'

'I want it back.'

'Are you mad, girl? This man is offering £25,000 for it.' In the stress of the moment she lapsed into further television-speak that, to her astonishment, her brain had soaked up. 'We're talking tax-free dosh here.'

'Yes, but whose?' Cathy asked calmly.

They heard Mr Hummel close the front door as he came back into the cottage.

Daisy Balcombe, who had been a woman of iron for many years and had been only temporarily nonplussed, got a grip on herself.

'If you're going to claim it is yours, I shall tell him its true origins.'

'You don't know them. One-cell Tel made it for me. And if you're claiming it as yours I shall tell him that.'

The two women stared at each other as the footsteps approached in the hall. There was just time for the two of them to realize that £25,000 was going to disappear in the course of this squabble which neither of them could win. It was a truth that dawned on Cathy first.

'Fifty-fifty,' she said.

Relieved, Daisy Balcombe nodded as Mr Hummel came into the room with a steel briefcase and a set of keys.

26

In an attempt to improve the bruised perception of himself which he imagined his friends now had, Toby Beauchamp invited everybody to a farewell dinner at La Palme d'Or. The mood might be sombre and the jokes uncomfortable, but he was relying on a few drinks to turn the evening into a memorable occasion.

He had reserved a table for seven, but the evening began badly when only six sat down in the converted farmhouse. Paul Vanner arrived alone.

'Where's Suzanne?' asked Toby.

'I give in,' said Vanner. 'Where is she?'

That morning she had watched a film called *The Stepford Wives*, and told her husband: 'They ought to make a film called *The Compton Sinbury Husbands* because you're a bunch of robots without anybody having tampered with you.' She then announced that she had no intention of dining that evening with 'a gang of tossers', climbed into her Mercedes and disappeared down the drive.

Vanner was not inclined to follow her, but her absence was an embarrassment now as he was used to arriving at occasions like this as one of a pair.

'Has she got a man?' Toby asked. 'She's a fairly voluptuous thing.'

'She could have a horde of them for all I know. Does anyone want some of this lovely wine?' In the relaxed atmosphere of La Palme d'Or, he seemed to have appropriated a bottle of Liebfraumilch all for himself and had suddenly noticed his mistake.

'Well, it was no use her waiting for Paul,' said Harry. 'It's not his department. He thinks that oral sex is when people talk about it.'

As they studied the menus, Toby said: 'I've decided to eat very well for a few weeks. I've been reading some books about prison and apparently the grub's not that hot.'

Looking at him across the table Nadine Kirby thought that concern had altered the contours of his face. He looked, she decided, like a man who hadn't made a serious visit to the lavatory for some time.

'Are you going to take part in one of those roof riots, Toby?' she asked. 'Shall we see you on television throwing tiles about?'

The waiter arrived to take their orders before Toby could react to this idea. He ordered a salmon steak and wondered if one had ever been seen in Her Majesty's prisons.

Harry spent more time than the others deciding what to eat. No gourmet, he was still lamenting the disappearance of brown Windsor soup.

When their orders had been taken to the kitchen, Gwenda Kennedy, who had been waiting impatiently, turned her attention to Paul Vanner.

'Come on, Paul,' she said. 'What's the problem?'

Vanner filled his glass. 'She's an alcoholic, Gwenda. I'd have thought you lot would have tumbled to that by now. Too much spare time and too much money.' He emptied his glass with two gulps as if the wine was a weak beer.

'What do you mean, she's an alcoholic?' said Gwenda disdainfully. 'She just likes a drink the same as you evidently do.'

'Likes a drink?' said Vanner. 'We're thigh-deep in empty wine bottles at the Manor House. You open a drawer to get your socks and discover a half-drunk bottle of Châteauneuf du Pape. You find abandoned glasses of wine behind the curtains. Last week I found a bottle of Piper Heidsieck in the tumble drier.' The wine in his own glass had mysteriously replenished itself. 'Why do you think my Ferrari went over the bridge?'

'In that case she needs treatment,' said Gwenda, 'and it's your responsibility to see that she gets it.'

'I knew an actress like that once,' Neil Kennedy told them. 'She spent £3,000 on a six-week course of treatment and a week later was found plastered in a phone box.'

'A six-week course isn't enough,' said Harry. 'It's not like learning origami.'

'Prison would be a good place to dry out,' said Toby. 'She could share my cell. I love her long dark hair.'

'I think you are all disgraceful,' said Gwenda Kennedy. 'What you have to ask is why did she take up drinking in the first place?'

'Oh, I can see who is going to get the blame,' said Vanner. He looked round at them, sensing their disapproval.

'It isn't entirely your fault,' Gwenda told him. 'She has a mind of her own.'

'Kind of you to say so,' Vanner said. 'Don't worry. I'm quite used to getting the blame for everything.'

'But there are certain duties you have now, and the first is to see that she gets treatment.'

'The first thing is to find her,' Vanner said, but it wasn't a job that he was going to pursue too assiduously. Soon after she had gone he had wondered whether it might be amusing to change the locks.

And later, chewing parsley to get rid of the smell of garlic, he found himself thinking about Cathy Gray rather than Suzanne.

When the waiter came to their table with the sweet trolley he wanted to know whether Neil Kennedy was the man in that television serial. He hadn't seen it himself as he worked in the evenings, but a customer had asked. Gratified to be asked, Kennedy said that indeed he was and turned to see a middle-aged lady gazing at him across the restaurant.

'I can remember when my fans were young,' he said.

'That was when you were young, dear,' said his wife. 'Now that you're thirty going on forty it's a different market.'

Neil Kennedy smiled ruefully at the others. 'My wife has an unkind tongue,' he said. 'When I get home I'm going to check the tumble-drier for bottles of Piper Heidsieck.'

'I must say that listening to you people doesn't make you

want to enthuse about marriage,' said Nadine Kirby. 'Which is unfortunate, because Harry and I are getting married next month.'

'How nice to hear some good news,' said Gwenda. 'Rachel will be pleased.'

'It's not every child of ten who gets to her parents' wedding,' Harry admitted.

'I hope it won't put a dampener on things if I send you a card from the dungeon,' Toby said.

'I should buy our present now just to be on the safe side,' Nadine told him.

One-cell Tel was reading *Crumpet* with his trousers round his ankles. Lawns were not mowed in November but this magazine was the next-best thing to his summer entertainment. In some ways it was better, because he had never got this close to Cathy Gray when she was handling her Flymo.

He was just reaching for the towel in a mood of some expectation when he heard her voice downstairs.

Cathy Gray had always believed that she would be famous by twenty, rich by thirty and dead by forty, but the world had not conformed to her schedule. Now, however, there was the hint of a breakthrough. Her picture was being studied by lonely men all over Britain, and for the first time in her life she had money.

She had given in her notice at the Refectory as soon as she received Mr Hummel's £12,500 and had gone straight into town to buy a yellow second-hand Volkswagen Golf. She had taken the trouble to pass her driving test at eighteen, having saved up for lessons, but she had subsequently discovered that saving up to buy a car was a more difficult exercise.

Now she drove even the short distance to the village shops and was thrilled by the luxury of car ownership. Driving back again, she had parked outside Terry Wallace's house despite the fact that she lived next door.

His mother invited her in.

'He's upstairs,' she said. 'I don't know what he's up to.'

'Don't worry, I'll go up,' said Cathy Gray.

One-cell Tel was hurriedly hoisting his jeans when she went in. He was wearing his usual yellow T-shirt.

'Hallo, Terry,' she said cheerfully, looking at his familiar erection. 'Amusing yourself by abusing yourself?'

The bedroom smelt like the lionhouse in the zoo. Nothing had been put away in this room – it lay all round the floor as if this was the aftermath of some terrorist outrage: a grimy pair of trainers, a Sony Walkman, a cassette of Phil Collins, a bottle that had once held Newcastle Brown, a curling sandwich, a pair of union jack shorts, a baseball cap with OLD FART printed in red letters across the front, a huge towel that looked from its rigidity and its colour as if it had been briefly immersed in a cement mixer, and an open copy of *Crumpet*.

'Why don't you mow the lawn any more?' One-cell Tel asked, zipping himself up.

'Unlike some things round here, it doesn't grow in the winter, Terry.'

'Well, it looks untidy to me,' he said miserably.

She sat on the bed and thought how unfair it was that when you found a man with a willy the size of a banana, he had a brain the size of a pea.

'Nice pictures?' she asked, pointing at the magazine.

He nodded, not knowing what to say. What was this woman doing in his bedroom? Why didn't she want him to make love to her as Suzanne Vanner once had?

One-cell Tel's life was in decline. What he had once described in a rare moment of lucidity as a series of beer-ups and bunk-ups was now short of both. The women were scarce and the jobs were scarcer. It was always harder to find work here in the winter, but something was happening in the country which made this winter worse than most.

Looking at him across his untidy bed, Cathy Gray wondered what confusion prevailed in his head, but when she tried to concern herself with his limited prospects and his hopeless dreams she found that she had exhausted her capacity to worry on her own unpromising future. Famous by twenty and rich by thirty was already half-wrong. But today she had had a wonderful idea that had brought her reluctantly to this fetid cell.

She asked: 'Would you like to make some money, Terry?'

A maniacal grin flickered across his face. 'Who wouldn't?' he asked.

'Well, of course,' said Cathy Gray. 'There's enough poverty on this awful estate. I've had an idea, Terry, that will make us both some cash.'

He looked at her suspiciously, as if any suggestion made in the privacy of his bedroom would have to be suspect.

'Oh yes?' he said.

'You remember that little gold model you made for me?'

'There was nothing little about it,' he said resentfully, massaging the bulge in his jeans.

'No, I'm sorry. It was enormous. I thought it was an elephant's at first. The thing is – can you make another one?'

'Why, because you lost it?'

'Not exactly, no. I found it and sold it. I can sell them, Terry.'

'Who'd want to buy one?'

'Oh, collectors of such things. I'll buy every one you make if you can keep your strength up. It doesn't seem to be a problem from where I'm sitting.'

One-cell Tel sat on the bed awkwardly.

'How much would you pay?'

Cathy Gray considered this carefully. She had no idea how much money she might get for any further models that One-cell Tel produced, and if she was buying them before she had sold them she could get left with an awkward stockpile.

'What about £100?' she said.

'Each?'

Cathy Gray nodded.

'I'd only have to make two a week.'

'Two a week would be plenty. You'd make them to the same standard as last time, wouldn't you?'

'Better.'

'Fine, Terry. We have a deal.'

She stood up, anxious for fresh air.

'When will the first one be ready? I don't want to rush an artist, but money's money.'

'Saturday.'

'That's wonderful, Terry. If you don't get a sudden attack of impotence we could have a nice little earner. I'll go into town this afternoon and buy you a supply of ginseng. I know it's a bit like buying a ladder for a giraffe, but I want to play my part.'

Absorbed suddenly into an instant family, Harry Grant was facing demands that he had never expected to hear during the long years when he lived alone. It wasn't only Sunday-afternoon drives in the direction of tea and cakes, or a request to spend an hour peering thoughtfully at a Scrabble board. One evening Rachel asked him in censorious tones why he had never written a book.

It was not a thought that had occurred to him. Churning out sufficient words to satisfy the voracious maw of the *County Gazette* seemed more than enough work for one man, and books meant months or even years of effort without the certainty of even a small payment.

But the idea was taken up by Nadine, who was reading a novel from the mobile library at the time.

'Why don't you have a go, Harry?' she asked. 'Some authors make an awful lot of money.'

'And some don't,' said Harry. His secret ambition had always been to eradicate work from his life and not increase it.

'Try, Harry,' said Rachel. 'I'm going to write a book one day.'

'I'll wait for that one,' he said.

But the subject was not allowed to drop.

'You could at least have a go,' Nadine said from her armchair. 'You don't have to write the whole thing. Do a chapter and see what people say about it?'

'How long is a chapter?' he asked.

'As long or as short as you like.'

Harry was finding that life was a question of compromises and submissions. His gentle refusals were soon eroded by the tenacity of women. Eventually it was agreed that the following morning he would sit at his desk until he had written the first page of a novel. He would bring it down at lunchtime, when Nadine and Rachel would sit in judgement on his effort.

Harry's desk, no longer in the front window downstairs, had been consigned to the smallest bedroom upstairs which was now known as his study. For some reason it was much more businesslike than the workspace he had used downstairs, where his typewriter had rested on a small table along with flowers, photographs and ornaments. In his new study there were files and old reporter's notebooks, a copy of the electoral roll, council minutes and several telephone directories. There was even a detailed map of the district pinned to one wall.

It was to this cosy den that he was driven with many encouraging comments the following morning, and instructed not to reappear until he had written one page of a novel.

He put a sheet of paper into his typewriter and stared at it with a blank mind. He found that trying to start a book when he didn't know what the book was going to be about was a daunting task. For an hour he frowned at the sheet of paper in his typewriter while his mind groped for ideas. He had once thought of doing a book of Spoonerisms, called *Cheese and Pips*, but that wasn't what was wanted this morning.

He tried to invent a story. He thought of a man driving off to get his car cleaned who was never seen again but couldn't figure out where the chap had got to. He thought of fictionalizing the memoirs of a monk but without some inventive obscenity would a monk have much to say? Perhaps he could set the book in a massage parlour in Mandalay, the scene of one of his most successful sex fantasies. In that exotic setting the bloody thing should write itself. His mind wandered from a monastery to the Vatican and after two hours he typed his first sentence: *I haven't had my leg over for yonks, thought the Pope.*

He tore the paper out of his typewriter, screwed it up and dropped it in his waste-paper basket. He was beginning to panic. Obviously he had been pitched into this too quickly; more preparation was required for the task of starting a book. But to go downstairs at lunchtime with a blank sheet of paper was unthinkable. He could see the disillusioned look on Rachel's face. Another hour passed as he struggled to collect his thoughts. The trouble was that he was used to telling a story in a hundred words. Who needed a hundred thousand?

As his watch dragged him closer to one o'clock he began to feel ashamed. He had earned his living writing words and no words would come. Downstairs they were maintaining a respectful silence for fear of disturbing his creative flow. A literary panel of two was waiting to deliver its verdict.

At ten to one he began to feel like a man who had been submitted to an exquisite torture. He stood up, stiff from three wasted hours, and stared at the books on his shelf. Plenty of people had found no difficulty at all in knocking out the odd three hundred pages. He took a book down and opened it and then he realized what he had to do. Soon he was typing at a furious pace.

When he went downstairs at one o'clock they were both waiting expectantly.

'Have you done it?' Rachel asked.

He handed her the sheet of paper.

'Give it to me,' said Nadine. 'Let me read this masterpiece out. Sit down, everybody.'

When they were all sitting she began to read from Harry's sheet of paper: *'In the late summer of that year we lived in a house in a village that looked across the river and the plain to the mountains. In the bed of the river there were pebbles and boulders, dry and white in the sun, and the water was clear and swiftly moving and blue in the channels. Troops went by the house and down the road and the dust they raised powdered the leaves of the trees. The trunks of the trees too were dusty and the leaves fell early that year and we saw the troops marching along the road and the dust rising and leaves, stirred by the breeze, falling and the soldiers marching and afterwards the road bare and white except for the leaves.'*

Nadine looked up. 'Harry, this is gibberish. No feeling, no punctuation, no anything. What troops? What year? What's all this about leaves all the time?'

'Quite,' said Harry.

'I think you'd better stick to journalism.'
'I think I better had. What do you think, Rachel?'
'Boring.'
'Let's have lunch then,' he said. 'I've done my best.'
He went upstairs and returned his copy of Hemingway's *A Farewell to Arms* to the shelf.

On the Kennedy lawn Lindy was trying to play croquet. The mallet was too big for her to swing between her legs and she stood to one side of the ball and swung the mallet like a golf club.
'Grandpa takes his teeth out at night,' she said. 'Couldn't I do that?'
'Not yet,' muttered Neil Kennedy. 'Try to hit the ball through this loop.'
She achieved this with a dexterity that surprised him – he had just failed at the same shot himself.
Croquet on the lawn with his daughter while *Hot Air Rises* climbed to third place in the television ratings seemed to represent a much more wonderful period in his life than any that had gone before. Even Gwenda had softened under the remorseless praise for his television performance and had begun to behave as if there was a talent there which deserved encouragement.
Neil Kennedy had decided that marriage wasn't a war, which was the fashionable idea advanced by Paul Vanner, but a long, sometimes uneasy truce. Disturbing bills, disgruntled progeny and disenchanted spouse were what you took in your stride during the bad moments while you waited for things to improve.
Gwenda emerged from the kitchen door and stood prettily framed by the patio's late roses. He wished he had his camera.
'Phone, Neil.'
'Who is it?' When you were riding high in the world of television there was always the possibility of exciting phone calls.
'It's your vulgar agent.'
Kennedy went into the house and picked up the phone.

'Good morning, Howard.'

'Maestro! How are you? Is the family well?'

There seemed to be a new respect in Howard's voice: this wasn't the good-natured ribbing of a forgotten star which was what conversation between them usually involved.

'They're fine, Howard. What can you do for me?'

'The world wants you. You're hot, kid!'

'Talk English, Howard.'

'Hollywood has cabled an offer. They've seen tapes of *Hot Air Rises* that I sent over and have the very part for you.'

'Would I have to ride a horse?'

'No, apparently they've started to make films over there now that don't have horses in. This is one of those beguiling comedies with Shirley MacLaine or somebody about an American millionairess who marries your archetypal Englishman. Clash of cultures. Separated by a common language. All that old moody. They're talking big moolah.'

'Is this English you're speaking now or what?'

'The offer I have here is half a million dollars.'

Kennedy looked at Gwenda who was stuffing the remnants of a late breakfast into her photodegradable pedal-bin liner.

'Half a million dollars?' he repeated for her benefit. 'Do you know who scripted it?'

Gwenda abandoned the pedal bin and stared at him with her hands on her hips.

'The usual two hundred people, I expect,' Howard was saying. 'They'll fly you and your family over for six months. Think of it, Neil! LA!'

Face to face, Howard was so gabby that even when somebody managed to get the odd sentence in he always tried to finish it for them, but phone calls cost money and now he fell silent.

'I'm thinking, Howard. When would this be?'

'They want you to fly out straight after Christmas and stay till June.'

'I'll just have a word with Mrs Kennedy.' He turned to Gwenda. 'Do you want to go to Hollywood for six months?'

'Yes please,' she said firmly.

'Mrs Kennedy says she could fit it in. Kindly cable our acceptance.'

'I want one of those whistles,' said Barnaby Barton, clutching a wad of £20 notes with both hands.

'Whistles, sir?' said the unctuous young shop assistant who was desperately anxious to be liked despite the unpromising appearance of his customer. His jacket was rumpled and stained, he wore no tie, and his trousers failed by two clear inches to reach the correct position on the man's unpolished shoes – a gap which revealed that, on top of everything else, he was wearing odd socks.

One hand let go of the banknotes so that Barney could jab a finger at a row of suits.

'Oh, I see. Rhyming slang. Whistle and flute. Very amusing, sir.' He looked at his customer doubtfully. 'What sort of thing would you have in mind?'

Barnaby Barton, uncomfortable in any shop, was quite lost here. His eye ran along the row of suits as if textiles were something he knew about. They all seemed to be blue, brown or grey and there wasn't much to choose between them.

But a letter from Lydia Baxter that morning had galvanized him into action. Undeterred by the photograph he had sent her, she announced that her son was bringing her to England for Christmas so that she could see the old place before she passed on. 'Dunc' had decided that, not wanting to put Barney to any trouble, they would be staying in an hotel only a few miles from Compton Sinbury.

Barnaby Barton took this message as a proposal of marriage. He discussed it over a pint of Guinness at lunchtime with One-cell Tel, who had only two pieces of advice. One was to buy some new clothes, the other to get his bungalow cleaned. Barney rather resented this advice, given its source. He had visited One-cell Tel's home on a couple of occasions and thought it disgracefully untidy. But he realized, looking back, that there had been a few funny looks from visitors to Southfork. Some, on entering his living room, had reeled back in a strange manner, as if they had been plunged unwillingly into an abattoir, before they had got a grip on themselves and stopped breathing through their mouths. And so he had spoken to Mrs Hockley, who cleaned for Mr Beauchamp, and she had agreed to come in once a week to see that his house was kept in order.

All he needed now was a new wardrobe. He looked at the suits and tried to remember what colour the men wore on television. There were a lot of smart men on the screen who got adoring letters from women. He decided that the favoured colour was grey.

The shop assistant fetched a tape measure.

'Do you always stand like that, sir?' he asked, as he struggled with some distaste to get the inside leg measurement.

He led his untidy customer to a changing cubicle. Even he was astonished at the difference a new suit made.

'I want shirts and ties,' Barney told him. 'I'm getting married.'

The shop assistant could only imagine what type of woman would contemplate wedlock with this shambolic figure; it wasn't a pretty picture. But he quickly produced a selection of shirts and ties, draping the ties over the shirts and holding both in front of the suit.

Half an hour later, Barney left the shop with two full carrier bags and went in search of a hairdresser.

When the telephone rang Paul Vanner was still asleep. After years of crawling out of bed while others continued to doze, he felt that he was owed a few lie-ins, and now that Suzanne had vanished there was nobody about to make him feel guilty as the sun rose and he failed to.

For a moment he wondered whether to ignore the ringing that had disturbed him. There was little enough chance that anybody would call him with good news. But the thing kept ringing as if the caller knew that this was a big house and it would take some time for anyone to reach the phone.

It was beside his bed; reluctantly, he picked it up. A voice with a flat Midlands accent said: 'Paul? It's Mervyn. I'm calling about Suzanne.'

This was difficult. How did you explain to your father-in-law that you had mislaid his daughter? But Mervyn's next remark removed this problem.

'I tried to get her to call you but she refuses. I knew you'd be worried.'

'How is she?'

'Terrible, Paul. She's got a real drinking problem. You haven't been in touch with the police, have you?'

Vanner pulled himself up on his pillow. He should be careful what he said. It was two days since Suzanne had swept out of his life on a tide of abuse and he had done nothing in the meantime to establish her whereabouts. Some people might think that odd.

'The police?' he said. 'It's not illegal to leave your husband.'

'Well, I suppose something could have happened to her. Women are being kidnapped, raped and strangled every day.'

Vanner's brain was working now and he could deal with this veiled accusation.

'To tell you the truth, I thought she had a man.'

'Not Suzanne.'

'Well,' said Vanner, 'she had one earlier this year.'

'I'm sorry to hear that, Paul. Very sorry indeed. It must have been the drink. Didn't you see the danger signs of too much boozing?'

'What are they?'

'Changing moods. Sudden irritability.'

'I'm afraid that wouldn't have stood out.'

A silence came down the line as this sunk in and Vanner could think of nothing to break it.

'There's a twelve-step rehabilitation programme based on total abstinence,' Mervyn told him. 'I'm going to try to get her on it. Alcoholism is a progressive disease that gets worse.'

Vanner didn't think that alcoholism was a disease. He thought that it was a weakness that some people were prone to – more strength, less drinking.

He asked. 'Do you think she wants a divorce?'

'That's what she says.'

'I'm not going to stand in her way. It's been pretty good

hell down here, Mervyn.' He very seldom called his father-in-law Mervyn, but it seemed necessary to emphasize what he was saying. 'It's been an unhappy home for some time.'

'I blame the hours you had to work, Paul. I don't blame you. If Suzanne's shop had succeeded it might have been different. She was lonely and needed an interest.'

'Her situation was hardly unique. Down here in the south of England there are men working horrendous hours. They've all got Range Rovers and Porsches but they're doing eighty- and ninety-hour weeks.'

'I know it,' said Mervyn. 'That's why you've got all the divorces.'

Vanner didn't know what else to say. 'Give her my love,' he suggested.

'I only wish that she wanted it, Paul.'

'Do you mean there's no chance of a change of heart?'

A cartoon came to Vanner's mind of a man who had built a powerful wooden barricade on the inside of his front door, on the outside of which his wife was saying 'I've come back, darling, to give you another chance.'

'No hope of that, Paul,' said his father-in-law. 'She even hates you when she's sober.'

When Mervyn hung up, Vanner rolled out of bed and went to the bathroom mirror to see how he had taken the news.

Last night he had been rendered rubber-lipped by eight pints of Old Peculier, but this morning he felt wonderful. He decided that a boiled egg and some buttered toast would be a suitable breakfast after the depredations of the night before which had been encouraged by the news that the country, somewhat unexpectedly, had a new Prime Minister.

Sylvia, the lone woman in the bar, seemed to resent Mrs Thatcher's sudden departure.

'How does it come about that when Thatcher wins by 204 votes to 152 she is told that she hasn't got enough votes and that there are too many people against her, but when a man gets 185 votes with 187 against he becomes Prime Minister?' she asked.

'Don't ask me,' said Harry. 'Nobody ever accused the Tories of behaving logically.'

'I'm going to miss the old bat,' said Toby. 'They've taken my mother-figure away.'

'That's right,' said Kennedy. 'Better shape up. We've got a headmaster in charge now.'

But Vanner, plucking a brown egg from its tray, reflected that two women had now departed from his life leaving him with a sense of space and freedom. Before he could put the egg in, the phone rang again.

He looked at it warily. The last conversation had not encouraged him to answer calls, but his curiosity finally got the better of him.

'Schupke,' said Schupke.

Vanner imagined that the money broker was ringing to tell him proudly what the Daytona was now worth, not knowing that it had developed amphibious tendencies since they last met.

'Good morning, Schupke,' he said. 'Where the hell did you get a name like that, anyway?'

'From my father,' said Schupke. 'It's how they do it in Britain. If I ever find the time to have children they'll be called Schupke, too.'

'Heaven forbid,' said Vanner. 'There's six billion of us on this planet already and most of them are hungry.'

'I'm a bit peckish myself, as it happens. How are you, Paul?'

'Do you want the long answer or the short answer?'

'Neither, really. I'm just treading water here. Listen, I may have some good news for you.'

'Impossible.'

'About your future.'

'I haven't got a future and my past isn't worth talking about.'

'I may be able to help you. Could you meet me for lunch?'

'I seem to have a bit of free time.'

'December five looks clear in my diary. The St James's Club.'

'This sounds really exciting, Schupke. Do you mean you're paying?'

'I owe you, Paul. The St James's Club. It's a block or two south of Piccadilly.'

'Pick a what?'

'Dilly.'

'Got you.'

When he put down the phone Vanner decided that he was beginning to like the feel of this day: two promising items of news and he hadn't even had breakfast yet. The egg cracked and leaked in its tiny saucepan and by the time he opened it there wasn't much more than the yolk left inside but he wasn't about to let that mar such a promising morning.

His marriage was obviously over. It wasn't something that he had sought, but now that the end had arrived he had an overwhelming feeling of relief. Having pushed for a life in the country, Suzanne had never really adjusted to it. Deprived of the excitement of the city she had found nothing better to do with her time than open bottles of wine. He felt no guilt at his pleasure, guessing, in a humbling moment of intuition, that she was as pleased as he was. She had complained that he neglected her sexually, but in the days when they did such things her withering remarks about his potency had not suggested that there was much pleasure in it for her.

The marriage had broken up because that was what one in three marriages did these days. Why should two people want to stay together for the rest of their lives, anyway? It wasn't natural, and those stout couples who managed it usually carried one reluctant partner who was too passive or too nervous to cut and run. A romance, a pleasant dalliance, was one thing; but a lifetime's commitment was an impossible demand. People weren't made that way.

He carried his washing-up to the sink and started to whistle.

27

Feeling like a man with terminal anthrax, Toby Beauchamp sat in the dock at the Crown Court and discovered a fear that he had not known before. For the first time in his life everything had been taken out of his hands; he had lost control, and no action or decision by him could influence what was about to happen. He was the helpless victim, and already a prisoner: behind him stood a burly policeman whose sole duty was to see that Toby Beauchamp went nowhere.

For an hour he had sat in another part of the court, listening to an animal rights' activist argue that a moral obligation overrode a legal obligation – a contention that found no support from the judge who jailed him for a year – but now he was in the dock and technically under arrest. The year that had begun with Manuel Noriega hiding in the nunciature in Panama City would end with Toby cowering in even more restricted accommodation.

He had made all the necessary arrangements. Documents had been drawn up which gave his solicitor Gavin Riley the authority to sign cheques and make decisions that would allow Beauchamp Developments to keep ticking over; his car had been sold, and he had locked up his house and told the cleaning lady to stay away until she heard from him.

Being laid off for a second time by Toby Beauchamp might have upset Mrs Hockley if she had not had other, more challenging, work on her hands: trying to restore Barnaby Barton's home to the standards of hygiene accepted by normal people made cleansing the Augean stables look like sweeping the step.

Outside the court Gavin Riley had introduced Toby to his

barrister, Barnes, who had shaken his hand with what seemed like repugnance. Toby was obviously already a substandard member of the human race, and he felt a childish gratitude when Harry Grant winked at him from the Press bench. The judge didn't seem to look at him at all, although he had eyebrows that were growing so wild that it was difficult to see exactly where he was looking. Glancing round the court, Toby felt the final humiliation: he was the principal actor in this drama but he was the one person whom everybody ignored.

He shifted uncomfortably in his hard wooden seat and felt a deep resentment at the cold, detached way that the people in the courtroom conducted their business. It wasn't their freedom that was at stake. It was just another day's work to them, then they went home to dinner and a bottle of wine.

A man Toby realized was the prosecuting counsel was now on his feet, outlining the facts in the case. 'What we have here,' he said in the ringing tones of the privileged classes, 'is a web of corruption that spread across half the county.'

In the Press benches the pencils started to scribble as columns of free copy began to pour from the lawyer's mouth. He looked a bit like Ray Milland before he lost his hair, Toby thought. He wondered what he would be like to drink with. He managed to produce a simulacrum of anger at the story he had to tell as if it genuinely outraged him, but surely if lawyers became this involved with every case it would affect their blood pressure?

Gavin Riley, sitting behind Barnes, was writing notes and handing them forward to the barrister at such a rate that Toby feared he would run out of paper. The jury, which Toby hardly dared to look at, listened to stories about secret meetings and cheques that found their way to the Isle of Man as if this was another soap opera devised to enliven their drab lives. Toby steeled himself eventually to have a look at the twelve good men and found that five of them were women.

It was impossible to tell what they were thinking. They sat poker-faced, staring at the prosecuting counsel who was inviting them to share his abhorrence at the behaviour of 'these cloacal creatures'. Toby doubted whether the jury knew what cloacal meant, and they must have been confused at the way he referred to the defendant in the plural. But the man was in full flight now and working himself up for a final fusillade. His exuberance carried him into errors of fact and terminology – when he referred to the poor ratepayers as being the main victims of the conspiracy in an attempt to involve the jury itself, Barnes leapt to his feet to point out that we had poll-tax payers now – but nothing could stanch his rhetoric. When he sat down Toby could actually smell the interior of a prison.

Harry Grant, who had volunteered to cover this case, felt that the odds on Toby drinking in the Flatulent Ferret tonight had gone out considerably in the last half hour. It had been an emotional prosecution that would have swept along those members of the jury who had never seen the inside of a court-room. He looked at Toby in the dock to signal some form of encouragement, but he was sitting with his hands in his lap, looking down at his shoes as if he had already had enough of these histrionics.

When Barnes stood up to defend the person he could hardly bear to shake hands with, the atmosphere was quite different. He was a short, young man with prematurely receding red hair, and his quiet, polite manner was a striking contrast to the rumbustious style of the prosecution. He addressed the jury as if they were his personal associates.

'My learned friend has spoken about a web of corruption, but he omitted to tell you that the spider has already gone to prison,' he began. 'My client was caught up in the system that existed and he could either accept it or go bankrupt. He played the game according to the rules that operated. They weren't his rules. He didn't frame them. The man who framed the rules was the planning officer at the council and this court has already dealt with him.'

Toby liked the sound of this. It wasn't entirely true but it was the sort of thing the jury needed to hear. It was true that Brynwyn Rolfe had hinted in the early days that he needed a new car and had gladly accepted the one that Toby promptly bought him, but since then Toby had forced quantities of money on him with the eagerness of a would-be lover swamping a determined virgin with roses.

The jury listened to Barnes with the same expressionless mien that they had accorded his adversary and it was impossible to tell which way they were leaning or, indeed, whether they were actually listening at all. The judge's degree of involvement was even harder to discern. Behind those eyebrows a man could doze unnoticed.

Toby decided to sit up, shake off his defeated air, and try to correspond in some way to the hard-working businessman and unfortunate victim that Barnes was now describing. He looked directly at the jury – a man not afraid to look someone in the eye – but they would not look at him. Was this a bad sign? Were they uncomfortable about what they were going to do to him?

The judge's summing-up seemed to Toby to be a masterpiece of detachment, and when the jury filed out and Gavin Riley strolled across to the dock for a chat, he was able to greet him with a smile.

'I thought Barnes was very good,' he said.

'That's why he's so expensive. You did want the best, didn't you?'

'You've done a great job, Gavin. What are the chances?'

'Of what?'

'Acquittal.'

'Flimsy, Toby. We're on a damage-limitation exercise here. Trying to keep you out of prison. I don't think jail would be your sort of thing. They have a tendency to run out of Stolichnaya vodka.'

'And what are the chances of that?'

'Justice Cocklecarrot is an amiable old cove. It probably depends on how his shares did this morning.'

He wandered off leaving Toby with nobody to talk to. He had never felt so alone in his life. Suddenly his constant companion, the large policeman, leaned forward.

'We can go below for a coffee,' he said.

Below there were cells but nobody tried to lock Toby in one. Instead they made him coffee and offered him a seat. Two policemen were playing cards.

'Is this all new to you?' the policeman who was escorting him asked.

Toby guessed that he wanted to know whether he had an inveterate criminal on his hands.

'Quite new. I didn't even know you had cells down here.'

'I meant in court.'

'I got done for speeding once.'

The policeman poured himself a coffee and nodded towards the cells. 'That's where you could be next,' he said cheerfully. 'It's where you're kept until prison transport arrives.'

Toby had never seen a cell before except in films, but now he looked at them with a horrified fascination. There were only three in the row, with inch-wide bars on the front, and a chair inside. He couldn't imagine anyone wanting to stay in one for long.

'Not exactly the Carlton,' he said, but his spirits were not conducive to humour any more. The move downstairs had been a short but significant journey, removing him from the real world. Isolation started here.

He sat down and picked up his coffee but immediately a buzzer sounded.

'The jury are coming back,' said the policeman, taking his still-full cup. 'It didn't take them long to decide.'

'Is that a good sign or a bad sign?' Toby asked.

'For you? A bad sign.'

As Toby mounted the stairs he heard the judge above him call 'Bring up the accused' but he arrived in the dock before anybody could act on his instruction. The jury were already back and this time a few of them didn't mind looking at him.

The judge asked the foreman, a middle-aged man in a sports jacket who it was subsequently learned was a bus driver, whether they had agreed on their verdict, and he said they had. And then, as each of the charges were called out, he said 'guilty' in a loud, clear voice.

Guilty. Guilty. Guilty. Guilty. Guilty. Guilty. The words were like hammer blows on the side of Toby's head.

Gavin Riley sat motionless, staring at the judge who thanked the jury and then asked if anything was known. The prosecuting counsel admitted, by way of reply, that the defendant had no previous convictions.

The judge shifted slightly in his seat and concentrated all his attention now on Toby Beauchamp. The eyebrows went up a little and two eyes appeared. 'The defendant will be upstanding,' he said. His voice had the gravelly texture of a man who loved tobacco.

'We have listened to a sorry story of what the defence called sweeteners, and the prosecution, more accurately, called bribes,' he said, leaning forward on his desk and jutting out his jaw. 'It is a sad day for the reputation of local government and, indeed, democracy in this country. If the people can't feel that decisions are being made in the public interest, and not because palms are being greased in the manner of some sleazy banana republic, our system of government will break down.' His eyebrows, which had maintained a certain loftiness during all this, suddenly dropped again. 'For your part in this disgraceful episode you must be punished.'

He paused and looked at Toby as if it were a toss up between the death of a thousand cuts or a more merciful bullet in the back of the head.

'However, I accept what your counsel has pleaded on your behalf, that you were to some extent the victim of an evil system already in operation, and I think that that can save you from a custodial sentence. I propose to fine you £10,000 on each of the six charges, making £60,000 in all.'

Before the significance of this had begun to sink into Toby's brain, Barnes was on his feet asking for time to pay. He was allowed three months.

Toby looked at Gavin Riley who was smiling broadly, and then he looked across at the Press bench where Harry Grant was giving him a thumbs-up sign.

The policeman stood up and opened the door of the dock.

'I'd sold my Porsche,' Toby told him.

'Pessimist, are you?' said the policeman.

Toby descended three steps and walked across the court to his solicitor. He wanted to shake Barnes' hand. The barrister turned and nodded stiffly, then took the proffered hand before stuffing papers into his briefcase and walking off.

'He's shy,' said Gavin Riley. 'But a wonderful advocate.'

'Why did he ask for time to pay?'

'It wouldn't have looked good if everyone thought you had a fortune stashed away.'

Harry Grant came over with his notebook still open.

'What's Barnes' Christian name?' he asked.

With the job finished, he put the book in his pocket and shook Toby's hand.

'I thought we'd lost you, Toby. I thought you were off to the choky.'

'Me, too,' said Toby. He was still dazed by the sudden gift of freedom. For weeks he had been preparing himself for a long spell in prison and now the future was not what he had expected. He felt confused.

'What happens now?' he asked.

'You've got to sign a couple of things,' Gavin Riley told him. 'After that you get my bill.'

Toby Beauchamp imagined that the day had cost him about £100,000 or the profit on a couple of houses. He relaxed for the first time since he entered this soulless building.

'What are your immediate plans, Harry?' he asked. 'I seem to need a lift.'

Harry put his hand on Toby's arm.

'The Mustang is outside,' he said. 'But first, I know a bar.'

Vanner caught the London train at an hour that was strange to him. Travelling up in the middle of the morning, there was none of the cramped tension of a commuter train. There was room to spread himself out and, instead of the depressing early-morning darkness which had enveloped the workers three hours earlier, there was a bright sun in the sky.

At Waterloo he got a taxi. He had never been to a London club before, but had read about them in newspapers and books. He imagined old men dozing over their port.

The St James's Club was in Park Place, south of Piccadilly. It looked much newer than he had expected. He went up spotless steps and found himself immediately alongside the reception desk and a sparkling brunette.

'I have an appointment with Mr Schupke,' he said. 'I'm Vanner.'

'He's signed you in,' said the girl. 'He's in the bar. I'll show you.'

Schupke sat at a table in a small bar downstairs, drinking Perrier water. His white face and blond hair gave him a ghostly appearance, and Vanner wondered how many nervous breakdowns he had had since they last met. He looked like a man who was destroying his health in pursuit of large quantities of folding money.

'Did the hypnotist cure you of drink?' Vanner asked, sitting down.

'Haven't touched it for months. How are you, Paul? I heard your bad news.'

He beckoned a waiter who brought Vanner a bottle of Carlsberg. At other tables businessmen were talking business. There were no old gentlemen drinking port.

'What did you hear?' Vanner asked.

'How your wife cocked up the Ferrari investment. How you lost your job. You seem to be surviving, though.'

'I'm not surviving, I'm sinking. How's work?'

'The usual hell. What I really want is to go to Rwanda and look at the gorillas.'

'You'd find it pretty similar to work, I should imagine. Why have you brought me to this flash place? We country folk don't get to the big city too often. What happened to the trams?'

'I'm an emissary,' said Schupke. 'I'm the bringer of good news. I'll tell you over lunch.'

When they had finished their drinks they walked down a corridor to the restaurant. A picture on the wall showed that Prince Philip had visited the club. His signature had been framed and hung on the wall below his photograph.

Vanner studied the menu and saw 'bangers and mash'.

'What is transpiring?' he said. 'A posh place like this and they offer you bangers and mash?'

'You have to go to a posh place to get that sort of thing these days,' said Schupke. 'I'm going to have some.'

They ordered two.

'Somebody wants to employ you,' Schupke said when they had started to eat. 'He wants me to sound you out.'

'A job would be nice,' said Vanner. 'I've discovered that I'm underqualified but was overpaid. I was also told that I would never get another job in the city.'

'Never say never. You've got a hot reputation, Paul, and Nigel wants you.' He mentioned the name of a bank in the city. 'Hundred grand plus commission. It may work out less than you were getting, but it's more than you're earning now.'

'Does he know how I lost my job?'

'Yes, and he thought it was a bit harsh after all those years. You didn't do anything illegal. You didn't do something that was against Bank of England guidelines. All you did was break internal regulations. It was the act of a desperate man and Nigel understands.'

'What's he like?'

Schupke munched his sausage. 'He's a chocolate speedway rider,' he said.

Vanner had never heard the expression before, but he could see what it meant. 'I thought he was married?'

'Yeah, to a Spanish waiter. But the bottom line is he'll give you a job. He's got a high opinion of you.'

'Only professionally, I hope?'

'What do you say?'

'Tell him it would be a privilege to join his organization.'

Schupke looked gratified.

'Well, that's fine,' he said. 'I only got time out for this lunch because Nigel's a client and the firm wants to please him.'

'Of course,' said Vanner, looking for the sweet trolley. 'I suppose the firm pays for you to belong to a joint like this?'

'They do. It's a good place to bring people away from the city's prying eyes.'

Vanner had almost forgotten that world where somebody else paid for those little extra items and called them perks: your club membership, your rail fares, your private health insurance, your car, even your children's education. The world of high-salary employment. He was glad that he was rejoining it.

He ordered a fruit salad.

'The gonorrhoea clear up all right?' he asked.

'Gonorrhoea?'

'An apple orchard in Dublin, I seem to remember.'

'My God,' said Schupke, laughing now that the business side of the lunch had been satisfactorily completed, 'you always remember the bad things.'

'Your life is so dramatic. Nervous breakdowns, hypnotists, gonorrhoea. I don't know how you find time to make money.'

'How's it been with you, Paul?'

'Apart from losing my wife, my job, and my car, you mean, and probably my house? Apart from that it's been marvellous.'

'Got a girl?'

'Sort of.'

'Try the rodeo position,' said Schupke. 'It's the new thing.'

'I was never that inventive in the bedroom. Too knackered from mixing with people like you. What's the rodeo position, anyway?'

Schupke finished his Perrier and looked whiter than ever.

'You enter her from behind,' he said. 'Then you tell her that the girl in the office does it better and see how long you can stay on.'

When he reached the Flatulent Ferret Vanner found that everybody was celebrating.

It was Harry Grant's stag night, but other people had reason to be in party mood, too. Neil Kennedy was celebrating the signing of a contract that would take him and his family to Hollywood, the magic world whose wild imagination had illuminated his youth; Toby Beauchamp was celebrating a freedom he thought he had lost, and the purchase of a new Bentley that would provide the luxurious travel that he unexpectedly needed to enjoy it.

In another corner of the bar, in a suit that already looked

older than it was, Barnaby Barton was celebrating the news of the date of Lydia Baxter's arrival, a disclosure that required a slight increase in the intake of Guinness.

One-cell Tel had hoped to be celebrating the sale of his first model phallus, but when he had finally succeeded that afternoon in immersing the relevant extremity in his bucket, he had become so enthusiastic about the soft, warm properties of the silicone–rubber moulding-compound that he absent-mindedly ejaculated and he had had to lie on his bed, bereft of desire for a few hours, with affluence postponed and lumps of silicone–rubber clinging like limpets to his pubic hair. He sat beside Barney now looking like a much older man who wondered where his next erection was coming from.

Several bottles of champagne had been placed into two ice-buckets on the counter and Harry Grant, tidier than usual with a new blue sweater and freshly cut hair, stood filling glasses for whoever approached.

Vanner came in and took a glass. He had things to celebrate, too. His career was back on the rails again, and quite soon, with any luck, Cathy Gray would come in and they would depart swiftly for the Manor House. Beneath his bed was a copy of *Crumpet*, but on it would be the real thing.

'Nadine is a wonderful lady,' he said to Harry. 'I'd make love to her when I'm sober and there's no higher praise than that.'

'Well, thank you, Paul,' said Harry. 'Forgive me if I don't pass the good news on.'

'Where's the honeymoon?' Toby Beauchamp asked. 'Two weeks in Babylon?'

'We're too old for a honeymoon,' said Harry. 'Also there's Rachel to look after.'

'People take their kids on honeymoon these days,' said Neil Kennedy. 'It's the new dispensation.'

'The elderly couple are spending their honeymoon in Lyme Regis discussing their bowels,' said Toby. 'Shall I write the *Gazette* wedding report for you?'

'It's time you featured in one, Toby. All that money and nobody to spend it on.'

'You haven't seen my solicitor's bill.'

'The give and take, the throb and thrust,' said Vanner. 'I've got quite keen on marriage since my wife left me. I can see the thing objectively now.'

'Marriage is like the London Marathon,' said Toby. 'A wonderful concept, but you wouldn't want to do it yourself.'

'Well, I do and I'm going to,' said Harry. 'And I don't want any of you lot in church tomorrow with a hangover.'

Cathy Gray came in wearing a smart grey two-piece that nobody had seen before.

'I'm not gatecrashing your stag party, Harry,' she said.

'She's come to meet me,' Vanner explained.

'That's fine,' said Harry. 'This is not a conventional wedding. Champagne?'

She nodded. 'What a pity that you didn't get married earlier, then my brother could have officiated.'

Harry was not convinced of this. 'The new vicar is a dear old man,' he said. 'It could be some time before youth gets another chance. How is Owen?'

'He's wonderful. His book's been accepted.'

'He's written a book already?' said Harry, aghast.

'Of course not. But he's been paid a big advance on the basis of a title and a synopsis, whatever that is.'

'And what is the title?'

'God is Dead: A look at outer space.'

Vanner's arm had slipped round her shoulder now in a proprietary fashion. 'It doesn't sound as if it is going to end up on the Vatican's bookshelves,' he said.

'The prospects of a movie aren't all that tremendous, either,' said Neil Kennedy.

'What's the next one going to be called?' asked Harry. *'Incest is Best?'*

Cathy Gray scowled at him. 'I don't think there'll be a next one. He's talking about getting a job in industrial relations.'

'Relations seem to be his thing.'

Toby Beauchamp opened another bottle of champagne with a loud pop. 'We're not really used to weddings round here,' he said. 'Death, divorce and desertion, but not your simple wedding.'

'It's a very old tradition in Compton Sinbury,' said Harry. 'People have been doing it in these parts for centuries. Kindly fill all these empty glasses.'

In the corner One-cell Tel had weighed up the situation. 'Harry Grant is getting married,' he said.

'I reckon Mr Vanner is getting married as well – to your friend Cathy,' Barney told him mischievously.

One-cell Tel looked at Vanner's arm draped over Cathy's shoulder and said: 'She's not my friend, she's my business partner.'

'I didn't know you'd got a job,' said Barney.

'I've got a job all right, but it's a secret.'

'Anyway,' said Barney, not to be outdone, 'I may get married myself.'

But his remark was lost among some raucous singing of 'For he's a jolly good fellow'. There were other people in the bar now who knew Harry and came over to congratulate him when they heard the news.

The following afternoon there were three dozen guests in St Thomas's Church to see him marry Nadine Kirby. Among all the guests the broadest smile was worn by Rachel Kirby, who was going to change her surname after the ceremony.

The little old lady who came through immigration at Heathrow looked like a refugee from an American television comedy. Her round suntanned face was partially obscured by a huge pair of blue-frame spectacles, and a red pillbox hat was perched atop her immaculately waved hair. She turned this way and that, anxious to get her first glimpse of Britain for nearly fifty years, but saw only swirling crowds most of whom, it seemed to her, couldn't possibly be British.

At her side Duncan Baxter pushed a baggage-laden trolley towards a sign that said TAXIS.

'This is it, ma,' he said. 'The land of your birth.'

'Itma!' said Lydia Baxter. 'That was the big radio show when I left. I wonder if it's still running.'

'Funny name,' said her son, steering his trolley through the unyielding crowd.

'It stood for "It's That Man Again". Tommy Handley, it was.'

Outside it was raining. That evoked memories, too.

'It was always raining. People said that was why the countryside was so green, but I could have taken it a little browner and drier.'

But as they sped down the M3 her predominant emotion was not so much excitement at being back in Britain as relief that the flight was behind her. It was only her desire to have a last look at England that had enabled her to overcome her misgivings about boarding a plane. After Lockerbie everybody knew that if you risked crossing the Atlantic in a jumbo jet you could be hurled into sub-zero darkness before falling five miles to your death. 'All travel is hazardous,' she told her son. 'I've held firm to that opinion since I fell downstairs as a child.'

But the speeding taxi, a proper car and not one of the old cabs, didn't worry her at all as it sped down the motorway's outside lane.

'They've certainly improved the roads round here,' she said.

Duncan Baxter nodded. He could happily have spent Christmas at home. It was a time that he particularly enjoyed, and his previous trip to this country had not persuaded him that the English had much talent for enjoying themselves, beyond pouring unwise quantities of alcohol down their throats. His picture of the typical Englishman as a man with a brolly and a bowler hat had been replaced, after visiting his father, by a fellow with a beer gut waddling to the pub. But he accepted this filial duty without protest. His mother was nearing seventy and she had brought him up on her own. He owed her a lot.

When they arrived at their large hotel in the country the rain had stopped and a weak sun appeared to provide a welcome.

'How far are we from Compton Sinbury?' Lydia Baxter asked when they had been shown to their room which had big windows and two single beds.

'Five miles.'

'I don't remember this hotel.'

'It was built in 1960.'

'The old country's not that broke then.'

She sat on her bed and began to count the English currency that she now had in her purse.

'I'm going down to fix a car rental,' Duncan told her.

'I wonder what happened to the half-crown?' his mother said.

The hotel stood in twenty acres of countryside and was much used for business conferences, wedding receptions and amorous weekends. It had indoor and outdoor pools, tennis courts and a large ballroom. At the reception desk Duncan Baxter encountered an efficiency which surprised him, and half an hour later a Toyota Celica arrived outside the hotel for his use.

But upstairs his mother, jet-lagged from an overnight flight, had gone to bed and was sound asleep, so it was the following morning, after an English breakfast, that he took her out in the car to see again places that she barely remembered. Road layouts had changed, new buildings had appeared and old ones had been demolished. In a field where she had once chased rabbits a new estate of identical houses had been built, and across another lay a new wide road.

Only in Compton Sinbury itself had time stood still. The village green with the duckpond, the pub at the bottom and the five-arch bridge over the river were all as she remembered. Some of the shops had changed but not all of them: the Refectory was still there and so was the post office. Duncan drove round the green several times while she gazed out at a scene that she had imagined often during forty-eight years in exile.

'Let's go in the pub,' she said. 'I always wanted to but wasn't old enough.'

They pulled in to the car park, alongside a red Ferrari and a new Bentley.

'There are some rich people living round here now,' said Lydia Baxter. 'All I remember is bicycles.' She got out of the Toyota. 'Of course there was a war on and you couldn't get gas.'

There were only two men in the Flatulent Ferret. Duncan Baxter realized that he knew them both but could not remember their names.

'What will you drink, ma?' he asked. 'Brandy and milk?'

'That'll do fine,' said Lydia Baxter. 'Old-worlde place, isn't it?'

'Brandy and milk, and a single Jack,' he told the man behind the bar. His experiments with British beer had not encouraged him to continue and he took the Jack Daniels gratefully.

'Duncan Baxter, isn't it?' said the younger of the two men who were sitting on stools at the bar. 'What on earth has brought you back here?'

'I'm escorting my mother,' said Duncan Baxter. 'I'm afraid I've forgotten your names.'

'Paul Vanner,' said Vanner, shaking hands with Lydia Baxter. 'Your son came to dinner at my house.'

'Indeed I did. You're Toby, aren't you? Thanks for doing that deal. How have things been in Compton Sinbury?'

'Paul got sacked, Harry got married and I got arrested,' said Toby Beauchamp. 'Apart from that it's been fairly quiet.'

'I'm going to have to sell the Manor House,' said Vanner. 'I'm seeing an estate agent in the morning.'

'Good God, I'd forgotten estate agent,' said Lydia Baxter. 'We call them realtors. I've got to remember my English. Drapes are curtains, and bobby pins are hairgrips, right?'

'We wouldn't have lent you the language if we had known that you were going to muck it about,' Vanner told her.

'Pity you gotta sell the house,' Duncan Baxter said. 'What sort of price will it fetch?'

Vanner shrugged. 'It's going down all the time. If I wait any longer it'll be a free gift at a petrol station.'

'Petrol, not gas,' said Lydia Baxter. 'It's all coming back to me now.' She sipped her brandy and milk. 'Any of you guys know Barnaby Barton?' she asked.

Vanner and Toby Beauchamp remembered together then what the connection was between Barney and these visiting Americans. They nodded, reluctant to say the wrong thing.

'He wrote me,' said Lydia Baxter. 'I used to know him.'

'If you're going to see him don't expect too much,' said Toby. If it took ten thousand monkeys one hundred and fifty years to write 'Dear Sir', he wondered how long it would take Barnaby Barton to write a coherent letter.

'Dunc's warned me,' said Lydia Baxter. 'He wasn't that bright when I knew him forty-eight years ago.'

'He's regressed,' Toby told her. 'You met him at his intellectual peak.'

Lydia Baxter looked at Toby and thought he reminded her of David Niven. The other man looked tired and overweight, but she had the impression that his weight made him look older than he was. She wondered what would have happened if she had never become pregnant and had stayed in this country. She would, perhaps, be sitting in this pub now, drinking a gin with her husband who would probably be a shop owner or an office worker. She regretted nothing.

There had been a brief romance once in America when Duncan was ten, with an Idaho potato farmer who had invented a device for blowing pills into goats; but the invention made no money and the farmer had hanged himself in a barn. That had been quite enough for Lydia Baxter; she had decided finally and for good that she was not intended to share her life with a man. When Duncan suggested that they wander down the road to see whether Barney was at home she left the pub with only the mildest curiosity.

Barnaby Barton was constructing a roll-up cigarette when the knock came on the door. He had mislaid his letter from Lydia Baxter and was no longer sure when she would arrive. He approached the door with his customary mixture of reluctance and suspicion and opened it to find a tall, powerful man with steel-grey hair and, beside him, a funny old lady with large blue spectacles.

Lydia Baxter looked at a man in brown corduroy trousers that were an inch or two short and held to a non-existent waistline by a piece of old rope. An old, blue denim shirt that was overdue for the wash had a pipe protruding from the top pocket. He had a red nose and crafty eyes that looked at them as if they were a pair of cat burglars.

'Hallo, Barney,' said Duncan Baxter.

Barney was as confused as usual but he slowly realized who this visitor was.

'It's Duncan, isn't it? Come in. Bring your friend in with you.'

They stepped into the room.

'Barney, this is your old friend, Lydia Baxter.'

'Hallo, Barney,' she said. 'How's the football-programme collection coming along?'

Barney stopped, suspicious of a trick. This was not the Lydia Baxter that he had been thinking about for forty years or more. There was no possible resemblance.

'Hallo,' he said nervously. 'Take a seat.'

Lydia Baxter lowered herself into an old armchair. The room was cleaner than Duncan had led her to expect but there was a bizarre smell which seemed to combine rotting food, used socks and anal air. The onrush of wealth didn't seem to have had much effect on Barnaby Barton. This was the home of a poor man.

'Would you like a coffee?' Barney asked, walking towards a door. He walked, thought Lydia Baxter, as if he was taken to pieces every night and put away in a drawer.

'Not for me,' she said quickly. She had read the papers. This country was riddled with food poisoning, salmonella, listeria, mad cow disease and God-knew-what. It was risky enough eating in a British hotel, without consuming the product of Barnaby Barton's kitchen.

'We've just dropped in to see you, Barney,' she said. 'I'm looking up several old friends, at least those who are still alive. My, this place has changed.'

But Barney was so preoccupied with how he appeared in this company that he wasn't listening to the conversation that was directed to him. He was wishing instead that he had had time to put his suit on with one of the new shirts. He was also having difficulty in believing that this cheery old lady really was Lydia Baxter.

'Do you need money?' he asked.

'Not any more, Barney. There was a time . . .'

'Did you get all that?' Duncan Baxter asked. 'Toby pay up? I see they're building out there.'

'I've put it in the bank,' said Barney. 'I'm getting interest.'

It was clear to Duncan Baxter that getting interest on your money was a novel concept to the man he could still scarcely believe was his father.

'What are you going to do with it?' Lydia Baxter asked. 'Why don't you buy a car? Improve your lifestyle.'

'I never learned to drive,' Barney said, returning now to the problem of the roll-up cigarette.

'Get a chaffeur. You can afford it.'

The idea of Barnaby Barton cruising round Compton Sinbury in a chauffeur-driven limousine brought home to his disorganized mind how different her idea of living was. The money was safe in the bank and he could have as many pints of Guinness as he wanted. That was what being rich meant.

'I don't want a chauffeur hanging around here,' he said. 'I value my privacy.'

Looking around at that privacy and wondering what prolonged bachelorhood did to a man, Lydia Baxter began to wish that her son would get married. Contrary to the graffiti, celibacy did appear to be an inherited characteristic. She decided that when she got home she would urge him to find a wife.

'Well, hasn't your son grown up fine?' she asked.

Barney nodded, embarrassed that she had raised the subject. 'He's a kind man. He made me rich.'

'Well, you enjoy yourself with the money,' said Lydia Baxter. 'That's my best advice.'

Duncan Baxter, saying little, sat on a rickety chair and tried to imagine how it was all those years ago when this couple met as lively youngsters and, in an isolated burst of passion, created him. He was old enough now to withstand the psychological trauma that such thoughts might once have produced.

When he suggested after an awkward silence that they ought to be leaving, his mother jumped to her feet. 'Yes, I want to visit Stella,' she said.

Barnaby Barton seemed relieved, too, to see the end of this visit. He got up immediately and made his way to the door.

Standing up, Lydia Baxter suddenly noticed a picture of herself, taken in 1942, on the mantelpiece. She went over and picked it up.

'Fancy you keeping this, Barney,' she said. 'Gee, I hardly recognized myself.'

Looking at the lady who was holding the picture, Barney could see why. He held the front door open for them and said: 'Nice of you to call.'

As they walked back down the lane towards the pub's car park, Duncan Baxter said: 'Well, what did you think of your old flame?'

Lydia Baxter started to laugh so loudly that he thought Barney could hear it in his bungalow.

'He needs a trepan, Dunc,' she said.

When Christmas came to Compton Sinbury even the ducks knew it. Their tiny thatched home by the duckpond on the green was festooned with fairy lights, and a 30-foot Christmas tree also covered in lights, was placed nearby. At the Flatulent Ferret, Barry dug out his lights, too, and draped them over the front of the pub as an inducement to trade.

At their home on the Meadow Estate the Kennedy family were in danger of losing sight of Christmas as they prepared for their stay in America. Gwenda was working her way through everything in the house to see what she should take and what she should leave. Neil Kennedy, in an uncharacteristic flurry of letter writing, was trying to arrange his life so that a six-month absence didn't alienate his bank, the gas and electricity boards, the local council, the telephone people and the several organizations that had trusted him with credit cards.

Lindy, who was oblivious to this upheaval, had set her heart on receiving a pet for Christmas. It was evidently not important whether the creature was a white mouse or a Rottweiler so long as it lived and breathed, and it fell to her father to explain that they were going on a long journey to live in another house for a while and could not take a pet with them. Lindy listened to this explanation with understandable impatience and at the end of it, with her usual uncanny accuracy, took a loving swipe at his testicles which laid him out for half an hour.

He was prostrate on the sofa when Gwenda answered a knock on the door and a few moments later Paul Vanner came in.

'You've been drinking,' said Kennedy, hoisting himself up to a sitting position.

'I'm well relaxed, pal. I've got to make the most of this leisure before I go back to work.'

'Any news of Suzanne?' Gwenda asked, showing him to an armchair.

'Our contact is through solicitors,' Vanner said. 'The letters aren't too gossipy.'

'What can we do for you, Mr Vanner?' Gwenda asked. 'We are fairly busy preparing for our American jaunt.'

'You keep going to America,' said Vanner. 'I wish I could.'

'Been there, done it, bought the jigsaw,' Kennedy agreed.

'Well, it's about your absence that I'm calling. The thing is, I've got to sell the Manor House. It's all part of the divorce equation. So what do I do? Move back to London? Buy a smaller house here? Live up a tree?'

'I should have thought a sleeping bag in the pub would take care of it,' said Gwenda.

'I want to stay in the village,' Vanner told them, 'until I find out where I stand with a certain little lady who shall be nameless called Cathy Gray. But I don't want to buy in case I'm moving.'

'I'm ahead of you,' said Gwenda. 'I said to Neil it would be best if we could find a short-term tenant. Deter burglars. Air the house.'

'I'm your man,' said Vanner. 'Mind you, the plunge from ownership of the Manor House to rented accommodation could damage my ego.'

'I'm afraid there's no swimming pool, but you could borrow Lindy's plastic paddling pool.'

'Most kind. Write down the rent on a piece of paper and the number of your bank account and I'll fix a standing order.'

'I think this calls for a small libation,' said Neil Kennedy.

'What doesn't?' said Vanner.

Half an hour later he walked erratically from the Meadow Estate and headed for the village hall where the opening night of *Cinderella* was proving a powerful counter-attraction to the evening's television programmes. To watch Cathy Gray glide sexily around Baron Hardup's decrepit old castle, Vanner had bought himself a seat in the back row – anticipating that a little of this production might go a long way and that his thirst might eventually triumph over his curiosity about its denouement.

Cathy Gray was playing to a packed house and Vanner wondered how many subscribers to *Crumpet* were among this sedate village audience. Her performance was surprisingly polished: the weeks of rehearsal under Daisy Balcombe's stern tutelage had produced something that didn't differ greatly from a low-budget offering on television.

Vanner sat with a dry mouth in the back row and watched Cathy Gray's long legs. The tattered old rags that she had to wear barely covered her bottom. When the Fairy Godmother – a woman who had once served Vanner in some local shop – transformed a rat into a coachman, and a pumpkin into a glittering coach, Cathy's metamorphosis was even more dramatic. Her gown of silver and gold, sparkling with pearls, made him itch to drag her away from this to somewhere warm and private.

'My spells can't last beyond the day I create them,' said the Fairy Godmother. 'You must return from the ball by midnight, for everything I have made will disappear then.'

So why, wondered Vanner a little later, didn't the glass slipper disappear? This flaw in the plot began to nag him. The coachman, the footmen and the coach had disappeared, and so had the other glass slipper. The shimmering gown had been returned to rags. But this odd glass slipper in Dandini's hand had mysteriously survived the midnight deadline.

His irritation at this discrepancy combined with his thirst to provide sufficient reason to go. He slipped out of the back door unnoticed and walked down the green.

The Christmas tree was surrounded by carol singers who were urging merry gentlemen to rest, a recommendation that found an echo in his restless heart. Neither God nor Father Christmas was going to prevent this holiday from being a lonely time, particularly as he believed in neither of them. He was always ambivalent about Christmas, anyway; there were more tears then than at any other time of the year. On Boxing Day he would go up to see his parents in the East End. They knew how to enjoy themselves up there. They were uninhibited – they even rowed with the windows open.

He stood for a while listening to the new carol, 'O Little Town of Bethlehem', and marvelled at the satisfaction that was being derived by the smiling singers. To be so easily satisfied was truly the secret of contentment.

In the Flatulent Ferret Neil Kennedy had already escaped from the pre-America arrangements and was drinking at the bar with Toby and Harry Grant. There seemed to be another celebration going on; there was champagne on the counter again, instead of the ordinary stuff.

'We're expecting a baby,' Harry told Vanner. 'Have a drink.'

'An element of premarital hanky-panky suggests itself here,' said Toby Beauchamp. 'They haven't been married a fortnight.'

'Is Nadine pleased?' Vanner asked.

'Delighted, particularly as we have Rachel as a babysitter. I'm delighted, too. I missed Rachel's upbringing.'

'Well, let's drink then,' said Kennedy. 'I'm going to have a vasectomy and sleep on the roof myself. I've tried children. Copulation without procreation is the family motto from now on. I must find somebody who can translate it into Latin.'

Harry Grant poured champagne and thought that life was turning out fine. The financial burdens that might have proved a strain had never materialized thanks to Nadine's widow's pension. They had even arranged a spring holiday with Rachel in Italy before the July birth.

Neil Kennedy, drinking champagne, was looking forward to the new year as well. The American adventure should see his career reaching heights that he had seen only briefly a decade ago, and afterwards he would be happy to return to this pleasant village where fame and bright lights meant absolutely nothing and the people you drank with were considerate enough to forget that they had seen you on television. A year had passed since he arrived in Sin and dramatic things had happened to people in that time but nobody had changed. There was an immutable quality about life in Compton Sinbury that he found reassuring, and it was a fine place to bring up Lindy. He had enjoyed taking her to the country market in the autumn where she had picked her own runner beans. Some children thought that food arrived in cans in supermarkets.

Vanner bought another bottle of champagne and put it in the ice bucket.

'I have to keep my landlord sweet,' he said.

'Cheers,' said Kennedy, filling his glass. 'When do you hope to sell your house?'

'People are coming to look tomorrow,' Vanner told him. 'The housing market may be on the floor, but the estate agent told me today that there are always people interested in places like the Manor House.'

'I hope you'll be selective about who you sell it to,' said Toby Beauchamp, lighting a small cigar. 'We don't want just anybody living here.'

'I'll bring them in here for vetting,' Vanner promised.

Toby didn't like to hear that the housing market was on the floor. He had his eye on a piece of land that would look all the better for having some old people's accommodation built on it. Of course, the necessary planning permission could no longer be taken for granted, but this could work in his favour. The council would not want to appear to be victimizing him. And now that people were retiring earlier and living longer, the country was reaching the stage where most of the population would be pensioners, and somebody had to house them. It was a truth that the council would be obliged to acknowledge.

'Where's that big striding filly of yours?' he asked.

'My friend Miss Gray is treading the boards at the moment. A starring role in the village hall. But she's promised to join me for a drink when the curtain comes down.'

'New woman, new home, new job,' said Toby. 'You young people are so adaptable.'

'It's a fast-changing world, Toby, my old son. Nimble feet is what you need these days.'

'Sluggish, torpid, leaden are the words that come to mind when I think of you.'

'New woman, new home, new job,' said Vanner. It hadn't occurred to him, until Toby had said it, that his life had been so thoroughly overhauled. The thought gave him a sense of excitement about the future.

When Cathy Gray arrived, glowing with the applause that she had received at the village hall, she was wearing a yellow silk dress with a men's style dinner jacket that the royals had taken to recently. She seemed to be spending a lot of money on clothes lately and Vanner – who believed that the plainest woman could arouse a man if she wore the right outfit – found himself stirred by the sight of bikini pants with tiger stripes that showed provocatively beneath her dress.

'Give me champagne,' she said. 'I'm a star.'

'You were wonderful, dahling,' said Vanner. 'Isn't that what you theatrical people say, Mr Kennedy?'

'I'm afraid they do. I'd better take Lindy to this pantomime tomorrow. I may discover that you should be coming to Hollywood with me.'

The bar was filling up now with the carol singers from the green and the audience from the pantomime and it was difficult to move.

'I think you ought to come and see my etchings,' said Vanner. 'You don't want to stay here mixing with *fans*.'

'There's nothing I'd sooner look at,' said Cathy Gray, 'as long as it's a private viewing.'

Harry Grant plucked a bottle of champagne from the ice bucket but it was empty.

'Barry – more champagne!' he called.

The new bottle appeared with surprising speed given the demands of the crowd and Harry struggled to release the cork. It shot into the air with a vulgar pop and he turned to offer a refill to his friends.

Neil Kennedy and Toby Beauchamp held out their glasses gratefully but two of the party had vanished. Paul Vanner had gone home early to enjoy the sexual demands of his girlfriend.